The Devil's Monk

Guardian of the Book

~

by

J.R. Russell

ISBN 978-0-9567029-3-7

Published by Skycat Publications, a subsidiary of Magdalene Technology.
www.skycatpublications.com

Designed and edited by Ian Kossick, Skycat Publications
Cover designed by Anne Mullord.

Printed by Lavenham Press Ltd, Arbons House, 47 Water Street, Lavenham, Suffolk CO10 9RN. Telephone: +44 (0)1787 247436. Fax: +44 (0)1787 247436

With thanks to my friend and leech Jackie Drakeford.

Bald's *Book of Leechdoms, Wortcunning and Starcraft* was written in the ninth century. It was a compendium of the prescriptions, potions, nostrums, incantations and astrological predictions collected over a lifetime by Cild, his father, a travelling leech. It dealt with most common conditions in the most common way then, with worts we now call herbs, but with knowledge we have since lost of when to collect them and how to apply them. In a thousand years, the names and natures of these herbs may well have changed. The original Book was lost in a fire, and the original words may have lost or changed their meanings. Bald knew what he was doing, and if he did not, there was no one alive to tell him. We do not know at all. Every wort, every medicine today, is both a cure and a killer. There is danger in ignorance, and folly in emulation. Do not, I beg you, try to be a leech, or take anything from the book beyond wonder and amusement. To use a phrase every child will understand: "Don't try this at home"!

J.R. Russell

Contents

SAXONS & BRITONS

AETHELFLEDA ...... Dunstan's patroness in Glastonbury
AETHELGIFU .... King Alfred's daughter, an Abbess
ALFRED .... King of Wessex
BALD .... a leech. Guardian of the Book
BOOT .... Doctor Oxa's maid
DUNSTAN .... a monk and a Saint
DUDA .... a churl
DUN .... famous doctor
EADBURH .... King Edward's daughter
EADGIFU .... King Edward's Queen
EADGYTH .... King Edward's daughter, married to Caech
EALHSWITH .... King Alfred's Queen
EATHELWYNN .... Abbess of Shaftesbury
EDMUND .... King Edward's second son, King of England
EDWARD .... King Alfred's son, King of Wessex
EMMA/AELFGIFU .. Eneda's daughter by Sigtryggr, Queen of England
ENEDA .... A thegn's daughter
GINNA .... Lyb's wife
GRIMWALD .... a councillor
LIOFA .... Lyb's son
LYB .... a dwarf, Eneda's slave
ODO .... Archbishop of Canterbury after Wulfhelm
ORM .... Governor of York
OXA .... a doctor
TOKI .... Lyb's wife
ULF .... Lyb's son
WULFHELM .... Archbishop of Canterbury
WULFSTAN .... Archbishop of York

VIKINGS

CAECH .... Sigtryggr's younger son, King of York
CUARAN......................... Caech's son, the last Viking king
GUTHRITH .... Sigtryggr's brother
GUTHRITH .... Guthrith's son
HAESTEN .... a Viking chief
OLAF GUTHFRITHSSON. Guthryth's grandson
MERFYN......................... a recreant monk
RAGNALL .... Sigtryggr's eldest son, King of York
SIGTRYGGR .... King of York

TERMS & PHRASES

BURH .... fortified town or other defended site
CATAFALQUE .... a raised bier or platform
CEARLS .... men - pronounced 'churls' and is the Saxon spelling
CONSANGUINITY .... related by blood
DANEGELD .... tax raised to buy off the Viking raiders
HAUBERK .... body armour
LEECH .... a herbal doctor
LEECHCRAFT................ the art of healing
LEECHDOM .... a medical/herbal treatment
LIMNED .... drawn or painted
NITHLING .... general term for creature
OREAD .... mountain nymph
OSIERS .... narrow-leaved shrub species of willow
STARCRAFT .... science of the stars
WORTCUNNING .... knowledge of the healing properties of herbs

PAGAN DEITIES

FREYA or FREYJA .... Goddess of love, beauty and fertility
LOKI .... God of mischief and destruction
THOR .... God of thunder and lightening
TY .... God of war and skies
VALHALLA .... Hall of Fallen Heroes in the Afterlife
WODEN .... chief Saxon god

SAXON SOCIETY

CHURL .... man
EARLDOMAN .... earl
REEVE .... official with local responsibilities
THEGN .... nobleman

Introduction

Bald is returning to the home he left fifty years before as a small boy travelling with his father Cild, carrying the book of healing nostrums that became his life's work. Their journey took them to the great libraries in monasteries and abbeys, adding to the knowledge in the book from the writings of the ancient civilisations of Egypt, Greece, Rome and Arabia. Cild, and after him Bald, used their skills to heal those in need where they could, and to ease the last days of those where they could not.

Britain at that time was a dangerous place for books and wisdom, for the waves of Viking invaders had no use for scholars, destroying the libraries along with the buildings that held them and those who lived there. The Saxon King Alfred was ailing of a mystery disease that none had so far been able to cure. As he weakened, so his plans for a peaceful and united country came under increasing threat. It was a time of intrigue, treachery, blunt politics, deceit and cunning, where killing was a skill possibly more valued than healing, and a man who knew how to make one look like the other would always be in mortal danger. Bald's plan of peaceful retirement would be shaken to the core as circumstances, Fate, God or gods set him on his travels again.

The Book of Leechdoms, Wortcunning and Starcraft genuinely existed. It dates from the ninth century. The original bore the inscription: "This is Bald's book that was written by Cild." Nothing more is known of Bald or Cild, but it was customary at that time for leeches – healers – to travel the country helping the poor and sometimes the not so poor with their treatments, based on a profound knowledge of herbal medicine allied with charms, astrology and faith.

King Alfred the Great, known as a scholar as well as a wise ruler, thought enough of the book to have several copies made by the monks, something that was rarely done at that time when few knew how to read and fewer could write. Fragments of it still exist in the form of a Victorian translation, from which the leechdoms and charms quoted in the text have been taken, keeping to their archaic spelling and punctuation.

The Devil's Monk covers that volatile period of British history from King Alfred through the reigns of Athelstan and Edward to the birth of Edwin. Set at the time of the Viking wars, and the striving to create a united England from the separate kingdoms that Alfred inherited, it spans the politics of religion between Woden and Christ as the declared faith of the inhabitants, showing how this changed the perspectives of healing and understanding of natural forces. During this period, some of our most famous abbeys were founded, and this is explored from the viewpoints of rich and poor, native and invader, pagan and Christian.

Bald himself has to survive an England full of dangers and superstitions, with only the book and his wits at his disposal. As well as his physical journey through the land, treating the sick, he has his own secret quest, and also a dangerous promise to fulfil made under duress to a dying Viking king.

Britain in the reign of King Alfred.

Book I

Fornjot's Palm

i

***B**ald woke naked under Nell Ball. He looked for the book where it lay wrapped in brown plaid near his head. That panic over, he closed his eyes to catch the remnant of his dream.*

The girl had gone; the feel of her stubble on his tongue remained. He had worshipped her again in the only way he could. He had known her again without knowing who she was. Known her as he knew Nell Ball, the earth-breast, the green hillock where he lay, in sheepfold country, old country, Bald's home country. He opened his eyes and thought he knew where he was.

In the book:

"If a man dreams he sleeps with his sister it betokens harm. With his mother freedom from vexation. With a virgin betokens anxiety. To see himself castrated betokens harm. To be in joy in dreams betokens uneasiness."

Who was she whom he knew so intimately, her body better than his own? He looked at his body, the scraped root of a tree, a rotten bough melting into earth, a rotted branch. It held no mystery. Every vein, every bone was written and limned in the book. He was a dead branch in a living field of flowers.

Bald was old. He was going home. Fifty years ago he had left home with his father, Cild, carrying the book which Cild was writing. The book was almost as big as the boy. They had passed Nell Ball on the first day.

Most of the south was forest. It had no name because it had no king. Only the harbours were well-inhabited, and the people went to church. Green domes like Nell Ball had names because elves lived in them, among the gold and bodies of giants. Cild had crossed himself when he passed, not a Christian cross but the old dagger cross of Saxnot. They were dagger men, Saxons.

In the book:

"Work thus a salve against the elfin race, and nocturnal goblin visitors, and for the women with whom the devil hath carnal commerce; take the ewe hop plant, wormwood, bishopwort, lupin, ashthroat, henbane, harewort, vipers bugloss, heathberry plants, cropleek, garlic, grains of hedgerife, githrife, fennel: put these worts into a vessel, boil them in butter and sheep's grease, strain through a cloth, throw the worts into running water. If any ill-tempting occur to a man, smear his forehead with this salve and put it on his eyes and where his body is sore; he will soon be better."

This is a leechdom. Cild was a leech and Bald after him, skilled in leechdoms, wortcunning and starcraft.

In the morning twilight, a dwarf was herding, a few scraggy sheep dragging their coats up the arc of the hill. On the indistinct edge of Bald's consciousness they could easily be elves returning to the barrow with sacks of gold.

He leaped up in alarm and reached for the book.

The dwarf saw a naked body rising from the grave, and shrieked. He turned to fly, tripped over his rags, rolled into a ball and came tumbling down the hill.

Heart-chilled, Bald dragged the plaid across his body and held out the book, crackling parchment between black wooden boards, to protect himself.

The ragged ball landed at his feet.

Bald spoke.

"Flee, flee, ho, ho, bile, the lark was searching!"

Then in case he was talking to a foreigner:

"Tetunc resonco bregan gresso."

Which even he did not understand.
He spat three times.
"I kiss the Gorgon's mouth."
He added for safety.
"Sanctus sanctus sanctus domino, deus saboath, amen, alleluiah."
It might be a Christian: who knows?
The ball unrolled like a hedgehog.
Bald saw the moon face of the halfwit progeny of an island race, a Briton.
The dwarf saw a book with two gnarled hands and a grizzled head with the long sharp face of a hatchet.
Neither was reassured.
Bald did not believe or disbelieve in anything. He was a leech and had seen men die who should have lived, and live who should have died. Elfling or changeling, the thing only made him angry with himself for fearing it.
"May the devil scratch your eyes out and shit in the holes!"
The dwarf heard something he understood and smiled the superior smile of those beyond the reach of insults. Bald had seen it on the faces of a saint and a prostitute on two different occasions.
An ancient charm ran through his head.
"Stupid on a mountain went, Stupid stupid was."
The few Britons who remained were slaves. Habitual inbreeding had reduced them from the upright inheritors of Roman arms and culture to a small dark unintelligible race of obscurantist herdsmen. Saxon language and civilisation had prevailed as effectively as Saxon swords and axes, and long enough for Saxons to consider themselves the true inhabitants of these islands. When Bald was young, the three kingdoms, Mercia, Wessex and Northumbria, had Saxon kings while King Edmund of East Anglia was, not surprisingly, an Angle.
Now of all those kings, one remained.
The dwarf still smiled.

In the book:
"Against mental vacancy and against folly; put into ale bishopwort, lupins, betony, the southern fennel, nepte, water agrimony, cockle, marche, then let the man drink."

Too much trouble.

"In case a man be lunatic; take the skin of a mereswine work it into a whip, swinge the man therewith, soon he will be well. Amen."

Not having the skin of a mereswine about him, Bald improvised and knocked the dwarf on the head with the book.

The smile went.

Bald wondered once again at the wisdom Cild had collected in their travels together.

Now the dwarf was looking at him reproachfully.

"You'll feel better soon. And for a fee I'll take a cup of milk."

The sheep had followed the shepherd. Taking a pannikin from his pouch Bald knelt by the nearest ewe and milked her.

Feeling the gentle udders he saw the girl again.

He drank and nodded towards the hill.

"Nell Ball."

The dwarf, who knew it was not, said nothing.

Stupid on a mountain went.

Bald pointed east where the sun was rising from the forest.

"Eashing."

The dwarf, who had come from Eashing way over the unfolding fields to the west, said nothing but he smiled.

"I give you to Woden."

Bald hooked the pouch on his shoulder, grasped the book, strode off towards the sun.

When he looked back the dwarf was indistinguishable from the sheep.

"I give you to Woden." It was the old double-edged adieu to friend and enemy alike – God keep you, God help you.

The forest held no fear for him. His heart lightened as he felt the warmth of spring and caught the sun flashing in the tops of the trees. Oaks, beeches, wild service trees abounded. Where the ground had been cleared by charcoal burners or the pigs of some passing herdsman, hawthorn, rowan and spindle veiled their spikes in a mist of tiny white blossoms. The beaten earth was criss-crossed by tracks of men and beasts, and littered with fallen branches. Everywhere, emerald buds appeared, and small birds darted from twig to twig.

He travels safe who travels naked. Bald had no fear of robbers. They could not take what he had. He could only lose it himself. Thought and memory fly over the world every day: I fear for thought lest he come not back but I fear more for memory. Bald was going home, and every stride took him further from home.

As a boy he had carried the book for his father Cild, but not this way. Memory misled him, the dwarf misled him, he walked with open eyes blithely into the familiar unknown.

In the book:

"Men said formerly when anything happened to them unexpectedly that it happened by chance; as if anyone should dig the earth and find there a hoard of gold and then say that it happened by chance. I know however that if the digger had not dug the earth or man had not before hid the gold there that he would not have found it. Therefore it was found not by chance but by fate."

He walked all day.

By evening he knew he was lost. The sun sank behind him and the forest opened like a curtain. Green water-meadows dipped into a wide dark winding river, and beyond it, shining like a knife, a Roman road cut straight across the land.

The slanting sunlight flashed on something lying in the river.

He stopped. Stared.

The light reflected by the polished strakes, a Viking longship lay there half-submerged. The sight of this gilded serpent so far from the sea struck him with awe as well as terror.

He crouched. Watched. Waited.

He had seen his father murdered.

In his youth they had travelled throughout the island as Cild collected leechdoms for the book. They went from abbey to abbey, monastery to monastery, where the wisdom of Egypt, Greece, Rome and Arabia lay in the cells like honey. Cild learnt the simple recipes of the poor for the ills of poverty, and the enigmatic charms of the rich for their imaginary ailments. He met the famous leeches Oxa and Dun, and wrote down the prescription the Patriarch of Jerusalem had sent the King of Wessex, Alfred, which failed, for as Bald knew, Alfred still suffered from a mysterious disease.

And where there were no leechdoms for the misery they met, Cild made them himself from his memory. Meanwhile the boy became a man and carried the book.

They knew the pagan seamen had come, and spread like the plague, from the burnt, maimed, raped, mutilated bodies they left behind, from the monks fleeing with the relics of their saints, from the smouldering monasteries and the ashes of their manuscripts. The pagans stole and took slaves, yes understood, so had the Saxons, but they killed like foxes for the sake of killing, and they destroyed knowledge. Their religion of beer and blood was profoundly pessimistic. Bald knew. It was his own to the extent he had one. The last battle was always going to be lost.

They were at Thetford in East Anglia when the great Viking army came, with kings this time, to conquer the whole island.

King Edmund was martyred. Cild was captured. Bald hid the book. He watched. Waited.

His father had knowledge, so King Ivarr sacrificed him to Thor, the god of laughter and the belch.

They split his chest open with an axe and wrapped his living lungs around him like the sheathed wings of an eagle. He became a blood-eagle, a trophy to stupidity. They killed the healer. They always do.

Bald watched.

The air was still. The longship glowed dying like an ember. There were bodies lying in the reeds.

There was no stink of death, no buzzards in the sky; it had happened today, he was the first one there.

He thought of gold.

The years between had made him hard as a tree alone and whipped by wind and weather. He was a leech and did a leech's work. He added nothing to the book. There was nothing more to add.

The pagans spread to Northumbria, Mercia, Scotland, Ireland, Wales. They would have taken Wessex and the south but for Alfred's battles, and his money to buy them off, and his persistence. They ruled one half of the island and waited for a greater army to come and take the rest.

Perhaps the longship in the river was the precurser of that army?

Bald was going home and could have gold for his old age. The thought of it subdued his fear.

Fear is a constant in old age. The moment we stop fearing one thing we fear another. Now he feared he would be too late to rob the corpses before dark. He ran down towards the river, splashing through the watery grass, raising droplets glittering in the sunlight like the golden coinage of his greed.

The first dead he came across were Saxons, in leather jerkins slashed and sodden with blood and water. He disdained to search them for the pennies in their pockets.

A Viking lay in the river a foot beneath the surface, staring upwards. The moving water made him look mysteriously alive. He was young. They were all young. The new army was here.

A dozen Vikings were strewn around in the sprawl of death.

Bald hesitated between them like a dog between two dinners.

He splashed from one to another, a demented dance in the growing darkness.

This man with a round peasant face had a Saxon spear stuck in his waterlogged body so each time Bald turned him upright he rolled back.

This man had a dagger in his chest that pinned his hauberk as tight as a miser's coffer.

This man hauled up from the mud and floated away and left Bald grasping water.

He saw the longship curving into the sky, and the sliver of a moon appear.

What a fool he was! That is where the hoard would be!

He waded into the river to where the water lapped the sunken stern. Some stars had joined the moon.

He pulled himself over the slippery gunwale into the belly of the ship. The oak keel stretched sixty feet in front of him, the oars and mast shipped neatly like the legs of an upturned insect.

He shivered with excitement and the chill of evening.

Where the longship was decked towards the prow, there was a heap of metal glowing softly in the lilac light, a catafalque, for on it lay the body of a chieftain cloaked in wolfskin, armed with a silver axe, his head cased in a gold-panelled helmet and mask made by the gods. Bald crouched like an animal, the hair rising up the back of his neck across his scalp.

This was the helmet the Viking Ivarr wore when he had sacrificed Cild. The body was Ivarr's son and the treasure Ivarr's treasure – until now.

Bald felt a surge of righteous gratitude to Woden and, as was his way, quickly added Jesus to be safe. He put down the book.

He crawled to the foot of the bier and saw it was built of silver plates, chalices, crosses, coins. His hand moved to touch the body's sandals and then, as if to take a pulse, the flesh. It was gratifyingly cold.

Bald stood. He, Bald the leech, looked down at the body of a Viking king. The light was going. This was no place to stay. Who knows what ghostly troop of warriors would descend from Valhalla to claim their own?

He could carry one treasure.

He leant forward to ease the golden helmet from the corpse's head. It was heavy and he tensed his body, his hands gripping tightly, his face above the corpse's face.

The helmet shifted, the gold mask lifted, the dead features beneath shone whitely.

Bald studied the face.

Broad forehead, beak nose, beard.

He moved his hand to raise the eyelids.

Before he could touch them, the eyes opened.

Bald nearly screamed.

Eyes fixed on eycs.

He felt for the silver axe, grasped it, raised it above his head.

Undecided. Cursed indecision of old age.

As a leech he knew the dead moved.

But the eyes he saw were definitely not dead. Kill him.

Second thought.

Cure him.

Curiosity.

How could a dead man live?

This man was Ivarr's son. Kill him.

The axe stayed poised in the moonlight. Descended slowly.

Bald was Cild's son. Cure him. Then kill him if you like.

He put his ear close to the man's mouth. A faint fluttering breath.

If not dead and nothing done, he would be dead soon.

He pulled aside the wolfskin. The body was clad in a white linen tunic edged with gold. The right arm and shoulder dark with a shadow from within.

He gripped the tunic at the neck and tore it open. In the faint starlight the arm and shoulder glowed a livid black.

In the book:

"Of swarthened or deadened body. If the swarthened body be to that high degree deadened that no feeling be thereon then must thou soon cut away all the dead and the unfeeling flesh as far as the quick so that there be nought remaining of the dead flesh which ere felt neither iron nor fire."

Fire, he needed fire.

With the axe he hacked the deck to make a stack of splinters.

He tore strips of linen from the tunic to make tinder.

He took flint from his pouch and struck it with the axe.

Fire smouldered, caught, flared. He chopped billets of oak from the gunwales and strakes to feed it.

He put his knife into the fire.

In the book:

"If thou must carve off or cut off an unhealthy limb from a healthy body then carve thou not it on the limit of the healthy body but much more cut or carve in on the whole and quick body so thou shalt better and readier cure it."

Using the pouch as a glove he held the knife red hot and turned to the stricken king.

The oak was beginning to burn fiercely and leaping flames lit up the sacrifice.

He cut shoulder to the bone, which he disjointed, severing the sinews, and round the arm leaving a bloody gaping hole.

He dropped the knife.

He took a burning brand from the fire and laid it across the hole. The flesh charred, the bone showed white, blood burned and sealed the severed vessels.

In the book:

"When thou settest fire on a man, then take thou leaves of tender leek and grated salt, overlay the places, then shall be by that the more readily the heat of the fire drawn away."

Bald hurried to the stern of the longship and slid into the water. The fire was beginning to feed on the ship itself, shooting flames into the dark river.

He waded to the banks of reeds and fleshy leaves, looking for wild garlic.

The white flowers showed him where they were. He reaped an armful and returned cursing himself for his stupidity.

The bow of the longship was blazing like the sun.

He raced to the king and thrust the mass of dripping leaves into the wound, binding it with strips of tunic.

The flames were stretching for the silver hoard.

Bald seized his knife and pouch. He reached for the golden helmet.

The fire burst through the deck and came roaring up again in a great lurid belch of smoke and flame to claim its own.

His hand hovered like a hawk between the helmet and the man.

God save us from indecision.

He grasped the man's hair and hauled him up until he could lift him bodily on his shoulder. He stumbled under the weight down the long belly of the ship to lower the man into the water.

He turned back to pick up the book.

He looked up into the fire and saw the treasure at its heart.

He grinned like death.

He slid into the river. Holding the book on his head with one hand and dragging the wounded king with the other he struggled to the shore.

All night Bald watched the Viking longship burning lower and lower until it sank and sent the treasure molten silver and gold hissing to the bottom.

Dawn, and the pale body of the king beside him.

In the book:

"A wound salve. Take clean honey, warm it at the fire, put it then into a clean vessel, add salt and shake it till it hath the thickness of brewit, smear the wound therewith."

No honey.

"If a limb be smitten off a man, a finger or a foot or a hand, if the marrow be out, take sodden sheep's marrow lay it on the other marrow, bind it well up for a night."

No sheep.

"A salve to the end that a wound may not foul; take briar on which hips wax, that is dog rose, chew the rind and let it drop on the wound, then it will not foul."

Bald went to look for briar.

He was coming back from the forest when he saw the second longship on the river.

He hid. Watched.

They found the king where Bald had lain him and picked him up and carried him into the longship.

Bald did not know if he was alive or dead.

He went back into the forest.

ii

Bald did not know it but the hamlet was his home.
Cild had never returned or talked about his family.

Bald wondered if he had a family, and half suspected he came from a long line of illegitimate leeches, of which he knew he would be the last.

He had a memory, or was it a dream, of a familiar motherly woman.

He had a memory, or was it a dream, of a hamlet somewhere between Nell Ball and the burgh of Eashing.

When the instinct to return to his birthplace overwhelmed him these were the images he sought.

Before that he had never given them a thought.

He had another dream, or was it a memory.

The night after he witnessed his father's death he dreamt the Vikings caught him and castrated him.

From that night on he had been impotent.

It was called the Knot.

In the book:

"If a man be restrained with a woman give him springwort for him to eat and let him sup up holy water."

He had eaten banks of primroses and drunk wells dry.

"If a man be too slow ad venerum boil water agrimony in milk then thou givest him courage. Boil in ewe's milk again hindheal, alexanders, the wort which hight Fornjot's palm then it will be with him as he would liefest have it be."

What was Fornjot's palm? Cild knew but Cild was dead.

Bald's life had been a search for Fornjot's palm.

Desire had not left him: on the contrary it had increased to a madness day and night. He knew the lubricity of dreams and the bitterness of waking.

His love, his great capacity for love, dried up while his lust raged impotently.

It made him what he was, a monk of the devil. A man of great faith in nothing.

The hamlet had changed in fifty years.

The huddle of daub and wattle huts on a scarp at the edge of the forest, once an Iron Age hill fort, had spilled down the hill in safer better times to the fields below, where sheep and cattle grazed. The woods in the low ground were copsed, there was a common for pigs, and a sandpit near a stream.

The land here, once Mercian, was now ruled by Wessex King Alfred, though that meant no more to the folk who lived there than to their animals. Their struggles were with nature and the gods, one on Sunday, others for weekdays. Jesus and the moon, Ty, Woden, Thor and Freya. Caution, patience, perseverance were in their blood.

They regarded the next hamlet with suspicion, and Eashing, where the King kept a garrison, with hostility.

When Bald wandered in, the day after the burning longship, he was in danger of being stoned as a witch until he set a child's dislocated elbow. Then he was tolerated as a witch.

He lived in a deserted hut in the old hamlet on top of the scarp. Folk climbed up with their problems, bringing eggs, milk, and bread in payment. You had to be ill to make that climb.

The longing for home left him and though he knew it could not be far he never went there. He passed the days in the forest and fields gathering worts for the leechdoms.

He passed the nights dreaming of the girl.

She had come to him first as a vague vision of womanhood and as he had grown older she had become more real. Now his nightly dreams ended in sweat, and regret that they had ended. All his longings for all the women in the world streamed into a single channel, as the sources of a river surge together into a fretful turbulent cataract.

He had thought desire would drop from him with age, but like an old yew tree it grew evergreen.

Spring burst into summer.

One morning when the sun was late and he knew great disturbances were taking place in the world, Bald was dispensing leechdoms to the few poor cearls and their women who had struggled up the hill.

In the book:

"For foot ache, betony, germen leaves (mallow), fennel, ribwort, of all equal quantities; mingle milk with water and bathe the swollen limb from the upper part lest the swelling go inwards; then take sodden comfrey and lay it on.

In case a man shall overdrink himself let him drink betony in water.

Against worms of the inwards of children, take green mint a handful of it, put it into three sextariuses of water, seethe it down to one-third part, strain then give to drink.

For breast anguish if a man have a dry cough, take a thin slice of lard, lay it on a hot stone, shed cumin on it, set it in a cowhorn and let the man drink in the smoke."

A boy ran up breathless, shouting "Bald! Bald!"

Bald took no notice, the drunk man cursed and one of the scraggy children threw a stone at him.

"Bald come down! Duda says come down!"

Duda was the least stupid of the villagers.

"Tell Duda to come up." Bald added "What's wrong with him?"

"Not him!" The boy was impressed with his own importance. "A horse!"

The poor folk gaped.

Bald frowned. A horse meant trouble. "Whose horse?"

"Hers."

"Who?"

"She."

A monosyllabic conversation goes nowhere.

Bald went into his hut to fetch the book and they all, forgetting their ailments, hurried down the hill.

The rest of the villagers, holding the tools they had been using as if permanently attached to them, were grouped outside a small stone chapel, ready to run inside at a moment's notice. They were staring at Duda, who was rolling on the ground clutching his leg in agony. Nearby, a native horse: dark bay, squat, shaggy, ugly, with an evil blue-brown eye stood on three legs, the left hind big with pus and pain, drawn up in resentment.

Bald arrived.

The villagers pointed, some to Duda, others to the horse.

Bald hesitated: no indecision this time but a reluctance to be kicked. A woman came from the chapel behind him, carrying a wooden bucket spilling water.

He saw a grey homespun cloak decked with multi-coloured ribbons go by. He thought she would go to Duda, but she walked past him and gave the water to the horse to drink.

Someone cried out, "But that's holy water!"

She turned. "It won't do him any harm."

"Give it to Duda!"

"Duda's a fool to go behind a sick horse."

Duda groaned.

"Where's the leech?"

They pushed Bald forward.

She faced him.

He supposed she was about thirty, a small figure, firm determined features, green eyes appraising him, fair tangled hair. She was no-one he knew or dreamt he knew.

"Well, come on, leech!"

He was offended by her fearlessness.

"Who do you want me to treat first, the man or the horse?"

"The horse." She laughed. "No. Go on. Poor old Duda."

In the book:

"A salve for every wound; collect cow dung, cow stale, work up a large kettleful into a batter as a man worketh soap, then take appletree rind, ash rind, sloethorn rind, and myrtle rind, and elm rind, and holly rind, and withy rind, and the rind of a young oak, sallow rind, put them all in a mickle kettle, pour the batter upon them, boil very long then remove the rinds, boil the batter so that it be thick, pour it into a vessel, heat then a calcareous stone thoroughly and collect some soot and sift it through a cloth with quicklime also into the batter, smear the wound therewith."

Sometimes, Bald thought, Cild overleeched his leechdoms.

The woman was holding the horse, gripping its long mane, so he went to look at Duda's leg. There was a hoof-shaped bruise on the thigh.

"Put butter on it."

Duda got up and limped away. Bald went to the horse.

He soothed it with his hand and lifted the hurt leg. There were deep cracks in the skin of the fetlock and heel, and hard fungus growths where pus had seeped out and solidified. It stank.

He touched the growths: they were hot, and, with a little pressure, oozed blood.

The leg twitched and he moved away quickly.

She asked "What is it?"

"Leprosy."

In the book:

"For a horse's leprosy take harewort pound it well then mingle with fresh butter, boil thoroughly in butter, put it on the horse as hot as possible, smear every day always apply the salve. If the leprosy be mickle, take piss, heat it with stones, wash the horse with piss so hot; when it is dry smear with the salve."

She looked him in the eye. "Anybody's piss?"

He shrugged.

"Anybody's butter."

She smiled and then he felt he knew her.

Her name was Eneda.

Duda told him when he went to see him she was the daughter of the local thegn whose small estate was carved out of the common land, which had always been a grievance in the hamlet. She had been a wild girl who had many lovers and disgraced her parents who died of shame.

She had gone with a gang of coiners fleeing from justice and had returned years later with enough money to buy a horse, a ram and a flock of geese. Now she lived in a broken-down house and Duda resented her independence. Besides, her ram was the only one for miles, and the wealth of the village depended on it.

Bald looked at the fading bruise on Duda's thigh and told him he could start work again. Then he went to see Eneda.

The sheep-track led him across cropped fields filled with summer sweet worts: small purple bugle, sharp yellow pheasant's eye, blue monkshood kill-or-cure, a whole odoriferous pharmacy.

He stopped to fill his pouch.

There was an innocence about the land, a youthfulness. Nature needs a touch of man, but not too much.

He picked a sprig of Roman camomile for Eneda, and a handful of sweet cicely for the horse.

If he had found Fornjot's palm, he would have been completely happy.

Why was he happy at all? Then he remembered he had not dreamt last night.

He shifted the book from under one arm to under the other.

No dream. What did that mean?

Nothing.

He stopped. What was he?

Nothing.

What could he give her?

Nothing.

What was he doing with his sprig of camomile and his handful of sweet cicely?

Making a fool of himself.

He heard the cackle of geese in the distance.

Old men were foolish. There was no leechdom for old age.

He turned to go back.

Stopped again.

Indecision.

All around, the earth was swimming in colour, light and warmth. There was a rustle of activity.

Nothing stood still, nothing went back.

Change, change was the order of creation.

If he wanted to, he could not go back, not the same man, he would not be the same man.

Thought never stopped, never went back, was always new.

Memory changed within itself, adding layer on layer of the patina of age, making itself more and more beautiful.

It struck him: Heaven is the past.

Unattainable.

He could not go back to anything except death.

So what was there to live for?

The lack of options appalled him.

Only folly.

He saw Cild again sheathed in blood, a sacrifice to stupidity.

Yet the fools had given nothing to their god because Cild's knowledge was in the book.

Man's life was folly and his death academic; all that mattered was in the book.

He turned to what had to be. The book had its own purposes.

Knowledge is the only constant in a silly world.

He proceeded in that doubtful faith.

He passed the famous ram in its pen, and envied it. The geese came rushing from a pond, like Furies until he flung the sweet cicely at them, and they decided to be geese again, and ate it.

The house was neat enough: a lower course of stone, timbered clay, straw roof, a wisp of smoke creeping from it. There was a small garden, and he recognised the shoots of onion, fennel, lupin, elecampane and parsley. He went round the back and saw a small paddock with a few fruit trees, apples and peaches, and the horse standing in the shade, whisking the flies off with its tail.

Did she live here alone? Was there a husband, or a lover, as Duda had more than hinted? That would solve his problem.

No it wouldn't.

Fornjot's palm would solve his problem.

And to be thirty years younger.

Somebody must be looking after the place!

As if in answer, the dwarf came from the house lop-sided, with a steaming bucket full of – Bald could smell it – piss.

The dwarf, Nell Ball, Bald owed him one.

He drew back behind a corner of the house and watched.

The dwarf put the bucket down next to the horse, lifted its swollen leg and dropped it in.

Sometimes the inevitable takes ages.

Bald waited for the explosion of pain that would send dwarf, bucket and piss flying.

It came with a satisfying scream.

Eneda ran out of the house.

The dwarf was scalded and stinking, and bruised all over from the way he hopped and howled. He fled past her and jumped into the pond.

Bald laughed out loud.

She turned to him, looking angry.

He still laughed. "At least he won't get leprosy."

He walked to the horse.

After a moment, she joined him. "It took us three days to fill that bucket."

"Give him cumin in four bowls of water fasting, and he'll fill it himself in a day."

He bent down to feel the horse's leg. He heard her say, "It isn't any better."

"I'm a leech not a saint."

He rose, and saw her across the horse's croup. If what Duda had said was true, her experiences had left no marks. Her face was young.

He still had the camomile in his hand and he offered it to her.

She frowned. "What for?"

"For nothing. For you."

She shook her head.

"All right, for nightmares, toothache, and sore nipples."

She almost smiled.

"You can use it to make your hair more fair."

She took it.

They walked towards the house. Bald wondered if what Duda had said was true. "Is your man at home?"

"He's dead." Short and sharp. She pointed to the dwarf in the pond. "Lyb is mine."

Bald stopped in surprise. "Your what?"

"My slave." She was angry.

He stepped back instinctively and trod on the row of onions in the garden.

Eneda nodded. "Well done."

He felt he was losing. "Who planted the worts?"

"I did. My mother taught me." She knelt to resurrect an onion. "You know about these things: what else should I grow?"

She was forgiving him, and he eagerly accepted.

"Chervil, comfrey, rosemary, hyssop, rue ..."

"Wait, wait! Come in the house and write them down."

The blank absurdity of it made him laugh. "What!"

"You can write, can't you?"

"I can write, but you can't read!"

"Give me your book."

He hugged the book close to him.

"Show it to me. Open it."

He held the book with its spine against his chest, and opened it as if it was his heart.
Eneda read aloud.

In the book:
"For a wormeaten or mortified body; dust of oak rind, dust of ash rind, dust of elder rind taken on the north of the tree, and the nether part warm dust of the root of helenium, dust of dock, peppers dust ..."

Bald said it was enough.
"No, no ... dust of rye, sulfurs dust, oil and horses grease, ship tar, of all of these equal amounts; mingle all cold together till they be well smudging ..."
She laughed.
He was offended. "So you can read. An ox can pull but it can't plough."
He closed the book.
"By the time you put all that together, the body would be dead."
Her eyes were laughing at him.
"Maybe it is."
He strode away from her.
"Leech! Leech! What about my horse?"
He could not answer. She had been too close. He feared what he could not do. He would not go there again.
When he saw her the next day, she had washed her hair.
The fairness of it hooked in his heart like a burr.
Lyb was sitting on a bench drinking water from a pitcher. He eyed Bald resentfully.
They went into the garden to plant the worts he brought her.
"Who taught you to read?"
"My mother."
"Not your father?"
"He was no scribe." She sniffed.
"He died young."
"No, he was almost as old as you."
Bald dug the ground angrily.
"She did." Her face was soft with remembrance. "Too young."
"You left home."
"Who did you talk to?"

"Duda."

She shrugged.

"Is he a liar?"

"He's a man, isn't he?"

"He said they died of shame." As he spoke, he knew it was a mistake. She raised her head and stared at him contemptuously.

"Can you die of shame? Is there a leechdom for shame in the book?"

Bald was ashamed, but he knew it was not fatal. He shifted away from her on his knees and went on planting, his head low, digging in the seedlings with his hands. He cursed himself for being human and not a god. He saw himself crouching there, grey stubble lined like a field in winter, scrabbling at the earth.

"I've never done anything to be ashamed!"

Eneda was standing defiantly looking down at him.

He bowed his head. "It's not a word I'd use."

He expected it to end there, but she went on compulsively.

"I was married! Tell Duda that from me."

Bald knew she was telling him not Duda. He could not think why, but the idea she was ready to confide in him grew leaves and budded.

"I was married in Winchester by Bishop Wigthegn."

It withered with the lie. She was lying to impress him, what for?

He rose and went to pick up the book. How often a lie achieves the opposite of its intention.

"Don't you believe me?"

He spoke sadly without looking at her. "You can't have been. A bishop wouldn't marry anyone below the rank of earldoman."

He walked away.

"Old man! Old man!"

He stopped and turned, an old man.

"Go into the house!"

Bald looked at the house. On the bench the dwarf had stopped drinking and was enjoying the scene.

"Are you too old for the truth?"

He shuffled towards the house, bending his head in the low doorway. He heard her coming after him, shouting at Lyb.

"Piss or I'll beat the piss out of you!"

Bald longed for the woman of his dream.

She came in like a fury, charging round the room, looking in jugs, pulling out boxes, searching for something valuable like a burglar. She found it and shook it at him – a shining key.

She dragged a chest out from under the stairs and crouched to unlock it.

She came to the table and slapped a parchment down in front of him.

It was a charter. It bore the royal seal. It was in Latin.

"Read that!"

He had forgotten all the Latin he knew. He tried to laugh it off. "I gave up Latin years ago. I could never find anyone to speak it with."

She spelt it out for him.

"To Ealdorman Eadric ... master of the mint at Winchester ... Alfred."

Bald sat silent for a long time, long after she had replaced the charter, locked the chest and hidden the key.

Eneda wandered round the room moving things, presumably for Lyb to put back later.

She finally stopped at the far side of the table.

"We were not exactly married."

He looked up. She was smiling. Without humour.

He thought of the walls between people. We live like monks in the cells of our bodies. In the cloisters of our thoughts.

"He was hanged for forgery."

"What?" He had not heard or had not believed what he had heard.

"Eadric was hanged. He went into business on his own. King Alfred hanged him."

Her smile was so bleak and cold he wanted to hurl himself across the table and hold her. He wanted to suffer too.

"Thirty years ago the Vikings killed my father."

It was pathetic! The girl had not been born thirty years ago.

"Strangely enough, I saw the killer's son not far from here ..." He had to talk to break the ice inside her. "He was a king. They were taking him for burial somewhere on a ship. There's a river here ..."

She was not listening still living in her own nightmare.

"You should have seen the treasure."

"What treasure?"

"A hoard of stolen silver. He must have robbed a hundred churches. And a gold helmet worth twice as much."

"Where is it?"

Her voice was tight as a bowstring. She leant across the table like the bow.

He was amused. "It's gone. I set the ship on fire. It sank."

"Let's get it!"

"It's at the bottom of the river."

"Lyb can swim, and if he can't, he'll learn!"

He laughed. "No, no, and anyway it must have melted in the fire. If it's still there it's worthless, a shapeless mass."

Eneda charged off round the room again, looking in jugs, pulling out boxes.

"What are you looking for now?"

"The frigging key!"

She shocked him. He would have to get used to it.

She found the key with a cry of triumph and rushed to open the chest. She came to the table and dropped a heavy bundle wrapped in cloth in front of him. Bald unwrapped it.

Inside gleamed grey the mould, dies and stamps of a coiner's trade, Eadric's legacy.

"We can make our own money."

Eneda's smile came from deep inside her and her eyes were shining like shillings.

iii

In the book:
"In the month of May the third day is mischievous and the seventh before the end of it."

Lyb went under for the third time. The rope round his waist ran to the bank where Eneda was watching. She saw the arrowhead of ripples where the river was parted by the sunken stern of the longship, and the butt of water where the dwarf had disappeared.

The horse was cropping grass nearby.

Bald stood with his back to the sun, estimating the length of his shadow.

In the book:

"On the twenty-first of May the shadow of a gnomon six foot long at nine of morning and three of noon is seven feet and at midday four."

"Bald."

"Today's the twenty-first of May."

"Bald, Lyb's drowned."

He turned. Ran. Seized the rope and hauled it in with all his strength.

With awful slowness the rope tautened, rose dripping, up came Lyb gasping and flapping. Like a mereswine, Bald thought.

He landed him among the reeds plastered with mud and stinkwort. Eneda went and looked at him. "Throw him back."

"He's holding something."

Bald prised the squat fingers open. It was a small square plate of gold engraved with the twisting tail of a serpent.

It must have dropped from the helmet before it melted.

He held it up.

Eneda snatched it from him and kissed it.

Lyb did not want to go back into the river.

He was full of water and had to piss, so she sent him across to the horse. He went, and then went round behind it and pissed out of reach.

Bald took the rope and waded into the water.

He found he could stand where Lyb had gone under.

He cupped his hands round his eyes and peered down.

A twisted silver cross the size of a man lay in the grasp of blackened ribs of wood where the river-smith had shaped it.

For a while he wondered whether or not to leave it where it was.

Until he heard her screaming.

He would feed her with silver, be her provider, her leech, provide her with a leechdom for her independence.

And himself? She would love him.

Worth more than silver.

He took a breath and plunged down with the rope, reaching for the cross.

The current teased him as he knelt under water feeling blindly for the shining crosspiece.

He embraced the cross with widespread arms and captured it with the rope.

He floated to the surface and tied the knot.

He waded to the bank where she was waving her arms in her excitement.

She grasped the rope and laid back against the pull of the river.

He saw the outline of her body under her dress.

He looked away and looked again.

"Come on!" She smiled. Her head was full of silver.

He moved behind her and picked up the rope. They leant back with all their strength.

Bald trembled at the nearness of her body. Her hair hung down and touched his thighs. There was an ecstasy in their joint endeavour akin to making love.

She slipped and fell back against him and lay on him laughing with the fun of it.

He thought now is the time, now, and fought against his thoughts knowing the time was never.

He rolled away, stood, called Lyb to bring the horse.

Eneda lay where she landed, laughing up at him. "You've got no strength!"

His body was corded with muscle plastered like an ash bole in the rain.

He felt the anguish of old age. The Knot.

He made a loop with his plaid and put it round the horse's neck.

He tied the rope to the loop.

Eneda stood at the horse's head.

He went back into the river.

Fool, fool, he was better off asleep and dreaming.

When he reached the sunken longship, he turned and waved.

What was the draw of this small wilful woman?

He saw the horse, lame, stumbling and she struck it with her fist.

The rope tightened. The cross shifted, turned and stuck between two blackened ribs of wood. The rope strained.

"Stop!"

He saw her strike the horse again.

"Stop! Stop!"

Folly folly folly. The rope would snap, the knot would slip, the game would be up.

"Stop you fool!"

He saw disaster clearly.

As it was, the ribs tore from the keel and the cross slid free from the longship like some underwater burial at sea. He took the two curved ribs back to the bank of reeds where the cross slid ashore.

Eneda came running down to see. She saw him and stopped.

"Fool yourself!" She went past him to look at the treasure. He wondered she had let him spoil her moment, why? Was he worth an insult?

She was squatting in the water stroking the silver as if she was a cat with a salmon.

He dragged the ribs of wood up to where Lyb was waiting with the horse. They tied them together to make a sled and then led the horse on slowly to draw the cross up onto it. Eneda followed, letting them do the work. She seemed moderate in her delight now that it was done.

Bald caught her looking at him differently, as if she realised there were things he could do better than she could, even that he could disapprove of her. The word 'respect' came into his head and he cursed it: he did not want respect from her.

"Well done." She said when it was finished.

Or gratitude.

Lyb was sent into the forest to fetch an armful of leaves to cover the treasure.

"Where's the gold helmet?"

Bald had forgotten it. "They must have found it."

"Pity." He noticed round her neck she had hung the serpent panel on plaited reeds.

It was a long slow journey home. The sled ran well enough across the water meadows. The forest track was corrugated by roots of trees and blocked by fallen branches. It was night when they came out from the shelter of the hanger that loomed over the village and Eneda's land. There were lights moving in the field between them and the house.

"Soldiers," said Bald, "Who else goes out at night?"

He picked out a dozen spearmen with lanterns coming towards him.

"Put Lyb on the sled! He's dead and we're going to bury him. Weep, woman, weep!"

Bald ran ahead waving his arms and shouting. "Halt – there's a dead body here!"

The men stopped as he appeared out of the darkness like a spectre.

The leader called out. "Who are you?"

"Bald the leech."

"We're looking for deserters from the army."

"He's dead! Can't you hear the woman weeping?"

Eneda wailed. The horse, smelling strangers, neighed.

"We'll take the horse!"

"Take it take it, but don't go near the man, he's got the flying venom! Faul faul he's got the elf disease! That's why we're here. We're going to bury him in pitch at midnight."

The soldiers backed away. The leader was reluctant.

"Bring the horse over here!"

"I will, but mind – it's got leprosy, a loose barrel and a bad temper."

"Give it to the devil!" The leader led his men towards the village.

"I give you to Woden," Bald murmured.

They got the silver home and hid it in the pond.

Bald went back to the village. The soldiers had taken Duda and some of the others. A great pagan army had landed in Kent and along the south coast. King Alfred was at Eashing. There was going to be a battle.

Bald was exhausted. He climbed the hill and went to bed.

Wars, battles, Alfred and the Danes meant nothing to him. Only Eneda. And in the middle of great wars we are concerned with our own problems, like little crabs caught in the tide bury themselves in sand.

He dreamt of nothing now at night or else dreamt and forgot.

Lyb built a kiln near the pond and lined it with sand. The opening was wide enough to take the cross, and a channel led to a spout for the molten silver to run into Eneda's moulds. Bald was impressed. All conquered people are despised, despise themselves, and try to emulate the conquerors. This is called progress.

They decided it was safer to coin the silver by day. Lyb lit a bonfire of last winter's rotten straw to cover the smoke. When the clay bricks in the kiln burned black, they hauled the silver cross from the pond and fed it inch by inch into the fiery opening. Eneda crouched by the spout with the moulds.

She looked up and saw Bald with the book.

"You look like one of those old men in the Bible."

Her life before he met her was a closed book. He remembered the libraries in the monasteries he had visited with Cild, all burnt now, only the book he held in his arms now remained.

He had never heard of a woman who could read.

If she knew the Bible, she was a Christian.

Jesus was a leech.

In the book:

"For a wormeaten or mortified body ..."

The book never gave up either.

She broke into his thoughts with a cry of joy. A thin trickle of blackened silver was running from the spout. She moved the mould to catch it, crooning like a mother as she coined the cross.

When a mould was full, Bald carried it to the pond and dipped it in. He turned it over an open sack and the blank coins fell out.

He ran back for another.

The smoke reddened their eyes. They shone with sweat. They worked like worshippers at a shrine without a conscious thought of what they were doing. Or cooks.

Midday. The kiln had consumed half the cross and squittered half a fortune.

"Eadric called it the devil's kitchen."

He saw her back through her sweat-sodden dress as if she were naked.

"You can't stop coining half-way through."

That's what hell is: doing what we like to do long after we like doing it.

They could not get the crosspiece in the kiln. Lyb had not bargained for that and so would stay subjected. They dragged it back and sunk it in the pond. They made him break the kiln to pieces and scatter the ashes of the bonfire over the burnt earth. They carried the sack of coins into the house.

It was evening and the acrid smell of smoke and scorched metal remained. Bald was going home. He was tired.

"Stay. Eat with us." He was not too tired.

He went down to the stream to wash. The sultry moon appeared enormous in the lingering smoke. He counted time by nights not days. He looked back at the house and saw her very small. She was bare to the waist bending down by the pond pouring water from a pitcher over her hair.

The droop of her breasts filled him with longing. He looked at his own cold leaden body killed by a dream, and knew the longing of a moonlit night.

Eneda lit the lamp and they ate a roasted goose's egg and worts from the garden.

She brought a stone jar to the table with the air of something special. It had a wooden stopper wrapped in stained linen. Bald was reminded of a bloody bandage. The stopper was loose and he smelt sour wine before she poured it. She raised her cup.

"To Freyja."

The goddess of fertility – Bald raised his eyebrows. As he was reaching for his cup at the same time, he knocked it over.

"Silly old man." She drank, grimaced, spat it out. He laughed.

In the book:
"For a light drink; bishopwort, wormwood, attorlothe, springwort, githrife, pennyroyal, fennel, beaten pepper, put all the worts into one vessel then put clear old wine into the drink then let the man drink and it is the better for him according as he oftener drinketh it."

He had the worts with him in his pouch and smiled to himself as he watched her watching him.
"Whose wine? Eadric?"
"My father."
He poured the concoction into her cup and she sipped it.
"It tastes like medicine."
"It will help you sleep."
"And you?"
"I have a long walk."
"Stay here." She gestured casually to a corner of the room.
There was only one room.
"Where does Lyb sleep?"
"With the ram."
Where else? The ram was more valuable than Lyb.
"And you?"
"There." She pointed to a heap of pelts on the floor.
Not in a bed like a Christian then but wild. For a second his fascination flared. In the darker darkness that followed his indecision stumbled.
"I don't know."
"You'll be quite safe." She smiled.
So she had thought of it too!
"So will you." It was a cheap riposte and he regretted it seeing her smile twist a little with contempt. He ostentatiously emptied his cup. "I'll be asleep." The smile went, the contempt remained.
He filled both cups again.
"How long have you lived alone?"
She did not answer. Perhaps she thought he was trying to measure how desperate she was.
"I mean why? It's unusual. It's unnatural."
"Do you think there is something wrong with me?"

"No."

"Then shut up. I'm alone because I want to be. Like you."

He did not want to be but said nothing.

"I've been alone since my mother. Eadric was a mistake. He wanted a whore. Since my mother died until ..."

She stopped.

Say you! Say until I met you!

"Until I bought Lyb." She emptied her cup. "This works." She got up and went outside.

Bald took the book and propped it up against the wall in the corner she had indicated. He lay down with his head under the book so he would not see her. Eneda returned, glanced at him briefly and blew out the lamp.

The room slowly filled with moonlight.

He lay with his eyes open listening and imagining.

He heard the rustle of her dress and imagined he saw her small body as pale and smooth as ivory.

He saw her kneel and bow in supplication to the moon.

The vulnerability of her arched back overwhelmed him.

He felt a fierce possessive protectiveness he had never felt for anyone before. And at the same time he felt a longing to be possessed and protected by her.

Her weakness was his strength, her strength his weakness. Only together could either be complete.

He heard her breathing. It moved him more than anything. The earth is never absolutely silent. Always a leaf falls somewhere.

He stared up at the book and saw her lying on her bed of furs, half animal, half woman, like a sphinx her face inscrutable in sleep.

The Egyptian Pamphilos invoked the sphinx.

"I invite thee tomorrow to the house of M or N to tie the artery to stop the haemorrhoids in the name of Stolpus."

As one leech to another.

Speaking across the centuries like the book.

Was Adam created with piles? He must ask the next monk he meets.

Or did he get them from eating too much fruit?

He heard her sigh as if she had been absent from his thoughts too long. He saw himself slide across the floor silently and kneel at her feet.

Then he began the familiar ritual of his dreams.

No incubus visited a host more intimately than Bald visited Eneda in his imagination.

He lay awake separated from her by age, inadequacy, fear and self-contempt, and at the same time he worshipped her with hands and mouth playing on her body with the expertise of an adept.

She lay unaware of his existence and hers in his waking dream, her other self twisting and turning, writhing in his embraces, succumbing to his ministrations and finally croaking out her ecstasy like a raven's spit.

She lay untouched in the moonlight.

He lay in the black shadow of the book watching himself celebrating an empty eucharist.

He was indeed the devil's monk.

On the second day they stamped the coins with Eadric's dies.

Eneda chose the design with care. Eadric's carelessness had been his downfall, short and fatal.

When Alfred succeeded his brother as king, the Danes had him pinned in a corner of Wessex around Athelney. He had bought them off with silver forced from the church, hastily coined and stamped AELFRED REX SAXONUM.

Years later after the peace of Wedmore had divided the island with the Danes, he had tacitly stated his greater ambition with the inscription AELFRED REX ANGLORUM.

England was to be his glory, not Wessex or even Saxonland.

This was the die Eneda chose.

The reverse showed two kings, Angle and Saxon, seated under two fronds of palm.

"Fornjot's palm."

"Whose palm?"

"Nothing."

She placed a blank coin in the centre of the grindstone they had dragged outside from the kitchen.

She held the cylindrical die pressed to the coin.

Lyb raised the coiner's hammer above his head. Bald had offered to do it. "You? You'd miss."

Now he stood watching.

The hammer flashed in the sunlight, hit true, rang.

The die leapt in Eneda's hand.

The coin shone with the face of the king.

She reversed the coin and held a second die pressed to it.

The hammer rang.

She tossed the coin aside and took another blank from the sack.

The hammer rang.

Again.

Bald picked up a struck coin and turned it in his hand.

Was this Alfred, the power, the potency of England?

Was this Fornjot's palm?

What was money? To him, nothing.

The pennyroyal had more power than the penny.

Yet the penny did more than Saxon armies, and defeated the Danes. That was real power.

The hammer rang and rang again.

Like a church bell. Or Thor's hammer on the anvil of the gods.

Money was more powerful than either. The king's money had subdued both Christian and pagan, church and Viking.

In the haze of sunlight he saw Eneda kneeling, flinching under the hammer blows, face glowing with intensity of desire.

Nature had betrayed him.

He would give his life for the life nature had taken from him.

He would die to have power, to be potent, to be one again with nature in the eternal tragedy of creation and death.

If this was Fornjot's palm it would make him potent too.

He dropped the coin onto the heap of struck coins. Eneda looked up at him and smiled.

The coining continued all day.

Lyb grew tired.

Eneda called to Bald to take his place. The heaps of blank and struck coins were about equal. Her hands were red from the friction of the cylinders.

He told her: "Rest."

"No." She shook her head impatiently.

He picked up the hammer. She bent down, her whole body tensed, waiting for the blow.

She was like a supplicant at his feet, and although he knew she knelt to another master he could not strike the blow.

"What are you waiting for?"

"I might miss."

She spoke without looking up. "You will if you think you will."

It was as if she had struck a spark in the black cavern of his brain, making his fear leap out of the darkness.

"You will if you think you will." He saw fear for what it was.

A shadow.

And if his fear of striking was a shadow – all his fears were shadows.

He swung the hammer and struck the die in her hands roundly so that it rang true.

His whole body felt the satisfaction of it.

She reversed the coin and placed the second die.

He struck it roundly.

She tossed the coin away and took another.

A strike.

A strike.

The blood surged in him excitedly. If he could do this he could do anything. He grinned with the feeling of power.

He struck. Shadows! He struck again.

He saw himself standing over the woman, striking, mastering, having, pounding.

He stripped his plaid from his shoulders, letting it hang over his belt. He stood astride. He raised his head to praise the god of money. He struck the die roundly.

No more thought. That was the gospel of it. Money does not think. Making money requires no thought, no reason, no purpose except its own. So why not making anything?

It had the brutal simplicity of Thor.

Swing the hammer. Strike!

Swing the hammer. Strike!

Don't think! Kill! Or fuck!

"Stop!" He looked down.

Eneda was watching him intently with a half-smile parting her lips. Her eyes were interested. She seemed conscious of the new power in him. She challenged him as if it challenged her.

Bald wanted to go on. "Why?"

She pointed to the sack. It was empty. The heap of minted coins was complete.

He became conscious of himself again. His heart was pounding. His arms were weak. He was spent. He swayed.

Eneda stood and steadied him, leaning against him to support his weight.

He felt the bulb of her breast press into his side.

He was overwhelmed with a great weakness.

He knelt, holding his arms around her, slipping down. He lay down.

"You did it." She knelt above him wiping the sweat from his face. "Old man." Her voice was soft and challenging.

He saw her hair and her breasts swinging inside the loose neck of her dress.

He longed for her to kiss him.

He felt her lips warm, firm, parted on the stubble of his cheek.

A great peace welled up in his heart and he wept.

She was puzzled and amused. "Why?"

How could he tell her?

"It's only money."

It was more than money. Fornjot's palm. Life itself.

The excitement of the day soured in the evening like dried sweat. They were both too exhausted to eat much. They drank the lees of yesterday's wine. The heap of struck coins lay in a heap in the lamplight waiting to be counted.

Their desires lay waiting behind their glittering eyes.

Bald felt the bile rising from the pit of his stomach and could taste the acrid bitterness of suspense.

Eneda was restless.

"Shall we do it? Count them?"

She went and crouched by the heap like a cat, clawing and putting the coins into piles. He watched her, trying not to think further into the moment.

"Come on!" Her voice was harsh and demanding. "We'll never get it done!"

Five would buy a sheep, ten a pig, twenty a cow, thirty an ox, a hundred Lyb, two hundred a Saxon cearl, two thousand an ealderman. Every man had his price, and every part of a man.

Bald, counting forty silver pennies, knew it was the price of his penis. He glanced at Eneda. She could afford it but would she get it?

In the book:

"Ad veneris. The extremest end of a fox's tail hung upon the arm."

Why would that excite a woman? The symbolism was obvious but the fox was dead.

By the time he had counted a hundred she had reached a thousand, two hundred, two thousand.

She could have bought Eadric from the king and saved his life.

Three thousand.

Four thousand.

King Alfred had paid the Vikings ten thousand pounds of silver to keep his kingdom south of Watling Street and the Thames.

That was the price of England.

Four thousand and twenty two pennies. A hundred foreskins and a cow. Now they lay behind them in piles of ten and there was nothing between them but their passions.

Eneda was looking at him intently: they were so close their eyes were focused inwards.

"What?" He heard himself ask her.

"I feel I've known you before."

Bald shook his head.

"I do. Could you have been here when I was a child? Did you ever live here?"

He shook his head again. He knew her but he did not know how.

"Perhaps I dreamed about you?"

She was smiling. He was serious. Dreams are true in everything except their interpretation.

"It doesn't matter."

She leant forward. She was so close her face disintegrated into eyes, nose, mouth, the surreal tessers of a well-loved mosaic.

He felt her lips on his.

"Why?" His voice was strange to him.

Her face resumed its proper shape and a flit of annoyance crossed it.

"Do you have to ask?"

He meant to say no no no, love needs no reasons, but he could not.

Instead he said, "I'm a leech."

He tried to smile and made his face ugly.

She moved away and sprawled upon the heap of skins that was her bed. "Come on then, leech me."

He thought, it did not suit her, she was playing a part dictated by desire, desire so powerful it suppressed her revulsion – so he thought. He crouched on hands and knees like an animal, and wished he was a dog or stag or ram or gander, and could go and gander her without a thought.

He felt nothing.

Where was the glorious freedom of the afternoon when he had Fornjot's palm in his hand and everything was possible?

He pushed over a pile of money. It could not buy what he needed. It could not stop him thinking.

Her sprawl had lifted her dress above her knees and her legs were splayed apart.

In the book:

"A leechdom for woman; take a fresh horse's turd, lay it on hot gledes, make it reek strongly between the thighs, that the woman may sweat much."

He left the lamp burning.

He thought if he saw her it would arouse him.

Fool.

He crawled to her feet and lowered himself onto his belly like a snake.

When he touched her foot she recoiled instinctively, but he grasped her ankles and pulled her onto her back. After that she lay still.

He touched her feet with his tongue.

It was dry like a snake's tongue. He could not salivate. All his glands were dry.

He tongued her legs, sliding his body between them, pushing up her dress until it rucked around her thighs.

She lifted her lower body patiently, like a patient, and pulled the dress up to her waist.

He folded her legs and opened her as if she was a book and lowered his head to read her with his tongue.

Eneda moaned her loneliness. This was not what she had meant. This leechdom.

She tried to push his head away but he was relentless, probing her wound to the depths.

She began to twist and turn between pain and joy, resentment and release. He raised his hands to her shoulders and clamped her to the bed.

She rolled her head from side to side and cried out meaningless cries he understood because he understood the music of her body. She shrieked like a victim, her body racked with joy and pain, and finally released her spirit, her sap, through the cut bark of her skin.

Bald lay for a long time as if Eneda had just given birth to him, still birth.

She rolled free. She went outside to squat in the water-grass at the edge of the pond and wash herself clean.

There was a sickle moon. It was the twenty-fourth of May. A mischievous day.

IV

He tried to think what she was thinking.

In the morning, she had gone around with a mischievous smile on her face, like a child with a secret, and he had returned to the hamlet depressed.

Perhaps she thought he was too old?

She had treated him with teasing condescension.

Perhaps she thought he was indifferent to women?

If he was, his heart was aching with indifference.

In the book:

"For pain in the chest. Take elecampane roots and bark that has grown again, and dry thoroughly and make into a dust and drive it through a cloth, and take honey and seethe it thoroughly; after that take the dust and mingle it therewith and stir together and put into a box and use when need be."

He took some, and felt more depressed than before. He knew sometimes the leechdoms made matters worse before they made them better.

He went out to the little group of old men, women and children who had climbed the hill with their complaints.

In the book:

"If thou wilt quickly cure a little wound, bruise and seethe in butter watercress, work it into a salve, smear therewith.

Against lice. Give the man to eat sodden colewort at night, fasting frequently, he will be guarded against lice.

For wamb (stomach) sickness and sore; a bowl full of linseed, rubbed or beaten, and two bowls of sharp vinegar; boil together, give to the sick man to drink after his night's fast. Again, lay chewed pennyroyal on the navel, and the pain will be still.

Blossomed worts are best to work, either for drinks, or for salves, or for dust."

From his perch, Bald looked across green fields, hursts and copses to the blue haze of the downs, and imagined he could see the sea. He knew about the world almost as much as he knew about the stars, and from the same source: Bede, whose books his father made him read. He had met monks with feet like leather, who had walked to Rome and back. He knew the world was large, but larger still were the moon and the stars, that ruled the tides, the seasons, nature, and the lives of men.

In the book:

"The thirteenth moon is perilous for beginning things. Dispute not this day with thy friends. The fugitive will quickly be discovered. A child born will be plucky, having a mark about his eyes, bold rapacious arrogant self-pleasing; will not live long. A maiden will have a mark on the back of her neck or on the thigh; will be saucy spirited daring of her body with many men; she will die soon. A man fallen sick on this moon will quickly escape or be long ill. A dream will be fulfilled within nine days. From the sixth hour it is a good moon for bloodletting."

He lay on his back looking up at the sky, so innocent, blue, no evil ought to live under it. Illness, stumbling age, the varieties of death contrived by men made no sense. He despised belief that suffering was noble, or death in battle was the doorway to the beerhall of the gods. They were the bedtime stories told for fools by poscrs such as priests and pirates. If god was god would god have time for a man? When nature, god's creation, was supremely indifferent to the individual? When the moon and stars, unseen but always there, gave the fugitive, the child, the saucy girl, the sick man and the dreamer, no choice, no chance?

Deeply fatalistic, empirical, accepting Cild's science and then only if it was effective, Bald lay in the sunlight, thinking.

He closed his eyes.

Now the sky was golden red and he was inside the universe of his dreams. His thoughts luxuriated and grew strange heads, the flowers of imagination, and they were all Eneda.

She was naked in the Eden of his mind.

Strange flowers stirred in the breath of desire. A bird sang the same note repeatedly: fate, fate, fate.

She drifted into his being, his blood, his heart, the warm

body-world he inhabited and was his own god and creation. She occupied him, filled him, was his essence. He felt love as a warm red liquid world in which he floated like a foetus.

An old man is a child in love.

And in the garden of his mind he saw himself walking among the flowers like Adam, a pre-apple Adam, nude and stupid. Then there bloomed in his dream a plant he had never seen before, with upright unbranched stem and pinnate head of full and fleshy leaves, which he immediately recognised and plucked and sucked the sap of Fornjot's palm. He felt power and the palm growing in him, an upright stem sprouting a fleshy head. He thought Eneda and she was with him warm and ready, encompassing and consuming him like fire, in golden red and joyous happy flames. He saw them united in a pillar of fire rising to the sky ...

Someone spoke his name and he awoke.

A man was crouching beside him shaking with fear and exhaustion.

He recognised Duda.

Even as he started up, he saw the pursuers, Saxon men-at-arms, breaking from the forest.

He pointed.

Duda called on god and turned to run towards the track that led down to the village.

The soldiers hurled their spears. One, by chance or fate, struck a rock and flew sideways across his path, tripping him and wrenching his ankle.

Duda lay palpitating in the dust like a stricken hart.

The soldiers soon came up to him and pulled him to his feet and struck him and he cried out, "Bald, save me!"

Bald was afraid.

The men were excited by the chase and in no mood to worry who they caught. The leader, a young thegn with a birthmark over his left eye and wearing an iron hauberk, looked at Bald suspiciously.

"Who are you?"

"Bald the leech."

"You know this man?"

"His name is Duda."

"He's a deserter."

Duda cried out. "I got lost! I fell behind and got lost!"

A soldier struck him across the mouth, drawing blood.

"He's a deserter. The King has ordered all deserters to be hanged."

The thegn looked round. There was a crossbeam sticking out from a ruined house. He pointed, and a soldier with a rope went towards it. Bald heard himself protesting. "Not without a trial. It's the law."

The young thegn grew more excited. "There's war not law!"

"Then I'll pay blood money for him. Twenty pounds of silver."

The soldiers heard and gathered round him in a circle. This was not only going to be a kill, but a drama and a kill.

"All right. Where is it?"

"Not here. I'll fetch it after nightfall. Alone."

"Where from?"

Bald was silent.

"How did you get it?"

"I found it."

"You mean you stole it. Found money belongs to the King. You stole it. That's a hanging offence."

The thegn looked round for applause and got it.

"I earned the money."

"First you found it, then you earned it. That's perjury. Another hanging offence."

More applause. The circle closed round Bald.

"I'm a leech! I'm trying to save a man's life!"

The thegn looked bored. "Stop arguing my friend." And to the soldiers, "Hang the deserter."

Duda screamed once before they gagged and bound him and dragged him under the crossbeam where the rope was dangling. They put the noose round his neck and hauled him up while one of them, a merciful comedian, grasped him and hung with him like a lover to shorten his agony.

When he stopped twitching they lowered the corpse and took the rope to use again.

Bald ran to him. Duda was dead. And yet Duda was not dead. In a mad paradox the hanged man's penis was erect and seeping life. Bald took his knife and opened a vein in Duda's arm to give his body peace.

He watched the blood seeping into the earth enriching it and knew there would be worts growing there next spring: chamomile, white borehound, wood sanicle, and pink vervain the holy wort, and men would be given life by Duda's death.

He did not resent death or hate death or fear death. Death was the supreme leech. Death ended all diseases. Death was the head of his profession: the last referral was to death.

He resented, hated, feared the men who usurped death's prerogative: the Viking Ivarr, King Alfred, the young thegn. They took the cure and made it the kill.

Drained of blood, the corpse lay sinking into the earth. Duda was a memory, and that would go with those who remembered him.

Bald thought of himself. It would not be long before he stopped thinking for ever. He tried to imagine it. He could not imagine it and laughed out loud at the absurdity of it all.

The villagers buried Duda next morning. Bald did not go down because he knew Eneda would be there. His despair was worse than ever. He heard someone coming up the hill and hurried into his house to avoid meeting them. When they did not call or knock he wondered who they were and went out and saw Lyb sitting on the ground.

He felt his heart turn over.

She sent for him. She wanted him.

Why did she want him?

He asked Lyb, who smiled.

Bald knew the dwarf hated him.

"When does she want to see me?"

Lyb pointed to the sun and then to the tops of the trees.

In the evening when he was crossing the fields he heard a nightingale on the edge of the wood. The song stopped abruptly.

He felt he was being watched and wished he had never talked of silver to the soldiers.

Eneda was waiting for him and barred the door after he entered. The window was covered with sacking. She took a taper from the fire and lit the lamp. The room glowed golden and he was reminded of his dream.

She looked beautiful to him.

She picked up a heavy sack and dropped it on the table.

"That's yours."

He put down the book and went and sat hunched up on the floor near the fire.
"Half." She said. "Count it."
When he did not answer, she opened the book at random.

In the book:
"In case that a man be withhheld if he hath on him Scottish wax and the small atterlothe let him drink it in boiled ale so that he may not be restrained."

He sat hunched, black in the firelight, etched in fire like a volcano.
"What is the Knot?"
His head turned angrily. She saw the fire reflect a red flash in his eyes. She went on.
"It's written in the margin in another hand."
He breathed hard, his voice grated. "Close the book!"
His harshness surprised her and she closed the book. She waited.
When he spoke again his anger was gone. "That is the Knot."
She saw the black cracked cover rubbed and scarred with age.
"It's the little death."
She knew he was talking about himself. She wanted to go to him but he was dark and unapproachable.
"It's the end not of life ... the end of love."
Eneda thought love was not the only love.
"Come and count your money."
"I don't want any money."
"Don't be stupid."
He was still resentful and full of doom. "I wanted money yesterday. You keep it." He had meant it to sound noble. It sounded petulant.
She went to the fire. There was some soup warming in a kettle. She filled two bowls. They sat on either side of the fire drinking from the bowls in silence.
He was troubled by her presence, more so than when she was only present in his thoughts. He put down the bowl.
"I don't want the money."
"After all the trouble we had making it?"
Bald shrugged.

"And what happened afterwards?"
He could not move. She was curious.
"When you help someone, save someone's life, what do you feel?"
He did not answer. "It must mean something to you."
"It means the book is right."
"You must feel something. Don't you feel anything?"
"No."
"If the book is wrong and they die?"
"No."
He watched her. She looked small. Her face in shadow. Childlike.
"What about me?"
He almost choked with the sudden swell of love from his heart. What could he say? Fear and impotence stifled him.
"What do you feel about me?"
She was looking at him. He saw the firelight glint green in her eyes, shine on her round face.
"I've given you the money."
"That's nothing! That's like Eadric! I mean you!"
"Me?" He seemed surprised there was such a creature.
"I'm nothing. You know what I am. You read it in the book."
"That? I can cure that."
Her matter-of-fact audacity made him laugh, a bitter bark of laughter.
"My grandfather was a leech."
Bald was surprised. There were not many leeches, even before the Viking invasions.
"What was his name?"
"Cild."
He knew it as she said it, as the spear of truth passed through him, creating and destroying, laying his love in ruins.
"Have you heard of him?"
Caution and a lifetime's apprehensiveness rushed to fill the hole.
Eneda was anxious. "Have you heard of Cild?"
Take care. A negative is harder to prove than a positive. He heard someone speaking with his voice.
"I met him once."

She became animated and excited, kneeling up eagerly in an attitude he would have loved a moment ago.

"Is he still alive? Tell me!"

"No, no he was ... my dear he'd be too old."

My dear he'd be too old. He cursed the old fool who was talking.

Tell her the truth. Tell her Cild was his father. Her mother was his sister. She was his niece, a fourth part of himself. Tell her he was crying out for her. He loved her! Tell her that and never tell her anything again. The barriers of closeness would come between them. The Knot would never be untied. He would tell her one day but now he had to kill Cild in her mind.

"But I heard he was killed at Thetford many years ago."

Her eyes glistened for a man she had never seen.

"My mother said he was a famous man."

How much did she know? He asked her, "Did he live here?"

"He was a leech. He didn't live anywhere."

"Did he have any other family, did your mother say?" Was there a boy carrying a book?

"She never said. She never knew him. Only what her mother told her."

His mother too. He looked at her and saw his mother. The memory/dream of his mother. "I'm sorry."

"I'm sorry too". She smiled. They were very close. "I think he was like you."

He felt her lips touch his cheek. He twisted round, reached out and pulled her against him hard, crushing her as if he would drag her into his heart.

She gave a womanly gurgle of triumph. "I've cured you. That didn't take long."

She was his niece. He watched her with the pride of possession.

Whatever happened, she was part of him and he of her.

With her back to him she slid her arms out of her dress and let it drop to the floor.

Her skin glowed red in the firelight.

He felt his flesh tightening.

The redness from the fire and the redness of her quickening blood.

Cild was gone.

Cild was there.

Bald saw the blood eagle.

The bloody membrane stretched round her body in the parody of god.

His blood turned to ice.

He shut his eyes but the image was burned in them, dying slowly from red to yellow to grey ashes to a ghost.

When he opened them Eneda was kneeling in front of him.

"Can't you bear to look at me?"

She kneeled up, womanly and practical, pushing off his clothes.

He waited fearing the sweet torture would not make him scream.

She traced his corded anguish with her fingers, making it more unbearable. He waited, letting her flow over him, but he was cold. He longed for Fornjot's palm. He tried to blot the thoughts out of his head. He strained his body, his face distorted in a grinning rictus in the grip of fate. The hanged man was erect like Cild in his glistening sheath! He hated himself!

He could see over her curved back the table and the book. It brought him back to sanity.

In the book:

"For a fiendsick man or demoniac, when the devil possesses that man from within, let him say, "Thine hand vexeth, thine hand vexeth. I pray thee Priapiscus that thou come to me glad blossoming so that I be shielded and undamaged by poison and by wrath."

He sighed and thought of her.

He bent his head and kissed her spine, her shoulders and her neck. He parted her hair with his lips and saw a mark on her neck and kissed it. He raised her like a child and lowered his head to worship her as he had done before.

Later when she was asleep curled against him, trusting him with her body, he felt almost happy.

V

The drunken axe and dagger gods slept with their sisters and nieces in the beerhall heaven they inhabited. They had no choice unless they fancied the monsters which lurked outside.

The great king-emperor Charles slept with his daughters and kept them single for that purpose. His granddaughter Judith was King Alfred's stepmother and sister-in-law, having married first his father Aethelwulf and then his brother Aethelbald.

Consanguinity has always been a temptation rather than a dissuasion.

So Bald thought.

Christianity raised barriers, he had a vague recollection, the Bible forbade almost everything, but he could not remember what they were. Besides, the principle concern of ecclesiastical courts was to preclude a debased progeny and a race of depraved inbred idiots like the incestuous Britons.

He looked to where Lyb was sitting on a low wall, stitching two hides together to make a saddlebag.

Eneda was exercising the horse in the paddock. Each time she came into view he admired her natural grace. She rode with a concentration that gave her an unusual gravity. Eneda did not think enough, he thought. He wished she gave as much consideration to herself as she did to the horse. She was impetuous, bold, wilful, headstrong, positive, alive! He wondered they could be so closely related and so different. He stretched in the sun, an old man, leathery as a lizard, warming his blood.

He had not told her yet.

Since he had given her all the money she had been very complaisant, letting him pleasure her when he willed.

He feared to tell her would be to lose that privilege.

He feared to say he loved her would lose her altogether.

He thought she thought he was what?

A dry old dog with one talent.

Or at the best, a father/lover without the inconvenience of being either properly.

Well, he would bear it. To be with her he would bear everything.

He had never felt so close to anyone before. His half-life had been lived in the apartness of his profession.

Few men love a doctor. They only see him when they are ill.

He is aloof, magisterial, costly and often wrong.

Above all, he is irreproachable from beyond the grave.

He is, Bald thought, a lonely man whose sole companion, knowledge, drives most men away.

Sheep, he mused, were shepherded by fear of the dog. The shepherd used their natural instincts to protect them and the fact, vital to medicine in men, that they were all basically the same and would react in the same way.

He thought all doctors must despise their patients or at best be indifferent to them.

He could not love them any more than they could love him.

So all his great capacity for love was lavished on Eneda, while he made sure she was unaware of it and he was the dry old dog she imagined him to be.

So he thought.

She came walking slowly from the paddock and sat on the ground next to him.

"Bald."

"Eneda."

"I'm going away."

He looked up as if he heard thunder on a summer's day.

"I can't go to Winchester because of Eadric so I'm going to London."

"Why?" He knew why: to spend the money.

"To spend the money." She was transparently honest when she was not transparently lying. "It's perfectly safe."

The earth was fresh on Duda's grave. There was a Viking army somewhere in the south. London was disputed between King Alfred and a Mercian ealderman who was his son-in-law. Pagan marauders, Saxon deserters, robbers, displaced men, masterless slaves, the human detritus of thirty years of sporadic war and the division of the island, all threatened the road and river between here and London. He said nothing, knowing she knew it as well as he did.

All she said was, "I've never been to London."

That was probably true. It was not a Saxon city. King Alfred had never been there. It was Anglian if anything, Mercian, Roman, Danish, a polyglot concretion of interested parties totally unlike any other city.

"Have you?"

"Yes." He had gone there with Cild to see the prosperous doctor Dun who practised there. He had waited in an anteroom under the eye of a superior clerk who had the conscientious satisfaction of protecting his master from sick patients.

"Well, did you like it?"

"No."

"You wouldn't!"

London offended his senses. By living close together in cities, men supplanted nature with man-made disasters and diseases. By building walls around them, they increased the pressure on the space inside. Human nature, denied nature, grew strange and dangerous tumours. Man caged used all his natural instincts against himself. This was good for doctor Dun and no-one else.

She laughed at him. "You don't need anything."

"And you?"

"Change."

"That's the last thing in the world."

"You can't stop me."

He could. He could tie her to him by the bonds of their relationship. He was old and would die soon. He could shackle her with guilt. She would stay, but she would not forgive him.

"You'll never get there on your own."

He was giving up his rest for her, the rest of his life.

"I'll take Lyb."

"You wouldn't reach King's Stone."

"Where?"

He laughed. "What do you know, Eneda? What do you want?" For him, need and knowledge went together.

"I want joy."

The word came out of the sky like a brightly-coloured bird.

Her lips were parted and he wanted to kiss her but her mouth was not granted to him.

"Joy." When he said it, it sounded like doom. Joy was as elusive as Fornjot's palm. "You mean pleasure." She looked contemptuous.

"Happiness?"

"More than that."

Joy was the prerogative of the gods. Joy was a moment's immortality.

"You can't buy that in London. You can't buy it anywhere."

"It isn't the buying, Bald, it's the spending."

She was right. Joy is effusion, the pouring out of genius, love, life, without consciousness of time, place or purpose.

He sighed, and planned the journey.

"The only way to get there safely is to pretend you're fiendsick, which you are – and I'm taking you to that old leech Dun if he's still alive. Lyb goes ahead with a yellow cross and a bell. You wear a veil and are in restraint. I am myself in this comedy."

"I didn't ask you!"

Eneda jumped up and walked away and stood like a dryad of the woods, proud and independent.

He felt a fierce joy in looking at her.

"Why do I have to be in restraint?"

"Because you're possessed by the devil. That's all these demons fear. A greater demon than they are."

"And when we get to London?"

"A miraculous cure."

"I mean will we be safe?"

"You have the greatest demon of all – money. They'll be delighted to take it from you."

She stood thinking for a moment.

"Go home. I'll send Lyb when I'm ready to go."

She went into the house.

Her presence stayed with him. He felt her blood in his veins, their shared blood. He would go with her to his death if necessary. Eneda was his god. He had tasted her body and imbibed her spirit. She quickened his heart.

As he walked back, he wondered perhaps if they reached London old Dun might have Fornjot's palm in his pharmacy?

The journey which he feared became more desirable. Whatever happened he would be near Eneda. His life, the last ell of it, was inseparable from hers.

Two days later, Lyb came to fetch him.

In the book:

"Smearing with balsam for all infirmities which are on a man's body, against fever, and against apparitions, and against all delusions; if a man become out of his wits then take part of it and make Christ's mark on every limb, the cross upon the forehead, and other also on top of the head.

The white stone is also powerful against stitch, and against flying venom, and against all strange calamities; thou shalt shave it into water and shave thereto a portion of the red earth, and smear thereon and bind with ewes wool.

When the fire is struck out of the stone it is good against lightning and thunder, and against delusion of every kind; and if a man in his way is gone astray let him strike a spark before him, he will soon be in the right way.

All this Dominas Helias, Patriarch of Jerusalem, ordered one to say to King Alfred."

"What's the matter with him?" Eneda asked.

Bald was smearing her with the black oil squeezed from the rose-balsam 'noli-tangere or touch-me-not', with a paste of alabaster, and with red ochre, and she was curious.

"The Patriarch or the King? From the cure I'd say they're both mad."

He stood back and looked at his work.

She wore a white smock torn and daubed with oil. Her legs and arms were bare and marked with red and black crosses. There was a black cross on her forehead. Her hair was standing thick with white paste and tied with strands of greasy wool.

"Well? What do I look like?"

"Don't talk. Or if you do, talk nonsense."

He turned to Lyb. The dwarf was in motley and carried a yellow banner with the word FAUL. They could not find a bell, so he had a pannikin and a spoon to bang it with.

The horse was loaded with the saddlebags heavy with silver. Long yellow ribbons hung from mane to tail.

Bald had added a touch of irony to his own appearance, wearing a close-fitting black cap that made him look sinister and domineering, and carrying a long peeled hazel switch. The book was secure in the fold of his plaid, slung across his back.

"Are you ready?"

"Come on, leech. Let's go."

"You forget you have to be restrained."

He took a length of rope and tied one end to her wrist and the other to the horse's halter.

"No! Why?"

"The devil has you in his power, remember? If you stray, I'll beat him out of you!"

"You won't if you want to piss again!"

She turned and he saw a glint of gold on her neck, and under it a dagger on a chain.

"Pull and the knot will break." If all Knots broke so easily! He looked around and sighed.

"Now what?"

In the book:

"This wort, which is called artemisia, and by another name mugwort, is produced in stony places and in sandy ones. Then if any propose a journey, then let him take to him in hand this wort artemisia, and let him have it with him, then he will not feel much toil in his journey. And it also puts to flight devil sickness, and also it turneth away the evil eyes of evil men."

He looked for the silver-green leaves but could not see them. He was seized with a terrible apprehension that numbed his feet.

"What?" Eneda was impatient. "Come on you old fool, or I'll have to pull you by the tail."

She slapped the horse and it started forward. Lyb ran ahead. Bald stumbled and nearly fell, feeling nothing but dread and the sting of her disdain.

They passed the summer field where the villagers cultivated their strips of land. The old cearls and women working there stared at them with alarm, crossed themselves and dropped to their knees, hiding their eyes from the look of evil.

It was high summer, and the forest welcomed them like a warm emerald sea alive with darting feathered fishes.

Lyb pushed ahead, finding the path among the many paths by instinct. Eneda walked by the horse, sparing it a double burden. Bald followed, and though he knew the artemesia could not grow there, he searched the forest seabed with his eyes.

They walked without talking until the sun was directly overhead and dropping puddles of light at their feet.

Eneda said, "There isn't any need for this charade." Bald strode along in silence. "How far is it to London? Will we be there tomorrow?"

"A week if we're lucky."

"Which way?"

"We can go by Stane Street or the river way."

"Which is best?"

"Neither. It's best not to go at all."

She put out her tongue and sulked.

The clanging alarm of the pannikin startled them. Lyb was out of sight. Bald signalled Eneda to wait and ran forward. As he broke through a screen of leaves he saw Lyb, and a gang of men barring the path. They had the brown grained leathery faces of their trade, charcoal burners, but from the staves and axes they brandished they had taken up a more violent and profitable business.

Bald shouted at them "Faul! Faul! Make way! Look out for your lives! There's a fiendsick woman coming!"

The burners moved menacingly round him. He smelt the acrid smoke on their greasy rags. He saw the danger in their red-stained eyes. They looked beyond him, and he turned.

The horse was coming with its tethered captive. Wild-eyed, stark-haired, stiff-limbed, jerking like a puppet Eneda played her part.

The burners fell back instinctively.

Bald signed the cross. "Signum cruces Christi conservet te in vitam aeternam amen."

The horse came on. Bald thought they were through and pushed Lyb to go forward. The burners saw the saddlebags and pointed, each urging the other on.

One of them took courage and seized the horse's halter.

"Take care! The woman has the devil in her I tell you." Bald put out a restraining hand. The other clutched the knife in his belt.

The burner reached for the saddlebags.

"Don't touch them!" He looked as grim as hell. "They hold the bodies of her dead children!" He had not known what he was going to say.

The burner lowered his hand but kept hold of the halter. He looked uneasily at his companions. They stood like cattle jerking their heads and grunting encouragement. The burner moved but Eneda moved first.

She stood at the end of her rope raising her arms piteously and tilting her head in grief. She took slow steps as a mother might towards her sleeping children. She began to croon.

"I it sell or it have sold
This swarthy wool
And grains of their sorrow."

She reached the horse and touched the saddlebags, caressing them with her fingers.

The burners stared at the crosses on her arms and saw tears trickle down her alabaster cheeks.

"May this be my boot
Of the loathsome late birth.
May this be my boot
Of the heavy swart birth.
May this be my boot
Of the loathsome late birth."

The burners were uneasy. Bald felt her sorrow and for a moment forgot it was invented. Eneda moved to the horse's head and the burner dropped the halter.

"Up I go
Over thee I step
With quick child
Not with a dying one
With one to be full born
Not with a fay one."

She took up the halter and led the horse forward.

"I will help thee
Fled Thor to the mountain
Hallows he had two
May the Lord help thee."

The burners followed her with their eyes and some had tears in them.

Bald hurried after her.

He caught her up and signalled her to stop and listen. When he heard birds singing, he spoke.

"Who taught you to sing the runes?"

Eneda grinned – a horrible sight.

"Everywhere I carried for me the famous kindred doughty one with this famous meat doughty one. So I will have it for me and go home."

He was astounded. It came from the book, word by word.

It was late but still light when they broke from the forest and saw the river and the Roman road, the ways to London. The river was low and the black skeleton of the Viking ship rose out of the lilac water meandering among little islands of lilies. Beyond the river, the road gleamed like the silver they had stolen.

"Which way?"

Bald wondered. The river was the safer as it ran through villages and towns, but would take twice as long. The road went straight across heath and downs and was beset by robbers.

"Look!"

Eneda's younger eyes had seen a movement on the road.

A column of black-robed monks was coming from the south. They walked slowly and bore heavy burdens and stretchers loaded with chests. The leading group under a great cross was armed. Those at the rear of the column led horses drawing a wagon carrying a stone coffin. Behind them was a straggle of old men, the weak, women and children, refugees.

Bald muttered.

"The battle's lost. They're coming up from Bosham with the bodies of their saints."

He had seen it before, when he and Cild had met the monks of Lindisfarne carrying the body of St. Cuthbert.

"The saints are dead. I wish they'd saved the books. Come, we'll be safer with them than on our own."

They went down across the meadows, forded the river and joined the company of saints at nightfall.

In the morning, when the poor folk saw Eneda, they fell back in fear, and let them follow the measured tread of the monks unmolested. Bald went among them.

It was true: the Viking army had swept ashore in a wave of

destruction, and was moving north. More ominous was that the Vikings who had settled north of the Thames were assembling an army, and there were reports of Viking warships in the river.

The monks were taking their sacred relics to a sister house in London.

Bald told his story of the poor madwoman and her dead children, and they put Eneda in their prayers.

They walked three days and three nights, pausing to beg for food from the hamlets they passed. As they neared London, the hamlets grew larger and the charity less.

The horse and Lyb's legs needed more rest, and they dropped back behind the rear of the column as it climbed the north downs, the last barrier to the city.

Beyond that lay safety.

Eneda begged Bald to let her wash. The crosses on her arms legs and face were smudged, her hair was stinking and crawling with lice.

He loved her more than ever.

"You say your grandfather was Cild and you and your mother never knew him."

She stopped scratching and nodded.

"Who taught you the charms?"

These words with no apparent meaning were the heart of his medicine. The words had more power than the worts or the stars, and they were often used together.

"Who taught you, Eneda?"

"I don't know. I have them in me."

They were standing on the rim of the great chalk saucer broken by the river which they could see when its windings caught the sunlight. The road went down into the wooded foothills of the downs, and the long sacred snake of the column was disappearing under the trees. Lyb was nearby, the horse was cropping grass, the rope looped to Eneda's wrist.

Bald took her arm and pointed to a distant brown smudge in the green and blue of field and sky. Caesar's Tower alone stood white.

"There's London."

"Can I have a wash?"

"No."

"To hell with you! Let Woden take you!"

"Cild was my father."

The famous kindred doughty one. He had to say it.

She stared at London but no longer seeing it.

"Your mother was my sister. I didn't know."

He looked at her mad face. Suddenly she turned and he saw her eyes wide with doubt and fear and a terrible growing monster of recognition as she searched his face for the truth.

"I didn't know."

She was mad, and now the madness was real and angry and resentful.

"How could you not know?"

"I left home when I was a boy."

"You came back!"

"I didn't know where I was. I'd forgotten."

"You came to find me!"

"I didn't know who you were. I found you by chance."

"There's no such thing as chance!" He acknowledged it silently.

"You found me!"

"I found the woman I'd always loved."

In his black cap he spoke his own death sentence.

The word made her more furious and vengeful.

"How can you love me? I'm your blood!"

The famous meat doughty one.

"That is why, Eneda. We are one blood. Cild is in you as he is in me. More so. You have the words in you. I have them in the book."

She was struggling with one truth after another, unable to bear any of them, twisting and turning, fiendsick, truthsick.

"You're my uncle?" Bald nodded. "And you're my lover?"

His eyes closed in resignation. He breathed out hope.

"You know what I am."

"You're a fool and a liar, I told you about Cild! You're a dog! You're a dog licking the bitch it whelped! A dog returning to eat its own shit!"

She started down the hill, the rope tightened and she dragged the horse after her. Lyb followed.

Bald stood struck by the bolt of her words. He had lost Eneda. The sun still shone but the day was black. He felt as if his heart had stopped and death was upon him.

He turned and stumbled back along the road.

He went some fifty paces.

He heard Lyb's cry – a scream of danger.

He ran back.

He saw the horse below leaping and bucking and Eneda fastened by the rope desperately struggling to untie the knot.

He saw Lyb running and darting under the horse's hooves trying to grab the halter.

He saw the horse rear up and strike Lyb to the ground and trample him. He saw Eneda swung round on the end of her rope like a piece of stick. He saw the horse bolt and drag her with it running and falling spinning and striking the ground.

He saw the arrow sticking in the horse's croup.

He turned and saw the bowman and a troop of Viking horsemen riding along the brow of the hill.

He looked back and saw the horse had fallen and was lying kicking out and Eneda tangled by the rope tossed by its hooves.

He saw the Vikings nearer. The dwarf dead. The horse dying.

Eneda white, inert, broken, one arm raised and falling like the broken wing of a gull.

He turned and fled.

An arrow struck him in the back and knocked him down senseless.

VÍ

"Loud were they, lo loud
When over the lew they rode;
They were of stout mood
When over the lew they rode.
Shield thee now; thou mayst save this nithling
Out little spear; if herein it be.
He stood under the linden broad
Under a light shield,
Where the mighty witch wives
Their main strength proved.
And yelling they sent darts
I again will send them another
Flying feathered bolt from the front against them.
Out little spear; if herein it be.
Sat the smith; he sledged a sword.
Little iron, wound sharp.
Out little spear; if herein it be.
Six smiths sat,
Slaughter spears they wrought.
Out spear; not in spear,
If herein there be, of iron a bit,
A witches work
It shall melt.
If thou wert on fell shotten,
Or wert on flesh shotten,
Or wert on blood shotten,
Or wert on limb shotten,
Never let be thy life ateased;
If it were an Aesir shot,
Or if it were an elfin shot,
Or if it were a witches shot,
Now will I help thee.

Here's this to boot of Aesir shot
Here's this to boot of elfin shot
Here's this to boot of witches shot
I will help thee.
Fled Thor to the mountain.
Hallows he had two.
May the Lord help thee."

He felt a heavy weight on his back pressing him to the ground. He twisted his head and saw ravens circling in the sky. They were birds of fate. The Vikings fought under the raven banner and glutted their pet with corpses. Woden had two ravens called Thought and Memory, who spied on men and advised him to kill them if they thought or remembered too much. Oh God! Thought and Memory hooded their wings and drove their horned beaks into his head. He had betrayed Eneda. Eneda was dead.

He thrust aside the book and saw the arrow stuck in it. Fear first – he rose and looked round quickly. Only the sun declining and shadows pointing long accusing fingers at him. Guilt second and shame – the book had saved his life as he fled. Hope a poor third – he hurried to the top of the hill. A flock of undertaker crows lifted like a pall from the horse's carcase. He stared. Eneda and Lyb had gone! Hope raced – they were not dead, the Vikings had taken them – and fell – he had seen them dying and while he lay unconscious the monks had returned to fetch them away for burial.

Either way he would not see them again. She had been suddenly torn from his life. He bled tears. Despair and the consciousness of his own impending death came with the darkness. He knelt to pull out the arrow from the book and the strange irony of it, that the book was itself the leechdom that had saved him, saved his sanity from the twin apparitions of hope and despair that threatened to destroy him. His life still had a purpose: to save the book.

He went to the west, thinking the Vikings were in London, but they were ahead of him moving along the valley of the river.

That late summer the pagan armies moved swiftly by ship and on horseback to encircle Wessex from north and south. There was a poor harvest, and what crops stood the Saxons burned, and drove their sheep and pigs into the forest to keep them from the Danes. Bald followed the invaders, and in the aftermath of fire and slaughter, he served the purpose of the book.

In the book:
"For a burn, take some of the netherward part of fennel beat it up with old grease, lay it on.
Again, take lily and yarrow, boil them in butter, smear therewith.
For the same put the white of an egg on frequently.
In case a man be badly burned take this wort celandine, pound it with goat's grease, and lay thereto.
Take hove and silverwood and brownwort and a bunch of the flowers of lustmock and vipers bugloss, boil in butter and wring the worts off, and put others in, ribwort bishopwort yarrow atterlothe, put them into the same butter, boil again strongly, wring them off; that will be a good wound salve.
If thou may not staunch a gushing vein, take that same blood which runneth out, dry it on a hot stone and rub it to dust, lay the dust on the vein and tie up strong.
If a man be wounded in his upper quarter or in his head and some bone be broken, take solwherf and white clover plants and woodruff; put into good butter, strain through a cloth, and so treat the patient."

The suppurating pus of burns, the blood of wounds, the acrid smoke and heavy scent of rotting flesh, infected man, beast and land.

In the book:
"For lent addle or typhus fever work to a drink wormwood, everthroat, lupin, waybroad, ribwort, chervil, atterlothe, feverfue, alexanders, bishopwort, lovage, sage, cassock, in foreign ale; add holy water and springwort."

It was a desperate leechdom and the addition of holy water revealed Cild's doubts about it.

Bald sickened. The land sickened. Autumn brought a plague of maggots blighting the leaves, acorns and beechnuts that were the last resource of men and cattle in the winter. Starvation added to the misery. The Saxons fled with their infections into the towns. Then as if nature or the gods conspired against them, storms of heavy rains flooded the rivers and made fords and roads impassable. The sole concession was the retreat of the pagan armies, in the north to camps at Benfleet and Buttington, and in the south to their ships. The rains stopped, and men's eyes turned skywards as if they heard the distant screams of eagles. An ice-sheet spread across the land and their prayers froze on their lips and turned to smoke.

Bald worked side by side with death and waited for his own last leechdom. It could not be long in coming. He had aged. His single garment was scarcely sufficient to protect the book. His skin was like parchment. His eyes betrayed the constant presence of Thought and Memory, seeing outwards the wretchedness around him and inwards the cringing guilty spectre of his impotence and cowardice. He looked for death as he had once looked for Fornjot's palm, and with as much success.

He drifted into Winchester with the snow. He came huddled among a crush of refugees and country carts creaking with provisions for the court, squeezing through the gateway in the Roman walls. The paving stones were slippery, the wooden houses hemmed him in, he could not see the tower of the Old Minster, or the taller towers of the New Minster and Nunnaminster built by Alfred and his queen. He lost his way in the narrow streets and had to ask if anyone knew Oxa the leech, and had to ask again and again until he found one of the five thousand souls who lived there. He hated cities but he was looking for death and Winchester was the centre of the quick death called justice and the slow death called civilisation.

He was told Oxa lived near the palace.

He followed the carts along a rutted street and saw a great new hall built of timber on old Roman foundations. The three minster towers were grouped at the end of the street. A solid stone house squatted between them.

A perky young maid opened the door. When she saw Bald she started to close it.

"Is Oxa here?"

"He won't see any more patients today."

"I'm not a patient, I'm a leech."

"Don't care if you're an octopus."

She shut the door. Bald hammered on it. She opened it an inch.

"I'm dying."

She shrugged with the arrogance of youth. "Come back tomorrow."

"God Woden take you! Tell Oxa Cild's son is here! Tell him he's going to cut his maid's tongue out for her insolence!"

He reached for his knife and the maid fled inside. He pushed the door open and entered the room. It was warm and red from the fire, and there was a heavy smell of cooked meat. A woman was lying on a bedstead suckling a baby. A portly young man in a prunella robe got up from a chair in the fireplace.

"Can't I have any peace?" He stared at Bald appalled as if a sarsen stone had strode in from Stonehenge and was melting on his carpet.

"I've come to see Oxa."

"Well?"

"Oxa the leech."

"I'm Doctor Oxa."

"Is Oxa dead? Are you his son? I'm Cild's son Bald."

"Cild, Bald – I don't know any of these people."

He waved his hand dismissively. Bald was succumbing to the heat of the room and the greasy smoke coming from the kitchen. He made a last effort and, lifting the book from the fold in his tattered plaid, he held it out.

"Cild was my father. He wrote the book."

"What book?"

"The book of leechdoms. Many of your father's cures are in it."

"Medicine has made a lot of progress since his time."

Bald was confused. "I don't know what you mean by progress."

"It's advanced."

"Knowledge is knowledge. It doesn't go backwards or forwards."

"It increases and obfuscates its forebears. Are you, for example, acquainted with the Medicina de Quadrupedibus of Sextus Placitus?"

Bald shook his head. "I thought not." Young Oxa turned away confirmed in his superiority. When he turned back he was surprised to see Bald still standing there. "I'm not going to buy your book!"

His assumption was insulting. Bald turned to go but his weakness overcame him and he dropped the book. He knelt to pick it up but could hardly lift the cover. He sagged to the floor.

Oxa did not hide his exasperation. "Don't die in here for God's sake! Boot! Boot!"
The maid ran in brandishing a roasting spit.
"Take him to the hospital!"

In the Medicina de Quadrupedibus of Sextus Placitas:
"There is a four-footed neat which we name taxonem that is brock in English. Catch that deer. Seethe his brain in three sextarii of oil in a new crock till the third part be boiled away; bottle off and preserve it. If anyone be troubled with head-racking pain smear him therewith for three nights, and though this man be in any chronic or incurable disease this manner will heal and cure him."

Bald did not notice much on the first night. He lay in a truckle bed under the stone vault of the abbey next to the old Minster. It was dark and cold. He felt as if he had been eviscerated and embalmed. The shades of monks drifted between the rows of beds each burdened with a wretched soul. He thought he was probably dead and in some Germanic afterlife reserved for cowards and impotents.

"For the man that suffer giddiness, a hares lung and the liver mingled together and myrrh by weight of four pennies and three of beer and one of honey; this shall be boiled in good vinegar and subsequently infused with sweetened wine, and after that let them drink and soon it healeth."

On the second night he knew he was alive because he had excruciating pains in his stomach.

"For sore of churnels smoke the man with goats hairs; rathely he will be whole of that sore.
Against churnels mingle a goats turd with honey; smear therewith; soon it will be better."

On the third night he thought he had gone mad, and through the smoke and filth in which he lay he saw the faces of Cild and Oxa and his mother's remembered face melting like candle-wax.

"For devil sickness and for an ill-sight, give to eat a wolf's flesh, well-dressed and sodden to him who is in need of it; the apparitions which ere appeared to him shall not disquiet him.

For sleep lay a wolf's head under the pillow; the unhealthy shall sleep."

He vomited. His vision cleared. He saw each truckle bed was hung with the rotting limbs and entrails of animals, and wretched pale infected occupants were expiring in this stinking slaughter-house. He cried out. He tried to move. His arms and legs were bound with rough bandages to the wooden poles of the bed.

A monk passed by, praying. "Dominus omnipotens, pater domini nostri Iesu Christi, per impositionem huius scripturae et per gustum huius expelle diabolum a famulo tuo Bald."

Bald shouted back, "May earth bear on thee with all her might and main!"

"A lithe drink against a devil and dementedness. Let him drink buck's piss."

Oxa came after they had gripped his head and forced a funnel in his mouth and poured the bitter fluid down his throat.

"There's nothing like learning by experience. If you recover I'll lend you my Sextus Placitus."

"You're killing me."

"On the contrary my dear Bald, the vegetables you were living on were killing you. Man is meant to eat meat. It follows that all his illnesses result from lack of meat. Good deer, hare, goat, boar, wolf, will cure anything. Do you know what I prescribed for King Alfred? Lion meat. The king of animals. Difficult to come by, expensive you say, but what else will do?"

"What's wrong with him?"

"You old leeches never found out, did you! You gave him nettle soup and worts, as if his great blood lacked camomile and elecampane. Meat is what he needed. Lion meat!"

"How is he?"

"You don't expect me to discuss my patients with you, do you?"

"I'm gaining experience of your methods."

"You are, and they're doing you good."

"Oxa, may I be released to wash myself?"

"The maggots will keep you clean."

Bald thought of Eneda, he remembered Eneda, and wept.

It was the start of his recovery.

His body purged itself. He purged his mind of the meat of guilt on which the ravens had been glutting. What had happened was fate. Their love – he romanticised it into hers as well as his – was fated to end because of their revealed relationship. He was the hero-victim of a tragedy.

There is nothing like dramatising one's defects to excuse them. And so, as he had deified Cild in his mind, he deified Eneda and sanctified his cowardice. He remembered his love as something ethereal. It could not have been lustful, by default.

Another defect became a virtue.

She died. It was fate.

The arrow lodged in the Book. That was fate, too.

She disappeared. That was awkward.

He decided Lyb had only been injured and had carried her body away. That was convenient.

He felt better already and by shitting out the gobbets of wild animals and pissing out their piss he made a complete recovery in three days.

It was hailed as Doctor Oxa's greatest triumph, a tacit comment on the usual results of his treatment.

Bald was released from hospital, and Oxa took him into his house as the living proof of his genius, with a nod to Sextus Placitus.

Bald was also useful to him as a scribe, and after a week he let him treat the more seriously ill of his poor patients who could not afford the Medicina de Quadrupedibus.

The snow lay thick on Winchester, and there were rumours King Alfred was dying.

Bald was unmoved. Oxa said little, though he was in constant attendance at the palace.

Bald was working in old Oxa's study under the roof, cataloguing his books and arranging in alphabetical order the jars of dried worts that crammed the uneven shelves. It was freezing, and the tiny dormer window was jammed with snow, blocking out the light. Each time he got up to fetch a book, he banged his head on the rafters. He could hear the baby crying downstairs and longed for the long summers of his childhood.

There was a Herbarium of Apuleus and another of Dioskorides.

He loved the names of flowers – apollinaris that is glovewort for sore of hands, maythe for sore of eyes, hart clover for foot disease, wolf's comb for dropsy (better than wolf's flesh), raven's foot for the inwards, agrimonia for blow of iron, woodruff for sore of liver, the herb centaurea maior that is churmel the greater or chlora perfoliata – he closed the book.

He picked up Bede's treatise on starcraft De Temporibus. He knew it by heart.

He opened a book of charms.

"Hail to thee mother earth
Mortals maintaining.
Be growing and fertile
By the goodness of God
Filled with fodder
Our folk to feed,"

He read in a book of prognostications of dreams:

"To see oneself taming a wild beast betokens the grace or thanks of opposers. To see wild beasts running betokens some vexation. To be washing in a bath betokens some anxiety. To see himself bearded betokens splendour. To have a white overcoat betokens bliss. To have a parti-coloured overcoat betokens an unpleasant message."

Bald would have been grateful for any overcoat.

He left the books and turned to the jars. Each was carefully labelled in old Oxa's miniscule script, and he had been sorting them for weeks. He had come to F.

Fern filix. Feverfue erythrea centaureum. Fieldrue thalictrum minus. Fenberry vaccinium. Fenugreek trigonella foenum graecum. Fennel foeniculum dulce. Furze – wrong place: he moved it. Fleabane pulicaria dysenterica. Foalfoot tussilago farfara ... he saw the little golden flowers that opened in the spring and turned to puffs of feathered seeds. The heart-shaped leaves made good cough syrup, and their white hairs could be heaped up and used as tinder. Foam-dock saponaria officinalis ... pink raspberry-scented flowers on a tall stem that could be boiled and used for soap. Fornjot's palm – he blinked, he did not believe it, and looked again. Fornjot's palm cauda pulli. He leapt up and banged his head but hardly felt it. Fornjot's palm! There was more writing on the label and he hurried to the window. Fornjot's palm cauda pulli. Sigmunds kraut. Foules tayle.

His hands were shaking.

What did it mean with names in Saxon, Latin, German and Old English?

Then it struck him. What did it matter?

The irony of it struck into his soul and corroded. He heard the laughter in Valhalla. This was an Aesir shot, the iron-tipped arrow of the gods. He had looked for it all his life, and now he had found it, his love was dead and he had no use for it.

He cursed the gods and put the jar back on the shelf.

The next day when he had climbed the narrow stairs and squeezed himself into the study, he sat on old Oxa's chair and mused on fate. His story had to have an author. It was too much to ask of chance – his finding Eneda, the treasure, the journey to London, her death and his survival, the discovery of Fornjot's palm! Who could that author be but a god who hated him? Woden could have done it but more likely Loki, the mischievous god of destruction. One thing was certain: it could not be Jesus. There was a suicidal Jesus who appealed to his dark nature, but there was not a cruel ironic one.

Jesus never laughed.

Jesus never committed incest or adultery, rape, murder or mayhem. So Jesus never knew what men know, or did what men do. He could never have had the knowledge to create the world. The old gods had. But they did not have the power to save it. The last battle was already lost!

Could Jesus, as some believed, save England from the pagan Danes?

There was a step on the stair: Boot in her wooden shoes. She came up pert and bursting out of her cheap dress, the sort of young girl he once hated and desired.

Once? He had been dreaming again. The great amount of meat he ate at Oxa's table fuelled his lusts. Now he dreamt of jolly rapes, of faceless girls with round breasts and buttocks pursued by giant penises, or giants with penises, he was not sure which.

Boot was breathless. "Baby's sick."

"Babies are often sick."

"She says do you come down and look at it."

"Let the doctor look at it."

"He's over at court again, poor old Alfred." She spoke as if the King were her uncle. "Come on Baldy."

He hated her and thought of her naked. He looked along the shelves to the jars marked F.

"Won't cost you anything to look at it."

He could look but could he do? He followed her down, it would be warm downstairs, and brushed against her in the doorway.

"Dirty old fart."

The baby was dribbling yellow slime. The mother's name was Mide. Bald shook his head. "Mide, what have you been feeding him?"

"Nothing."

"Nothing, Mide? He's as fat as a pig."

She was Irish and took it as a compliment. She shifted her fat breast. "He was hungry."

"That won't harm him."

Boot spoke from the doorway. "Doctor had a chop for breakfast and gave him the bone to suck."

"That bone?" said Mide, "I wondered where it came from. I thought the dog brought it in."

She patted the baby complacently, and it brought up another gob of bile.

In the book:

"For inward griping and small guts ache; take betony, and wormwood, marche, radish, fennel; pound all and put into ale, then set it down and wrap it up; drink at night fasting a cup full."

Bald went up to mix the leechdom. While it was setting, he took down the jar of Fornjot's palm and turned it in his hands.

Fornjot's palm cauda pulli. Sigmunds kraut. Foules tayle.

He read it like a charm, meaningless but full of power.

He pulled the book towards him. It opened where he knew it would.

In the book:

"Boil in ewe's milk again hindheal alexanders, the wort which hight Fornjot's palm, then it will be with him as he would liefest have it be."

He looked casually along the shelves. Hindheal eupatorium cannabinium with its purple florets and rough-edged stem. Alexanders smyrnium clusatrum with yellow umbels and hairy roots. Where could he get ewe's milk?

He shook the idea out of his head. It was academic. He was too old. Boot would laugh at him.

He smiled thin-lipped like a connoisseur. He knew how to stop women laughing.

It would be an experiment with a sound scientific basis. Besides, it was probably his last chance.

He put the jar back on the shelf and took the gripe-water downstairs. "Mide, you must ask the doctor for some ewe's milk for the baby."

Oxa came home looking worried.

"I can't understand it. He's eaten a whole lion. I can't get another until spring and the road to Jerusalem is open again.

It might be too late."

Bald thought it might be too soon.

"In the meantime I've prescribed boar's meat."

In the Medicina de Quadrupedibus of Sextus Placitus:

"Against spewing and nausea and napping, take boar's suet and seethe in three sextariuses of water till that the third part is boiled away; add thereto boar's foam and let the man drink; he will be whole. And he himself will wonder and will ween that it be some other leechdom that he drank."

Bald did not care. Alfred had murdered his friend Duda. Instead he said, "Mide needs some ewe's milk for the baby."

"Where am I to get ewe's milk in the middle of winter?"

There was a flaw in the leechdom. A man could not be cured of impotence for Christmas. "Goat's milk?"

"If she must. Tell her to send Boot to the palace kitchen and ask for it."

There was a nice twist to it. The girls would supply the rod for her own back.

Oxa was still worried. "I want you to come with me tomorrow."

Bald was surprised and flattered. "I'll give you my opinion."

"No you won't: you won't say a word. I told him how you were cured by the Quadrupedibus, and he wants to see you."

Bald declined the offer of Oxa's fur coat for his visit to the palace. He thought any change would be a compromise with his conscience, and he went in his ragged plaid. He wanted to take the book but Oxa would not allow it.

It was midwinter, and there were candles in the windows of the huddled houses, and sprigs of holly and mistletoe, to propitiate the old gods. In the meantime, the Old Minster bell was ringing and the monks were parading the relics and banners of their saints to propitiate the new. Oxa and Bald stood shivering up to their ankles in slush as one of these processions passed by with the grisly remains of St. Swithun, chanting prayers for the King's recovery.

Snow fell silently and relentlessly, and the sky pressed down as if to stifle prayers and snuff out candles.

They crossed the street and entered the great hall by a side door. Bald was impressed by the vastness and wondered why men always tried to exceed nature. A forest had been felled to provide the beams and trusses, the wall panels and the huge curved rafters. Another fed the two great open fires that blackened the roof-space with smoke until it crept out through chimney-holes. The narrow windows were filled with panes of horn, yellow in the winter daylight.

This echoing cavern was swarming with people respectfully jostling about like bees. Men-at-arms, tradesmen, tax-collectors, minor thegns, monkish clerks, clerkish monks, officials, justices, merchants, younger sons, and those who gravitated to government because they had no talent for anything else, performed a polite and elaborate dance with the sole purpose of approaching nearest to the raised and curtained dais at one end of the hall which was guarded by a line of grim veterans.

It was there that Oxa led Bald along one wall with the preoccupied air of a man who, if he was not the most important person in the room, was certainly the second. The veterans knew him and, with sideways glances at his tattered friend, let them both through.

As the curtain closed behind him, Bald suddenly felt overawed and underdressed.

The great people gathered round the bed in the centre of the dais had a dignity and humanity underlined by their grief and distress. They were mostly the same age as the king who lay there. He was fifty and had reigned for nearly thirty years.

Prayers were being said, and they stood with heads bowed, their eyes misty with tears and the smoke of incense.

Oxa pointed them out to Bald in whispers, hoping to inflate his importance with theirs.

"That's Plegmund, Archbishop of Canterbury – Bishop Waerferth – the big man in the way is his household thegn Aethelfrith – there's Lucuman the reeve and there, do you see her? That's the Queen, Ealhswith, and her daughter the abbess Aethelgifu. Her other daughter's married."

The prayer ended. A soldierly man went to the bed. "Edward: he'll be King next. His brother's with the army."

Edward was talking excitedly. "The crews of two pagan ships wrecked on the coast have been captured."

Bald felt the hair stirring on his head.

"What shall we do with them?"

The voice came from the bed, the croak of the raven. "Hang them."

He knew it. They were the same. Pagan and Christian. Ivarr and Alfred.

Edward and his officers came by them, intent on execution. He was younger than Bald had first thought. Ambition and the exercise of power had aged him.

The others had made way and there was an open path to the bed. Oxa stepped into it. In his fur hat and coat he looked like one of his own prescriptions.

Bald followed. His appearance, gaunt, grey and ragged, disturbed them as if death had entered the room. He watched them watching him.

Lucuman and Aethelfrith had, like Alfred, stood in the shield-line in battle after battle against the Vikings. They were broad, notched and hewn, like the swords hanging from their belts.

Plegmund and Waerferth were councillors more than churchmen, with the smooth faces of politicians peeping out from their gaudy carapaces.

As they approached the bed, Ealhswith the Queen looked enquiringly from Bald to Oxa.

Oxa explained, "My Lady, this is the man Bald whose life I saved."

Her mouth curled at his crassness.

Bald heard the abbess Aethelgifu speak softly. "Do you owe your life to Doctor Oxa?"

He answered, "I owe my life to God but Oxa took a lien on it."

He turned to her and saw the shadow of a young profile under her veil and he could have sworn she smiled.

An elderly man came from behind the bed and asked him, "Bald, what is your occupation?"

"I am a leech."

There was a stir of interest and Oxa interrupted. "He's not here in that capacity! He's here as proof of my success!"

The elderly man went on, "As a leech, what do you think of Doctor Oxa's practice?"

He felt the old conflict of truth and the devil waging in him. He caught Oxa's anxious eye. Caution taught him never to spring a trap.

"Master, there is a little wort hyoscyamus niger we call henbell which has a wonderful manner. The juice puts to flight the sore of ears and kills the worm in them. The same wort pounded and laid on will take away the swelling on a body. Taken in wine it heals sore teeth. If a woman's breasts are sore, work it with butter and smear it on. For lungs addle, the juice with other worts will heal a man. And the same little wort can kill him in the time it takes a swallow to cross the sky. How can I judge this wort except by its effect?"

They looked at him in silence.

"Well said." The voice came from the bed.

Oxa was standing in the way. Bald moved and saw Alfred.

The hands that lay outside the covers were red and puffy, and the fingernails were yellow. The body beneath was clogged with fat. The face was florid, choleric, with swollen cheeks and bulging eyes, and hard veins ridging the forehead. A mane of white hair was stiff with animal fat. Bald leant down and smelt fetid breath coming from between purple lips and yellow teeth.

He drew back quickly and the full horror of it struck him. He was looking at the parody of a lion.

The eyes were watching him. The rest seemed dead.

Then the last thing he expected happened. He wept. He could not help it. He hated the King but this thing lying here was a man. Tears stood on his face like dew on a stone.

They noticed.

Oxa muttered, "That's enough." And then importantly, "The king must rest."

On the way home, Oxa told Bald the elderly man was Grimbald, a scholar from Rheims. "He's an old fool like you. What was all that rigmarole about henbell? Nobody understood a word of it."

Boot had brought the goat's milk and Bald quietly stole it. That night he left his garret and crept across to old Oxa's study. He struck a flint and lit a scrap of rag soaking in a bowl of oil. He put a tripod over it, and a dish he filled with goat's milk. He took down the jars of hindheal, alexanders and Fornjot's palm. He was totally absorbed in the experiment, his eyes glittering in the granite valleys of his face.

He opened the jar of hindheal, and the faint scent of apples came to him. He shook out the dried pink florets and brittle faded leaves. There was a piece of stem six inches long, curved like a black rib. He crushed some leaves and flowers between his fingers and added them to the goat's milk.

The jar of alexanders contained a thick brown root which still had some suppleness. Old Oxa had known the umbels, leaves and seeds were used for foods and flavourings, and only the root held the wort's potency. Bald scraped a heap of shavings with his knife and put them into the milk, which was beginning to stir with heat.

He could not suppress a shiver of excitement as he took up the jar of Fornjot's palm. The best part of his life was invested in its contents. He turned it to the light and noticed with a twitch of anxiety that the paste which sealed the lid was cracked. It opened easily.

He tipped it slowly. Nothing.

He tapped it on the table and tipped it further. Nothing.

He turned it upside down and banged it. A few grains of dust drifted out and disappeared.

He grimaced at his fate. The gods had not forgotten him.

Old Oxa had used it all for himself, or more likely fumbled with the lid and the precious wort had disintegrated and turned to air. He brought the jar up to his nose. It smelt like a burial mound he had once discovered. There was a dessicated corpse on a stone shelf. The flesh was like leather. The penis was a foot long.

He turned the jar and looked again at the label.

Fornjot's palm caula pulli. Sigmunds kraut. Foules tayle.

The milk boiled over and frothed and spilt, dousing the burning rag.

In the blackness he cursed the milk, his fate and Fornjot's palm. Rage welled up in him. Why? Why was he always being punished? What had he done?

He knew the answer already. Nothing. But it did not help.

It struck him – there was no reason and there was no reason why he should be the only one outraged by the gods this night!

He felt along the worktop and his fingers found the stalk of hindheal.

This would do!

He rose and hit his head and added to his anger.

He found the door and felt the stone steps strike cold on his bare feet.

He went down.

The fire was glowing in the room and he made out the mounded figures on the bed. He made his way to the tiny scullery where Boot slept.

He stood in the doorway and then moved in to let the rosy light reflected from the fire fall on the bed.

The covers were rumpled and rucked up, revealing a pair of big pink buttocks.

Bald grinned like the devil.

He gripped the stick of hindheal like a dagger, took two steps to the bed, and eased it gently between the buttocks. He heard a grunt.

He pushed it in and was rewarded with a groan of pleasure-pain.

He jammed it home.

An arm swept the covers aside. A fat body turned. A face full of surprise at this unexpected rape appeared. It was Oxa.

Behind him Bald saw Boot.

VII

Bald took the book and left Oxa's house that night. He wanted to leave Winchester, and wound his way by cold starlight through the maze of streets. The great gates were shut. There was a brazier burning by the watchman's hut, and the watchman told him the gates were only opened when it was light enough to distinguish honest folk from thieves and robbers. He begged a corner of the watchman's fire and squatted down to wait.

The fire was banked with turves that smouldered away opening caverns of glowing embers. He stared into it without thinking. After a while, two fiery eyes appeared, then two red cheeks and a gaping mouth, a fringe of flame encircled the whole, and he saw the likeness of a lion. Alfred had been in his mind all the time.

He had never seen lion-features on a man, nor did he know of any disease that would cause them, certainly not a native one. He thought of Cild, and wondered if there was anything about it in the book.

The only reference to Alfred was the leechdom the Patriarch of Jerusalem had sent him years before. It was a jumble of balsamic remedies for colds, magic, and Christian image-making, and it seemed like madness.

The watchman threw a turf on the fire, almost putting it out. He cursed, and stirred the embers with his shoe. One ember stuck to the rough leather like a burr and burnt his toe. He jumped up and saw a heap of snow at the foot of the gateway, and kicked it, and stubbed the same toe on the stone underneath. He grasped his foot in agony and burnt his hand on the ember. He sat down swearing and looked at Bald, challenging him to laugh.

What is madness, thought Bald, but reason back to front? Perhaps the clue to the disease is in the leechdom? Perhaps the disease is known in Jerusalem? The lion-features were a symptom, and they had prompted Oxa to prescribe lion meat as a cure, and the lion meat came from Jerusalem. First he had to find the Patriarch's letter in the book.

He took the book from his plaid and turned his back on the watchman so that the firelight fell on the pages.

The watchman was immediately suspicious. What was this ragged old fellow doing with a book? Only saints and scholars could read, and he looked more like a disciple of the devil. The more he looked at Bald, the more obvious it became to him that the book was stolen. The old man certainly could not read it. From the watchman's point of view, he was holding it upside down! Now look! He was turning the pages rapidly, pretending he was reading! What a fool! The priest in the Old Minster took the whole of Mass to turn one page of the Bible. The watchman glanced through the doorway of his hut. It was growing lighter. The guard would be here soon.

Bald found the Patriarch's letter. It lauded the properties of scamony, gutta ammoniaca, gum dragon, aloes, galbanum, balsam and petroleum, without specifying what they were. He thought the good Patriarch might have misunderstood the king's condition, and the prescription might do very well for embalming him. Then came the charm against apparitions and delusions, the black, white and red crosses on face and limbs with which he had disguised Eneda.

The ravens of Thought and Memory swooped down on him with a vengeance, and he relapsed into gloom.

The next thing he knew, a shadow fell across the page. He was seized from behind and the book was wrenched out of his hands. He struggled against his assailants but there were too many of them and he was dragged away past the watchman who advised him he was going to be hanged and another time to steal a book he could read.

The guard took him to the prison in the old Roman fort. From his cell he could see the prison yard and the gallows tree hung with the corpses of the Viking sailors.

At first he thought Oxa had accused him of stealing the book to get his revenge. But Oxa was an honest man, if an egregiously stupid and opinionated one. He looked in his mind for his accusers and saw the gods arrayed against him. Somewhere deep inside the earth he was being judged by fate, and the mysterious women who brooded over man's destiny called the Mothers. If his judges were women, he was finished.

The cell was cold, he had not eaten, and he missed the presence of the book, realising how much it had become a part of him. His body hurt and he had no power to ease the pain. He could not sit or stand or lie down in peace, and alternated between the three as if he was demented. Since he had lost Eneda the only purpose in his life had been to keep the book, and now the book had gone too. There was only one alternative, and in his mad perambulation of the cell, he began to consider it.

He had seen many deaths. The best came young and by surprise: the worst old, painfully and slowly. It was perhaps an irony more appreciated by the leech than the patient, but the young died with hope and the old with despair. They were the last illusions. Heaven, whether among warriors or choirs of angels, was for the young. The old, of course, thought heaven was hell. He did not want to live with gods he disliked and even despised.

In order to avoid heaven, he would have to kill himself. He thought it would be a scientific experiment of considerable importance to him, answering most of the questions of the universe and all those of religion.

He felt for his knife, but they had taken it, and he could not open a vein. He could hang himself with his plaid, but they were going to do that for him. Starvation would take too long. He had good poisonous worts in his pouch, but they had taken that, too. He could run at the wall and dash his brains out. His madness stepped in to protect itself, and he decided against it.

In the middle of these delirious ramblings he thought he saw a man dressed in black enter the cell carrying the book. He stopped and stared. The man opened the cover of the book and read aloud.

"Bald habet hunc librum, Cild conscriberet. The Latin is atrocious but the meaning is clear. Who is Cild?"

Bald's vision resolved itself into Grimbald the scholar, who repeated: "Bald owns the book, Cild wrote it. Who is Cild?"

"My father."

"He was a man of wide knowledge and great foresight. I assume he's dead? This book is invaluable."

Bald reached for the book eagerly and Grimbald parted with it reluctantly.

"I hope you will give me the opportunity to look at it again."

Bald tucked the book into his plaid. It gave him confidence.

"It dies with me."

"So little lifetime, so much wisdom? What would your father say?"

"Don't hang my son."

"What for? Sodomy with a vegetable? Doctor Oxa complained to the king about you. He showed it to us. Was it rhubarb?"

"Hindheal."

"That's almost poetic. However the king takes a very serious view and the archbishop believes you've profaned virtually the whole book of Leviticus."

Grimbald gave no indication whether he was serious or not, and Bald in his confused state was not sure.

"Why did you do it? To cure his haemorrhoids?"

"He's a bad leech."

Bald had not meant to say it. The truth found its own way out.

Grimbald was surprised.

"He cured you."

"My own body cured me, and the king's body would cure him if you gave it a chance."

Again the truth forced itself out of him.

Grimbald regarded him gravely and waited for him to purge himself of his natural reticence.

"Oxa's father was a good leech. A good leech looks first at the man he is treating, and then at the book. He chooses a leechdom for the man that will help him cure himself. He never goes against the body. The body knows what is good for it even to death, the last great good. A bad leech looks at nothing but the book. He gives the same treatment to every man, young or old, strong or weak. It means he is only as good as the book he chooses."

He glanced at Grimbald, who nodded for him to go on.

"Cild collected the words of many leeches, many from the past, and from many countries. No one man knows everything. Knowledge is a universe in which a man is an atom. Oxa's book is one man's opinion, one man's obsession."

"That does not necessarily make it wrong."

"No, master, but you must go by results. A good leech gives a leechdom and if it has no effect or a bad effect, he stops. A bad leech gives double."

"Do you think the Medicina de Quadrupedibus is wrong?"

"If you give a man an animal, you give him the goodness of the animal and the badness of the animal. With worts and herbs and flowers, we know all their properties. There are no bad worts. With an animal, we do not know. The animal could be infected. It is certainly dead."

He stopped.

Grimbald was thinking deeply. He had the weak eyes of a scholar in the thin face of an ascetic. His manner was off-hand, but his brain was perceptive and his wit caustic. He beckoned to Bald.

"There are others who must hear this. Come with me."

They went by ways Grimbald knew, skirted the palace and entered the abbey of St. Swithun. There Grimbald left Bald in the care of two monks, who washed him, cut his hair and beard, and garbed him in a scholar's gown of black broadcloth trimmed with ermine. The plaid that had given him long service disappeared. The book he never allowed out of his sight. He ate a plain dinner in the empty refectory and was led, with growing wonder, up stairs and along stone corridors, to a panelled room lined with books, where Grimbald was waiting for him. There was a second door, half-open, leading to another chamber.

Grimbald spoke loudly.

"You're going to see the king. Take care what you say. Don't talk about Oxa: he's well-respected in Winchester and still the king's physician."

Bald thought for a moment.

"Master, give me back my plaid and let me go."

Grimbald shook his head firmly.

"No! I believe you can heal the king."

"Believe in god, master, and you'll have more chance of being right."

"Do you believe in god?"

Bald's eyes narrowed and his mind raced. In this place it was dangerous not to. Grimbald noticed his hesitation.

"It's difficult for a leech, isn't it? And a scholar. We know too much. We know the minds of too many men." He waved at the bookshelves.

"I will tell you why I do. There is a war now going on, and if we lose, all learning and knowledge of the past is going to be lost. The Vikings are destroyers, and their gods are destroyers. Christianity and civilisation have come to mean the same thing, like Rome and civilisation once did, and I believe in civilisation."

"I don't, so let me go."

Grimbald was surprised.

"You're a bookman, Bald, you must."

"Must I, master? The Vikings murdered Cild: they turned him inside out for what they believe in. And Alfred murdered a friend of mine for what he believes in. Damn all beliefs, I say – and I'll swear to god I never said it!"

There was a small sound, a murmur, from behind the half-open door.

Grimbald was adamant.

"You must heal Alfred. He's the only man who can save us!"

"I can't. I don't know what disease he's got. I've never seen it before."

"Find out what it is, man! You're a leech! Heal the king!"

"No I won't heal the king!" He heard the same small sound again. "But yes, I am a leech. I'll do what I can for the man, that's all he is."

Grimbald turned and pulled the door fully open. The queen Ealhswith and the abbess her daughter were standing there.

Bald waited to hear his fate from these women. Eahlswith looked severe.

"Don't say that to my husband."

She turned and led the way into the chamber that lay behind the great hall of the palace. As he passed the abbess Aethelgifu, Bald could have sworn he saw her smile again.

The king's bed was screened from the hall by a large tapestry depicting a hunting scene and the wholesale slaughter of wild animals that always delighted Dr. Oxa's heart. Alfred was lying dictating to a monk, and they waited for him to finish. Bald watched him. His languor, unhealthy colour, puffiness, spoke of a long-established debilitating disease. He did not seem to be in pain but his body was probably full of poisons. The lion-features were baffling. Bald knew of diseases that caused swellings, and others that distorted the face and ridged the veins, but not one that stamped itself so terribly on a man. He felt inadequate, impotent again, and cowardly. He had said he would try. He was a leech, not a saint. But if the king died now he knew who would be to blame.

Alfred dismissed the monk and turned to him.

"I've been writing my Will."

Ealhswith went to the bedside and spoke to him quietly. Bald heard him give a long sigh of resignation. Ealhswith turned to him.

"The king will see you."

She made way for Bald and motioned to the others to leave the room with her.

Bald stood in silence by the bed, feeling Alfred's eyes on him, searching for weaknesses, he thought. He became conscious of a foul stench issuing from Alfred's body and said suddenly, "You need a good shit and a bath."

The red eyes glared at him.

"And not to lie in a barn where everyone can breathe all over you but in a little room on your own."

He gained confidence. "And a diet of worts I'll make for you. And I'll draw a chart of the best times for bleeding off your old poisonous blood."

"Will that cure me?"

"No it won't cure you but it will stop you dying until I can find out what will."

Alfred lay still for a moment.

"You know, it's usual for a man to call me 'my lord' or 'your worship'."

"Will that cure you?"

"No, but I will die with dignity." He smiled.

Bald started. He saw something he had seen before. Where the smile creased the swollen cheeks, tiny drops of pus seeped out and trickled into wrinkles which he noticed were lined with little funguses of dried pus.

He reached out his hand. Alfred flinched.

"Don't touch me! Oxa never touches me. Aren't you afraid of being contaminated?"

Bald leaned forward.

"No man is alien to me."

He gently felt the swollen face, running his fingers across the ridged forehead and down the encrusted cheeks. His face was close to Alfred's.

"No woman is a friend."

Alfred smiled again and Bald felt hot blood gathered beneath the skin. Where had he felt that before? He straightened up.

"Will you do what I tell you ... my lord?"

When Alfred spoke, Bald heard a great sadness in his voice and sorrowed for him.

"They won't let me have a mirror. I can't think of anything better than knowledge or worse than ignorance, can you?" He paused. "Isn't that the only war worth winning?"

Bald suddenly realised that this man had been fighting all his life for the one thing Bald believed in. His impotence was nothing. He would heal him. If he let him.

"I will do what you tell me. Send Grimbald in."

Bald breathed loudly like a bugle summoning all his powers. As he moved away, Alfred said, "Don't tell the queen."

"What, my lord?"

"No woman is a friend."

Back in the book-lined room Grimbald was waiting with Ealhswith and Aethelgifu. Bald sent him to the king.

He was thinking furiously. Where had he seen a man whose swollen tissues oozed pus and hot blood? When? Most of all, what disease did he have? His thoughts came like conscripts, reluctantly and out of step. He became aware Ealhswith was waiting for him to say something.

"I don't know, lady, I don't know."

"That's a good place to start, don't you think?" It was Aethelgifu who spoke.

Grimbald came back.

"My lord says he wants to be in a smaller room. He has ordered a close stool and a bath."

Ealhswith was surprised. "What is to happen to Dr. Oxa?"

Grimbald smiled thinly. "He's going to be sent to Jerusalem for another lion."

Bald was reminded of something he wanted to ask the queen.

"Lady, do you remember the embassy from the Patriarch of Jerusalem many years ago? He sent a leechdom for the king."

She smiled. "We were always getting bad advice from people who wanted to help."

"They brought a prescription and eastern medicines. What were they for?"

He spoke eagerly and the others caught his eagerness except for Eahlswith, who laughed.

"I don't know if I should tell you."

"It's important, lady."

"If it's important, I will. They were for his piles."

He looked so disappointed that she laughed again.

"They stayed here for a whole year. There was a monk, Brother ... Brother ... I forget his name but he treated the king every day. Brother Lepidus! He was dark-skinned and had ..." she faltered. "He had bumps on his face and hands ... and he died."

She looked ashamed. "But it was twenty years ago."

"What did he die from?"

"I don't know. Nobody knew. Why?"

Bald did not answer. Now thoughts came rushing to the colours. A monk from Jerusalem, dark-skinned, with bumps on his face and hands, in close contact with Alfred for a year. He could have given him the disease. The venom had slowly distilled in his body, spreading year by year and finally bursting out through the skin. The answer was not in the mummery of the Patriarch's prescription, but in the monk who carried it – and carried the disease from Jerusalem and died of it! The good intentions of the good Patriarch had resulted, by the will of the good God, in the good king's death! But what was the disease?

Aethelgifu was laughing under her veil and the queen admonished her.

"Forgive me, I was wondering how Dr. Oxa is going to get to Jerusalem. Do you think he'll ride the Quadrupedibus?"

They laughed. Bald did not. He did not understand the joke.

But then he suddenly shouted.

"The horse!"

That was where he had seen pus and blood seeping from the swollen fetlock! Eneda's horse! And the horse had leprosy!

They were looking at him with uncertain half-smiles, as if he might be mad. And for the moment he was because he knew that what Alfred had was not leprosy. He knew leprosy. Leprosy was the white roughness, headroughness, tetter, scaliness, and he knew the name came from the Greek 'lepos' a scale. He almost fell down in his despair, tottering to a chair and putting his head in his hands.

Grimbald asked, "A horse? Do you want him to eat a horse?"

The queen and the abbess were looking at each other anxiously.

If the leech was mad, what chance had the patient?

"The book!"

He had put the book on the table before he went in to see the king. He seized it and tore it open, turning the pages furiously. Grimbald recognised the symptoms of a man in search of a word and motioned the two women to leave him alone, and they left the room together.

In the book:

"Some give leaves of aloe when a man willeth to go to sleep, as much as three beans every day to be swallowed; and drinks like these, and more powerful ones if need be, are to be administered; especially in the early spring before the evil humour, which is collected in winter, spread itself through the other limbs. Many men have not attended to this, no nor do ye; then there come of evil humours either hemiplegia or epilepsy, or the white roughness which in the south hight leprosy, or tetter, or headroughness, or erysipelas. Hence one must cleanse away the evil humours before the mischiefs come and wax in the winter, and run through the limbs."

Bald pored over the words until it grew dark and a servant came and lit the candles made of pure beeswax which scented the library with honey. Aloes were in the Patriarch's prescription but without any special emphasis. They were not a native wort, and came from the east. This was one clue. The other was in the words "which in the south hight leprosy" suggesting that Cild knew another disease called leprosy in the north, or more likely in the east. There was no other reference to it, and the leechdoms in the book for leprosy were for the disease Bald knew, the white roughness.

Grimbald came in around midnight with a plate of cheese and a flask of wine. Bald showed him the passage in the book.

"What is your problem?"

"I know the king's disease is leprosy and I know it's not leprosy."

"How do you know it's leprosy?"

Bald did not like to admit that his diagnosis was horse-drawn, and tapped the side of his nose.

"And how do you know it's not leprosy?"

Bald tapped his finger on the book.

"Have you considered there might be two forms of leprosy?"

"Master, they're different. They're as different as ..." He looked about for a comparison and chose the cheese and wine.

"One is white, one is red. One is cold, one is hot. One can be healed ..." He did not finish.

"If the diseases are different, I don't see it matters what you call them."

Bald grew reticent. He was like a man who knew where a great treasure was hidden, and was trying to borrow a spade from his neighbour. "The name describes the disease. If I know the name, I know the leechdom." Grimbald looked unconvinced.

"The name has a power in itself." He looked round warily and flinched from the shadows on the wall. He spoke softly so as not to be overheard. "If I know the name, I know the charm."

Grimbald was disappointed. He had expected some god-defying revelation. "I thought you only used worts and medicines."

"I do."

"Then why do you need charms and some such nonsense?"

Bald looked around and moved an inch or two away from Grimbald in case god's aim was not quite true.

"No nonsense."

"My dear Bald, I thought you were a scholar."

"No, you're a scholar, master. What you do hardly matters."

Grimbald was offended.

"Knowledge is the only thing that does matter."

"Not all knowledge is in books. Man has a brain and a reason and a spirit and an unreason. I've cured a man with a stone because he believed the stone would cure him. All healing comes from inside, master. The book cures the body: the charm cures the spirit."

"You mean it raises the spirits?" Grimbald smiled slightly. Bald merely looked worried. "So you do believe in something?"

"I believe, like everyone, that I'm immortal, though I know I'm not."

Grimbald nodded. "So the charm speaks to the immortal part of a man? I understand. What is the charm for leprosy?"

Bald was silent.

"Well, well, that's your affair. What is the problem with the word itself?"

"Cild writes of the white roughness in the south called leprosy. That's our native leprosy. The king's leprosy comes from the east. It was carried by the monk from Jerusalem. But how can it be called 'leprosy' which comes from the Greek word 'lepos' meaning a scale?"

"I know what it comes from. There is some advantage in being a scholar. Look at the word, my friend. What would happen if it was not derived from the Greek but from the Latin?"

"From the Hebrew if you like! I don't know!"

Grimbald went to the table and took pen and paper. He wrote down the letters with spaces between them – L E P R O S Y – and pushed the paper in front of Bald.

Bald stared at them until they danced.

Grimbald leaned across and added an O after the E and an A after the P. It read L E O P A R O S Y. He spelled it out.

"Leoparosy. Derived from the Latin Leo-parus. Lion-equal. Lion-like."

They were both deeply affected by the discovery, though Grimbald hid his excitement under a mask of irony.

"Your nose was quite correct."

Bald kissed him.

VIII

"I have wreathed round the wounds
the best of healing wreaths,
that the baneful sores may
neither burn nor burst,
nor find their way further,
nor turn foul and fallow,
nor thump and throb on,
nor be wicked wounds,
nor dig deeply down,
but he himself may hold
in a way to health.
Let it ache thee no more
than ear in earth acheth."

Winter clamped the land, and men waited anxiously for spring and the king's recovery.

Bald was given a room in the abbey with access to the palace and the small chamber now occupied by the king. He instituted a regime of diets, baths and blood-letting. He limited official business to an hour a day, though he allowed Alfred to continue his translation of Boethius' *Consolations of Philosophy* with the help of Grimbald. It surprised him Alfred was a scholar. One day he asked him how it had happened.

"I was the youngest son of four. Nobody thought I'd be king, so they let me waste my time by reading books."

As a boy, he had visited Rome, and been greatly impressed by the power and grandeur of the church. His brothers had died: some in the wars with the pagans, and at twenty-four, he had found himself the king of little more than a county, hemmed in by enemies. Seven desperate years saved the south and west of the island from the Danes. There followed twelve years of relative peace in which he established laws, strong government, and a defence system of fortified towns and strongholds. He believed the given wisdom of the past was the cement of the ruling caste, and Christianity the tie-bar and thatch of the people.

So much Bald knew. His patient was a man, but a man above other men, and he worked all hours in Alfred's library searching for a leechdom for what he called the lion disease.

In the book:

"For a leprous body, delve up sorrel and silverweed, so as to draw it out long, pound all well, boil in butter, add a somewhat of salt; that will be a good salve for a leprous body, wash the man with hot water and smear with the salve.

A bath for a leper, boil in water ash rind, quickbeam rind, holly rind, the foultree or black alder rind, rind of spindle tree, sedge, ploughmans spikenard, marrubium, bathe therewith and rub the body with hayrife."

Though Bald used Cild's leechdoms, he knew they were for the white roughness. The lion disease came from the east and somehow the cure had to come from the east also. He looked at the Patriarch's prescription again. Scamony, gutta ammoniaca, gum dragon, aloes, galbanum, balsam, petroleum. They were all unguents, oils or spirits. He began to think it might not be madness and that the Patriarch had sent the antidote along with the poison.

He wondered if the medicines might still be lying somewhere in the palace. He asked those nearest to the king without success. He asked Alfred.

"I remember Brother Lepidus. He had a swollen face and mottled skin." His own poor face and skin were swollen and mottled. "No, I don't know what happened to the medicines. It was twenty years ago. They will have gone to dust and lost their potency by now."

"Who was your leech then, my lord?"

"Oxa, the father not the son."

Bald went to see Oxa. Boot giggled when she opened the door and he was greeted by the familiar stench of burning flesh. Mide was lolling on the bed while the baby played on the floor with a dead hare. Oxa was in a conciliatory mood, considering Bald's new position at court. He could not help bragging.

"You know I'm going to Jerusalem for another lion?"

Bald would have asked him to bring back what he wanted, but Oxa would not return for a year.

"I hear you've diagnosed his worship's illness as leprosy. Far be it for me to disagree with someone of your great authority, but a mere student knows leprosy is the white roughness! However, if you say so! There's an excellent prescription in the Medicina de Quadrupedibus."

"For leprosy and for a beaten body, take the water which is inside a goat, and which it at whiles outpoureth; mingle the wet with honey and salt and always at even wash and rub the man's head and body with that."

He took Bald up to the study and watched him carefully.

"What are you looking for?"

"A medicine chest that came from Jerusalem about twenty years ago."

"Well, everything's just as the old man left it. You've been up here more often than I have."

Bald searched the shelves of books and jars, though he had never seen such a chest. He knew old leeches liked to hide their secrets.

The room was under the angle of the roof, and there was a little triangle of space unaccounted for in the panelled wall behind the chair. He took out his knife and ran it along the edges of the panel.

"What are you doing? Look out! You'll pay for any damage!"

He levered the panel out. There was a small cache crammed with dusty rolls of parchment. He pulled them out and found a dark wooden chest inlaid with brass. He knelt down, feeling his heart beating with excitement. He wiped the dust away and saw the stems of brass were entwined in strange and beautiful Arabic letters.

Oxa was dancing about behind him.

"What is it? Whatever it is, it's mine!"

Bald dragged the chest out and hoisted it onto the table. Oxa immediately tried to open it, but the lid was cunningly concealed.

"I'll go and get an axe!"

"No! It's not yours, it's the king's! The Patriarch of Jerusalem sent it to him."

"Well it's mine now!"

"Oxa – it could hold the medicines that will cure him. Think of the credit it will bring you – if they work."

"If – after how long? Twenty years? No thank you. You take it. Only ... if they work, Bald, tell him I gave them to him."

Bald carried the chest downstairs. In the doorway when Mide was out of hearing, Oxa coughed and asked him:

"Bald, why did you stick that thing in my bottom?"

"Master, it's not generally known, it increases potency."

"Does it? Well I'll tell you something – it works!"

Bald carried the chest back to the palace. He put it on the table in the library and studied it. The wood was dark and had a faint exotic scent. The brasswork was intricate, and appeared to be in one piece, enclosing the whole chest in its arabesque tracery.

Bald knew little about Arabia. He counted in Roman numerals. He saw it as a distant pagan shore, and Jerusalem as a domed city where a white god had met a demeaning death at the hands of foreigners.

Grimbald heard about the chest and came to examine it. He knew as little as Bald but scholarly scruples intervened and he forbore to mention it.

"It's undoubtedly the chest sent by the Patriarch. Why don't you open it?"

"I can't. The lock's hidden somewhere."

"Do you understand the writing? Why should a good Christian send a sealed chest anyway?"

"To stop the contents from being stolen."

"Medicines?"

"Gold, frankincense and myrrh were medicines. I rather think money itself began life as a medicine."

"Only one gave it to the doctor."

Grimbald left. Bald stared at the chest for a long time, tracing the filigree leaflets with his finger.

"Easter lilies."

He turned and saw Aethelgifu watching him. She wore her habit, an adaptation of her own of a monk's habit, and a coif that framed her face. He saw her unveiled for the first time. Good humour gave her features, which were rather large for a woman, a pleasant appearance, and Bald was reminded of a friendly sheep. He was disappointed. Behind her veil she had a mystery which was revealed as no mystery.

She repeated: "Easter lilies. The flower of Our Lady."

"Where?"

"There." She pointed to the brasswork.

He shook his head and let his disappointment show in a scowl that made him more hatchet-like than ever.

"Yes they are." She pointed. "Here are the leaves and here are the flowers, like angels' trumpets."

"Arabic letters." Bald muttered.

"And look, where the stigma is, there's a little cross. You turn it like this."

He heard a metallic click and stared amazed as Aethelgifu pulled back the stigma and lifted the brasswork on top of the chest.

"You can open it now."

"How did you know that?"

"Brother Lepidus showed me when I was small."

Simplicity itself! Bald thought – how we see what we expect to see and mislead ourselves and miss the obvious. The Christian Patriarch would not have sent a box of Arabian magic. The Arab who made it would not have drawn a lily that did not look like a letter.

He slowly lifted the lid. It slid up smoothly. It was so close-fitted that he heard a slight hiss of air as it opened. He smelt a sweet and pungent scent. Aethelgifu cried out, "I remember!"

The chest was lined with cedarwood and had six compartments, each containing a vial. The seals on the stoppers were intact. He closed the lid quickly.

"I remember so well. When I think of Our Lord I think he must have smelt like that."

He looked at her sharply. Her eyes were closed and she was smiling. He was in the presence of innocence, and it disturbed him.

He showed the chest to Alfred. He too saw Easter lilies and smelt the odour of sanctity. He was deeply moved. He lifted out the vial of petroleum.

"To think this came from our Saviour's own city. This oil might be the same the woman poured on His head in the house of Simon the leper. Tell me Bald, how did you know without knowing?"

Bald did not know, and said nothing. He was himself in awe of the mystery of his craft. He examined Alfred. The diet was reducing his fatness, and the bleeding renewing his blood. The baths were having the greatest effect. His hair was free from animal grease, and his channelled skin showed white streaks of healing.

Alfred was absorbed by the discovery. The vials were marked in Greek, and he called Grimbald to translate them. Petroleum. Galbanum, a resin of ferrula asafoetida, which came from Syria. Similarly scamony, the resin of convolvulus scamonia. Gum dragon was another resin, and balsam an extract of impatiens balsaminia. Aloe came only from the Mediterranean area and was a compound of the gelatinous leaf-sap. Gutta ammoniaca was missing. Bald thought it was a volatile essence in which to dissolve the resins to make a tincture, and he could use a spirit to as good an effect.

The king was anxious to proceed with the cure. The days were growing lighter. Spring would bring new dangers. He had finished translating Boethius, in which the turbulence of a great life was compared unfavourably with the peace of a philosophical one. He ended with his own prayer.

"Strengthen my mind to your will and to my soul's need, and confirm me against the devil's temptations, and keep far from me foul lust and all iniquity."

Bald was impressed with the scholar-king who over the years had put his name to translations of Gregory's *Pastoral Care* and Augustine's *Soliloquies* and ordered other books into the common language "most necessary for all men to know". He was more impressed by the man who confessed to foul lust and all iniquity, even in the person of a dead philosopher. The executioner had a soul.

So he prepared the first salve, instilling drops of oil and scrapings of resin into his distillation of old wine. He applied it to the king's face and body that night. To Alfred, the holy oil had a double significance and the healing process came as much from his mind as from his body.

The abbess Aethelgifu came to the library the next morning.

"Don't expect a miracle."

"But I do!"

As a child, she had fled with her father from the Vikings and taken refuge in the marshes at Athelney. She had seen the Saxons rally to him and win the battle of Eddington that saved the kingdom.

"I do indeed, and why not, my dear leech?"

"Because I'm not a saint."

She smiled broadly and it worried him. He thought luckily sheep are not carnivorous or she would have eaten him for breakfast.

They went to the king's chamber. Alfred was asleep. It was a grey misty morning and the light was like dust, and yet his face was glowing, and shone as if the skin was stained glass in the abbey window. Aethelgifu was transfixed, and murmured several Aves. Bald thought he had probably made the salve too strong. There was nothing to do but wait, and blame the Patriarch.

They returned to the library where he opened the book and stuck his head in it.

In the book:

"A bath for blotch, boil ten times the worts in a basin and separately betony, nepeta, marrubium, agrimony, yarrow, mint, horseheal, hindheal, churmel, earthgall, dill, marche, fennel, of all equally much, work then a stool of three pieces of wood, with a hole below, sit on a bucket and robe thee over from above with a garment lest the vapour escape; pour the prepared hot liquor under the stool into a bucket, let it reek on thee."

Aethelgifu was singing:

"Sit ye my ladies, sink,
Sink ye to earth down;
Never be so wild
As to the wood to fly."

When he looked up, she smiled, and sidled along the side of the table provocatively, never taking her eyes off him.

Was she trying to seduce him? Impossible, in more ways than one.

"Have you been to confession recently?"

She was!

"I go every day."

No she was not.

"I have so many sins."

The innocent always have.

"It's better to start with a clean sheet, don't you think?"

He had never had one, clean or dirty. He did not judge himself.

But she was trying to seduce him – into church. He had to put a stop to it.

"I have the Knot."

"What's that?" Her smile faded a little.

"I can't believe."

"In what?"

"What you believe in."

"Miracles?"

"Among other things."

"Angels? The company of saints? Heaven? Love?"

He wanted to say God, but knew it would hurt her.

"Hope."

"Oh you must!"

"It seems a great folly to me to rely on a wish. If men got better because they hoped they would, there'd be no need of leeches."

"If we didn't hope we wouldn't come and see you anyway."

She smiled indulgently.

"It's self-deception, lady." He tapped the book. "There's not a pennyweight of hope in here."

"Bald, you're deceiving yourself." She was still smiling, but her voice was deeper and more purposeful. "Don't you know God writes every book?"

He thought quickly. He knew only four or five books: the Herbarium, Bede, Augustine, God might have written two of them.

"Not this one. Cild wrote it."

"Who's Cild?"

"My father. He's dead. He wasn't God because the pagans killed him at Thetford."

"They killed Jesus at Jerusalem."

He saw Cild spreadeagled and Christ with outspread arms and was uncomfortable. She still smiled.

"You're a child of God and you're allowed to hope. As to your Knot, I'll undo it."

She left in a waft, and he caught a whiff of female sweat. She had been excited. He had to put a stop to it.

Everyone said it was a miracle. The king improved daily. The salve penetrated to the source of the poison and dried it up. The lion-features melted in the heat of the salve.

Alfred endured the pain of the cure patiently. Suffering was half of it, as he believed his lusts and iniquities were as much the cause of the disease as his abnegation of them was the cure. Bald saw only that his patient was recovering. He was besieged with patients. The whole court suddenly fell ill in order to be treated by him. And of course everyone was cured. He was so lauded that when a minor friar had a heart attack he crept to his cell and died rather than go to Bald and lay a death at his door. Aethelgifu alone stayed healthy, and in between the archbishop's piles, the reeve's warts and the queen's insomnia, he was pleased to see her. He went to church. He had to. With success came envy, not from Oxa, who thought so well of himself he could not envy anyone, but from the little leeches who called themselves doctors because they had once been to Paris or Maidenhead. The bone-setter Withbec was one of them. He put it about that Bald was a witch and a devil's man, and made himself so unpopular he had to flee across Watling Street to the Danes.

To his surprise, Bald liked the church. The music and the ritual suited his new personality. He was putting on weight and gravity. He had not known respect before; he never expected renown. He thought it came too late, and then that it could never come too late. Aethelgifu was delighted with him, and he began to think he need not put a stop to it. If the king's daughter loved him, why not? She was an abbess by virtue of her rank, not by virtue of her own. She could be unabbessed in order to be married. Disordered, as it were. As for the Knot, then let her do her best. He knew how to amuse her.

Then there was another miracle. Winter broke and spring came early. Edward the prince, the reeves and ealdermen were leaving for the armies besieging the Danes in Benfleet in the east and Buttington in the west.

Alfred rose from his bed. Leaning on Bald's arm, he went to the great hall to receive the homage of his soldiers. They knelt while Archbishop Plegmund blessed them. The king's recovery and the story of the holy oil inspired men with a spirit of unity under God. It was a potent force, and when they stood and clashed their swords and axes against their shields, shouting Alfred's name, Bald felt a power to rival that of nature. He was seduced. One God seduced his spirit. One nation under God seduced his mind. He shouted "Alfred! Alfred!" with the rest.

Alfred came to see him in the library.

"I want to do something for you."

Bald immediately thought of Aethelgifu, and saw the resemblance between her and her father. Alfred's face was pink and tight-skinned, but it conformed to the bones beneath. The redness had gone from his eyes, his lips were firm and his teeth white. His white hair curled round his head.

"How can I pay you? What do you want?"

So it was not Aethelgifu. That was yet to come. What did he want? A polite 'nothing' came to his mind, but he rejected it as ungrateful.

"I want a copy of my book, my lord. Several copies."

"Your book?"

"My book of leechdoms."

"Show me."

Bald pushed the book across the table. Alfred sat down and opened it.

"Who is Cild?"

"My secretary."

Bald felt he had to live up to his success. He owed it to himself. Alfred turned the pages, becoming absorbed in them. He murmured:

"Leechdoms against all infirmities of the head ... against neck ratten ... for breast pain ... heart pain ... loin ache ... thigh ache ... foot ache ... you have the whole man here."

He closed the book reluctantly.

"You know parchment is scarce?"

Bald felt a lurch into disappointment.

"It would take a monk a year to copy this."

He fell in.

"The scriptorium has enough work of my own for the next twenty years. They are writing the chronicle of my reign."

He drowned.

"I'll order only six copies, and that's more than Boethius."

He was saved.

He told Aethelgifu. They were walking in the cloisters that linked St. Swithun's with the Nunnaminster. There was a pale yellow sun, and daisies pricked the green. She was less impressed than he had hoped.

"My dear Bald, you remember you said you didn't believe in hope? Well I don't really believe in leechdoms."

"I've changed."

"Prayer is a hundred times more effective."

"A leechdom cured your father."

"It came from the Patriarch in Jerusalem. Jesus might have written it."

He said nothing. If she had gone down on all fours and started cropping the grass he would have said nothing. She was the king's daughter, and his success had sprouted aspirations.

"You ought to write a book of miracles."

He suppressed the unwelcome truth that he had never written a book of anything.

"What a consolation that would be to the terminally ill."

He made a mental balance of his life. In one scale the book.

He had done more for the book than Cild could have expected. In the other, Aethelgifu, God, his new prunella gown, and an earldom.

"I'll write a book of miracles, lady, and I'll call it my life."

"How lovely!" She exploded with delight. "And then you must take the last great step to make your life complete."

He stumbled, imagining a step up. What step? The step to the altar?

"What step is that, dear lady?"

"The step to the altar."

His eyes filled with tears of triumph and gratitude. He had gone to church. He had turned to God. He had hoped. Now he was rewarded. He wondered which earldom Alfred would give him. He fancied Sussex.

"I'm sure my father will give you an abbey."

"You mean an earldom." What a sheep she was!

"No, no, an abbey. This one perhaps."

"That's impossible."

"Bishop Waerferth's older than you."

"If I'm an abbot, how can I get married?"

She danced in front of him.

"When you take holy orders you go to the altar and you're married to Jesus."

She was a sheep – a sheep in wolf's clothing! He could have poleaxed her! The old Bald rose from the dead.

"Holy orders? I'd rather marry you first!"

He left.

She stopped. Her jolly face crumpled. She cried.

Aethelgifu said nothing to her father but she was always quiet and thoughtful when Bald was in the company, and she never looked directly at him. He had stopped it.

Everyone was exuberantly happy, and they went about congratulating each other. Great news came from the armies. Benfleet was stormed, and the Viking chief's wife and two sons were captured, together with ships, stores and women. Buttington was starved out. The Vikings fought a desperate battle in which the reeve and ealderman Aethelhelm were killed. Large numbers of Danes were slaughtered, and the rest went and sacked Chester before returning to the north and east. The Viking chief was coming to Winchester himself to sue for peace.

His name was Haesten.

Everyone was happy except Bald.

Alfred was busy with the Viking's visit. Aethelgifu avoided him. Grimbald, when he heard Bald was having six copies made when his Boethius merited only three, looked at him with the particular contempt scholars have for those whose books sell better than their own. And in the general mood of exhilaration, nobody was ill any more.

Bald was bored. He feared the purpose of his life was over.

IX

Haesten came to Winchester on the first of April.
Bald was in the great hall, where the king, council, and court were waiting to meet the Viking chief. The guards were much in evidence, and many in the assembly trembled at the thought of seeing the marauder whose name was feared from Paris even to Rome. Stories of his atrocities had been circulating for weeks. He rivalled Ivarr the Boneless and the terrible Sigtryggr king of York in notoriety. His wife, a formidable woman with hair in more places than was customary, stood with her two oafish sons behind Alfred's chair. Bald suspected the king would be glad to get rid of them. They had lived there since being taken prisoner at Benfleet. There was a stir of apprehension as the doors were opened. The crowd outside made way and there was a spatter of applause. The Saxons respected violence.

Bald was standing among the churchmen and scholars. He was taller than the rest and had a good view of the hall. He was one of the few who had seen a Viking king and lived, and he tasted the bitter expectation of hatred.

A plump elderly man in a white tunic entered, smiling and acknowledging the applause. He had a gold circlet on his head. He might have been a bishop. He was followed by a group of handsome young men, also in white, and an escort of young warriors carrying garlands of spring flowers which they handed out left and right as they passed.

Was this Haesten?

Alfred rose and went to greet the elderly man. The surly Saxon veterans received their garlands uneasily. Grimbald, who was standing next to Bald, murmured, "Rejoice, rejoice, we've tamed the beast."

Bald was less sure. The gloss had rubbed off his broadcloth and the ermine was moulting. Clothes mean only what the wearer intended them to mean.

Alfred was leading Haesten's wife and sons forward to present them to him. Haesten did not look overjoyed and went to greet the queen and Aethelgifu who was sitting next to her. Archbishop Plegmund approached the Viking, who suddenly knelt down in front of him to receive his blessing. This unexpected gesture provoked surprise and more applause. Alfred raised Haesten and embraced him, and the archbishop led the way towards the abbey where Haesten was going to be baptised and given the royal Saxon name of Aethelstan.

Bald did not attend the ceremony. He did not want to see a man forswear the gods he had forsworn himself. He stayed in the hall and watched the slaves strew the floor with rushes and carry in the long tables and benches for the feast that was to follow.

He caught the smell of roast meat and thought of Oxa, who was already on his way to Jerusalem. He envied him. A journey anywhere would be a relief. Success like young wine left him with a headache. He thirsted for the spring, the forest, the flowers, the feel of the book against his back. He decided to ask Alfred to let him go.

The peace celebrations lasted for a week. Haesten, or rather Aethelstan, agreed to withdraw his army to the Danelaw, the old kingdoms of Northumbria, East Anglia and Essex, occupied by the Danes. In return, he received danegeld. The amount was secret but silver was in short supply that year, and gold was unobtainable. Hostages were exchanged, and the handsome young men in white stayed in Winchester while an equal number of young Saxons were to leave with Haesten.

Bald had no chance to speak with the king that week. He spent much of his time in the scriptorium. Fifty monks had been assigned to make the first copy of the book. It had been carefully taken apart and a number of pages allocated to each of them. He was amazed at the speed and precision with which they worked. It was a factory of books, the first anyone had seen on the island. At the end of the week, the first copy was finished and the book was stitched together again. On the king's instructions, the old wooden covers were replaced with oxhide. Now he had the book again, Bald was even more eager to speak to Alfred. But Alfred spoke to him first.

It was a fine day and he was summoned to a council in the palace garden. Plegmund, Waerferth and Grimbald were there with Edward and the king.

He was asked how old a man could be and still father a child.

"Sixty."

"How old do you think Haesten is?"

"Sixty."

Alfred shook his head. Edward was angry.

"If you let him marry Aethelgifu, he'll have a claim on our kingdom."

"It won't affect you, Edward, you're my son."

"It will if they have a child!"

Bald thought they are going to let the Viking put aside his hairy wife and marry the king's daughter so that their child would inherit the whole island. He spoke out.

"If he did, it would be an idiot."

Grimbald muttered, "There's an idiot in every village in England."

"It would unite the country." Alfred voiced Bald's thoughts.

Edward put his hand on his sword. "I'll do that!"

Plegmund said, "We don't want to be ruled by an idiot."

Bald thought nobody does, everybody is. An idiot or an executioner.

The council broke up. Bald went up to Alfred.

"My lord, can I ask you a favour?"

"Anything you like."

"I'd like to leave Winchester."

"Good. I'm leaving myself soon. Now there's peace I'm going to tour the kingdom and raise some money. You can travel with the court."

"I'd like to leave court."

"Nobody leaves court, my friend." Alfred smiled. "They go where I send them and they come back. I need them all. I need you."

"You said anything you like."

"I meant anything I like." He was still smiling, but Bald felt the chill. He persisted.

"My lord, I've work to do. The book is finished copying. The book has work for me to do."

"Don't you think I have work to do? Does your work compare with mine?"

"I can't do it unless I collect fresh worts, my lord."

"Tell a slave what you want and he'll collect them for you."

"They must be picked at different times for different leechdoms. Can a slave prepare them or administer them or know which leechdom is for which disease?"

"Bald, I know all this. You can, and that's why you stay with me. Anyway, what is there in the world that I won't give you?"

"My freedom."

Alfred reddened and his face distorted with anger. For a moment Bald thought the old lion was back.

"Even god can't give you that without denying himself! You're no more free than a leaf is free! It grows from the bough and serves the tree, and when its service is over, it dies. That's what freedom is: death! Do you want your freedom now?"

"No, my lord."

"Then don't ask for it."

He went, the old murderer.

A raven flew down from the tower of the Old Minster to see if Bald was dead and it could peck his eyes out.

He was surprised when Alfred sent for him the next day. He went to the courtyard where the Vikings were preparing to leave. Their horses were coming from the stables quietly on unshod hooves. Two oxcarts were being loaded with provisions, and a third with heavy coffers of danegeld. The young Saxon hostages, the sons of ealdermen and thegns, were saying their tearful farewells to their families. Alfred and Haesten were standing apart. As he approached them, Bald saw Alfred was red and angry.

"You've got your will, Bald. You're leaving me and going with Aethelstan."

Bald wished he had never spoken. What new delights had the gods contrived for him?

"Am I a hostage?"

Haesten intervened. Dane and Saxon spoke virtually the same language.

"You'll be my guest."

Bald thought of the little henbell, that looked so innocent and housed a deadly poison.

"Forgive me, master, I'll stay with my lord Alfred."

"You'll swing, Bald! Ride away! The king of York has asked for you by name, and I'm giving you to him. Come back when you've cured him!"

Alfred left in a temper. Haesten shook his head.

"You Saxons are so violent."

"Master, how did the king of York know my name?"

"You're a famous leech, my friend. Everyone knows you cured king Alfred. Now, will you ride a horse or go in one of the wagons?"

Bald would have preferred to walk in the opposite direction.

"The wagon, master."

"Excellent. You can look after my wife."

Bald would have preferred a horse.

He took his scholar's robe and exchanged it with a Saxon soldier for his plaid. He took nothing else except his pouch, his knife and the book, and so left Winchester much as he had come there six months before.

They headed south. Bald expected them to go north, but he was not a Viking. Their natural element was the sea.

They rode quickly. He found himself jolted and jarred in the back of the oxcart with Haesten's wife. The cart fell into a rut and they were flung together. He had to prise himself away and then bear her toothless grin for the next mile.

When they entered the forest, the pace slackened, and Bald got down and walked alongside the wagon. Sunlight splashed through the young green of the trees and made the many-coloured carpet of flowers sparkle. Free of walls, free of the heavy robe, free of Alfred, Bald strode along in the old way. His fears began to lift with his spirits. The Vikings were talking and laughing with the hostages like young men anywhere. What are the girls like in Trondheim?

Haesten was riding ahead of the wagons and he looked round and waved to Bald with a smile. His geniality warmed Bald's blood, and he thought he might do something for his wife.

In the book:

"In order that the hair may not wax; take emmets eggs, rub them up, smudge on the place; never will any hair come up there."

There was a rotten tree lying near the track. He dug under it with his knife and uncovered an ants' nest. He took a dock leaf and scooped up a handful of the eggs. Climbing back into the wagon, he offered them to Haesten's wife. She took them, and he rubbed his finger on his upper lip and chin to show her where to smear them. She nodded, grinned, and ate them.

Bald sighed with resignation and waited for the scream that would bring Haesten and a dozen warriors down on him.

The hairy one smacked her lips and pointed to her mouth for more.

It was evening when they came out of the forest onto the hills above the Solent, and saw the silver mirror of the sea. The men dismounted. Wood was collected and a great fire lit. They unhitched one of the oxen and led it aside. Bald watched idly and then with uneasy prickling attention. He caught the flash of metal in the firelight and saw that under his white tunic each warrior was armed with sword or axe. Two of them took the ox's horns and pulled back its head while a third upswept his sword and cut its throat. The big black animal stood foursquare with its life gushing out. Bald felt his own blood draining, leaving him numb and cold. Before it fell, the knives were out. He turned away.

They broached a cask of ale and drank from a bowl which they passed around among the hostages. They handed out gobbets of oxflesh on sticks, which they thrust into the fire and ate still dripping blood. The hostages swilled and laughed. One leant into the firelight, and Bald recognised the young thegn who had hanged Duda. They were much the same, Saxon and Dane, swillers and killers. The fire burnt down and they slept where they lay.

Bald ate a handful of worts he had picked on the way, and crept underneath the cart, where he lay with the book underneath his head. He thought of escape, and then again that he was old and slow, and the Vikings young and quick. They were stupid, and might kill him and then remember their king had asked for him. Haesten was not stupid, and now he was a Christian perhaps he would keep his promise and the peace.

He slept.

He dreamt he was in the middle of a storm, with rumbling thunder and streaks of lightning.

In the book:

"In the present year, if it thunders on a Sunday, then that betokeneth a great bloodshed in some nation. If on the next day, Monday, that storm betokeneth that a royal child shall be put to death. If it thunders on Tuesday, then that betokeneth failure of crops. If it thunders on Wednesday, that betokeneth death of tillers of the land. If it thunders on Thursday, that betokeneth death of women. If it thunders on Friday, that betokeneth death of sea animals. If it thunders on Saturday, that betokeneth death of judges and bedfellows."

He woke suddenly. What day was it? As the dream-panic went, he heard Haesten's wife snoring in the cart above his head and saw the moon shining through the treetops. It was Monday the twenty-sixth of April.

In the book:

"On the twenty-fifth and twenty-sixth night of the moon's age, a dream betokeneth future terror and troubles, and in nine or ten days it shall be fulfilled. Turn your head to the east and ask for mercy."

He did.

The dawnsong woke him again, and in the grey light he saw a group of warriors going into the forest. Haesten was with them. He thought they were probably going to collect wood.

The birds sang to welcome the victory of light over darkness. He wondered if a similar victory would ever dawn over the island. He was going into darkness, ignorance, the storm from the north. There was a spattering above, and the boards of the oxcart leaked foul rain. Bald swore, seized the book and rolled out of range of Haesten's wife.

The camp was astir. Bald saw the warriors had put off their white tunics. Some wore Norse homespun, but most had gaudy jerkins boasting successful raids across the sea in Francia. Their mood had changed, and they kicked and pricked the hostages with their swords, herding them into a tight circle under an oak tree on the edge of the forest. He looked round and down towards the sea. In the opalescent greyness, two serpent ships were lying off the shore. He thought of – nothing. Death had erased Eneda from his mind.

The warriors returned from the forest. They too had changed into their war-gear and carried boughs and garlands of oak. Haesten wore a helmet and gripped a short ceremonial axe.

Bald felt his skin crawl with the familiar lice of fear and indecision. He wanted to shout no, no, not again! He wanted to shut his eyes. He wanted to run. He wanted to die. But sound, sight and movement were frozen, and his heart went on beating.

They took the hostage Bald knew they would: the young thegn, the child born under the thirteenth moon. They forced an oak branch under his arms and across his back. They put a chaplet of oak leaves on his brow. They tore open his tunic, bearing his breast. Haesten stepped up to him and said, "I give you to Woden." He raised the axe and chopped him like a tree, slicing through his breastbone.

The pinioned arms pulled his ribs apart. Haesten reached into his chest and drew out his living lungs and stretched them back over his shoulders like the sheathed wings of an eagle.

The sun rose.

The Vikings hurried down to the sea, whipping the oxen and hustling their captives, who no longer rode but ran like slaves.

Bald was flung about in the cart but felt nothing but dread of what the gods had ready for him.

The ships were drawn up to the shore and loaded with treasure and provisions. The oxen were slaughtered and the carts broken up for fuel. The captives were shackled in one ship. Bald went with Haesten and his family in the other. The horses were led aboard, hobbled and tethered. The warriors took on their other role as oarsmen and, before the sun was halfway up, the ships slid out into the Solent.

One terror drives out another as a new pain masks an old one.

Bald had never been to sea.

He crouched in the block-hole where the mast would be stepped in the centre of the ship, wondering what it was like to drown. He was too frightened to move, fearing the trampling hooves of the horses, the sweep of the oars, and his own clumsiness that might tumble him over the side. Haesten found him and pulled him out of the way, for the ship was heading out to sea and the crew was ready to raise the mast and break out the great sail in which he was curled like a louse.

Haesten led him to a seat in the prow and sat beside him.

The sail spread and caught the wind. The curved beak carved the sky. The ship's breast sliced the curling waves. Bald felt he was on the back of a giant eagle in flight. He glanced at Haesten and saw a speck of blood on his bishop's chin. In flight and in the company of the devil.

Haesten returned his look.

"What's in that book you carry?"

"Leechdoms." He added quickly, "Leechdoms that could help the king of York." He edged to one side until he looked and saw the sea beneath him, and edged back again. "It's not particularly Christian."

"There's nothing wrong with being Christian. I've been baptised three times. It's never done me any harm."

He should have been a bishop.

"On the contrary, I was a Christian when I robbed the churches in Paris, and I was one when I looted a pretty little town near Rome."

"You're not one now."

"You saw that? No. Christianity doesn't travel very well. It's not in tune with nature. It tortures trees into crosses. It eats its god, which is barbaric. And it denies the goodness of this life with a promise, and who believes in promises? If you were a good Christian, you'd let your patients die and go to heaven."

"I'm not a good Christian."

"Neither am I." Haesten laughed quietly. "Are you a good leech?"

Yes or no, Bald thought, and I am in trouble.

"If I was a navigator and I said I know the ship and I know the stars, and if the gods give me good wind and waves I'll bring you safe to harbour, would I be a good navigator?"

"You'd drown. I know the winds and waves as well."

Bald wished he had just said yes. But Haesten was in a philosophical mood.

"You must know more than the gods to live long and do well. That's the secret, Bald. And don't let them know you know it."

He went back, and after a moment, the great sail swung a degree or two and took them south of a bill of land Bald had barely seen.

At nightfall, the Vikings ran the ships into a river estuary, and went ashore to feed and water the horses. The Saxon captives were not allowed to land.

Haesten seemed to like Bald's company and led him to a fire and a meal of oxmeat his men had prepared for him. He offered Bald some wine.

"It's from Francia. I stole it myself. One day I'll go there and plant vines, and grow old with my vintages."

"If that's all you want, master, why did you leave your homeland?"

Haesten thought for a long moment.

"It was my fate." He added after another moment, "And yours."

At dawn they were at sea again, and soon rounding the south-east corner of the island. Bald thought sailing was easy.

In the book:

"If any thole or endure nausea on shipboard, let him take the same wort pulegium and wormwood, let him pound them together with oil and with vinegar; let him smear himself thereof frequently."

Pulegium was dwarf dwosle or pennyroyal, and as scarce aboard ship as Fornjot's palm.

Bald suffered.

He expected Haesten to go ashore that night but the wind was coming off the land and it was as much as the Vikings could do to keep course to the north for the following three days.

Bald had always borne other people's suffering with courage. His own defeated him. When the war with wind and tide forced the crew to take down the mast and resort to their oars, he crept back into his block-hole and prayed to whichever god came into his head. When he was not praying, he was cursing. He cursed Alfred, Haesten, the ship, the weather, all the gods he prayed to, and finally himself. In the last, he was right because his suffering was largely self-inflicted and self-indulgent. He bemoaned his fate instead of accepting it.

Bald was incapable of standing on his own. It is the paradox of strong, solitary men that they need a prop, a dream, an art or a religion. Bald needed the book, and the book in the present circumstances could only offer him dwarf dwosle. So he collapsed bodily and mentally and lay drivelling in his own vomit.

Three days of open sea and then the ships came under the lee of East Anglia, and put into the estuary of the river Orwell. This time the hostages were allowed ashore. Bald feared another sacrifice, but Haesten was pleased with the progress they had made and that appeared to be enough. Who decides god needs appeasing? The priest. So who knows more than god? Haesten was right, Bald thought.

The warriors seemed to relent towards their captives, and ate and drank with them as before. Bald watched them laughing together as if nothing had happened. There is nothing quite as convenient as memory, he thought, forgetting he had forgotten Eneda.

The voyage resumed under a May sky and the shelter of the great land mass. A bright breeze blew them north, and even Bald forgot to be miserable. He went to find Haesten in the prow.

"Master, has the king of York got leprosy?"

"No."

That was a pity. When a leech has a cure for a disease, he likes to find a patient with it. Some leeches give it anyway.

"What has he got?

"You must tell us when you see him."

Bald did not appreciate the threat implicit in Haesten's answer. He suddenly felt superior to the little fat man.

"There used to be a famous library at York. And Bede's library at Jarrow. And Cuthbert's at Lindisfarne."

"Bald, can you swim?"

"No, master"

"Then don't tempt me. You think us ignorant because we have no books. What good have books ever done?" Bald was cautiously silent.

"They only preserve the lies of the past. When you see York, you'll see the truth of today, a new people free from the past, free from oppression, free from prejudice, free from lies. Since we've been there, men have prospered and made money and lived in peace. If that is ignorance, amen. I call it independence."

The ships sailed north along the great sweep of coastline for four more nights.

Bald began to recognise individuals in the warrior-crew. There were some greybeards, but most were young and open-faced, farmers' sons, he thought, who sought a richer harvest in foreign fields. Haesten's words, freedom and independence, echoed in his head. They were the words refused by good king Alfred, and here they were in the mouth of a savage bishop. He began to think fate might be kinder than he expected, taking him to York.

That was a mistake. Know more than the gods, Haesten had said, but do not let them know it. When he woke on the fifth morning, the ninth after they had first set sail, there was no land in sight.

The sky darkened. Thunder rolled. Black clouds pressed down on the sea, which rose to meet them.

"Roaring the raging sea
drove with its fair sails
many a proud ship
of the beah giver
broken on land.
Blew with its loud blasts
on the brine skimmers
full fraught with warriors
fiercely the sea storm
stirred by the wizards
up on to Scotland
scattered and tossed
broad barking billows
threw brave men of battle
with shields and war gear
shivered and torn."

The Vikings knew the sea, and rowed their ships through the dragon's mouth, and sent blood-eagles screaming to the sky to rend the clouds and come home safe – with Bald, wrapped in the sail to protect the book, looking like a corpse.

And so they slid into the Humber estuary and safety, for some. The sail was lowered, and the men bent to the oars with a will. They were going home.

Far away, a woman waved from the shore, and the children running along the water's edge were Danes who had been born where they now lived. It was Ivarr's army, the Ivarr who had slaughtered Cild, that took York, destroyed the library and the school, ruined the cathedral, and returned to East Anglia. These settlers had come ten years later in waves of incursions from Denmark.

It was a fair journey up the Humber to the river Ouse and so to York. Farms and settlements lay along the banks on either side, and the hills behind were speckled with sheep and lambs. It was May, the best month, Bald thought. Haesten came and stood next to him in the prow, looking more episcopal than ever.

"They're what we call bondi, free farmers. They're all equal and are valued equally; no ealderman owns them, Bald. They own land according to their means. If a man has a team of oxen, he has a ploughland, if he has one ox he has an oxgang, an eighth, and if he has no ox, he has an eighth of that, a manslot. Most of them join their land together and then go to the folk-court to argue who owns what."

"Who rules them?"

"They rule themselves, my friend. They meet and decide by counting the number of spears raised for and against."

"Who wins?"

"The majority of course."

Bald gaped. He had always thought that the more men agreed, the more likely they were to be wrong, but then he was an intellectual.

"What about the king?"

"What about him?"

"Doesn't he have a say? Doesn't he hang a few every now and then to keep the rest in submission?"

"What do you think we are?" Haesten was hurt. "The king is the war-leader, and he's chosen by the warriors. They tend to stay with the same family. The devil you know is better, don't you think?"

Bald thought he did not know the devil at all.

"That's almost civilised."

"It's more than civilised, Bald, it's fair."

As they neared the city, the river filled with trading vessels going to and from the continent. Bald had been to York before. He had walked there with Cild, and copied leechdoms from the library. York was the military capital of the Romans in Britain, and he had wondered at the vastness of the legionary fortress and the wall. The Saxons were puny builders by comparison; the cathedral was a pile of wood and the jumble of houses looked as if they had fallen off it.

He did not expect the York he saw that day.

The Ouse ran through the city, where it joined the Foss. In the angle of the two rivers, the Danes had built a walled trade centre packed with narrow houses, workshops and stores. Trading vessels served this hive like bees. Leather was fashioned here, wood and horn were shaped into cups and bowls, metal was hammered into knives, axes, jewels were set in gold, cloths were woven, and moneyers struck coins to pay for it all. The Danes, who had no money of their own, took to the new religion and the old, and their silver pennies carried both the cross and Thor's hammer.

Houses now covered the area up to the fortress, smaller than Bald remembered it, and the cathedral, less significant since the roof had fallen in.

The Viking ships ran ashore under the new river crossing. The horses and hostages were disembarked and the treasure unloaded and left under guard. Haesten and Bald walked ahead through Ousegate into the city. Bald was amazed at the noise, the smells, the activity. Haesten was right: here men prospered, made money, lived in peace. He saw many Saxon faces among the Danes and foreigners. Haesten was amused.

"You thought we were all blood-crazed bull-headed idiots, didn't you?"

"No, master."

"It's in your books, that's why. And who writes them? Alfred."

Bald thought he had some personal experience, but did not mention it. Haesten guessed.

"You judge a whole people by the first one you come across."

They passed some slaves in shackles being driven down to the river. Haesten did not notice them.

"We are in a fair way to becoming a new force in this country. In this part of it anyway. We make good men."

They had come to the aggregate of buildings that housed the court of the king of York. It was late in the day, and Haesten had to arrange for wagons to collect the danegeld. He left Bald with a warrior, and instructions to take him to the king.

"Master, who is the king? What do I say to him?"

"Don't you know? Sigtryggr Ivarrson, king of Dublin and York."

The warrior led Bald inside.

Sigtryggr king of Dublin. The terror of the name blocked out any other association Bald might have made on hearing it. It whirled in his head as he blindly followed the warrior through passages and rooms of people to a chamber on the far side of the fortress. The sun was setting and bright yellow light shone through the embrasure, leaving a bed where a man was lying in shadow.

At first, Bald could not see for the light. He moved to the foot of the bed and, as his eyes became accustomed to the shadow, he knew the gods had played the trick he least expected and most feared. He had seen the man on the bed before: broad forehead, beak nose, beard, lying on a catafalque of treasure on a funeral ship.

King Sigtryggr Ivarrson, the son of Ivarr, had been going on his last journey from Dublin to York when Bald had saved his life by cutting off his arm.

But the man lying on the bed had two arms.

X

Bald stared in a terror of incomprehension. Had Sigtryggr grown another arm? He could not find an answer except in magic and unreason. He forced himself to look closer, and moved to the right side of the bed.

Though the light was fading, he could see a difference between the hands lying on the covers. The right hand was smaller by half than the left. It was pale and waxy, and the fingers were unnaturally stiff. He reached down to touch it and recoiled from the clammy coldness. He folded back the sleeve of the loose gown Sigtryggr was wearing. The forearm had the same unhealthy waxiness. The muscle was wasted, and the tendons pulled tight under the skin.

He pressed the flesh softly, and the indentation made by his finger remained.

The terror of unreality was displaced by the greater terror of reality itself.

He turned to the warrior who had remained in the room.

"Call Haesten! Call the king's family."

He pulled back the covers on the bed. Sigtryggr was breathing heavily, drugged, he thought. He opened the gown and pulled it back to uncover the right shoulder. The upper arm was yellow and shrunken, and the skin stretched up to where it had been crudely stitched to Sigtryggr's skin. Where the dead flesh touched the living flesh, there was a raw red ring of infection.

Bald shook his head in disbelief. Someone had tried to graft a dead man's arm to Sigtryggr's body!

His first feeling was rage at whoever had committed this sacrilege against nature. He tried to repress it. His own position was precarious. The Danes must have trusted whoever it was. For him to refute this man would be dangerous, to undo his work fatal if Sigtryggr died later. He told himself he must do nothing yet.

Yet how could he leave this travesty alone? This was the work of some ignorant and pretentious leech with just enough learning to make him lethal! Worse – what crass arrogance the man must have to believe he could give life to a dead limb! Worse still – what stupidity and assumption! What an outrage against the profession and practice of leechdoms! This puerile doctor had no right to impose his incompetence on another human being. He had committed an atrocity little short of murder. And in the name of healing! He was an enemy of sense, reason and humanity. Bald's rage rose, and overwhelmed all his cautions and fears for himself.

He turned to the bed and drew his knife to right the wrong that had been done.

"Stop him!"

He was seized and flung to the floor. The knife was prised from his hand and held to his throat.

"Don't kill him yet."

He could not see who was in the room, but he could hear the tread of feet and men's voices.

"Father, father, wake!"

"Is the king safe?"

"Who is it?"

"What did he do?"

"He had a knife in his hand."

"Look after the king. Call Withbec."

"Call Wulfhere. This is a Saxon sent to kill the king!"

"Who brought him here?"

"Haesten."

"I don't trust Haesten."

Bald felt death was very close. There was an agonised groan from the bed as the disturbance woke the king.

"Father, we've caught the murderer. Bring him here!"

Bald was dragged up and thrust towards the bed, his arms twisted behind him by two warriors. Blood trickled from his neck where the point of the knife had penetrated. There were torches in the room, and he grimaced and blinked his eyes. He saw three Vikings with strikingly similar features which resembled those of the king. Two were young and one old, and they all had death in their eyes.

A worried pale-faced man in a clerical robe hurried in. Bald saw with surprise the cross around his neck.

The old Viking spoke.

"Wulfhere, question this man. He's a Saxon. He had a knife and was going to kill Sigtryggr."

"God forbid! Excuse me." The cleric signed the cross several times. He approached Bald tentatively.

"Wicked man, who are you? Speak the truth like a good Christian. I am Archbishop of York and I'll know if you're lying."

Before he could answer, Sigtryggr groaned again, and Bald saw he was watching them.

"I'm Bald the leech."

"You're lying. Will you swear it? What were you doing?"

"I was going to cut that monstrosity off his body."

Wulfhere turned to the others. "He's admitted it. Is that all?"

Bald realised Wulfhere was more afraid of the Vikings than he was himself. He looked at the old one.

"The king of York sent for me. Ask Haesten – he brought me here."

"Yes, but what for?"

"To heal him."

"You say, and Haesten will too, I expect."

"Let him answer for himself. I'm a leech."

Wulfhere held out his cross. "Swear it."

"I'm not an oath-taker."

"Take him out and hang him!" It was one of the young men.

"No, Caech." The other. "Maybe he's telling the truth."

"Brother, we have a leech already."

"Yes, one that suits you better than he does our father."

Bald began to realise each one was more concerned for himself than for the man lying on the bed.

A young man entered in a doctor's gown pulled on hastily over his nightshirt. He had a shock of ginger hair on a narrow head not much wider than his scraggy neck. Pale blue eyes of the shifty sort peered out of slitty holes in his sharp face. He was slight but wiry and had bandy legs. He complained in a whining voice, "I was asleep."

"Withbec, do you know him?" The old Viking pointed at Bald.

Bald felt the sharp one's gaze and saw his eyes go left and right as he tried to balance one lie against another.

"He's a witch and a devil-sucker! He tried to kill good king Alfred – I say good because I'm honest – and when a better doctor than he is, Doctor Oxa, who's dead and gone to heaven cured him, he took the credit."

Bald was upset. "Is Oxa dead?"

"He went into a lion's cage in Jerusalem, and it ate him."

Raw luck, thought Bald. He eyed the man. He must be Withbec the bone-setter, who had fled to the Danes from Winchester.

Haesten entered the room. "What happened here? Guthrith?"

Guthrith was the eldest of the three Vikings. He pointed to Bald.

"He had a knife. He was going to kill Sigtryggr."

Bald was exasperated. "You keep saying that! Look, Haesten – whoever sewed that arm on the man is killing him!"

They turned to Withbec, who edged nearer to the bed as if for Sigtryggr's protection. The pale blue eyes flickered.

"The arm is good!"

"It's dead, you fool."

"It was alive when I put it on him. You killed it by witchcraft!"

Bald shrugged. Haesten intervened.

"This is a dispute between doctors. Let Sigtryggr decide." He went between Bald and Withbec to the foot of the bed. "Sigtryggr, Bald the leech is here. I brought him from Alfred, who says he healed him. Bald accuses this leech. This leech accuses Bald. You must choose between them."

Sigtryggr struggled to raise himself, groaning with the effort, dragging the dead arm up the covers. Pain dug deep lines in his face. He groaned again. "Bald, is Bald here?"

"I am."

"Withbec begged him, "Don't let him touch you. He's the devil's man!"

Sigtryggr turned his head slowly from one to the other. Withbec forced himself to smile a nervous seductive moue of fear. Bald scowled.

"I choose Withbec."

The bone-setter giggled and the pale blue eyes condemned

Bald to death. Sigtryggr raised his left hand and beckoned him to come nearer. Withbec leant over the bed confidently.

The great hand stretched out and seized him by the throat, and locked.

Withbec writhed and twisted and struck out, but Sigtryggr's arm was like oak.

Bald watched with horrible fascination. Withbec's face was going the same purple as his doctor's gown. His eyes bulged. His mouth dropped open and his tongue lolled out. His struggles became twitches and then spasms as death danced in him. Sigtryggr gripped him until he was still. Then he unlocked his hand and the bone-setter dropped to the floor.

The warriors had released their hold on Bald, and they went and dragged out Withbec's corpse.

Sigtryggr swung his head round to look at Bald and fell back on the bed exhausted.

Bald saw the great black ox that stood foursquare after it was dead.

Haesten turned to him. "Ask for everything you need. Don't fail. You know what it means."

Bald nodded. The blood-eagle.

"I need fire and water and clean rags – and honey!" He unslung the book and laid it on the bed, kneeling to turn the pages.

Guthrith had already summoned two household slaves, young girls, Ginna and Toki, and sent them on this task. He came to Bald and spoke quietly:

"I'm the king's brother, and Ragnall and Caech are his sons. Speak to one of us."

Bald thought, he does not trust Haesten.

They all left, Wulfhere making a token sign of the cross before retreating. Caech came back.

"Whatever happens here, you have a friend."

Bald wondered. A moment ago they would have killed him without a thought, and now they were his friends. Did they want Sigtryggr dead or alive?

He went to look at him. Sigtryggr had fallen into a deep sleep. Good. Two menslaves carried in a burning brazier, two more a ewer and basin. Ginna and Toki brought clean rags and a jar of honey.

In the book:

"To heal a wound, as thou wouldst the part which as yet may have some feeling, and be not altogether dead. Thou shalt with frequent scarifying, whilom with mickle, whilom with slight, wean and draw the blood from the deadened place. Cure the scarifyings thus; take bean or oat or barley meal, or some of such meal as to thee seemeth good so that it will serve, add vinegar and honey, seethe together and lay on, and bind upon the sore places. If thou shouldst wish that the salve be stronger add a little salt, bind on at whiles and wash with vinegar or with wine. Apply the leechdoms according as thou seest the state of the body. For a mickle difference is there in the bodies of a man, a woman, and a child; and in the main or constitution of a daily wight or labourer and of the idle, of the old and of the young, of him who is accustomed to endurances and him who is unaccustomed to such things."

Bald cut the stitches and discarded the dead arm. For four nights he scarified the infected flesh, applied the salve and cleansed the wound with wine. The shoulder healed. The king slept. Withbec was a bad memory.

Ragnall and Caech were frequent visitors. Bald noticed they appeared together as if neither trusted the other alone with their father. The double kingdom of Dublin and York lay in the balance. Guthrith, Ragnall and Caech were all possible claimants, and Bald suspected Haesten too. All depended on his keeping Sigtryggr alive.

On the fifth morning, Sigtryggr was sitting on the stone seat in the window embrasure. Bald examined his shoulder. The scars had healed, and new skin was forming where the arm had been. Sigtryggr turned his great head.

"So you're Bald the leech."

"Yes, master."

"I owe you a life."

Bald was worried. The Viking way of cancelling a loan was to cancel the lender.

"And you owe me a death."

What did he mean? A race who wrote only in runes tended to be cryptic, and Sigtryggr was not given to words. He repeated it.

"Bald, you owe me a death."

"What do you mean, master?"

"The first time."

Bald's thoughts flew in confusion like trapped birds in a cage. He had understood from Haesten that the king had asked for him because he had healed Alfred. Had Sigtryggr somehow recognised him from the burning ship? How did he know his name? He echoed, "The first time?"

"Yes. I had a war-wound and was ready to die and go to Valhalla. Instead you cheated me, worse, you thief! You took my sword-arm. Now I have to die like a woman."

Did these Vikings think of nothing else but death?

"Master, I'm a leech. The gods decide who lives and who dies."

"You took my death from me. Remember what you owe me, and pay when I demand it."

Sigtryggr turned to the embrasure and gazed at the golden morning as if he saw the hall of heaven.

Bald returned to his room. Ginna and Toki were cleaning it, and he sent them away. He lay on the bed and listened to the ravens talking in his head.

The Viking knew. How? Sometimes a sick man saw more than a whole one. He knew, and had sent for him not to save his life from the fool Withbec, but to give him back his death! Why? And how, except by killing him?

Bald despised the beerhall theology of Valhalla and belief in the bloody hangover in which the world would end. But he knew that by cutting off his sword-arm he had deprived the Viking of his manhood. He tasted the irony of it. He had made Sigtryggr impotent in the one thing that mattered to him. There was no Fornjot's palm cauda pulli Sigmunds kraut Foules tayle to restore an arm. Only the fool's arm that cost Withbec his life.

How would it end?

The tiredness of four nights' waking drifted him to sleep.

In the book:

"If it seems to you in a dream that you see bees carrying honey, it shall prove to be the earning of money from wealthy persons. If bees sting him, that signifies that his mind shall be much disturbed by foreigners. If he fancy he sees bees fly into his house, that shall be the destruction of the house."

In his sleep, he sensed someone was watching him. His face was turned towards the door. He slowly lifted his eyelids and saw a figure in the doorway. He jerked awake and opened his eyes fully. There was no-one there. But he swore he had seen the figure of a dwarf. And it was Lyb!

He lay back on the bed. Had he seen it or dreamt it? Either way it meant trouble.

In the book:

"To do away a dwarf, give to the troubled man to eat thost (dung) of a white hound pounded to dust and mingled with meal and baked to a cake, ere the hour of the dwarfs arrival, whether by day or by night it be; his access is terribly strong and after that it diminisheth and departeth away."

Bald sent Ginna and Toki to the kennels. The Viking kennelman thought they were joking.

"A white hound?"

"Yes, master."

"The leech wants its shit?" The girls giggled. "You Saxons are uncivilised!"

Archbishop Wulfhere came to see Bald. He wondered why he did not offer him a piece of cake, and took one when he was not looking.

"I don't suppose you could give the church the credit for the king's recovery? He might give us a new roof for the cathedral. What an awful end for that poor young man."

Bald was unsympathetic.

"I know you disapprove of me, but if I hadn't stayed here, York wouldn't have an archbishop."

"Have you seen a dwarf here recently?"

"Heaven forbid! I do some good, you know. I've baptised quite a lot of them. They don't seem to mind."

"They have their own baptisms in blood."

"Yes, but one has to be broad-minded in these matters. When I tried to remonstrate with Sigtryggr, he said we did much the same to Jesus. I told him there weren't any Christians then, but he didn't understand. He said how could he be a god if he wasn't always there? They're very literal, you know."

Bald was too, but said nothing.

In the book:

"In case that the upper part of the belly is filled with evil sordid humour, a thing which happeneth to the man who in much continued drinking take nutritious meats or who spew, and chiefly after meat, and who are subject to nausea, they are all overblown as with wind, and the wamb is extended and they frequently have breakings. To these men one must give oxymel with radish; that is a southern leechdom; and then they soon spew up thick corruption, and it is well with them."

Guthfrith arrived as Wulfhere was leaving. He came straight to the point.

"How long has Sigtryggr got to live?" Bald shrugged. "There must be a peaceful succession."

"Why are Dublin and York together?"

"Ivarr, Sigtryggr's father, seized them both. We settled them with our people. Now Dublin's threatened by Norsemen, bloody terrorists!"

Bald acknowledged the double-edged irony of the gods.

"Can you find out from Sigtryggr who's going to succeed him?"

"I'm a leech, master, not a lawyer."

"Tell him he must decide because he's only got a few months left."

"If the butcher told the ox the truth, there'd be no beef and probably no butcher."

"Get the right answer and I'll have you in my council. You can be archbishop if you like. Wulfhere wasn't looking well."

"It was something he ate."

Later in the day Bald was not surprised to see Haesten. The old pirate gave him a piece of gold.

"I'm going back to Francia. I'd like to take you with me but Sigtryggr won't part with you." Bald was pleased to be spared another sea journey. "There's too much intrigue going on here for me. I'm a simple man." He spoke confidentially, "Don't trust Guthrith. Mind you, they're all false-hearted." He looked as bland as a bishop. "Be careful. Your best friend is Sigtryggr. Or his mistress."

It was the first Bald had heard of a mistress. "My wife sends her farewells."

Bald asked Ginna and Toki whether they knew the king had a mistress. They giggled, and he got no sense out of them.

He began to think how he could escape from this nest of Vikings. He liked York. It was more open than Winchester, and the new citizens were frank and outspoken. But crowns create corruption wherever they are.

He was in the market place when he suddenly found Caech, the king's younger son, next to him. The safest place for intrigue is in a crowd. Caech spoke with a smile as if he was ordering a bunch of carrots.

"I want you to give me a poison to kill a man and make it look as if he died naturally."

"There isn't one, master. Any leech will know the cause of death."

"Not if the leech is you, Bald."

He smiled again and walked away. Bald felt he was in a whirligig, the spinning cage in which witches were tormented.

What could he do? Who could he tell?

Haesten was going. Guthrith or Ragnall? The poison could be intended for one of them. Or both. And then Caech would know who had told them. He could give Caech an anodyne and pretend it was the poison. And then again Caech would know, and when the victim did not die, he would. He could tell Sigtryggr. Haesten had said he was his best friend. But Caech would deny it, and who would the king believe, his son or a Saxon leech? And would that stop Caech from getting his revenge? The market place was spinning round him. The vendors' cries were deafening in his ears. He cursed his luck in coming to York. He spun – he fell!

A crowd gathered. Sometimes a sick man sees more than a whole one. Bald saw the legs of men, the skirts of women, and then, pushing to the front of the crowd, the face of Lyb.

He fainted!

There were bees buzzing in his head. Some carried honey: others stung him. All flew into the house.

He woke in a delirium in his room in the palace. His mind wandered backwards and forwards searching for a way out of his quandary. Sometimes he was conscious, other times he found refuge in fantasy, and he could not tell which was which.

Were the men who came and went Guthrith, Ragnall, Caech?

Could he hear Ginna and Toki whispering together? Who was the stranger who stood in the lamplight? Did Wulfhere sprinkle holy water on him? Who shaved his beard?

Or were the men giants on the ceiling, the whispering the buzz of bees, the stranger his cloak hanging from its peg, the water rain through the window, and the razor the ceremonial axe wielded by the manslayer? The meandering river of thoughts ran into the desert of indecision and died. The poison in his mind spread through his body, paralysing both. He lay silent, unmoving, unthinking, like a trapped animal, a cat in a cage killing itself. He gave up. There was no answer.

He became seriously ill. His body no longer functioned. His retreat into impotence was complete.

Sigtryggr came himself. He dragged the bench across the stone floor and sat facing Bald.

Bald heard thunder and thought god had come to visit him.

"You have what is called 'stupiditus Saxonum'. There's another name for it – the Knot. You can't move. You can't speak. You can't think. You are bedrugged. Something is strangling your mind with a chain of terror."

Having stated the obvious, god left.

Bald lingered, growing weaker.

His brain dried up. His mouth was dry. His eyes glued up. When the word came to him, he could not speak. When he tried to move his arm he could not move even his finger.

Hearing is the last of the senses to go. The word is first and last. He heard a woman sing.

"Here came entering
a spider wight:
he had his hands upon his hams
he quoth that thou his hackney wert:
lay thee against his neck:
they began to sail off this land:
as soon as they off the land came
then began they to cool:
then came in a wild beasts sister:
then she ended:
and oaths she swore,
that never this could harm the sick

nor him who could get at this charm
or him who had skill to sing this charm,
amen, fiat."
She wiped his eyes with watercress.
"Steem hight this wort,
on stone she grew,
standeth she against venom,
stoundeth she head wark;
stiff hight she also,
stoundeth she venom,
wreaketh on the wrath one,
whirleth out poison."
He opened his eyes. He saw Eneda.
She wiped his mouth. He spoke her name. "Eneda."
She wiped his head with watercress. He knew she was Eneda.

xi

Bald was too weak to question Eneda, and found consolation in the simple knowledge she was still alive. How and why could wait. He felt gratitude, but also the reawakening of guilt.

He watched her as she moved quietly round the room or sat in the window in the summer sunlight. Did she still hate him for not revealing their relationship? Did she forgive him for running away when she was in danger?

He tried to find answers in her attitude. She was caring but careful. Her carelessness for appearances that had so attracted him had gone. He thought the last year had probably been a bad one for her and had made her compromise with fate. He cursed himself, the treasure, London and the Danes, for shackling her spirit with the chains of caution.

She was cool towards him. One day she told him she had not wanted to see him again. When she knew he was in York she kept to her apartment to avoid meeting him. She had told Lyb to watch him. Only his sudden unexplained collapse had induced her to come out of hiding.

Bald was silent. It was answer enough. She hated and had not forgiven him. He loved her all the more for it. She was right.

And yet she had saved his sanity, if not his life.

He noticed new lines in her face and a trace of grey in her hair. Her dress of grey silk, the gold circlet she wore, the grooming, and, he guessed, the governance she was under, had aged her. He dared not ask her how she had come to York or what her position was in the court, and she did not tell him.

He regained his strength slowly. Eneda was his leech, mixing his salves and drinks. She used the book, which was only fair for Cild's granddaughter. When he disagreed with her prescription – for which two doctors agree on everything? – he was silent, and took his medicine. Lyb washed him and helped him dress.

The dwarf now had a hoofmark on his head from nose to ear, which made him more grotesque than ever. Ginna and Toki were terrified of him, and he chased them for amusement. Since Eneda's appearance, Guthrin, Ragnall and Caech had stopped coming to see him. His only other visitor was Wulfhere, who sought anyone's company providing he was not a Viking.

One day when they were alone, he asked Wulfhere about Eneda.

"Don't you know? She's the one who told Sigtryggr about you. He trusted Withbec, but she made him send for you."

So she had thought of him but for Sigtryggr's sake.

"Haesten had her at Benfleet before we captured it. She had a piece of the royal crown, heaven knows how! He gave her to Sigtryggr."

Bald felt the gentle touch of fate.

"She's been here two or three months. I suppose you know she's his mistress? I can't stop it."

He knew it, but the word hurt him. He wished his impotence on Sigtryggr, and guessed Sigtryggr wished his impotence on him.

He could hear the Mothers chuckling to themselves as they twisted the skeins of life around each other.

That was how Sigtryggr knew Bald had taken off his arm. Eneda had told him to explain how she came by the gold serpent from the helmet.

When he was well enough to leave his bed Eneda no longer came to his room. Lyb brought the salves and potions, and he administered them himself. This was the signal for the reappearance of Caech, and the return of the problems that plagued him like a swarm of bees.

"I've come to congratulate you on your recovery. Life's so uncertain, isn't it? We need our friends. I'll call on you in a day or two for the favour you promised me."

"Master, I've nothing here for your purpose. I must collect these things and I can't leave the court."

"You're making difficulties for yourself, Bald, not for me. Two days."

He left.

Bald felt himself slipping back into the abyss of despair. He had to tell someone.

It was evening, and the pale shadow of the moon before the sun had set was like a dying face. Lyb had brought his supper and was leaving. Bald followed him. The ancient fort was a nightmare of passages and rooms added over the centuries until even the old slave who had served a dozen kings their dinners got lost and was berated for the coldness of the beef. Lyb, with the instincts of a mole, knew the dark underground by smell and went off apace with the empty plates. Bald, whose stride was four of the dwarf's, was left behind and lost him. He waited in the gloom and saw Lyb coming back, and hurried after him again. He found himself outside his own room, and then the one he knew was Sigtryggr's, but Lyb had disappeared and there were three more rooms in the corridor. Which would Eneda have chosen, Eneda, independent, self-possessed? He chose the last one, and entered the room without warning.

He saw her in lamplight. Her hair was down and she wore an old homespun nightdress. Surprise made her look young, wide-eyed like a child.

"Why are you here? Are you ill? What's the matter?"

"I'm well, it's not me. I must talk to you about Sigtryggr."

"Oh, that." She sounded almost disappointed as if she was expecting something like it. She went past him to close the door. "I have to thank you for saving Sigtryggr's life."

"You could have done it."

"I'm a woman."

Now she saw him in the light, and he looked old and worried. A sympathy, an unconscious empathy between them, made her gentle. She led him to a chair and stood looking down at him.

"Well – uncle Bald."

He grimaced, believing she hated him and was mocking him. But he had to confide in her.

"Caech has asked me for a poison. I have two days to prepare it. And afterwards I have to say it was a natural death."

Eneda frowned and was silent for a moment.

"I thought it would be Guthrith."

"What?"

"Who wanted Sigtryggr dead. I thought it was the brother, not the son."

"Will you tell him?"

"I don't know."

"You must tell him, Eneda."

"Then Caech will know you told me."

"Does that matter?"

"Yes it does."

He felt a sudden flow of blood, warm blood.

"Perhaps he wants it for someone else: Ragnall or Guthrith?"

"No, it's Sigtryggr. Ragnall and Caech act as one. They have no reason to kill Guthrith."

"Then you have no option."

"And Caech will have no option but to kill you."

"True." He laughed once, short and ironic. "We're leeches, my dear. We save other people's lives."

She looked angry and he knew she wanted to protect him. At that moment he felt so close to her that he wanted to reach out and touch her, not as a lover but as a part of himself, the part he had never really had, friend, mother, sister, wife. Self-sorrow swelled and overflowed into his eyes.

"How did we come to be like this?"

She did not answer and turned away, he thought because she despised him. If he had looked he would have seen her tears.

Reality prevailed in her first.

"We must be careful. My own position here is not too safe. He's an old man, and he cares more for his sons than a woman."

"A mistress."

"That's what they call me. It's a title more than an office." She made herself smile.

"If you don't say anything, you consent to his death."

"I didn't do that before, and I won't now!" She was angry again.

"What, then?"

"Caech wants a poison. Which poison?"

Bald shrugged. "There are as many poisons as there are worts. We can kill as easily as we cure."

"Is there one with a certain antidote?"

"Nothing is certain."

"Nearly certain."

"Wolfsbane."

"And the antidote?"

"Stavesacre."

"Give Caech wolfsbane. Give me stavesacre."

The anger made her sparkle.

Bald looked up at her as if a star had suddenly appeared in his sky. He breathed again. The shadow lifted from his face. She smiled to see him so and he spoke quickly before her mood changed.

"Eneda, what I did was love, the only love I could give you. When I knew what we were, I loved you the greater because we were part of each other. I should have told you but I was afraid what you'd think of me. I am everything you said."

He got up slowly. He was still weak and unsteady and she reached out to hold him.

"I'm to blame as much as you."

"No blame, Eneda. Where the gods are concerned no human is to blame."

She suddenly laid her head against his body and he closed his eyes in gratitude. He raised his hand to touch her hair but stopped and gently moved her away.

"I must go tomorrow and find what I need."

"I'll come with you. No fear. He knows you're my uncle."

This time the word held no hatred and no mockery, and he welcomed it.

She still went to the door and made sure that no-one was there.

"Do you know where you are?"

Bald nodded. "At last."

He went back to his room. He did not sleep. He was content to be near Eneda.

They left the palace at dawn. They took Ginna and Toki and Sigtryggr thoughtfully provided a guard, and Caech another. Lyb trotted behind carrying a basket for the flowers they were ostensibly going to pick. They followed the river upstream. When they reached the open meadows beyond the cultivated fields outside the city, Ginna and Toki ran off chased by Lyb. They disappeared in the long flowery grass, and their squeals came from further and further away.

The sun rose. Between the osiers the Ouse glowed a dusty gold as motes of mayflies drifted down to be swallowed by the ripples. Following the golden girl through the soft brush of grasses that fringed the riverbank, Bald was as near the heaven he had read about in Bede as he was ever likely to be.

"The heaven locketh up in its bosom all the world; and it turneth ever about us, swifter than any mill wheel, as deep under the earth as it is above it. It is all round and solid and painted with stars."

Eneda, glancing back, was strangely comforted by the tall gaunt haunted figure so near to her in blood.

The woods closed in on the river and in the shadows she saw the tall purple spikes of wolfsbane. She dropped down as if tired among the deadly spires. Bald sat beside her.

The two guards, seeing their charges had no intention of running, relaxed and went down to the river to throw stones at anything that moved.

Eneda reached out to take a stalk. Bald snatched her hand away.

"It's death!"

He cut the stalk with his knife, letting it fall. He dug out the root and trimmed off the earth before picking it up with his knife and putting it in his pouch.

He looked round. The guards had seen nothing. Eneda gave a puff of relief and smiled at him nervously. He thought it was a good time for another confession.

"I thought the horse had killed you."

"It will take more than a horse."

"That's why I didn't come back."

"It's lucky you didn't. The place was full of Vikings."

"Did they take you with them?"

"I was painted white and covered in crosses, remember? They thought I had the flying venom. They hoofed it."

He was silent, waiting for her to tell him.

"God Woden, it nearly killed me. Lyb dragged me down the hill to the woods. Then he went back for the saddlebags."

"I thought he was dead."

"He was rearranged a bit."

"And you?"

"He covered me with moss. When I came to, I thought he'd buried me."

"It's an old leechdom. Moss draws out the humours."

She was silent. He lay on his side. The sunlight gilded her like a saint in a missal.

"After three nights, the moss was black and I was white as a corpse. I gave Lyb money to buy a handcart. I lay on the saddlebags and he wheeled me into London."

"Weren't the Vikings there?"

"It was only a raiding party. The army had moved up the river. London was safe."

"Where did you go?"

"Doctor Dun. It was the only name I knew. You'd said you were taking me to Doctor Dun."

"How did you find him?"

"There's a street in London where all the leeches have their houses. His was the biggest."

"I can hardly remember him."

"He's a little fat man with small feet and hands like a juggler. He can write a bill, fold it and slip it into your hand while he's saying goodbye. He dyes his hair black and has a nose a chicken could lay an egg on."

"He made a good impression."

"I told him I was Cild's granddaughter and he said he didn't treat paupers. They don't in that street."

"What then?"

"I showed him the money."

The money then was gone, thought Bald.

"It's gone. By the time I was well again, and by an extraordinary coincidence, his bills added up to the exact amount I had. Four thousand and twenty-two pennies."

He laughed.

"Don't laugh!"

He could not stop laughing.

"I couldn't even buy a second-hand dress!"

He laughed so loudly that the guards came up from the river to see what they were missing. Eneda said, "I've just told him he hasn't a penny."

"Stupid Saxon!"

They walked on along the river. Bald followed at an aptly beggarly pace, and after a while she dropped back and walked beside him.

"What does it look like?"

In the book:
"This wort which one nameth stavesacre, and by another name lousebane, hath a leaf as a vine, and a straight stalk, and it hath seed in green pods of the size of peas, and it is three cornered, and it is austere and swart; it is, however, within white and bitterish to the taste."

"It's very like briony."
"Black briony."
"That's a poison. What is the leechdom?"

In the book:
"For the evil humours of the body take fifteen grains of the seed of this wort, pounded in lithe beer; administer it to be drunk; it purgeth the body through spewing; and after that the sick hath drunken the drink he shall go, that is walk about, and bestir him before that he speweth, and when he beginneth to spew, he shall frequently swallow some lithe liquor of beer, lest the strength of the wort burn the throat and choke him."

Bald glanced at her. She was memorising it. When she was serious, small lines formed at the corners of her mouth. He suddenly thought he knew her face better than his own. What did he look like to her? She caught him thinking, and smiled.
"We'll find another Viking ship."
"I think one found you."
"Haesten!" She said it like a curse.
He did not want her to say any more. He knew. He tried to comfort her.
"You don't say no to Haesten."
"It was fate. He'd have killed Lyb. He'd have killed me if I hadn't had the little piece of gold, do you remember?" Bald nodded. "I couldn't stay in London. There was a ship going to King's Stone. Haesten captured us. You don't know what he did to one of the men!"
Bald did know, but said nothing. She stared as if she still saw the blood-eagle.
"He took us to Benfleet."
"The Danes wintered there."

"He gave me to his wife. You can imagine how she treated me."

Bald wished he had kicked the hairy woman. He wished Haesten dead. He wished God existed. He wished all the evil in the world destroyed.

She looked wistful, like a child. "We go on living."

"There's a part of us no-one can touch. Not even a leech."

She smiled. "Our souls?"

"No, nothing as grand as that. Just us."

He did not look at her as he said it. He felt her hand touch his arm. It gave him life, that touch.

"Haesten brought me here and gave me to Sigtryggr as a present. Sigtryggr had to have an arm to prove he was a man. He was dying. I told him about you. Then in the spring, the Saxons took Benfleet. Haesten was going to see Alfred and I made him ask for you."

She stopped and turned to him urgently.

"Sigtryggr must not die, you know that!"

He looked at her as if it was for the last time.

"We don't command death, my child, we obey it."

They found the stavesacre growing in a thicket on the way back to York. Bald lingered behind the others and cut the seedpods with his knife. Ginna and Toki returned, and Lyb followed with a basket of flowers. The girls were restrained and self-important, and Bald thought the dwarf had probably ensured the survival of the British race. He glanced at Eneda almost unconsciously. She was walking ahead of him, and something in her bearing alerted him to a possibility he could hardly conceive. Ginna and Toki were trotting either side of her, and she put her arms around them maternally.

Bald realised she was pregnant and she knew it. That was why Sigtryggr's life was so important to her. She was carrying his child!

His first reaction was a feeling of jealousy and anger as if she had betrayed him. But he was old, and passions did not last long. He felt sorry for her. But why? She did not look sorry for herself; on the contrary, she had a gravity and serenity, which he had attributed to caution but which came from confidence.

He shrugged. It was fate. But what if Caech knew and wanted the poison for Eneda? No, only a leech would see the signs, and then only if the connection was made in his mind. He wondered if he should speak to her about it. That was another problem.

When he returned to his room, he sent Ginna and Toki to fetch the things he needed: a pestle and mortar, a covered jug, a quart of ale. Guthrith came in as he was pounding the root of wolfsbane into a paste.

"That looks good. Can you eat it?"

"I wouldn't advise it."

"Have you spoken to Sigtryggr? Have you any idea what's in his mind?"

"Yes: you are."

The lie came instantaneously. Perhaps he said it to distract attention from Eneda, or to get rid of Guthrith, or to confuse Caech. Perhaps a god put it into his mouth. He regretted it but it was too late. Guthrith already saw himself as king. He became devious and dangerous.

Bald was reminded of Alfred.

"I'll reward you, of course. What do you want most? I mean when Sigtryggr is dead."

"I leave it to you, master."

"You're a wise man."

As he left, Bald thought – and you are a fool. He put the paste into a small jar and sealed it. He carefully washed the implements he had used. His thoughts returned to Eneda. Would Sigtryggr marry her? Would Ragnall and Caech let the child live?

Suddenly the whole scaffold of questions and concerns collapsed. He was an old man! Why did he have to bear this burden of probabilities? Eneda was using him to keep Sigtryggr alive. She did not care for him – no matter how many times she called him uncle! What was he doing, making poison for conspirators and antidotes for a king? His place was among the common people, who needed his leechdoms. He was a healer, not a killer!

He went to the window and looked out at the city. It was a summer evening and lights were springing up like daisies on a lawn. Briton, Saxon, Dane, what did nature know or care? And nature was his master. He resolved to leave York, yes, and leave Eneda. She had her child, her lover, her protector, the son of Ivarr who had murdered Cild! Should he tell her? No, let her find out. The child would have the killer's blood, and the healer's blood, too!

Bald was tired. He went to bed. He could not sleep for the cares and indignations of the day until the early hours, and then he was disturbed. Wulfhere blundered in and fell against the table, rattling the jars. "Bald, I've been to a party! Guthrith told me I wasn't looking well and ought to retire. Give me something for an upset stomach, there's a good man."

Bald thought of wolfsbane, but got up and made him a spewdrink from a few stavesacre seeds and ale.

"Guthrith was in a high and mighty mood. They're as wicked as one another: pirates, all of them! Sigtryggr was drunk. He won't last long, I don't wonder."

He drank the spewdrink.

"What do I do now?"

"Run."

Wulfhere leant towards him and belched in his face.

"Why do we drink when we know it's bad for us?"

"To kill the worm, master."

"Yes, Eve has a lot to answer for."

He lurched out, and Bald heard him running down the corridor.

So Guthrith was boasting of his good fortune. Let him go to Woden.

Caech came in the morning bringing a man he said was an Irish leech named Merfyn. Bald gave Caech the sealed jar.

"You must use it before midnight or it will have no effect."

"Tell him what it is and I'll not trouble you again, my friend."

Merfyn was a short balding man or else, Bald guessed, a recreant monk whose tonsure was growing out. He was furtive, with weak eyes, and blue lips betraying his bad heart. He looked uneasily at the worts and jars on the table.

"I hope to God it's not too difficult."

"Where did you study?"

"Dublin and around." He pulled a dirty scrap of parchment from the pocket of his old frayed gown. "I have a charm here from the Irish leech Pythagorus. It's cured thousands."

"Read it." Merfyn shuffled. "Can't you read?"

"I can, but my eyes can't."

Bald took the parchment and read it aloud.

"Taz azuf zuon threux bain chook."

"I'll sell it to you for a penny."

Bald gave it back. Merfyn came closer. His blue mouth stank of decay.

"I won't tell a soul."

"What?"

"The stuff you gave him's no good, is it?"

So he was a bad spy as well as a bad leech.

"Try it."

Bald offered him a harmless leaf of fieldwort. Merfyn backed away.

"What is it?"

"Sigmund's kraut."

"Will it do the job?"

"A hangman gave it to a man and he dropped dead."

"By gob that's powerful! What's the name you said?"

"Sigmund's kraut."

"That Sigmund must have been a powerful strong man. Where will I find it?"

"If you're a leech it will find you."

Merfyn was confused. He shuffled all round the table until he breathed on Bald again.

"I am and I'm not. When I'm called to a sick man, I say a paternoster and refer him to the Almighty. If he recovers I charge him a penny. If he dies I charge him tuppence. He can't argue if he's dead, can he?"

Bald longed to kick him. Instead he gave him a handful of fieldwort. When he failed, Caech would do it for him.

He finished making the spewdrink and Eneda came for it.

"Have you heard? One of Caech's hounds has just died." She took the covered jar. "How shall I know when to give it to him?"

"I told Caech it won't work after midnight. Give it to Sigtryggr when he comes back from the hall."

"Are you sure it's strong enough?"

"It will empty a cesspit." He was still jealous and resentful, and she sensed his anger. She wanted to console him.

"Things are going to change for us."

She meant the child. He almost told her it was cursed, that one of its grandfathers had slaughtered the other, that the blood-eagle was in its blood! She looked so shining hopeful. She touched his arm.

"You're tired. Go and rest. It will soon be over."

"What if Caech tries again?"

"Caech will be nothing soon. Guthrith, none of them. You'll see."

She meant her child would be king. What hopes women have for their children! What belief in the future! She trusted Eadrich, she trusted Dun, she trusted Sigtryggr, she trusts me, Bald thought. And we are men, and not to be trusted. As soon as this was over, he would go.

That night, after the usual carousal in the beerhall, Sigtryggr was as sick as a dog. Guthrith died like one.

XII

Bald stayed in York. He did not mean to stay. On the contrary, he kept thinking I'll go tomorrow, but each tomorrow gave him another reason for staying. Eneda needed him. Ginna and Toki were pregnant. Sigtryggr was declining into drunken obesity. Caech was a constant threat. Wulfhere had chronic indigestion and complained Danish dinners were killing him. Above all, his own indecision and the habit of indolence kept him dawdling there.

Summer passed. This was the golden summer of Alfred's reign. Old kings do not fight. They are more afraid of their heirs than their enemies. Danes, Mercians, Saxons, Angles, began to merge their identities by intermarriage. The languages were interleaved. The war gods slept, and Christianity absorbed the old religion, adding runes to crosses and savage rites to festivals. The century was gently coming to an end.

With the first cold wind of autumn, Sigtryggr declined rapidly. Bald had given him a year and, by accident, Eneda. Her pregnancy was by now well advanced. The old king called Bald to him.

"I know the danger to her and the child. I'll send Ragnall to Dublin. Caech must stay here but he'll do nothing while Ragnall is alive. I have made provision for her."

He shifted his bulk and swung his head round like an ox.

"If you'd let me die, the child would not have been born. From now on, the child is yours. I swear I'll come back and give you to Woden if you fail."

Bald suppressed the protests clamouring to get out. He feared Sigtryggr might anticipate his oath.

He had brought a salve for the king's shoulder but Sigtryggr waved it away.

"Now I claim the debt you owe me."

Bald felt a clutch of terror round his heart.

Sigtryggr lay back. His left hand scrabbled at the bedclothes.

Bald had seen the same movement made by dying men, as if to draw the sheet across their faces. He became concerned.

"Shall I call Caech, master? What do you want?"

He would have said a priest, but Sigtryggr was a king/priest and the master of his own destiny.

The hand found what it wanted, pulling back the sheet to uncover a silver axe.

Bald stared with horror. Ivarr had slaughtered Cild with such an axe.

Then he knew what he owed Sigtryggr before Sigtryggr said it.

"I must die in battle, Saxon. Me – or you."

The hand drew the sheet back over the axe.

Bald understood. He was to be the executioner, but no-one was to know. No-one would suspect him. He was to be the executioner or he would be the victim.

He knew Sigtryggr was waiting for an answer. He looked at the great diseased body, already rotting like a dead tree ready to fall. He had killed men before, usually inadvertently, but sometimes with a stronger leechdom than necessary, which he could claim was an error. He had nearly killed Sigtryggr. The blow he had not struck then had to be struck now.

Not now. It was still daylight. He said, "You."

There was no expression on the ox-face. Sigtryggr would wait.

Eneda was in the garden when he went down. She glanced up at the casement of the king's room.

"How is he?"

He did not answer.

It was an evening between seasons when everything was still: the turning of the tide, the moment before a petal falls from a rose, when there is no wind and the world stops breathing.

She sat like a lady in a tapestry with her handmaids, their stomachs swollen as they always are in tapestries, and a hare on the lawn. How could he answer her and say he is no worse, he will die tonight?

She sighed. "I hope he lives to see his child."

What hope! Sigtryggr had said me or you. There was no hope in that for either of them.

She sensed his unease.

"You've saved him twice, uncle."

Three was a terrible number. Gods came in threes. Fates came in threes. Three was the signal for action.

"I'm ready."

She had gone from him to Sigtryggr. He had given her a life. Now, as if to compound Bald's impotence, Sigtryggr had given that life to him.

The child is yours.

"I'm going to give Ginna and Toki their freedom. Lyb too of course."

He would give Sigtryggr his freedom to get drunk every night to the warsongs of the skald singing in Valhalla!

"I'll buy a farm. Lyb will be a bondi." She smiled at his sour face. "What are you thinking about?"

The panic that had been gripping his heart suddenly broke out. He bent down and whispered urgently.

"We must go away tonight! Leave York! I mean it! It's too dangerous to stay here any longer!"

She looked at him serenely.

"Don't be ridiculous."

She laughed the knowing womanly laugh that always infuriated him.

"You're jealous, uncle. You don't have to be. The baby will be yours as well."

Now she had said it too. What blindness!

Then he realised blindness was happiness and not knowing was heaven. Foreknowledge was the worst thing that could happen to a man.

Hell was not a devil-pit, or the nothingness of religious unbelievers, but the knowledge of the future. If there was a god he would be in hell, not heaven.

The day was ending. A cold breath of wind stirred the garden. A petal fell.

Wulfhere would not go to bed. He made a habit of coming to Bald's room from the beerhall and boring him beyond sleep.

"Alfred sent me a copy of his translation of Pope Gregory's *Pastoral Care*. What am I supposed to do about it? How can I preach Christian morality to men whose idea of heaven is an everlasting orgy?"

"Preach it to the women."

Wulfhere was shocked.

"You mustn't give women ideas, you know. Once you tell them what a sin is, they'll want to do it!"

He went at last. It was almost dawn.

Bald began the ritual of a kingslayer. He blew out the lamp and stripped off his clothes. There would be blood. He dipped his fingers into a pot of woad and streaked his face and body to break the whiteness and hide himself in shadows. He opened the casement and stood waiting for a sign.

In the book:

"To see one or many stars betokeneth joy. To see a star fall betokeneth death to one."

He went to Sigtryggr's room.

The casement was open and he could see the dark bulk on the bed. He went to the left side and felt under the covers for the axe. He drew it out and stood hefting it in his hands.

Sigtryggr's head was raised on pillows, a dark block in which Bald saw two glimmers of light. Sigtryggr's eyes were open.

It had to be.

Bald drew back the covers and knelt astride the gross body.

It was an act of love.

He looked into Sigtryggr's eyes and said,

"I give you to Woden."

He raised the axe in both hands above his head and brought it down with all his strength on the left side where the neck joins the shoulder and the great artery lies.

The axe went deep and stuck in the flesh. Bald put both hands on Sigtryggr's head and thrust it back half-severed.

Blood spouted out and Sigtryggr died.

Bald took the axe and laid it on the body. He went to the window.

Sigtryggr's blood spread over his right arm and chest.

He waited for a sign. The stars had gone, and in the east there was a streak of rose-red dawn.

He returned to his room and washed the crime away.

There was no inquest. Caech was suspected but nobody dared speak. The Vikings furnished a ship with grave goods and built a shelter for Sigtryggr's huge coffin. Caech put a treasure in it, and each man gave a gift: a brooch, a buckle, a coin.

Bald watching wondered did she know? She had Cild's blood in her. They rowed the ship upriver towards the high ridge of land that lours over the moors.

They dragged the ship out of the river and up to the highest point, where they sank it in a trench and covered it with a barrow. Here Sigtryggr lay, threatening to the last.

Long after, men called the place Ship Town.

Ragnall returned from Dublin and was declared king. Winter brought new concerns for the Danes, who were increasingly attracted to trade and agriculture, and complained about the incursions of Norsemen on their settlements as acts of savage aggression.

As she had promised, Eneda bought Lyb and his two wives a farm outside the walls of the city, where they were free from the strictures of Archbishop Wulfhere. Lyb still came to the palace to attend her, while Ginna and Toki compared their roundness and fed the pigs. Bald now had to stay in York. Sigtryggr's oath bound him to care for Eneda and her child when it came. As the cold months closed round the palace, and neither Ragnall nor Caech showed any concern about Eneda's presence and condition, he began to think necessity favoured him. He had a comfortable apartment, some company, and the prospect he had never expected of becoming a father, if only by proxy. Know more than the gods, said Haesten, but do not let them know it.

The merchants of York traded extensively with the continent. One day a man approached Bald with the offer of a parcel of dried worts from Francia. Apparently they had been intended for Sigtryggr, who had sent for them on the advice of Withbec. The man wanted money and so Bald, who never had any, went to see Eneda.

He found her in her room, sitting near the fire while Lyb massaged her feet.

"I don't know why Sigtryggr wanted them, but you must have them, uncle."

She took the silver pennies from her casket and gave them to him. She was getting very near her time.

"Who will have a baby first, Ginna, Toki or me?"

"Knowing the perversity of women, you'll all have them at the same time, and drive me mad."

"When do you think?"

"A week, perhaps."
"When will that be?"
"Middle of December."
"What are the bad days?"
"The seventh and twenty-first."
"And the good ones?"
"Thirteenth and fourteenth."
"What will he be?"
"Pious and righteous."
"I'd rather he was a king."
"He'll be a king too."
"You're making it up."
"It's better if I do, Eneda. Nobody really wants to know what's going to happen."
"I do. I do know he's going to be a good king."
Leaving her room, he met Caech in the corridor with Merfyn.
"I was looking for you, friend Bald. Would you believe this fool has lost the cure-all you gave him?"
"It can't be got now, master. It has to be found in the summer, and only lasts for a day."
"You mean nobody dies of a cold any more? I think my father sneezed."
Bald was silent.
"Well, I owe you a favour."
Bald bought the parcel and carried it up to his room. He wondered what Sigtryggr could have wanted. When he opened it, the answer stared him in the face. Fornjot's palm!
There was an abundance of it, dried, packed and labelled with care: cauda pulli.
The old king was worried about his virility, and Withbec had learned one leechdom at least. Foules tayle. He would know that!
Bald thanked the gods again. Now he was past caring, they had provided. What on earth was he to do with it?
With an old man's misanthropy, he thought there was enough copulation in the world as it was.
He burnt it. It went up in smoke.
On the tenth of December, Ginna and Toki gave birth almost at the same moment. Bald delivered two boys, neither of whom resembled Lyb in the slightest.

He always wondered about women. They lived in two worlds, their own and that of men, and seemed to have the best of both.

Eneda was late. Her small body could hardly bear the burden of the boy-king she hoped for.

Bald was always with her, and Lyb slept in her room. As the days passed, Bald became desperate.

In the book:

"In order that a wife, that is a woman, may quickly bring forth, take seed of this same coriander, eleven grains or thirteen, knit them into a thread on a clean linen cloth; let then a person take them who is a person of maidenhood, a boy or a maiden, and hold this at the left thigh, near the natura, and so soon as all the parturition be done, remove away the leechdom, lest part of the inwards follow thereafter."

Desperation is a poor counsellor.

On the thirteenth night of the month the fire was banked up in Eneda's room. She lay pale and sweating under the covers on the bed. Bald had been watching over her for three nights. Lyb was lying under the heavy cloth drawn across the window.

Bald went to his room to prepare a drink and fell asleep at the table.

In his sleep he heard a cry.

He woke.

Had he heard it or dreamt it?

He hurried out.

As he came into the corridor, he thought he saw Merfyn running away past Sigtryggr's room.

The door to Eneda's room was open.

He rushed there and stood in the stifling firelight. At first glance everything looked normal and he began to think he had been dreaming.

Lyb was asleep by the fire.

Eneda was lying where he had last seen her. Her face was turned away from the flames and she seemed to be at peace.

He walked to the bed.

He laid his hand gently on her forehead. The skin was cold and flaccid. He turned her face to the light.

Her eyes were wide and her mouth dropped open.

His blood congealed.

He put his mouth to hers to feel her breath on his lips.

There was no breath.

With frantic haste he tore the covers back and pressed his ear to her swollen breast.

There was no heartbeat.

He saw on the floor one of her pillows. It was indented with the impression of her face.

He cried out and Lyb woke.

The dwarf leaped up and ran to the bed. He clambered up and put his swollen lips on hers, breathing into her mouth.

Bald gripped his hands and tried to remember a prayer, a charm, to bring back the dead.

But no magic, no charm, no leechdom, no great love, could bring Eneda back again.

Lyb was crying like a child in great gulps.

The child!

Bald stripped the bedclothes and ripped open Eneda's nightgown, pulling it apart. He laid his head on her swollen stomach and heard the beating of another heart.

He knew what he had to do.

He gripped his knife.

Lyb seized his arm, mouthing No! No!

"She's dead! The child is alive! We have to save the child!"

Lyb released his grip.

Bald laid the knife on Eneda's stomach and cut a cross through skin and flesh, opening up the cavity of the womb and revealing the curled shape of the child. He cut away the surrounding tissue, having no care for the mother, she was gone, and releasing the child cradled there. He put in his hand and drew the child out, plucking the living creature from the dead.

It was a girl.

Lyb held out a sheet and took the child, wrapping it tightly.

Bald picked up the money casket and thrust it into his hand.

"Go! Never come back here! Raise the child as your own. Don't tell anyone who she is. Go, go!"

Lyb took one last look at Eneda and ran out of the room.

Bald turned back to the rifled corpse. The sheet it lay on was soaked in blood. He pulled it out, screwed it up and pushed it into the cavity of the stomach. He drew the nightgown together and fastened it with its sash. He straightened the limbs and covered the body with the bedclothes.

Then he stood, chest heaving, looking down at the dead face.

"The thirteenth moon is perilous for beginning things. A maiden will have a mark on the back of her neck or on her thigh; will be saucy spirited, daring of her body with many men; she will die soon."

He could not grieve because it was fate.

When morning came and the discovery was made, Bald said Eneda had died in childbirth and the child had died with her.

Caech came, looked at the swollen body and went.

Late in the day, Bald asked Caech to let him take Eneda's body and bury it.

"She was a Saxon, master. I beg it as a favour."

"Do what you like, kingslayer."

Bald took his plaid, his pouch and the book.

He carried the body, wrapped as it was, out of the palace, out of the city, across the fields, through the woods, and beyond into the ancient forest.

He collected wood for a pyre and burnt the body to ashes. No-one would ever know the child was born, and was alive.

As he scattered the ashes, he said:

"I give you to Woden."

His voice broke, and he wept at last.

He walked away, deeper and deeper into the forest.

Book II

St. Aelfgifu

i

In the book:
"The eyes of an old man are not sharp of sight; then shall he wake up his eyes with rubbings, with walkings, with ridings, either so that a man carry him or convey him in a wain, and they shall use little and careful meats, and comb their heads, and drink wormwood before they take food."

As the outer light by which we live closed in on Bald, so his need increased for the inner light by which we die. Twelve years had passed since he walked away from York. He had not returned, fearing to compromise the child by his presence. He had nothing to give her but the dangerous knowledge of her lineage. He had resumed his solitary pilgrimage in the fading light.

King Alfred was dead, Plegmund, Grimbald, Eahlswith and Wulfhere also. Edward ruled England, recognised by the Mercians, the Welsh, the Scots and the Danes. Ragnall and Caech had retreated to Dublin. There was peace of a sort, the sort of peace a patient has between attacks. It was this that tempted Bald towards Ermine Street and the north, to see Eneda's child while he still could see her.

It was late afternoon in summer, and the bondis and their slaves were busy with the harvest. York lay crumbling like a giant sandcastle washed by the sun. Bald skirted the city and came to the strips of fields on four sides of the mud and wattle farmhouse Eneda had bought for Lyb and his double family. Six small figures were toiling among the stalks and sheaves of barley. One was taller than the rest, a girl with fair hair that shone like a crown among the awns, who made his heart falter. Here was his blood: the kingslayer and the blood of kings.

The others were dwarfed and dark. Bald was surprised. Ginna and Toki had had normal children.

On the edge of the field he hesitated. Should he cross their lives or leave them be? He held their fate in his hands. So he thought. He could turn away now and let them go on living in peace and ignorance. Or he could give them the knowledge that could make or destroy them.

He hesitated, fatally.

One of the boys looked up and saw him. He pointed. Then Lyb was running across the stubble towards him.

Bald scorned his own stupidity. He no more held fate than a baby held its mother. Indecision, impotence was his fate, and now it was theirs too.

Lyb came up and grasped him round the knees.

They called her Emma. She had Eneda's look, her laughter, her challenging eyes, and something more – a quality of calmness, self-possession, that for all the sixty years between them made Bald wonder. The girl was fit to be a queen, he thought.

Her brothers, as she called them, Ulf and Liofa, were like twin retainers. They lived in Emma's eyes. She did not need to speak or they to answer for them to serve her. It was their nature. A nature, Bald observed that night, assisted by Lyb. Before they went to sleep in the byre with the goat – old habits, Bald thought – they each took a cup of milk from their father's hand and drank it as he watched. Suddenly Bald knew the source of their deformity. The dwarf stunted his progeny as probably his father had done his. The ground roots of daisies or knotgrass boiled in milk, given since birth, inhibited growth. This was the secret of their survival in times when a ram, a goat or a dwarf was a more precious commodity to a Viking than a saint or a scholar.

Emma could not read. She spoke Saxon with a mixture of Norse in the Northumbrian accent of Ginna and Toki. Bald was horrified, and hurried to amend her education. There was already a school of Alfred, an authority emanating from the south, Winchester Christianity, that laid down the standards of reading, writing and thinking. For all his independence, Bald was part of it. He was a man of the book.

Emma loved the book, and turned over the heavy pages in the sunshine in the barley field, and Bald lay on his side, feeling the stubble against his skin, watching her.

"Read to me, uncle."

She was her mother, and more. She looked beyond the moment. She wanted to know the word and the meaning of the word and the why of the meaning of the word. She asked him questions he could not answer, questions he had never thought of asking Cild.

He knew the book by heart.

In the book:

"If a man be overlooked, and thou must cure him, see that his face be turned to thee when thou goest in, then he may live; if his face be turned from thee, have thou nothing to do with him."

"Liofa killed a mouse. Where did it go?"

"Into the ground."

"Not its body."

"Into the air."

"Is it still a mouse?"

"You're going to ask me is a man still a man after I've killed him."

She laughed. "Is he?"

"I hope not."

"No, no! Why do you hope not?"

"One life is enough."

"What? And never see her again?"

"Who? Who, Emma?"

"My mother."

"What have they told you?"

"She died when I was born."

"And your father?"

"He's with Woden."

"That's probably true."

"But she's here. I've seen her."

Bald felt the fear of the unknown crawl like a spider down his back.

"Where?"

"Once da' took me to market and he was in the alehouse and I went to the big church inside the walls."

She had passed her father's palace and entered the Roman fort!

"There's a painting of some old men and some criminals being punished, one of them looks like you ..." She teased him gently.

"And she's there, wearing a grey dress tied with ribbons."

"There?" His voice was ghastly.

"In the picture. In a house of her own. I think she's meant to be unhappy but she's smiling."

"But you never saw her. How do you know who she is?"

"She's my mother."

She spoke so simply and certainly he could not deny it. She smiled. "You'll see her too. Da' will take you next market day."

"He won't go further than the alehouse. You take me."

That night as Bald lay looking up at the stars he wondered at his sudden intrepidity. True the grandsons of Ivarr were in Dublin, and York was governed by Archbishop Wulfstan and the Witan, but it was always dangerous to return. What was he frightened of? Remembering or forgetting?

They entered the city by Petergate, the main street from the north that passed through the Roman fortress. Bald knew the place well from his stay at the royal palace. Lyb and his pigs would have gone in the shadow of York Minster, past the palace and on to the market in the densely populated angle of the two rivers. Bald and Emma, she dancing in the sunlight, he an upright shadow, took the path to the great west door.

The timbered nave rose on Roman stone like a ship on the stocks, clustered about with wooden buildings housing the school, the library and the mint. Wulfhere had saved the church in York by his collaboration with the Vikings. His successors, Wulfstan was the latest, had taken on the authority and prerogative of kings.

To enter the nave was to go from hot stone-reflected sunlight into the dark silence of a grove of trees. Small light penetrated the glassless apertures of the eastern apse where a monolithic altar served its latest god.

Emma ran forward, free of faith and uncaring of sanctity, past the tombs of archbishops and the sarcophagus of Guthrith murdered by Caech, and stopped in front of a decorated section of the plastered wall. Here was the depiction of a crucifixion against the background of a Roman city, with an emaciated Christ roped to a tree-cross like a gallows, between two thieves, and St. Peter, the Minster's patron saint, prominently facing in the opposite direction. The four gospellers sat with their animals under Roman porticos, and in a house of her own, gazing out of the window with a quizzical smile, was a woman in a grey dress tied with parti-coloured ribbons. Above her head was written MARIA VIRGO. The scene was an undramatic statement of fact as if the artist had drawn it from life.

"There she is."

Bald came up behind her. The woman did indeed bear some resemblance to Eneda.

"She's not your mother."

"Who is she then?"

"Maria Virgo, the mother of God."

"Woden?"

"Christ."

"Who's he?"

Bald pointed to the crucified Christ. Emma frowned.

"The hanged man?"

"A man. He was hanged. Many are." He thought of Duda.

"Why was he hanged?"

"For being God."

The paradox puzzled her.

"If he was God, why didn't he stop them?"

"Perhaps he was an unleech. There are times when it's better for a man to die." He thought of Sigtryggr. This girl was his daughter. She would understand. "Like a warrior."

"Was he a warrior?"

"No, he was a leech."

"And an unleech?"

"You're going to ask me how can he be both? My dear, he unleeched himself, and Christians say that's how he leeched the world."

Emma stuck out her bottom lip as Eneda might have done.

Bald smiled.

"I don't understand it either."

"Only if it worked."

Bald knew it did not work and the world was as sick as ever.

There was a bustle of priests and boys: a service was beginning and the two pagans crept out quietly.

Emma had a real love of learning, and if Cild's endless leechdoms for "dry fig" or "sore of head" were too much for a summer's day she had the sense to let Bald go on repeating them from memory.

She studied his face.

Old age had cut deep lines like runes on a standing stone. He seemed to be turning to stone himself, with eyes of silica and bloodless skin stretched across his skeleton. The skull was like a rock, a venerable fountain of knowledge.

Lyb and her little mothers Ginna and Toki were forgotten. Ulf and Liofa went berrying without her. She clung to Bald, her tutor and the mystery of her past which she would one day divine.

He watched her with amusement melting into love. His love, devoid of passion, yearned for an object of dependence, a prop for his old age and a recipient for his wisdom.

And so in a few weeks they grew together as ivy and an ancient wall grow together, depending on and supporting each other.

Winter came. Great snow and cold and unprecedented frost. Horrid signs besides. The heavens seemed to glow with comets. A mass of fire was observed with thunder, passing over Ireland from the west, which went over the sea eastwards.

Ragnall and Caech ruthlessly restored their fortunes in Dublin. Their armies were recruited from Norsemen, land-hungry Norwegians who had landed on the inhospitable shores of Cumbria and were ready to fight for a more agreeable life across the Pennines.

They were shipmen, and took the sea route to the Clyde and over land, dragging their ships, to the Forth. On the way, they sacked Dunblane and won a battle at Corbridge against the

Scots before moving south on the Roman road to York. Ragnall returned to claim his father Sigtryggr's kingdom. His half-sister lived obliviously in his way.

It was hard enough for the little household to survive the winter. Rivers froze. Earth was bound with iron. Deer retreated to the depths of the forest. Foxes tiptoed through snow searching for the tell-tale thaw betraying a warm trembling mouse or more luckily a hare. Ulf and Liofa brought the pigs, goat and chickens into the house, where they stank only slightly less offensively than Lyb. Little water, little food, little fuel. Cold white landscape. Nightscreams of animals.

"Read to me, uncle."

Bald turned the pages of the book and recited the leechdoms by heart. It grew dark and he went on and she knew he could no longer read. She asked her brothers.

"What will he do when he's blind?"

Ulf said, "Walk with a stick."

Liofa went out and cut and peeled a long switch of hazel.

Bald asked Emma to take him to the Minster.

The snow was frozen, and they walked high above the land. When she saw the city walls, Emma cried out. Bald was alarmed. "What? What?"

"They're building up the walls! They're breaking the houses and using the wood to make them higher. Is there going to be more snow?

"Not snow, my sweet." Apprehension gripped him.

"Why are they doing it?"

"There's going to be war."

They hurried on. Petergate was barricaded and they had to cross the frozen river and enter York by Ousegate. There was activity everywhere. Men muffled against the cold dragged wattles to the walls. The smiths were busy under black snow hammering spears. Bald called out: "Who's coming? What's it for?"

"Ragnall's coming back!" "The pagan's coming back!" "Ragnall the pirate!" "Ragnall and Caech!"

Those answering were Danes, grandsons of pagans and pirates, calling their Danish king a pagan and a pirate.

"Who's Ragnall?"

"Someone you must never meet."

Priests were praying frantically in the Minster. A group of Saxon ealdermen and Danish jarls was gathering round a young energetic churchman Bald guessed was Wulfstan. They were arguing whether or not to defend the city or yield and spare the slaughter.

"He'll slaughter us anyway! He's Sigtryggr's son!"

"Who's Sigtryggr?"

"Take me to the picture."

She led him to the crucifixion scene. Bald peered at the woman called Maria Virgo. Had the picture been there when Eneda was alive? Did the painter know her? What was she doing in a Christian icon? He sighed and turned away.

"What is it, uncle?"

"It's growing dark earlier."

"It always does just before the spring."

In the book:

"It is needful for us that we hold the holy Easter tide by the true rule, never before equinox and overcoming of darkness."

Cild took that from Bede, but how did she know it?

When they returned to the farm, Bald told Lyb he had to leave and take Emma with him. She looked too much like her mother. If Ragnall saw her, or Caech if he was coming, he would recognise her.

The dwarf shook his head defiantly.

"It has to be. We'll go to Eneda's land in the south. She'll be safe there."

Lyb pointed to himself.

"No, my friend, your life is here with your family."

Lyb took Bald's arm and pulled him towards the door. Outside, Ulf and Liofa were breaking ice to melt for water. He pointed to them.

"And who'll look after you?"

Lyb held up one finger.

"No, neither of them, they're too young. You've done your service, Lyb. You're free."

But the dwarf still frowned with worry.

Bald had to tell Emma she was leaving her family and her home without telling her why. The knowledge of her birth was dangerous in itself. Her father Sigtryggr was the grandson of the great Norse warrior Ragnar Lodbrok and his wife Kraka, a witch who spoke birdspeech and helped Ragnar with her magic. Ragnar had invaded Northumbria and been defeated in spite of it, and died in a snake-pit, sentenced by king Aella of York. His sons Ivarr and Haelfdene had followed him, and Aella ended as a blood-eagle. Ivarr sacrificed him as he later sacrificed Cild. So one of Emma's forefathers had murdered another. How could he tell her that?

How could he tell her that she was a child of fate and her half-brother had murdered her mother and sought her own life in the womb? How could he tell her he himself had slaughtered her father like an ox? That evening, as the fire hissed and smoke stung their eyes, he told her his life was in danger and he had to leave before the Norsemen came. She did the rest herself.

"There's no way you can go on your own! You're too old!"

He could hear Eneda shouting.

"You're blind! Oh yes you are! You pretend you're not, but you are! You'll fall into the first hole you come to!"

Lyb had warned Ginna and Toki and the two boys and they stayed silent. There were tears in the little mothers' eyes, and Ulf and Liofa looked wretched.

Emma was excited and frightened and sad all at once. She flew about, organising and consoling, lecturing and crying.

Bald watched her. She was thirteen, or he would have called her Eneda. Then later, when he saw her alone outside in the moonlight, he knew she was not Eneda.

He had decided to leave before the spring, and the floods that would make the road south impassable. The decision made, there was no reason to delay. They were going the next day.

Emma had gone out. The others were crouched by the fire, talking quietly in the old British tongue nobody else understood. Bald went to the doorway to breathe in the cold black air.

Emma was standing on a heap of snow like a barrow covering the midden. The moonlight made her ageless, like an illuminated angel in a missal.

He held his breath.

She looked unreal. There was a cold radiance about her. She never lived on earth.She raised her head to the hood of night and said one word: "Mother."

It was not a question or a prayer, but the affirmation of her oneness with the earth, the moon and the stars, the acceptance of her destiny, the token of her faith in the woman called Maria Virgo.

ii

They left York at dawn, crossed the frozen river Wharfe near Tadcaster and saw the low greystone minster at Barwick in Elmet as the light was fading.

Bald avoided Ermine Street and the straight road south knowing they had to find shelter for the freezing nights. He had been this way before, and hoped the monks of Barwick would remember him.

They made good progress walking on the crust of frozen snow that covered moor, bog and mire, following the brown-stained track from York to Leeds.

In the book:

"There are two days in every month in which whatever is begun will never reach completion. In March when the moon is six days old, or seven."

The moon was rising when Bald knocked on the minster door. A monk peered through the grill.

"I'm Bald the leech."

"And the child?"

"My niece."

"She can't enter here. Take her round to the hospital."

Bald cursed. He should have dressed her as a boy. No woman was allowed beyond the precincts.

He led Emma to a wooden side-building containing two truckle beds and little else. The monk appeared with a lamp and a small brazier full of glowing charcoal. Bald turned to Emma.

"I'll bring you something to eat."

"It's all right, uncle, I have some left from home."

When he looked in later, the room was warm and she was asleep in one of the beds. Nobody told him a traveller had died in that bed from shivering fever the night before.

In the morning they continued on their way. Bald planned to cover the twenty-four miles to Monk Bretton by nightfall, but Emma began to lag behind and it was almost midnight when they passed Cudworth and entered the abbey grounds.

The moon was in the first quarter and the sky was clear. The ruins of the abbey rose like jagged teeth. Monk Bretton was deserted. They had no option but to go on and hope to find some moorland croft or hamlet where they could shelter.

Bald had often walked through the night and slept by day. The stars were better signposts than the sun.

"Can you go on for a while?"

"Yes, uncle, I feel quite well."

The while brought dawn, and the first signs of a thaw. The snow was grey and pitted in the dales and to the west the heads of the peak district were tonsured with melting caps of white.

She called out and collapsed a few steps after that.

Bald ran back and lifted her in his arms. The sweat was standing on her brow, and she was shaking.

God what a fool he was!

He swung round looking for a sign of habitation.

To drag a girl out here in winter!

The moors stretched away on every side.

To run from fate into the arms of fate!

Where was the next stopping point? Wirksworth Abbey twenty miles away! He had to go on; he could do nothing here except bury her!

In the book:

"Against the cold fever, take this wort spreritis, seethe it in oil, and at the times at which the fever will approach to the man, smear him therewith."

What was spreritis? Hope!

What was hope? Nothing!

"Mother of God protect your child!"

She was shaking in his arms. He walked on grimly. He walked on with one fixed destination in his mind. Wirksworth. He walked on blindly, and the snow trailed into valleys and melted, and the moors sprang villages and folk came to their doorways and stared, and he staggered into the small town of Bakewell and found himself surrounded by soldiers and men from the south, and someone said his name.

"Bald?"

He stopped. Consciousness came back slowly to his eyes. He saw the only man he knew in England standing before him, and he held out Emma's limp body in supplication to Edward the king.

They talked of nothing else for days. Bald the leech who cured Alfred and everybody thought was dead, walking off the moor with a mysterious young girl and giving her to the king! Edward had looked embarrassed but had taken her and handed her to the man next to him, Archbishop Wulfhelm. Wulfhelm had passed her to his chaplain with orders to take her to the queen's lodging and send for the Eucharist. Who could she be? Bald had accepted the king's offer of shelter, but had said nothing.

Edward was at Bakewell with the army, at the end of a long campaign to subdue the Welsh, the Scots and the Northumbrians. He had fortified Nottingham, Derby, Manchester, Chester and now Bakewell, in a line of strongholds protecting the roads from the North. Ragnall's return had frightened his former enemies, Constantine king of the Scots, Ywain king of the Strathclyde Britons, and Ealdred of Bamborough, into recognising him as their overlord. Now he was waiting for Ragnall to come as enemy or friend.

Bald thought Edward looked old, but he had always looked old, taking his kingship and the continuation of his dynasty as a god-given duty. He had married three times and had five sons and seven daughters. He had campaigned endlessly to raise the house of Wessex to the kingship of England and had all but succeeded. Ragnall's return to the north was a challenge he had to meet to secure the sovereignty of his sons. The struggle between the grandsons of Ivarr and the grandsons of Alfred was beginning.

Bald was anxious to see Emma and smear her with spreritis before another leech got his hands on her. He went to the queen's lodging in Bakewell minster – no nonsense about no women here! – and was brought into the side chapel converted into a nursery for her young family.

Through the arched window the folds and fells of the peaks rolled like a soft green sea under a pale blue sky.

Queen Eadgifu called the children together. Eadburh with her gospel in her hand, Edmund, a boy of ten dressed as a man, Eadgifu and Eadred her little brother, merely toddlers.

They stared at Bald as at an apparition.

"This is the good leech who saved your grandfather's life."

Edmund held out his hand self-consciously.

"Thank you."

"Lady, how is the girl? I must see the girl."

"In a moment." Eadgifu waved the children away. "Tell me first, who is she?"

"Nobody. My sister's grandchild."

"Where were you going with her?"

"Nowhere. Lady, I must see her! I must treat her cold fever!"

"Don't worry. My priest is with her."

A priest! He would give her three paternosters, a drink of holy water and typhus!

"I'll see her at once! Where is she?"

He turned and rushed out like a madman.

"Edmund, go and show him."

The boy caught up with Bald in a corridor and led him to a cell in the upper storey.

As Bald burst in, the young smooth-faced monk leaning over the bed had barely time to cry out "What the devil!" before the devil seized him and hurled him against the wall.

Bald knelt by Emma. Her skin shone like alabaster. He touched her forehead. Cold, cold. He struck his head with his knuckles.

"Spreritis!" What was it?

"Anagallis arvensis."

"What?"

The monk was lying awkwardly on the floor.

"Anagallis arvensis. Scarlet pimpernel."

"It can't be. It has yellow flowers."

"Yellow, blue or white."

"Spreritis is not scarlet pimpernel! It's not in the book!"

"The book is wrong." The monk picked himself up. "Bald didn't know everything."

Bald stared at him as if he was mad.

"I'm Bald."

"You didn't know scarlet pimpernel can have yellow flowers. But it's a comprehensive book. We have a copy at Glastonbury."

Bald was astonished. He felt a flush of pride. Then jealousy.

"You've read my book?"

"Some of it. It's rather long. Shall we see if they've got any in the herbarium?"

On the way down, the monk said his name was Dunstan. Bald stared at his back, hating his youth, his confidence, and the possibility that he could be right.

In the book:

"This wort which is named spreritis hath diminutive leaves, and tufty, and it sendeth forth from one root many boughs, and they are laid near the earth, and it hath yellow blossoms; and if thou breakest it between thy fingers, it hath then a smell as myrrh."

In the herbarium Dunstan found the jar marked anagallis arvensis. The leaves were small and might have been tufty, the root had several stems, and the flowers were like dried blood.

Bald gave an ugly grin, part triumph, part disappointment.

Dunstan snapped one of the stems and held it to his nose. He sneezed.

"It's pimpernel. The name comes from the Latin 'piper' meaning pepper."

"Maybe, but it isn't spreritis."

"If it works it is. Where's the oil?" He rolled up his sleeves. "And if it isn't, God will turn it into spreritis."

They carried the steaming infusion up to the cell and Bald went in alone.

Edmund was still there, standing pale and wide-eyed, staring at the figure on the bed.

"She's dead."

Bald put down the bowl of oil and pushed the boy out of the room. Heartsick, he hurried to the bed and pressed his ear to Emma's heart. He put his eyes close to her mouth to feel the stir of breath. He lifted her eyelids to look for life and her eyes were white.

The fear of death chilled him, gripped his heart and made him shout with pain.

He fought against it, forcing himself to think, to act, to leech. With shaking hands he drew back the bedclothes and unlaced the nightgown Emma wore.

Her body was unformed, small, unmarked like a child.

He cupped his hands and dipped them in the warm oil. He poured it over her as if he was anointing her. He spread the oil around her, lifting her, raising her arms and legs as if he was washing her corpse.

He smeared the oil on her face and the palms of her hands. He felt the coldness coming from her body into his, and the pain in his heart increased.

With hopeless hands he drew the nightgown together.

He knelt back on his heels. His head drooped in despair. He raised his hands to his face.

She was dead and he was dying.

He had found her only to kill her with his stupidity. He groaned.

"I give you to Woden."

As he spoke he caught the scent of myrrh.

He smelt myrrh on his hands.

He looked at his hands glistening with oil and felt a warmth in his hands.

A look of wonder came into his face. The hands had been an embalmer's hands and now they were the hands of a healer.

His pain eased. Warmth suffused his body, giving him life which he could give to her.

His breath came shorter and his eyes glowed opaquely as if a light had been lit in his skull. He knelt forward and opened the nightgown.

Her child's body was warm, and the whiteness softened with the flush of blood pulsing beneath the skin.

She moved.

Emma was breathing. Emma's heart was beating.

He dipped his hands in the oil and bathed her in oil.

It was spreritis!

Thank God! Thank God! Thank God!

And he did not mean Woden.

Bald was washing his hands when Dunstan entered the room. The monk went to the bed and looked down at Emma sleeping. He sniffed the air and nodded. He came across to Bald.

"Have you ever thought of taking holy orders? It's never too late, you know. I suppose I was born to it. One of my uncles is bishop of Wells, and another bishop of Lichfield. My cousin Aelfeah is bishop of Winchester. My brother Wulfric is a friend of the king's son Athelstan. Since I was ordained I've had several visions and two miraculous escapes from death. I've seen the devil, you know, dressed as a woman, or rather, undressed: he wasn't wearing very much!"

Bald turned away.

God might be God but his priests were insufferable.

It was reported that Ragnall had taken York without a fight and was approaching Bakewell to meet King Edward. The Danes who had settled in the north accepted Ragnall, and he was a powerful threat to Edward's dynastic design. The king sent for Bald and asked him what he knew about Ragnall.

"Ragnall will make peace; Caech will make war."

Edward nodded.

"I wish my council was always so brief."

He looked at Bald steadily.

"How old are you? You were older than my father when he died, and he was over fifty."

"Master, I've lived too long, like a blind old dog."

"Most men would say it's impossible to live too long."

"Most men would like to be king. But you know the burden of being king, and I know the burden of being old."

"I know they seldom go together."

Bald was anxious to leave Bakewell before Ragnall came there. He longed for the summer of the south, Eneda's cottage, and Emma dancing in a field of flowers.

His dreams were fitful, Emma was too weak to move, fate was inexorable.

Ragnall arrived bringing with him his cousin, the murdered Guthrith's son called Guthfrith, and a company of York councillors led by Archbishop Wulfstan. He was escorted by the royal prince Athelstan and received by Edward as king of York.

Bald stayed in the minster where he could watch over Emma.

Ragnall made peace, as he had predicted, and accepted Edward's overlordship. The celebrations lasted several days and all seemed to be coming to a safe conclusion when the queen suddenly fell ill. Everyone hurried to the minster, and Ragnall sent his own leech to attend her.

Bald was worried. Emma's room was close to the queen's and the corridor was crowded with priests and courtiers.

He was not asked his opinion of the queen's illness. There were new ideas, new fashions. The new young men from Alfred's schools looked at Cild's leechdoms as rustic remedies and old wives' tales. Cures could be achieved by prayers. Visions and miracles, charms and amulets were more effective for educated gentlefolk than worts growing by the wayside. Knowledge was being eclipsed by religion and faith in nature by faith in God. Healers were beginning to be regarded as witches.

So Bald lurked behind the door while Dunstan prayed and St. Cuthbert's relics were brought from Chester-le-Street. The groans of the poor queen were drowned in chants and prayers audible in Emma's room.

"Uncle, why don't you go and tell them they're wrong?"

"I never interfere with God."

Nevertheless he went into the corridor out of curiosity.

A procession was issuing from the queen's room with swaying crosses in a cloud of incense.

Bald stared.

Among the monks was one whose appearance he dreaded.

The monk wore a brown habit among the white, like a shrike among doves, and when he turned, Bald saw his pasty face and blue lips.

It was Merfyn!

Bald shrank back but not before Merfyn saw him with a start of surprise.

Bald cursed himself.

He returned to Emma's room, his heart uneasy and his head filled with thoughts of murder and escape. When he saw her too weak to lift her arm, he knew they were impossible.

Nobody expected Eadgifu to recover. The monks began to anticipate the renown of a royal sepulchre in the minster, the body of a queen and an endowment to match, a new chapel at least, and candles and masses for a century or two.

When she did recover, they bore adversity patiently and redoubled their prayers for the king.

Bald did not see Merfyn again. He avoided the court and only visited the minster at night. He began to think Merfyn was as loath to see him as he was to see Merfyn. As the days passed, Bald gained in confidence. Then he heard Ragnall was planning to return to York, while Edward was going on to Chester. It was evening, and he was approaching the minster when he stopped by the standing cross in the burial ground outside. It was a stone cross with a circle round the centre and he saw it against the soft lilac light of early summer over the moors. He saw the shaft sculpted with a vine-scroll that became a serpent entwined about a man, a Viking motif recalling the fate of Ragnar Lodbrok at the hands of king Aella of York. He looked up the shaft to the circle at the top. With eyes that now saw less of nature and more of faith, he saw not the Celtic cross but the ring of Thor and the sword of Woden. He tried to rub the brutal emblems from his eyes but they saw no better. What did it mean, this message from the gods?

He hurried into the minster.

There was somebody with Emma.

When the flash of suspicion faded, he saw it was the queen's daughter Eadburh reading to her from her missal. She rose.

"Stay child, stay."

He stayed himself only a few moments. It was good the royal family was interested in Emma as their protection would be extended to her. He had left the minster and was returning to his lodging in the town when he was met by the archbishop's chaplain and summoned to the fort. There were soldiers silhouetted on the walls and a mounted troop rode out under the gatehouse and headed west into the fading light. More soldiers were assembled in the courtyard.

The chaplain led him up a wooden staircase to the room above the gate. Fresh torches flared in his eyes, and it was a moment before he could distinguish Edward and Athelstan, both armed, among the officers and the two archbishops Wulfhelm and Wulfstan among the councillors gathered there in agitated silence.

They were waiting for him. Nobody said a word. Edward motioned him to follow and led the way to an inner chamber guarded by soldiers. They drew aside the hangings over the doorway as the king entered. Bald was next.

By candlelight he saw a body sprawled across the bed in the frozen paroxysm of violent death.

He recognised the distorted purpled face of Ragnall.

Athelstan, Wulfhelm and Wulfstan entered the room. Edward spoke.

"How did he die?"

Bald knew before he moved forward and saw the pillow on the floor. He bent over the body, smelling the gaping mouth.

"He was drugged and smothered."

Ragnall would not see Valhalla.

"Master, look for a man called Merfyn."

Wulfstan was surprised.

"Merfyn is Ragnall's own leech."

"He's Caech's man."

Athelstan spoke to an officer at the door.

"And speak to Guthfrith."

Wulfstan was surprised again.

"Guthfrith left for Dublin two days ago."

"He's gone to fetch Caech."

"But how did he know it was going to happen? Oh, I see!"

Wulfstan was becoming familiar with Viking politics.

Wulfhelm spoke.

"This has been made to look as if we did it, to raise up the old hatred of Danes for Saxons, so when Caech comes he'll have an army waiting for him. If only he'd been murdered in York!"

Wulfstan was outraged.

"York is a Christian city!"

"Just."

The archbishops of York and Canterbury glared at each other.

The officer returned and spoke to Athelstan.

"They can't find Merfyn!"

Bald felt secretly relieved the poisonous monk had gone. It meant he knew nothing about Emma, he thought. He did not care about Ragnall and Caech, Dane and Saxon, York and Canterbury. He longed to be away with Emma out of the north, out of the winter, out of the darkness. He edged out of the room where the others were talking about marching to Chester to meet the threat from Ireland. He pushed his way past the soldiers in the corridor. He stepped out onto the wooden staircase and felt a hand on his shoulder. It was Athelstan.

"Don't leave and don't try to take the girl away with you."

Bald's voice was tight with suspicion.

"Why not, master? She's nothing and I'm a blind old man."

"You saw what happened in there quickly enough."

Athelstan was angry as a proud ambitious prince would be at anyone who dared question him. He tried to hide his anger with a false jocularity.

"No, no, my family owes you a favour and they love your little niece – Emma, isn't it? That's not a Saxon name."

Bald was silent. What did Athelstan know about Emma, yes, and about Ragnall's death?

"You can be my leech. By the way, Ragnall's death was an accident."

Athelstan was gone. It was an order. Bald stepped down the staircase slowly. He did not want to risk an accident.

With the alacrity of a team of oxen the court left Bakewell and took the road to Chester. They were two days out when the solid wooden wheels of the cart carrying the convalescent queen broke down and the royal family was left like gypsies on the roadside. Emma stayed with them. Summer sprinkled the moors with sheep-defying worts: mugwort, waybroad, lambscress, attorlothe, maythen, nettle, wergule, chervil and fennel.

"These nine can march on
Gainst nine ugly poisons.
A worm sneaking came
To slay and to slaughter;
Then took up Woden
Nine wondrous twigs,
He smote then the nadder
Till it flew in nine bits."

Emma blossomed in the sun and jumped down from her cart and ran through the fields with Edmund and the two little ones. She brought the wild bunch of worts to the queen.

"Oh you little savage! These worts the Lord formed not Woden. He is wise and holy in heaven. Where did you learn such nonsense?"

"Uncle Bald taught me."

"He's not your uncle, child. You have blood in you."

Emma was puzzled until she decided Bald was too old to have blood in him any more, and she was nearly right.

Bald walked on with the king's servants. On the sixth day out, Edward fell from his horse. Wulfhelm took charge and ordered masses to be said for the king at Nantwich. Edward appeared to recover, and it was not until they reached Farndon-on-Dee that Bald was summoned.

The king had no feeling on his left side.

In the book:

"For the half dead disease and whence it cometh.

The disease cometh on the right side of the body, or on the left, where the sinews are powerless, and are afflicted with a slippery and thick humour, evil, thick and mickle. The humour must be removed with bloodlettings, and draughts, and leechdoms.

Carry the man to a very close and warm chamber, rest him very well there in shelter and let warm gledes be often carried in.

Warm at whiles the sore place at the hearth or by gledes, and smear with oil and with healing salves and rub smartly so that the salves may sink in.

At whiles lay on and bind on pitch, and wax, and pepper, and grease, and oil, melted together. At whiles lay on and bind on the sore swollen sinews goats treadles mingled with honey, or sodden in vinegar; then the paralysed and swollen sinews dwindle.

Work him a wort drink which driveth off the evil humour in the sick man.

At whiles, when he may endure it, let him blood on the inner part of the arm, and scarify his shanks.

A noble leechdom."

"Some books teach for the half dead disease that one should burn a pinetree to gledes and then set the gledes before the sick man and that he then, with eyes disclosed and open mouth, should swallow the reek for what time he may; and when he is no longer able, he should turn his face away a little and again turn it to the hot embers and accept the glow; and do so every day, till the part of the body which was deadened and injured come again to its former health."

As the leechdoms became more heroic, Bald became more desperate. Edward could not speak and only his eyes showed how he bore his tortures, staring at Bald until he could bear it no longer.

He spoke to Athelstan. Wulfhelm and Dunstan were there.

"I'm making it worse for him, master. Nature is his best leech now."

"Will nature cure him?" Bald shrugged.

"There's still God." Wulfhelm was hopeful.

"A miracle." said Dunstan.

Bald was sad.

"Pray for his soul, my masters, and leave his poor body to die."

They tormented Edward for a few more days, pressing relics on him and making him breathe incense instead of pinewood and he died anyway. Bald opened the body, removed the internal organs which were buried at Farndon except for the heart, and embalmed the rest for the journey to Winchester.

Athelstan was anxious to go south to be crowned at the King's Stone. He was apparently not concerned about Caech or the threat of invasion, and insisted that Bald and Emma should accompany him.

iii

Winchester was a building site. Work was being completed on the New Minster. Nunnaminster was enlarged and dedicated to St. Mary. The royal palace had been extended to accommodate Edward's large family and Athelstan had plans for more grandiose apartments to suit his new style: King of All England.

There was new building all over England. Alfred's fortified burhs were becoming towns. New money was building new houses. New monks were building new monasteries.

Foreigners were much in evidence and Bald, picking his way along the High Street, was jostled into the gutter down the centre by a variety of continentals. He took to swinging a staff to aid his whitening eyes and shouting "Sorry I'm British!" at those whose legs he thwacked.

He was lodged in the abbey and attended court only to get an occasional glimpse of Emma. Although he was officially the king's leech he was seldom in the king's company. Athelstan was usually closeted with churchmen, not for his soul's sake but they were drawn from among his friends and were his ministers and some said his minions too. Rumour ran he was not married because he had too many queens.

Emma lived in the palace and went to school with Eadburh and Edmund under the patronage of the widowed queen Eadgifu. Dunstan was one of her instructors and she was soon going to be baptised.

Athelstan sent for Bald to question him.

They were in the old part of the palace where it merged with the religious houses in an accretion of grey stone cells and chambers that seemed to have grown out of the sea. There was no natural light, only a pervasive gloom darkened by guttering candles a foot high. Faceless monks ran like mice along the channels leading to a domed chapel where they left Bald to wait.

He peered around with marble eyes. The chapel seemed to be an ossuary crammed with old bones and scrolls of parchment, ancient weapons, and such an assortment of junk as might be left after a sale of empires.

Athelstan bustled in in good humour. Bald thought he looked like Alfred before the cure: florid, leonine and crafty.

"I've had no time to talk to you since we left the north."

"No, master."

"Why don't you address me properly? That affectation of bluntness impresses nobody."

"I call you what the disciples called Jesus."

"Yes, but that was before the resurrection. Speaking of Jesus, have you seen this?"

Athelstan took a lance that was resting against the wall and handled it casually.

"Duke Hugh of Paris sent me this. He wants to marry one of my sisters. Do you know what it is? It's the lance of Longinus, the Roman soldier who pierced Jesus with it. It belonged to Charlemagne!"

He gave more credit to Charlemagne than to Christ.

"You see this sword? Constantine the Great had it. There's a nail from the Cross set in the hilt. Can you see it? There!"

"I can hardly see anything."

Athelstan took a baulk of timber and put it in front of Bald.

"A piece of the true cross. The cross, man! That could cure your sight. Don't touch it!"

Bald withdrew his hand and peered at the wood closely.

"It's oak."

"What?"

"Oak, master. Does oak grow in the Holy Land?"

"How do I know? My brother Otto the Emperor of Germania sent it to me. And King Charles of Francia gave me this on his wedding to my sister. The banner of St. Maurice the martyr."

He flourished a Roman eagle and flung it aside and picked up some rocks. "From the Mount of Olives and Mount Sinai!"

He dropped them and pulled out a scrap of cloth that floated like a cobweb.

"The veil of the Virgin Mary!"

He waved his hand at the ossary.

"St. Peter's finger. The thighbone of St. Bartholomew. The head of St. Justus. St. Denis's toe. Look, look at these treasures! Look at all this holydom! And all these wills and treaties, charters and contracts! Look at all this power!"

Bald looked in vain. He could not see much and what he saw was junk. Athelstan pawed his relics.

"Do you know why it's power? Because it's belief. All men believing in one. All men believing in me." He gradually became less agitated. "What do you believe in, Bald? Shall I show you?"

He went to a chest in a dark corner. Bald waited for some dusty knuckle to appear but Athelstan returned with a piece of silk skilfully embroidered with the figure of a woman holding a bowl of fruit and surrounded by ducks and fishes and woodland animals. It shimmered in the candlelight and Bald thought he saw the woman walking in some ancient Eden.

"The goddess of nature. You see, I have that, too. I'm going to give it to St. Cuthbert's shrine one day."

"Yes my lord, let it rot in darkness."

"I'll let you rot in darkness. Who's the girl called Emma?"

Bald was shocked into silence.

"She's King Sigtryggr's daughter, isn't she? The monk told me. The Irishman."

"No, my lord. Emma's my great-niece."

"That may be true but she has royal blood in her. All my sisters married kings, except those who married God. I'll find a husband for her."

"No, my lord, she's a common girl ..."

"The Viking Caech, perhaps?"

"Caech's her brother!" As he spoke Bald cursed himself. Athelstan had trapped him!

"Yes, old man. Caech is her brother." He turned away, his business done. Bald leant towards him.

"Lord, swear you'll never give the girl to Caech. I beg you, lord."

"Why not?"

Bald shook his head; he could not answer. He slowly stood erect and opened his eyes and stared at Athelstan.

The king could hardly face that stare that seemed to come from beyond the grave. He looked away, muttering.

"Or what? You won't cure me like you cured Alfred? You'll kill me?"

"I'm a leech, master."

"No I won't give her to Caech. I'll swear it if you like."

Athelstan put his hand on the cross in front of him.

Bald reached out and pressed the king's hand to the wood.

"King, you have sworn. On the cross if it is the cross. On oak it is, and oak is sacred to Woden."

Athelstan looked uneasy. Woden was still a green presence in the charnel house of his mind, for the kings of Wessex traced their ancestry back to Woden.

The word flew round the palace. Where there were monks, no secrets were safe. A vow of silence demanded to be broken, much like a vow of chastity. It was the paradox of Christianity, Bald thought, that God created sin by forbidding it. Thou shalt not was a terrible temptation to thou shalt. When Dunstan seized the devil by the nose he seized the instrument of his own desires. Bald knew all about dreams.

In the book:

"Seek in the maw of young swallows for some little stones and mind that they touch neither earth, nor water, nor other stones; look out three of them; put them on the man on whom thou wilt, him who hath the need, and he will soon be well. They are good for headache, and for eye wark, and for the fiends temptations, and for night visitors, and for typhus, and for nightmare, and for knot, and for fascination, and for evil enchantments by song."

Cild must have smiled when he wrote that leechdom. First catch your swallows.

Emma found herself the object of a general fascination she did not understand. She sought out Bald and met him on the city wall facing eastwards towards the great forest of Andred that covered the south of England like a soft brown blanket in the autumn sunshine.

"What am I, uncle?"

He wanted to say "my love", but it was no longer enough.

"Is it true my father was a king?"

"Yes."

She was excited and flushed and her green eyes challenged him.

"And what was my mother?"

"She was a common whore."

What made him say it? What made him hurt her as he had? To stop her feeling dangerously proud? To punish himself for loving Eneda?

"Well that should teach me."

Emma laughed, though there were tears in her eyes.

"They didn't tell me that."

"It's better not to be too great, Emma."

"I'm not great! I'm smaller than Ulf and Liofa! I've got no mother, no father, no one."

He took the rebuke. He had earned it.

"I didn't mean you but what other people think of you. You're a child, but to Athelstan you're an asset, a pawn that could be queen one day, and to Caech you're an enemy."

"How can I be anyone's enemy?"

"In this world you don't have to try. You won't even know it until you feel the knife in your back."

"I wish I'd never left Lyb and my brothers! I wish I'd never met you!"

"You're right to wish it. I've never done anyone any good in my life."

And at the moment he meant it. He saw himself as the figure of fate bringing disaster, the kingslayer, the devil's monk, Bald of the bald life.

Her face softened and she grinned at him.

"You poor old man!"

She put a friendly hand on his shoulder. He was glad of that small hand and wished it to stay there always.

"You should hear what they say about you. You were the best leech since Dr. Dun."

Second best to a high-priced pickpocket! Thanks, reputation! Thanks, fate! So Dun was dead ... he shuddered in a chill wind that did not blow.

"Emma, whatever they say, whatever they make you do, please never leave me."

"You don't have to ask."

It was a funny little formal exchange without the meeting of eyes. She kissed him lightly and they sat together on the wall looking eastward towards the forest of Andred now glinting like a copper shield in the declining light of autumn.

"My mother will take care of us."

She was forgiving him for calling her a whore.

"Yes Emma, I believe she will."

The copper darkened.

"Dunstan's worried now."

"And why is Dunstan worried?"

"He's been teaching me about Jesus."

"Don't you believe what he says?"

"I believe it, uncle, but I'm not sure he does. He prays all the time as if he isn't certain. He sings psalms all night long because he's afraid of going to sleep in case Jesus isn't there. If Jesus is there, he's there."

The copper turned to black.

"Is he there?"

"Oh yes, they're all there."

Bald was surprised.

"All?"

"The mother, the father and the son."

What new trinity was there in the eyes of her soul? What was Eneda doing in the picture?

"Is that what Dunstan's teaching you?"

"Not quite. It's what I'm trying to teach him."

She rose gravely and turned to the sunset.

"And what about my old friend Woden?"

"You are old-fashioned. Look uncle. The black wood is Woden. The golden world is God."

They stayed facing different ways a little while. Bald doubted if it was Christianity, but it was believable.

He looked round and up and saw Emma in the golden red sky, no child, no woman even, but the nature goddess in the silken shawl.

We all see what we believe.

Two nights later Bald was shaken awake in his cell by an excited Edmund.

"Bald! Bald! Come quickly!"

"What is it? Whatever it is will be better in the morning."

"She could be dead by morning!"

They rushed out of the abbey into the street. A silent group was gathered in the moonlight outside the palace staring up at the tower of the Nunnaminster.

Edmund pushed Bald to the front where Dunstan seized his arm and led him to the queen standing shivering in her nightclothes.

It was all black to Bald.

"What? What?"

"Look up!"

He raised his head. On the periphery of his vision he saw something white in the sky.

A voice called out. "It's an angel."

"No you fool. It's the girl!"

"What? What?"

Queen Eadgifu spoke quietly.

"Emma is on top of the tower of the Nunnaminster. The watchman saw her climbing the scaffold left by the builders. We all rushed out. Bald, she's standing on the parapet by the weathervane. Shall I call her?"

"No. If she looks down, she'll fall."

Dunstan was excited.

"I did this once myself on a church in Somerset: we were talking about it only the other day."

Bald turned to him blindly. "Send these people away! No-one follow her!"

"I was delivered by God."

"Shut up or I'll give you back to him!"

The crowd refused to disperse and stood staring up in horrified expectation. Bald heard them gasp in unison.

"What happened?"

"She went to the edge." Edmund spoke. "Is she asleep?"

Dunstan started to sing quietly. "Gloria in excelsis deo."

"She won't hurt herself unless she wakes up, then she'll fall."

"Poor girl."

Bald turned his head towards Eadgifu.

"No, lady. Lucky girl. The gods are holding her."

"God, Bald. God is holding her. There's only one."

"I can see at least six angels."

But he was lying. He only saw two.

"She's coming down!"

They watched in amazement as the little white figure walked without a falter to the narrow platform and climbed down the spindly ladders hooked to the tower. They could not have been more surprised if she had floated down, so gently she descended.

Bald held out his hands.

"Is she down? Where is she?"

Emma walked towards them. She was wide awake and seemed surprised herself to see them there.

"What, my lady? You should be in bed, uncle."

"Emma, Emma."

"What do you think you were doing, child?"

"Where?"

Eadgifu turned Emma towards the Nunnaminster and pointed upwards to where she had been almost directly above their heads.

"I went to see my mother."

The queen saw the Virgin. Bald saw Eneda. Dunstan saw an angel. Edmund saw Emma.

They took her inside and put her to bed. Eadgifu called a meeting with Bald and Dunstan.

"What does it mean?"

"Just before I became a monk, before I took my vows, I climbed a church tower in my sleep. I believe it was a sacrifice, I was offering myself as a sacrifice. I call it the white martyrdom."

Eadgifu looked doubtful.

"I thought the white martyrdom was what you called the vow of celibacy?"

"Yes my lady, I believe the two are connected."

"It's not celibacy!" Bald growled at him, "it's exactly the opposite. Young girls! Sacred poles in high places!"

Eadgifu raised her eyebrows.

"No, no, Bald, please. The tower is dedicated to St. Mary the Virgin. That would be the last thing on her mind."

So it was left, and so it was at court, with the truly religious believing Emma was blessed and the truly honest guessing she was menstruating.

Bald had his own idea and went to find her alone.

"Do you want to be baptised or not?"

"I have no choice."

"That's true. They won't leave you alone. Remember it's words and water. I knew a man who was baptised three times for convenience."

"Dunstan says it will wash away my sins."

"He's an old woman. You know the book, Emma. All the ills of mankind are in the book and there's not one sin. Only Christians have sins. Do you want them?"

"I want Jesus."

Yes, yes, Bald thought, dripping blood like Cild, the need of sacrifice to man to cure himself, leechdoms were never enough. What deep disease is in ourselves that needs such drastic medicine?

"Why?"

"I don't know. It's my nature, I expect."

Nature? The gods of nature killed each other, not themselves!

"Nature's here and now. It's not another life in another place."

"Here and now."

She nodded eagerly and he was reminded of Eneda and the money.

"Did you see your mother the other night, on the tower?"

She shook her head rather sadly.

"I think she saw you. Somebody did."

"I saw the Mother. I saw Maria Virgo."

Bald heard the capital M and tried to analyse them in his cell. The Mothers would have been deep in Sigtryggr's being long before the bully gods of Valhalla. His own craft he admitted was a woman's craft and the first healer was a hermaphrodite. Was his own impotence a nod in that direction? Had Emma stumbled on a secret, a sort of spiritual Fornjot's palm to give life to the soul as that did to the body? Could he find it before he died?

Only if he stayed with Emma.

Emma was baptised on Christmas day. She forswore the pagan gods. She was given the royal Saxon name of Aelfgifu.

Dunstan came to see Bald because he thought he had leprosy.

"By Woden, stop complaining," said Bald, "or Emma will get it too."

Emma and Edmund were often together. Old courtiers smiled indulgently and Aethelstan's imperial missionaries had a moment's regret for lost innocence when they saw these two children of fortune in the firelight. Edmund was coming twelve and next in line for the crown, Aelfgifu was two years older and a Viking princess. They even looked a little like each other, as if the lines of Alfred and Ivarr were being spun together by the twist of fate.

Edmund and Emma, who hated the name Aelfgifu and refused to answer to it, were oblivious of the glow in which they lived. Winter in Winchester was fun. After lessons – Emma was first in everything except moral precepts which she had started late – there was a race to the frozen river to skate, or to the snowbound slopes to sledge, or to the forest and the cathedral-quietness of great trees where Emma enchanted the boy with her knowledge of the book.

In the book:
"Erce! Erce! Erce!
Mother earth
May the Almighty grant thee
The eternal Lord
Acres waxing
With sprouts wantoning
Fertile brisk creations
The rural crops
And the broad
Crops of barley
And the white
Wheaten crops
And all the
Crops of the earth.
Grant the owner
God Almighty
And his hallows
In heaven who are
That his farm be fortified

Gainst all fiends, gainst each one,
And may it be embattled round
Gainst baleful blastings everyone
Which sorceries may
Through a land sow.
Now I pray the wielder of all
Him who made this world of yore
That there be none so cunning wife
That there be none so crafty man
Who shall render weak and null
Words so deftly neatly said."

Then if he was not besotted by the muddle in her mind she danced between the trees, bending to collect fallen seeds and plant them, and sport her budding body to befuddle and stir up his desires.

"Aelfgifu."

"I shan't answer."

"Emma, then."

"What, Edmund then?"

"Where do you come from?"

"First the man's brain is formed in his mother's womb.

In the second month the veins are formed and the blood floweth and he is divided into limbs.

In the third month he is a man without a soul.

In the fourth month he is firm in his limbs.

In the fifth month he is quick and waxeth and his mother is witless.

In the sixth month he gets a skin and the bones are growing.

In the seventh month toes and fingers are growing.

In the eighth month his breast grows and his heart and his blood and he is altogether.

In the ninth month he is brought forth.

In the tenth month the woman does not escape with her life if the bairn is not born, since it turns in the belly to a deadly disorder and oftenest on Tuesnight."

"I meant did you come from York or somewhere else?"

"I come from the icy sea and eagle-spread salt spray across the ocean."

"Seriously."

"Seriously Edmund. I shall call you Seriously Edmund."

"Then I'll call you Aelfgifu."

"And I shan't answer."

Emma did not answer to the expectations of the court. Encouraged by Dunstan, Queen Eadgifu and the virtuous Eadburh who had renounced the world at the age of three, she suddenly declared her intention to take vows and enter a convent at Easter.

This did not suit the plans of Athelstan. He sent for Bald once again. He was in a brittle mood amongst his holydom and tapped the skull of St. Justus with St. Peter's finger.

"What's all this religious nonsense going on?"

"Some about God. Some about horses."

"I can cope with horses. Can't you give her a leechdom for it?"

"She'll leech herself. Her body is changing and it frightens her. She wants to stay a child and all the time she's growing into a monster with breasts and hair and desires."

"A woman!"

"A human being. Children are gods and very old men without desires. So she looks for somewhere she doesn't have to grow up."

"The church?"

"The mother church, my lord, where she can hide her body."

"I can't have that. You say she'll leech herself?"

"Desire is stronger than fear and life is stronger than death."

"It is in your case."

"I didn't mean anybody's life, but life itself. Her womanhood will triumph over everything."

"God, God will triumph, Bald. God is a man!"

"If he is, my lord, he is an old man."

"So you think I should do nothing?"

"Yes, master. But do it before Easter."

In February the court moved north to Tamworth, the ancient capital of Mercia. It was early in the year and everybody wondered why. Athelstan gave no reason, but messengers were already on the roads to Dublin and York.

iv

Eadgyth was Athelstan's eldest sister and he persuaded her to leave the monastery at Polesworth where she had spent most of her forty years and come to Tamworth to see him. She joined the royal family in the old palace built for King Offa a hundred years before. As she swept along the draughty passages, Athelstan's young ministers made way for her because she was a virtuous and portly maiden.

Athelstan was standing with his back to the fire in the hall, keeping the heat from the rest of the family. Emma was shivering on the edge of the group, trying to thread an embroidery needle with numb fingers. Edmund was sitting nearby gazing at her.

Eadgyth brought a cold wind in with her.

"Well, brother, I hope you have a good reason for bringing me here."

"The best reason in the world, Eadgyth – our country's welfare."

"That's in the hands of God."

"Yes it is, and I have the approval of the Archbishops of Canterbury and York for what I'm talking about."

He looked round for everyone else's approval.

"The union of the kingdom of York with us."

Emma pricked her finger and paid more attention.

"How do you mean to achieve it, brother?"

"What better way than by a marriage?"

There was a stir of surprise, and Eadgifu and the children turned to look at Edmund and Emma.

"Indeed. May I ask who's getting married?"

"You are. You're going to marry Caech."

The stir became a whirlpool of consternation. Caech had a fearsome reputation, several wives and a son as old as Edmund.

Emma knew most about him and was the most concerned. Eadgyth was quite oblivious.

"Who is Caech?"

"King of York, but more than that, he's the accepted leader of the Danes who settled here in Alfred's time. I'm talking about the union between north and south."

"Why have you chosen me for this honour?"

Athelstan had expected the question. He could hardly tell her she was his last unmarried sister apart from the children and would have to do.

"My dear Eadgyth, do you know what this means? The conversion of a pagan king and of all the Norsemen and their families brought over here from Ireland and the west by that wretched man Ragnall. There are several thousand souls which only you can save."

Eadgyth was interested but modest.

"I'm sorry, Athelstan, I can't possibly think of marriage at my age."

"Don't think of marriage, think of the great service you will do your country and your God. The greater the age, the greater the honour. Saints have been made saints for less."

She flushed, and it reminded her of something.

"What about my vow of chastity?"

"I don't think it will be troubled. He's old, and I have it on authority that he's not long to live. But to be safe, Wulfhelm will absolve you and we'll have it ratified by the pope."

Emma could not believe what she heard. Bald had told her enough about Caech to make her hate his name. How could Athelstan sacrifice his own sister in such a blatant way? How could Eadgyth possibly agree? But Athelstan knew women better than most men who love women. He knew their ambition, though nearly always repressed, was as great as any man's. He knew Eadgyth was very like himself.

"What will my title be?"

"Queen. And when you're a widow, abbess of any monastery you care to name."

"Polesworth."

Eadgyth probably had a few accounts to settle.

Caech arrived in Tamworth shortly afterwards, tactfully leaving his latest wife and son in Dublin with his cousin Guthfrith. He brought gifts for everyone. The illuminated gospel he gave Athelstan was called the royal bible.

He had a gift for Emma. When she was brought reluctantly into his presence, she was introduced as Aelfgifu, a young lady of good breeding, so as not to embarrass him.

Emma found herself curtseying to a short, stout, red-faced man with a fringe of yellowing hair. His eyes were bloodshot, and a cast in one made him look asquint. He was not the terrifying picture Bald had painted, but no husband, even for a forty-year-old nun.

When he saw her, his mouth twisted, baring his broken teeth like a dog. It was meant to be a smile, but she saw the mouth of hell.

He held out her present, a small gold box decorated with an ivory crucifix and the inscription "What is within will release us from sin". She returned to her place and tried to open it, but the lid was stuck. She did not notice a monk with blue lips in a putty face watching her.

Bald had not been let into the hall, and was waiting anxiously in her room.

"It was all right until he smiled at me. He gave me this."

Bald seized the box from her and opened it with his knife.

"Don't break it, uncle."

There was the dust of a wafer inside; some soul had gone without communion the day it was looted. He gave it back to her.

"Can I keep it? I'm sorry for Eadgyth."

"Be grateful it's her he's taking with him, not you."

"Is he really my brother? Is half of him like me?"

Bald saw the dangerous fascination of this line of thought.

"Now Athelstan has no more use for you, perhaps he'll let us go."

"I have to take my vows and be a nun."

"If you must swear, Emma, swear to be free like your mother. Come with me and take your vows in the forest. Serve the book, yes, this book, that does give life. Jesus was a leech before he was a god. I tell you, I'd rather cure one body than let it die and save its soul."

He rested after this long speech and carefully avoided looking at her. He felt Eneda's presence. After a moment, Emma asked: "What did she believe in?"

He hesitated to say money.

"Air, fire, earth and water."

"Nothing else?"

"That's everything in the world."

"No god?"

He thought for a long time until she thought he had gone to sleep.

"Uncle?"

"I believe in fate."

"What's that?"

"I don't know." He meant his own impotence but he could not say it.

"How can you believe in something you don't know?"

He turned his eyes to her and saw her face like the sun seen through the thickness of an autumn mist.

"I know the book. I believe it is all the truth.

I know I'm blind. I believe I see your face.

I know I'm going to die. I believe I'll love you forever."

He heard her catch her breath and knew she was crying. He heard her say, "I swear I'll never leave you for anything."

He was content.

Athelstan and Caech were often together and it was rumoured they had agreed a perpetual treaty uniting the kingdoms of north and south. Caech had to be baptised before his marriage to Eadgyth, and the chapel in the palace was filled with monks and courtiers for the great occasion. The two archbishops were to conduct the service, and Athelstan was standing sponsor to the old pagan. Everyone was fascinated by the prospect of seeing him renounce his old marriages along with his old gods.

Bald was sickened by the sanctified hypocrisy of the whole business and was out in the street when he was called by Dunstan.

"Bald, we need your help."

"Is someone ill?"

"No. We have to make six copies of the treaty by tonight and there aren't enough scribes. You can write, can't you?"

"My eyes are bad and I haven't written anything for years."

"Never mind, the Danes can't read."

Bald followed Dunstan to a room where some monks were working at a table, painstakingly writing in the minuscule script. He was given pen and parchment and a page of the treaty. He peered at the letters until they assumed their proper shape and then began to copy them. After the customary titles, prayers and pledges came a list of placenames that made him blink and yawn. He worked for an hour and was nearing the end of the page when a name stood out and made him stare – Aelfgifu!

He read the clause in which it was set. "The abbess Aelfgifu to receive the abbey of Thetford."

He had good reason to remember Thetford. His father Cild had been sacrificed to Woden at Thetford, and he knew there was no abbey there. There were other royal ladies called Aelfgifu, one of Athelstan's sisters, but no abbess, and why was she mentioned in the treaty? He sat staring at the letters until they blurred and marched across the parchment, meeting at the capital T of Thetford.

Did it refer to Emma? And if so, why? And why Thetford?

The T grew larger and the letters appeared to circle the cross at the top.

Suddenly Bald saw the vision he had seen outside the minster at Bakewell. The T – the Celtic cross –became the sword of Woden, and the circle the ring of Thor!

The clause in the treaty was a cover for the transfer of Emma from Athelstan to Caech!

Any future question of her fate could be answered. She went to the abbey of Thetford. Any search would be frustrated because the abbey of Thetford did not exist.

Bald felt the sweat break from his body and the bile rise in his stomach.

In spite of his oath on the cross, Athelstan was going to give Emma to Caech, which meant to death, as part of his bargain with the devil!

What could he do?

Emma was guarded by Athelstan's agents. The church was implicated because Wulfhelm and Wulfstan were witnesses to the treaty.

His own impotence overwhelmed him, his hand retracted scraping the pen across the parchment leaving a trail of despair.

"What, brother, finished already?"

Dunstan looked over his shoulder.

"You've spoilt the parchment. It's your eyes. I must do something about them one day."

"My eyes!"

Bald sat upright, staring. His eyes were as white and sightless as the paper in front of him. He was blind.

Then a mystery was revealed to him.

It was as if his eyes had been obstructing his vision, and total blackness enabled him to see more clearly than he ever had before. He saw with the eyes of his mind exactly what he had to do. He felt for Dunstan's robe and gripped it, pulling him closer.

"When is Caech going to be married?"

"Tonight."

"Take me to the hall tonight. I'll be a witness."

In the evening, while he was waiting for Dunstan, he felt in better mind than ever he could remember.

Now he could not see at all, he had no fear of darkness.

Now he had lost all desire, he had no dread of impotence.

Now he knew death was imminent, a step away for a blind man, he could sacrifice his life.

And that is what he was going to do.

He had wanted to speak to Emma, but she was dressing for the wedding, when she and Eadburh were to be Eadgyth's attendant bridesmaids. Athelstan, with superb disdain was honouring her to the end.

So Bald sat waiting.

He thought of praying but decided against it. Athelstan was forsworn, and if Jesus or Woden was offended let Jesus or Woden punish him, Woden more likely than Jesus.

Bald thought he was better on his own to die as he had lived, alone. He was certain he would die, either immediately or in a day or two. Would Emma be saved?

There his certainty ended and he did pray, but not to Jesus or Woden.

"Woman save your daughter
Mother your child."

He felt a presence, a warmth, a comfort.

He was glad he could not see because then he would have known there was nobody there.

Dunstan came.

"Why are you wearing that old plaid and not your leech's gown? What do you want with your book? It's a wedding not a funeral. Why are you carrying a stick?"

"I'm blind."

Dunstan examined his eyes, mumbling to himself.

"Woman's milk is good for blindness."

"In babies, Dunstan. Read the book."

The hall was filled, ale was flowing, and flaming torchlight fell on the red faces of Athelstan and Caech and their followers, on the churchmen and ealdermen, jarls and men-at-arms.

Eadgyth, conscious of her new dignity as Queen of York and taking precedence over the dowager queen Eadgifu, was coolly watching Caech while secretly praying to Jesus he would drink himself to death or at least impotence.

Caech, with the advantage of a squint, was watching Eadgyth and praying something similar to Woden.

In terms of ambition and mutual dislike, they were perfectly matched.

Emma sat in a borrowed dress among the ladies. She wished she could be with Edmund and the children. The clucks and lascivious chuckles around her made her uncomfortable. She knew the book, and what men and women did, and the leechdoms that followed, and found the theory odd but unamusing. She did not understand the red-faced women or the nods and winks and licked lips of their common experience.

She saw Dunstan lead in Bald and sit him at a table among the minor officials and lower orders of priesthood.

She was soon herself the object of interest of some Danish ladies from York who were astonished to hear about her.

"Sigtryggr's bastard? A princess? No! Her mother was a slave!"

"She should be dead by all accounts."

"Sigtryggr was murdered in his bed."

"The mother met a violent end."

Her father murdered! Her mother too!

"Have a jelly, Aelfgifu."

A surge of vengeance rushed into her heart and she shouted: "Who killed them?"

"Hush, child." Eadgifu leant across and patted her hand. "It's not polite to ask a question like that at table. I hope nobody heard you."

Bald was desperate to be heard.

The clamour round him was intensified by his blindness.

The clash of pewter, gabble of unmeaning words, scrape of benches, the general belch, all dinned in his head.

He had his own speech ready, carved in the tablet of fate.

He knew there would be prayers: great devils knew how to pray, and then he would hurl his words at their heads.

Two from him along the bench, though he did not know it, sat Merfyn.

The two archbishops, Wulfhelm of Canterbury and Wulfstan of York were reconciled, each convinced of his own primacy. The ancient division of north and south, aggravated by the Danish invasions, had been bridged. The fate of a girl was nothing compared to the repletion of their episcopacies. They rose together and held up their hands for silence.

Gradually the clamour in the hall subsided.

They waited for absolute silence.

Wulfhelm waited too long and Wulfstan began to pray: "Dominus dominusque ..."

Wulhelm was annoyed and rapped the table.

Wulfstan stopped and glared at him.

Wulfhelm composed himself. He drew in his breath.

"Caech is a woman-killer! Athelstan is an oath-breaker!"

Bald's voice echoed from wall to wall.

"Caech murdered Aelfgifu's mother! Athelstan swore he would not give Aelfgifu to Caech! He's going to do so! Caech is a woman-killer and Athelstan is an oath-breaker!"

Bald was standing in his ragged plaid, the book slung from his shoulder, leaning on his staff like an Old Testament prophet.

Those nearest shrank from him, those furthest craned to see him.

All felt the shock of terror and the chill of worse to come. No-one dared speak or even look round for fear of being associated with these terrible accusations.

Bald waited for the arrow or spear to end his life. He believed by accusing the kings in public he would make it impossible for them to dispose of Emma.

Emma had some wit of it and jumped up and ran across the hall to clasp him. He slowly and symbolically drew his plaid around her. One dove moves and the flock rises. Suddenly everyone was on their feet.

Men-at-arms from both camps rushed at Bald, seized him and hurried him, unresisting, up to the table where the kings were sitting. Emma was dragged from him and held apart.

Athelstan was purple with rage. Caech rose to see his accuser. He stared askance at Bald and the light of comprehension came into his red eyes. He spoke with increasing anger.

"This man is Bald the leech! He's a wanted murderer. A kingslayer! He slew King Sigtryggr! Kill him!"

The Danish guards drew their swords and would have struck Bald but the Saxon guards intervened. He was jostled and turned and was facing away from Athelstan who managed to croak through his rage: "Bald! Look at me!"

"I'm blind."

"That won't save you."

Athelstan channelled his rage as Caech dissipated his, and was the more dangerous of the two. He looked for advantage where Caech only saw revenge. He spoke with greater composure. He addressed the hall.

"You know this man Bald makes a virtue of plain speaking: well, so do I. But I also make a virtue of justice under the law. He must prove his plainspeech is true. The law is that he will be tried by ordeal. Put him in a cell. Confine the girl to her room."

Athelstan's authority was absolute. Bald knew he had gambled and lost. A trial by ordeal was held in silence, except for the screams of the defendant. He resisted the guards. He leant across the table.

"King, free the girl."

"I will free her, if you survive the ordeal."

The soldiers closed around Bald and took him away.

That night Dunstan came to see him in his cell.

"I have some news. I don't suppose it's any use offering you last communion?"

"Is it bad?"

"The worst. Caech chose which ordeal you have to suffer. Drowning is bad and choking is bad, but fire and boiling water are the worst. He chose boiling water"

"God will protect me."

"It's a lot to ask when you don't believe in him."

"Then I'm dead. Go and see Emma."

"I can't see her. No-one can see her."

"Dunstan, I need some worts and medicines, a leechdom for a dying man. Will you get them for me tonight?"

"If I can. Are you sure you won't let me baptise you at least?"

"I will if I live. Now listen to what I need."

In the book:

"... take this same wort serpyllum, and ashthroat or vervain, one bundle, and by weight of one ounce of the filings of silver or litharge, and roses by weight of three ounces, then pound all together in a mortar, then add thereto wax and of grease of bear and of hart, by weight of half a pound, seethe all together ..."

"Serpyllum?"

"Organy."

"Silver filings?"

"Get them."

"Bear's grease?"

"Will you go through the whole leechdom again?"

"What's it for?"

"Rheumatism."

"But tomorrow you'll – well, you'll probably be dead."

"I don't want to wake up in heaven with rheumatism."

Dunstan left.

He returned at dawn with the worts, the silver, the roses and the grease. He brought a mortar and a crucible for Bald to seethe them over the fire in the cell. He watched Bald working them together for a while. When his back was turned, he blessed him.

The ordeal took place in church because God was the judge. The archbishops officiated and Athelstan was a witness. Caech was not present but sent a monk to represent him: Merfyn. Tamworth minster was crammed with magnates from both communities, for the charges were notorious, the ordeal spectacular, and the outcome sure to be satisfactory. A great cauldron filled with boiling water stood above a burning brazier before the altar. Steam hung in the cold morning air. Prayers for the departed were already being chanted because they knew if the terrible blistering did not kill the man, the shock would.

There was a stir as Bald was led in by his guards. He walked slowly along the length of the aisle. He was newly blind and still turned his head towards sounds as if he could see.

"There are many people here."

They took him up to the cauldron and left him between two hooded monks who were to be his executioners.

Everyone in the minster knew his arm would be thrust into the boiling water. If the skin blistered then God found him guilty. If the skin remained unmarked then God found him innocent. If he was guilty and still alive, he would be hanged. Nobody considered the alternative.

The monks in the choir began to pray.

The two who were his executioners stripped the plaid down to his waist and gripped his right arm. They pushed him forward between them until his arm was poised above the boiling water.

Wulfhelm spoke: "God judge this man."

They seized Bald by the shoulders and forced him to bend down and sideways, plunging his arm deep into the cauldron up to the armpit.

There was a gasp of anticipation.

The church held its breath in the presence of God.

Silence.

Why was he not screaming?

Athelstan left his chair and came to see the arm was completely immersed. He recoiled from the scalding steam.

The monks prayed. One paternoster, two, three.

Now the arm would not just be blistered, the flesh would be boiled and stripped from the bone.

Athelstan went back to his chair. Wulfhelm called out.

"Enough!"

The two monks released Bald and retreated.

The church waited for the judgement of God.

Bald slowly straightened his body and withdrew his arm from the cauldron.

He turned and raised his arm for everyone to see.

The skin smoked and glistened, but there was not a mark on it.

There was the scent of roses.

With arm raised he turned from left to right.

Men were struck with awe. Some fell to their knees. Some prayed aloud. The two archbishops stared at the naked arm and glanced nervously at the naked Christ crucified behind the altar.

Athelstan leant forward like Herod when he saw the head of John the Baptist.

Wulfstan was the first to speak.

"The man is innocent. God has saved him from injustice."

"No! It's witchcraft! He's a witch! The arm's bewitched to be sure!"

Merfyn came forward screaming.

Merfyn ran up to Bald and felt his arm.

Bald turned his blind eyes on him, knowing him from his voice.

"Merfyn!"

He seized the monk with both hands. Merfyn struggled in his grip.

"I accuse this man of murder! God judge him!"

He forced Merfyn to the edge of the cauldron, holding him with one hand and pressing his head downwards with the other.

Merfyn felt the scalding steam and screamed.

Then the scream was stifled by an awful choking gurgle as Bald thrust his head into the boiling water.

No-one could move.

The monks were praying. One paternoster, two, three.

Bald released him.

Merfyn sprang up. His head, face and neck were a great white blister which bubbled as the steam from melting flesh escaped through ears, eyes, nostrils and mouth. His brains were boiling.

His body span and twisted in agony, teetering towards the two archbishops who backed away in horror, staggering towards the altar, falling, writhing, subsiding, twitching, dying.

Bald stood as if he had descended from a cross.

All men looked from one man to the other. The judgement of God was apparent to all. What was the judgement of the king?

Athelstan got slowly to his feet. He breathed a deep breath as if to reassure himself he was alive.

"The monk was guilty. Bald is innocent. He is free."

He turned away to leave the scene of an ordeal which had been an ordeal for all who were there.

Dunstan ran forward to Bald and grasped his hand.

"Who's that?"

"Dunstan. It was a miracle!"

"Take me to Emma."

"Emma? Emma's gone. Caech left before dawn and took Emma with him."

V

Tap, tap, tap. Ermine Street, the road to York, a blind man tapping his way north from one worn slab to the next, tripping, stumbling, seldom stopping. An old man, cheated by life, cheated by death that ought to have put an end to his futility long ago, following his fate. As the year changed, Bald marched on.

He felt completely isolated by blindness, and deserted by the gods. He had no hope Emma was still alive or he could save her. His mind was empty, his spirit gone, he no longer drove himself, but followed.

There were many travellers on the road, merchants in company, monks returning to their monasteries in the north, drovers with lean cattle looking for new grazing, families moving, those going to pray at shrines, the possessed and the dispossessed, the drivers and the driven.

Bald did not want for food or water. The old religion and the new fed fools and strangers.

In the night of his eyes he dreamt dreams of the past.

His mind was like a funerary urn containing the ashes of his life, painted with images, turning slowly, so he kept meeting himself in stillness. Cild's sacrifice, Sigtryggr's amputation, Eneda's passion, her face imprinted in her pillow, Emma's promise – all still, eternal art.

He carried the book like a damned soul bears its old obsessions, and like the book, his life was closed.

North of Nottingham, a family visiting relatives took pity on him. They were the grandchildren of Ivarr's pirates. Now they spoke anglo-saxon, farmed in Norfolk, paid tithes, prayed in church for Athelstan, and were more English than the English.

They tied a rope round his neck, and let their youngest child lead him like a dog. He did not care. It saved him from falling into ditches. He saved them, once.

In the book:

"For bite of adder, take the same viperina, pound it, mix with wine, give to drink; it healeth wondrously the rent and driveth away the poison; and this wort thou shalt pick in the month which is called April."

A child's shrill scream cut through his dreams. He heard a cry.

"It's a snake! Egill's been bitten by a snake!"

He blundered into the boy who led him. Egill was his older brother. He heard the woman sobbing and the man calling out for help to passers-by. It was far from him and the narrow world of his blindness. He squatted down to wait.

The woman's cries grew louder and more desperate. He heard them shouting for a leech.

He had been a leech, but in another life. Why should he return to a world where he had been so cruelly treated?

The woman was calling on God.

Let God leech the boy. What could he do, he was blind?

The boy was groaning in pain. Bald frowned. The blood should have washed out the poison unless the wound was blind. Then it must be opened or the boy would die. The leechdom was there in his head.

"For bite of adder, take the same viperina ..."

Viperina, adder wort, polygonum bistorta.

"... this wort thou shalt pick in the month which is called April."

It was April.

They were weeping. There was so much sorrow in the world.

The old gods drank. The new God gave his blood to drink.

The wound should bleed. He heard himself call out: "Does the wound bleed?"

"No! His arm is swollen. He's pale and feverish."

Bald pulled the young boy to him by the rope.

"Run into the field and find the wort with thin pointed leaves and long thin stems with fine pink spikes at the top like a brush. Pull it up and bring it to me quickly."

He called to the woman:

"Mother, take me to your son and put my hands on the place where the snake bit him."

"Why? What can you do?"

"I'm a leech."

The woman came and led him to the boy and put his hands on the swollen arm.

Bald felt the swelling and knew the wound was blind. He slipped out his knife. The man shouted:

"For Jesus' sake, he's going to cut off his arm."

He made three cuts above the swelling and squeezed them open and put his mouth on them to suck out the poison.

He felt a blow on his back and the woman cried out, "Let him be!"

"What's he doing?"

Bald spat out poisoned blood.

"I'm doing what I'm here for."

The young boy ran back and pushed a bunch of worts into his hand. He felt the leaves: long and pointed. He chewed a leaf and knew the bitter taste of viperina.

He took the pulp from his mouth and pressed it into the wounds.

"Woman, scrape the root and crush it into wine. Give it to the boy to drink."

He chewed more leaves, and when the wounds were covered in the mulch, he bound them.

Egill was better by the evening.

When his parents went to look for Bald they found the young boy dragging the rope along the ground.

Bald could not wait for them. He had to get to York.

It was market day. The streets of the city were crowded with folk from the countryside come to sell their produce.

The river was so tightly packed with ships it was like another street. York rivalled London as a commercial centre, indeed it had the advantage of shorter sea-routes to its trading partners.

The tide of dominance was turning to the north and the neap of expectation was a kingdom of England with its capital in York.

Bald was carried along the busy stream and landed, in answer to his pleas, outside the alehouse. He stood in the doorway waiting for Lyb to follow his natural instincts and pass that way. He had no plans, only the urgency for action pulsing in his blood.

Curing the boy Egill had cured his despondency.

Since his reawakening on the road, his instincts had sharpened to compensate for his blindness. He smelt Lyb coming. The same smell of stale urine and pigswill that used to revolt him made him call out with excitement.

"Lyb! Lyb!"

He heard the dwarf shout in anger and was suddenly flung against the doorpost and pummelled about the stomach. He had the worst of premonitions.

"Oh god is she dead? Tell me, Lyb!"

A storm of blows fell on him and tears filled the pools of his eyes and overflowed the white sightless pebbles.

Emma was dead. What inner light kindled on the road went out. Someone dragged the dwarf off him.

"She's dead all right, uncle."

"Liofa? It wasn't my fault! Athelstan gave her to Caech!"

"Who gave her to Athelstan?"

Bald could not answer. Fate was no answer. Guilt was silent. He could only mourn.

"Liofa, take me to the minster."

Liofa took his hand and led him like a child while Lyb followed venting his anger with swipes and kicks in the air behind his back. They went the way along the wharves to the old Roman wall where the minster rose within its Christian compound.

Liofa told Bald that Caech had returned over a month ago. The rumour had spread he had Sigtryggr's daughter in his power. Ginna and Toki had returned to the palace to work but there was no sign of Emma. Instead there was a new queen, deserted after her absurd wedding, spending her days and nights in prayer. Ulf and Liofa had searched the city, and every hole and passage, cell and prison.

"We're like the rats, uncle, we can go everywhere."

"No sign? No name? They call her Aelfgifu."

"Nothing. She's not in this world any more."

What was left of his heart was wrung with anguish. One last tear.

They stopped.

"Where are we?"

"The minster. Can't you see anything?"

Bald sighed and shook his head.

"I'll try and find out what they did with her body."

Lyb cursed him. "Faul! Faul!"

He flinched from a word so old they say God cursed Adam with it, and fled blindly into the minster. The dwarves followed to the door but would go no further.

Bald stood trembling in the stillness.

He thought of his last visit there with Emma and the mystery of the painting on the wall. He made his way to where he thought it was, and knelt, and touched the stone.

A priest saw a blind old man kneel by Guthrith's tomb in the central aisle and passed by reverently, unaware the old man thought he was somewhere else and was searching in his mind for a goddess.

The woman of his dreams, Eneda, Maria Virgo, the figure in the Byzantine shawl, each came like the pattern in the horn shutter of a lantern between the source of thought-light and the eyes of his mind. They were projected by the light but were not the light. What he now sought in his blindness was beyond the images that had satisfied his sight. It was the light itself, the light that shines in our dreams. He felt if he could see that light he would see Emma again when he died.

A sound encroached on the stillness, a shuffling of feet and swish of robes, a muttering of endless ave Marias. He smelt the sweat of unwashed women and guessed a swathe of nuns was passing by. He tried to concentrate his mind on the Maria Virgo he thought he saw before him. Perhaps she would tell him where Emma's body was?

He heard a surprised whisper.

"Uncle?"

The absurdity of it! Was he the virgin's uncle?

"What are you doing here?" Emma's voice!

He tried to turn but felt a small restraining hand on his shoulder.

"Stay still! Meet me here tomorrow before matins."

She moved in the general murmur and was gone.

He gaped. His whole body gaped!

Was it Emma or her ghost? Had he heard her or dreamed her?

He sniffed the air and smelt the unwashed purity. It was Emma! Emma was a nun!

Light! Light!

That was why Liofa had never found her. He would not go into a church! That was why she was still alive. Caech would never kill a nun!

He rose resurrected with a joyous shout and wild laughter, and strode back along the aisle with an accuracy born of blindness towards the door.

The priest stared with astonishment. A miracle at Guthrith's tomb? Had God gone mad?

Bald emerged from the minster. Liofa and Lyb moved forward to guide him.

"Come home, uncle. My da's forgiven you."

"Lyb, come here, Lyb. Have you forgiven me?"

He felt about until he found the dwarf and seized him.

"Faul you horseturd! Faul you fool!"

He raised his stick and beat him.

"Emma's in there! Emma's alive and in the church!"

He was laughing and shouting and beating.

"Faul! Faul, you fools! You Britons will always be slaves!"

He started dancing on the green in front of the minster. Passers-by were becoming suspicious and Lyb and Liofa grabbed him by the arms and hurried him away as quickly as they could.

All the little family laughed except Lyb who sulked and rubbed his bruises. How smart she was, that Emma!

Bald made a salve for Lyb with honey and goat's treadles.

"Just like her mother."

He was in the minster before dawn. He made Ulf take him to the painting before the boy fled from the naked god on the wall.

Emma came a little after and knelt beside him.

He felt her youthful presence like the air in spring.

He spoke in excited and urgent whispers.

"Emma."

"Yes uncle."

"Is anyone else here?"

"No."

"Let's go now! Come, my love, let's escape while we can!"

"Why?"

"Why? Because your life's in danger every minute."

"No it's not. My soul perhaps but not my life."

Bald was confused and angry, as if the girl had struck him.

"What? Don't be so stupid! Caech will have you killed."

"No, uncle. I'm protected by Queen Eadgyth and Archbishop Wulfstan."

There was a touch of pomposity in her voice which infuriated him. He blamed it on the church.

"Do you think those sainted doves will save you from a blood-eagle?"

"I don't know what you mean. The king was worried I'd get married and his son Cuaran would have a rival for the succession. When I take my vows, that will be over."

Bald was astonished she was so calm. The Vikings in his memory axed their rivals.

"Perhaps it saved you for the moment but now you can leave with me and you'll be free for good."

He waited for an answer and the longer he waited the more concerned he was.

"You want to be with me don't you? Emma, I need you."

He turned his blind eyes on her, not knowing her eyes were closed and her lips were moving in silent prayer. He waited until he could wait no longer.

"Emma, I'm blind."

She kept her eyes closed as if she could not bear to see him.

"I can't, uncle. God will guide you."

Resentment flared in him.

"You said you'd never leave me!"

She answered gravely and her voice trembled as if reflecting the troubled look in her face.

"I'm another person. When I said that, I was Emma. Now I'm Aelfgifu."

"Emma! Aelfgifu! I'll give you another name. Ungrateful!"

She spoke sadly. "That's my burden."

"You're speaking like a saint, a child! What pious rubbish!"

He turned and seized her arms and shook her.

"You have one life, a whole life, before you. Live it! Live it while you can! I tell you, my life was taken from me when I was your age. I've had no life. I had no choice, but you, you Emma, you're making yourself impotent. You're cutting yourself off from life. What for? Tell me what's better than life?"

"I dedicate my life to God."

"What is God?"

She was silent. The god on the wall was silent. The whole minster was silent, the whole world.

"Shall I tell you? And I'm nearer the answer than anyone on earth. God is the power of life, the living essence of the earth, the cunning in the leechdom, the machinery of the stars, the hand of fate. It's in the world, Emma, not a picture on the wall of a stone prison. God's the eternal yes to everything."

He had not known what he was going to say, but as he said it he knew it was the truth.

She tried to speak.

"Jesus was his mother's child ..."

"Jesus was impotent – look!"

His frustration burst into fury. He flung out his hand and struck it against the wall, making it bleed.

"If Jesus was God he'd have killed them all!"

"Uncle, your hand's bleeding."

She reached out and took his hand, but he snatched it away.

"Uncle, Jesus was a leech, you said so."

"Leeches die."

This said so much of his despair she could say no more. Her green eyes pleaded with him but he could not see them.

He turned his stone head and spoke as if from the grave.

"I give you to Woden."

He went away. She made no attempt to help him and watched him sadly until he found the door and went out.

She turned to the altar and the elongated Christ that never was a man. She had made her sacrifice but felt guilty because the god on the wall looked dead to her.

Bald did not know what to do.

Emma was only fourteen, and impressionable, but he had recognised Eneda's stubbornness in her voice. He knew he could not change her. He feared Caech. While Eadgyth and Wulfstan might moderate him sober, one drunken fury would be the end of Emma.

His own existence was of no consequence, except that it had gone on too long. He lived in the communal grunt and wallow of the farm until the hot summer drove him out to become a hermit. He slept in woods and fed on worts he found by shape and smell. His senses sharpened by experience and he became conscious of the being, as opposed to the being seen, of nature. He began collecting worts and practising leechdoms, first for the forest folk and farmers and then for poor city people who could not afford the city leeches. A rumour spread of a blind leech who performed miraculous cures by touch, and a track was beaten in the dust from York. Lyb discovered his well, which was polluted, had magical properties, while Ulf and Liofa accepted the pennies Bald refused from grateful patients.

In the book:
"The third moon is not good to begin works, except to root out what is grown up again; to tame cattle, to castrate boars; do not sow a garden that day since idle worts will be produced. What is stolen will be quickly found. He who takes to bed will quickly be up again or will suffer long inconvenience. A child born that day will be spirited, greedy of others property; rarely he will become old; he will die by a bad death. A maiden likewise, and she will be laborious; she will want many men, and she will not be old. A dream is vain. It is not a good moon to let blood on."

Three women came cloaked from York, though the day was hot, with a discreet escort of servants. One was a portly matron who made numerous stops and drank a pint of Lyb's water which might have been Lyb's water. The second was a nun with an unsightly growth of hair on her face, who was, by chance, Haesten's daughter. The third was a young novice who kept her face veiled out of modesty or to hide her smiles.

Whilst the matron was resting by the well, the novice slipped into the house and spoke severely to Ginna and Toki about their questionable British morals until their blank expressions made her burst out laughing. Then Emma pushed back her veil and kissed her little mothers and called to Ulf and Liofa her brothers and Lyb her da' and told them she had come to say goodbye. In a month she would take her vows and leave the world. The kisses turned to tears.

Ulf and Liofa were to lead the ladies to find Bald in the forest. Ulf went ahead: Liofa came behind. His head was on the level of Sister Haesten's middle and he could not help seeing the jewelled cross she wore on a ribbon bouncing as she walked. It was a cruel temptation, as it had been to Haesten himself when he killed the abbot who wore it. Luckily Emma lingered by him. She was not sure how Bald would receive her visit.

They found him on his knees beneath the trees, spreading fresh-cut worts to dry in the sun. Yellow celandine, pink viperina, white dittany, silverwood, selfheal, hartclover, woodrose, wolfscomb, only a few amongst the vast variety that flowered in his simple world. The matron arrived and spread herself on the multicoloured carpet. Eadgyth asked for a leechdom for her friend.

In the book:

"In case the menses are suppressed; boil in ale brooklime and the two centauries, give her this to drink and breathe the woman in a hot bath and let her drink the draught in the bath; have ready prepared a poultice of beer dregs and of green mugwort, and marche, and of barley meal; mix them all together; shake that up in a pan and apply to the natura and to the netherward part of the vulva, when she goeth off the bath, and let her drink a cupful of the same drink warm, and wrap up the woman well and leave her so poulticed for a long time of the day, do so twice or thrice whichever you must. Thou shalt always prepare a bath and give the potion to the woman at that ilk tide at which the catamenia were upon her; inquire of the woman about that."

The queen turned to her companion.

"When is that, Sister Haesten?"

"The third moon."

Bald was trying to sort out his scattered worts and did not see the coin Eadgyth offered him.

"Here, leech, for you."

She put it into his hand. He fingered it for a moment.

"Lady, I know that head. Beware of the man with that head."

She went white. It was Caech's head and the coin was newly minted with the hammer of Thor on the reverse.

"Be careful what you say."

"Those near him should be careful. Take the money and give it to the poor."

"I've never seen anyone quite so poor as you."

"Me, woman? You're treading on my riches."

Emma thought it was getting out of hand.

"Uncle, you're talking to the queen."

"Are you here too? Yes, I suppose so. You're all suppressed."

"I've come to say goodbye."

He was silent, pulling at the flowers, scattering the petals.

She looked at him as if to commit his graven face to memory, then she moved away.

Sister Haesten bent down for a whispered consultation.

In the book:

"In order that the hair may not wax; take emmet's eggs, rub them up, smudge on the place; never will any hair come up there."

He had given the same leechdom to her mother.

Liofa followed the queen and her party back to the city. In a narrow street he darted up to Sister Haesten, seized the cross and tried to cut the ribbon with his knife. She cried out and grabbed hold of him. He stabbed her. The knife caught in the folds of her habit and barely scratched her skin. He ran. There were men-at-arms at both ends of the street and he was arrested and dragged to prison. He was fourteen years old.

VÍ

In the book:
"Thunder cometh from heat and wet. The air draweth the wet to it from beneath and the heat from above, and when they are gathered in one, the heat and the wet within the air, then they battle with one another with an awful noise, and the fire bursteth out through lightning and damageth crops if it be more than the wet. If the wet be more than the fire, then it is of advantage. The hotter the summer is, the more thunder and lightning there is in the year."

Because his victim was a nun, Liofa was judged by the ecclesiastical court presided over by Archbishop Wulfstan. Emma had witnessed the assault and was greatly distressed but she hoped for mercy from a Christian court. She knew Caech would have been merciless. She had been there when Caech made one of his infrequent visits to Eadgyth.

"Oh yes, I know the attack was aimed at me!"

"You were nowhere near the place."

"These dwarves serve the bastard in the corner and she wants to see me dead."

"What? The poor girl will take her vows in a few days' time and spend the rest of her life in a monastery!"

"I'd get the truth out of him!"

"Don't worry, the church will do that."

There was a righteousness in the queen's voice that made Emma shudder. Caech glowered at her, and when she turned away to the window the northern sky was glowing with fiery lights.

Liofa was tortured as a matter of course. There was no defence, and the only purpose of the court was to make him confess and repent before he was punished. This he did immediately but the torture continued long afterwards because nobody thought to stop it. It amused the torturers, good monks who were capable of anything except shedding blood, to stretch the boy. In three days he was stretched by three inches. Then he was carried before Wulfstan and condemned to death. The church would not kill him, so he was returned to the king's prison for justice to be executed. He was going to be hanged on the same day Emma was going to take her vows as a nun. She found herself stretched mentally between the theory and practice of the church. Liofa was guilty, the punishment was terrible, where was Christ?

As the day ended, the strange lights in the northern sky shone more fiercely with darting flames that made men search their hearts and consciences for reasons not to be destroyed.

Bald had returned to the farm. He could not see the red glow in the sky but felt the air heavy with heat and moisture, and knew a great storm was coming.

The small folk did not grieve. They grudged. Liofa was a pledge in the perpetual battle they fought against the world of giants. The old Britons, alone of all the races in the island, had known the golden age before the so-called civilisation of Rome. They were the only natives; all the rest were invaders. Britain had been taken from them, and they had been made slaves. From then on, their struggle to exist was itself a crime, and so robbery, deceit and murder were no crimes but part of the struggle. Oppression decriminalises the oppressed in their own eyes. It is no crime to steal from the state: everybody does it. So Liofa was a hero and a martyr. Lyb killed a pig and they feasted silently on the night of the execution.

Thunder rolled across the moors, and the lights flashed and flickered and bolts of flying starlight crashed to earth.

Some soldiers came running from the city, their faces streaked with sweat, calling out for Bald.

Lyb was still up and dragged Bald from his bed by the fire.

"What, is it day already?"

The captain said the queen sent for him and he was to come at once.

"Let her come here."

Bald heard the clank of metal and changed his mind. He took the book and pouch by habit and set off with them.

A hot wind was blowing, and there was the crack and roll of thunder. A great tree that had stood three centuries creaked and split, crashing to the ground and sending up a cloud of birds, and bats, bugs and beetles. They were blown back to York with the wind behind them and Bald in the middle, ragged and blown like a spectre against the red-streaked sky.

They entered Petergate and passed the vast bulk of the minster, creaking and groaning like a ship at sea. They were going to the palace, to the queen. Bald wondered what disaster was waiting for him.

Emma was awake. Sister Haesten had been breathing in her bath. The wind rattled the shutters and blew out the candles. Fiery shapes danced on the stone walls of the abbey.

Liofa was asleep. He and the hangman were the only two asleep in York. Both were drunk. The hangman was a Viking and usually drunk, and had entertained the dwarf who was going to entertain him tomorrow. Eadgyth was awake. She and Wulfstan were waiting agitated in the corridor outside the king's apartments which Bald knew well. Frightened courtiers and slaves appeared in the flashes of lightning like spirits awaiting the last judgement.

The captain brought Bald along the corridor to Eadgyth.

"Leech do you hear me? The king is unwell. He has been drinking. He sent a slave to fetch Aelfgifu; I fear he means her harm. Luckily the slave came to me."

Bald thought, she shows good Saxon courage, Eadgyth.

"I came to see the king. He started raving at me. He was - he was Viking, do you understand?"

Blood-eagle. Bald understood.

"Suddenly there was a great crash of thunder and lightning I think it struck him! He clutched his head and screamed! His head was – his head was split and he held it together with his hands! Oh God! He sat down and I left. I sent for you."

Wulfstan came close to Bald.

"We know you have reason to fear him."

"We don't want him to die!"

Eadgyth gripped Bald's arm. He felt her strength, her will, her Christianity. It actually meant something to her to keep this monster alive.

"Someone must come with me and tell me what he sees."

"I'll do it."

Wulfstan took Bald's arm and led him to the door and into the room. Bald heard the thunder rumbling and thought of Sigtryggr on his endless voyage across the moors. Sigtryggr's son was stricken in this room where he had struck Sigtryggr. He could hear Caech's breath breaking and gurgling in his throat.

Wulfstan gasped and started to pray.

"In nomine domini nostri ..."

"Tell me what you see."

"I can't describe it."

Wulfstan's voice was scored with dread.

"The king is sitting bent forward with his arms crossed over his head."

"Is he conscious?"

"Bald, I can't see! The candles are smoking. The only light is from the sky. Holy God!"

"What?" There was a crash of thunder.

"The clothes are ripped from his back. There's a burn mark on his back like – we're not meant to see such things!"

"Like what, man?"

"A cross. I can't see. The sky's red."

"Is there any blood?"

"No."

"Look at his head."

"It's covered by his arms."

"Move them."

"They're knotted and trembling. I can't touch him."

"Does the burn go up to his head?"

"Yes."

"Look closely. Is the head broken?"

Bald heard Wulfstan's breathing quicken and then stop as he drew in his breath.

"Yes, I think so. There's something white coming out between his fingers."

"You can come away now."

Wulfstan came close to him.

"Can you save him?"

"If it is his fate. I need four men to hold him. Send a monk to fetch eggs and honey and a length of tow, also the wort betony if they have any. I'll get the rest tomorrow."

He heard Wulfstan leave the room. He turned towards the rattle and scrape of Caech's breathing.

"Master, I'll help you live, but there's something you must do. The thief called Liofa: spare his life."

No answer but the rasping breath.

"And send the girl Aelfgifu away, she's a pagan like you and me and not fated to enter a monastery."

No answer.

"That's my bargain, master. It's a devil's bargain, agreed by silence."

Caech was silent.

"It is agreed."

People were entering the room. Wulfstan spoke and then Eadgyth.

"The men are here. The things you asked for are coming."

"Can you save him, leech?"

"For three days, lady, after that I don't know."

"We'll pray for him."

"There can be no executions and no vow takings while he lives."

"No, you're right. All things wait for the judgement of God."

In the book:

"For broken head, take betony, bruise it, and lay it on the head above, then it unites the wound and healeth it; and if the brain be exposed, take the yolk of an egg and mix a little with honey and fill the wound and swathe up with tow, and so let it alone; and again after about three days syringe the wound, and if the hale sound part will have a red ring about the wound, know thou then thou mayest not heal it. For the same take woodroffe and woodmarche and hove, and boil in butter and strain through a coloured cloth, apply it to the head, then the bones come out."

The storm broke.

Caech lay with his head wrapped in tow.

Liofa woke in his cell and was told he had been reprieved.

Emma returned to her cell wondering why God had not called her.

The minster was illuminated with candles, and twenty masses were sung for the king's recovery.

It rained for three days.

On the fourth day, the king's room was filled with jarls and ealdermen with divided loyalties. Wulfstan and Eadgyth entered with Bald.

A monk-leech unwound the tow from Caech's head.

The split was wide, and filled with what looked like scrambled egg. There was a red ring round it.

Everyone left the room apart from Bald and the monk.

Riders sped out of Petergate for the west and Dublin to summon Guthfrith and the king's son Cuaran.

Riders clattered across the bridge to the south and Tamworth where Athelstan, alerted by Eadgyth, was waiting with his soldiers under arms.

The monk rewound the tow and left. Bald sat in the window feeling the afternoon sun on his face.

He heard the harsh breathing stop and start. It was only a matter of time. He thought, in the end it's only a matter of time. We have our seasons and then no more. Was it any better to live to winter than to die in spring?

"Kingslayer."

The word was rough-sculptured breath. He thought he knew what Caech wanted.

"There's no need, master. You've been slain by God. You'll go straight to Valhalla."

"For my funeral ship."

"What will you have me do?"

"Burn York."

Eadgyth gave her husband a Christian funeral and his body lay on a catafalque in the minster. A week later, Athelstan's soldiers entered York, and meeting some resistance, set fire to the palisades on the walls. The flames spread to nearby houses and caught the summer-dry stocks supporting the ancient wooden hulk of the church which went up in a giant crackling explosion of Viking laughter, fire and flames.

Athelstan came and sent Eadgyth back to Polesworth. He left Edmund in York and marched north to meet Constantine king of the Scots, and then west to subdue the kingdom of Strathclyde and chase Guthfrith out of England.

In the meantime Liofa lay in prison under sentence of death and Emma went to see Edmund.

The air was still acrid with smoke and floating ash.

Edmund was embarrassed and conscious of his importance as regent of York. He sweated in a purple robe of state.

Emma was self-conscious. Her head had been shaved and was now growing a stubble that itched under her veil. Her novice's habit was tight, and stained with sweat under the armpits.

They were waiting.

"Edmund, will you tell me what's happening?"

"What?"

"They won't let me be a nun and they won't tell me why."

"It's Athelstan."

"Athelstan what?"

He knew more than he wanted to say.

"Athelstan what, Edmund?"

"Nothing."

"Seriously Edmund."

She said it with a smile, but childhood was over and it made him irritable and resentful.

"He wants you to be free to marry someone."

"Marry someone! Who?"

"I don't know."

"Why?"

"I suppose because your Sigtryggr's daughter. You have a claim to York."

"He's taken York."

"He collects things. He's careful. He's got a collection of relics."

"Thanks."

Sarcasm was lost in the gap that had grown between them.

"I shan't marry anyone!"

"It's not up to me."

"But if it was? Edmund?"

"I don't know."

But he did know and it was obvious. She knew too. It was their marriage that separated them. They stood for a long time looking past each other as if fate for once was wrong and two lines destined to meet were going to pass by.

Wulfstan entered the room.

"Sister Aelfgifu, I've looked into the matter and the sentence of the court must stand."

"But he didn't kill anyone."

"Only by the grace of God."

"Well only by the grace of God don't kill him!"

"I don't: the church never does. It's all in the hands of the king."

She turned to Edmund.

"You see? It's your responsibility."

"Athelstan said no. I'm sorry."

"He's not here. You can change the sentence. Edmund, Liofa's my brother!"

She forgot herself and moved towards the boy, pushing back the veil so she could look at him directly.

He saw how ugly she looked with the stubble and sweaty skin and clumsy adolescent body. He saw all that and he loved her.

"I can't!"

"You can! You're going to be king, everyone knows that. You can!"

Wulfstan smoothly intervened.

"No, Aelfgifu. I'm afraid even his grace cannot alter the sentence."

"I'm not Aelfgifu!"

She was not. She was Eneda's daughter.

"If the church won't help my brother, I don't want to be in the church. If Christ won't help him, I don't want to be a Christian. And if you, Edmund, won't help him, I won't marry anyone, not even you. No, I'm not Aelfgifu, I won't be Aelfgifu. I'm Emma!"

She pulled off the veil and threw it on the floor and stamped out of the room. Wulfstan shook his head. "Viking blood."

Emma did not return to the abbey. She walked up Petergate past the smouldering heap of wreckage that had once towered over York, and went out of the city towards the farm.

Later, when Edmund sent for her, the slave returned to say she was missing. He was alarmed. He was frightened of losing her, and he knew Athelstan would be furious.

He sent out soldiers, Saxons not Danes, who knew where she would be.

"When you find her, tell her I've changed the sentence. Liofa will be exiled for six years. Tell her that and bring her back."

They searched the city and the surrounding countryside. When they came to the farm, Emma and Bald had gone.

VII

They were hunted.

Athelstan would not be thwarted. He had added 'basilicus' to his titles, emperor, the first and only emperor of England. He needed Emma to oppose to a new claimant to the kingdom of York, Guthfrith's son Olaf, a direct descendant of the Viking Ivarr. The Danes settled in East Anglia and Northumbria resented a Wessex overlord and looked to Olaf Guthfrithsson as their natural king. Emma, Ivarr's granddaughter, married to Edmund, would give the semblance of unity to Athelstan's empire.

They were hunted like deer in winter through the forests of the north. Bald fled by instinct westward, away from the Roman roads. He was indifferent to night or day and Emma had to make him stop and rest at some peasant's hut or woodcutter's fireside. They repaid their hosts with simple remedies. So Emma learned to be a leech acting as Bald's hands and eyes.

When the nights grew cold and there were no friendly habitations to be found, they lay under his plaid together by their own open fire. She had no fear or inhibitions. He was so far from desire, which in his blindness was a forgotten country, he had only the comfort of her warmth.

Sometimes she stirred in his arms, like a bulb under the frozen ground, and grasped him in the innocence of sleep. He lay passive and inert, the ancient brainstem blinded. He did not dream.

They were hunted, and heard the hunters' horses on the iron ground, hooves ringing and the baying of hounds.

In the book:

"If anyone have with him this wort which we named peristereon, he may not be barked at by dogs."

Vervain, or holy wort, was worshipped and used in sorcery. Bald had a little dried dust in his pouch and scattered it to confuse the scent.

As the leaves fell, they lost the protection of the forest and were driven westward, climbing now into the foothills of Wales. The shepherds they met were hostile and spoke no Saxon, hurled stones and cursed them in a language composed entirely of consonants. Like ancient Hebrew, the vowels were lost somewhere in history.

One misty morning, they suddenly came across a man who drew his knife. Emma shouted. Bald swung his staff and by God's help or Woden's struck the man senseless. They took a goat and fled.

Under the shelter of a crag, Bald butchered the goat and left the meat to freeze. In the morning the blood was like rubies.

Bald had always been a creature of the woods and in that winter Emma changed from the adolescent plump novice of York to a rather angular oread, as shy as a deer, and as desperate. Survival sculptured her like a bronze newly discovered and shining with the patina of ages. She learnt survival was the business of man, and learning art and politics were the business of god.

They climbed the gorse-covered hills and lay up in hides of dead bracken, and left their enemies far behind.

One bright day early in a new year, they fell among thieves.

Bald had ventured down from the hills for food. Emma led the way along a green fold towards a small hamlet caught in the curve of a river. The small stone houses were little bigger than the shelters the Welsh built for their sheep. They lay scattered in an irregular ring like an ancient monument.

Bald stopped and sniffed the air.

"Horses!"

"No. There's only the smoke from the little houses. No place for horses to hide."

"How far is the forest?"

"No forest, uncle, the hills slope down to a river. Let's go on."

"I don't trust these people."

He stumbled on. He did not trust his own instincts.

The day was cold and bright and calm. Some sheep brought down for the winter huddled in the fold. There were no people.

Emma left Bald and went towards the nearest house to ask for food. As she approached, the rough wooden door flung open and a horse and rider burst through the doorway and charged towards her.

She turned and fled.

Too late.

Riders emerged from all the houses, small dark men on wild ponies which they rode without saddles or reins, grasping the long manes and gripping the flanks with bare legs and feet. They wore belted plaids and carried spears of ash.

Bald heard the thud of hooves and caught the stench of men and horses. He called her name and felt Emma throw herself against him.

"What are they?"

The riders circled them and he felt the brush of horse or man and flinched from the snorting nostrils and trampling hooves.

"I'm Bald the leech. I'm no harm to you. Look, I'm blind."

Emma clung to him.

"What are they, uncle?"

"God knows!" Which god?

Hands gripped him. Emma screamed. He felt her being dragged away from him and clamped his arms around her, shouting.

"Leave the girl! For Christ's sake!"

She was prised from his side, torn inch by inch away by many hands.

"Hold me, uncle, hold me!"

Her body, arms, the stretch of cloth were slowly drawn through the clasp of his hands and fingers.

"Emma!"

He heard her cry and then even that was gone in the churning of the earth as the riders went as suddenly as they had appeared, like raiding jackdaws.

The inner light by which he lived went out. Blackness took hold of his mind as it had his body. He was as good as dead.

He did not know how long he stood in that damned place.

Nature itself dragged him back to some sort of consciousness.

Cold and hunger penetrated the numbness of his feelings.

He moved at last, like an insect with its antennae probing the way with his staff. He touched the wall of one of the houses and felt for the doorway. The single room stank of horse and man. The villagers who lived there must have fled.

A residual warmth drew him to the hearth where he found a flat loaf of bread and a pannikin of water.

He lay down.

He would not let himself think of Emma or what fate she was undergoing. Fate was wordless, ruthless, pointless.

The riders were fate.

He thought the end of his life was worse than the beginning, and the beginning was worse than death, whatever that was.

It would be better to be dead, if Emma was dead, whatever that was.

He slept like one dead.

When he awoke, he could not tell if it was day or night. He reached out and felt the cold charred wood in the hearth. He knelt and dipped his fingers into the water, and washed his blind eyes by habit. He groped for the book and staff and rose unsteadily to his feet.

He had a purpose.

He shuffled to the doorway and felt the cold wind coming from the north. He went outside.

The river had to be to the east.

He walked with firm steps until the grass petered out beneath his feet and he was treading on sand and stones and he could hear the water rippling.

He welcomed its iciness.

He had long expected death. Only Emma had stood between him and death of one kind or another, at the hands of Athelstan's soldiers, at the teeth of wolves, or at the fatal grip of winter. Now he would finish what fate had started and drown the last stubborn trace of life in his body.

He waded out into the river and felt the current tugging him and the river calling him with a thousand whispers.

He waded deeper, and a numbness crept up from his feet to his calves and thighs, like a slow poison.

A little further and he would fall, and be carried down a congealing corpse to meet Cild, or Sigtryggr, or Caech, or all, or none, or Eneda ...

Then, as if nature was a watchful dog, he had an unbearable griping in his belly and a fierce tenesmus in his bowels that drove every purpose from his mind but one!

In this, his last moment, his first instinct reasserted itself with an all-powerful impulse that had to be obeyed.

He turned and struggled back against the current, running and splashing through the shallows, until he reached the bank and stumbled and squatted like a child, head bowed, hands clenched, defeated by nature once again.

When he had relieved himself, the will to die had gone. Die he would, blind and alone. Let nature do it. He even felt a perverse sort of satisfaction.

He dried himself and sat down to wait.

He had a certain ironic pleasure in trying to decide what would kill him first: the cold, hunger, wolves, the villagers returning to their ravaged cottages. Would he feel axe or knife, or stone most likely? The last thing he expected was the hand that touched his arm.

He barely felt it, so light it was like a dead leaf, but he knew it was Emma.

It was Emma, and Emma was alive. It was Emma, and Emma was silent. He should have felt relief, gratitude, thanks to God! Instead he felt the hand of fate crushing him, so light the touch, so heavy the meaning.

She was only a young girl, and this, and this.

"I found some houseleek growing on a roof. I squashed it and put it on the place. What else shall I do, uncle?"

In the book:

"For sore of womb take this wort houseleek, pound it and lay it thereto; it alleviates the sore."

He felt her hand tremble. Rage rose in him and he shook. Did god ever blush? God? What god? Nature … nature … nature. He breathed again. What leechdom was there for a rape? None. For the consequences then?

"Comfrey."

"It's winter." Her voice was like a sliver of ice in his heart.

"The yellow pansy grows in winter, we call it bonewort and find it in the cracks of stone of a wall. The yellow, Emma, not the white. Make a poultice of the leaves and push it into your cunt. Stir the seed in water and drink it and wash yourself again in it. Come back when you've done it."

He felt her hand tighten when he said the word. He wanted to shock her. He wanted to bring himself down to her level. He wanted to feel what she felt.

He could not even see that chasm, let alone span it.

Rape is instinctive to man and so the consequences are unimaginable. It struck him there was no love in nature, no place for love. The riders raiders rapists were a force of nature designed for survival as impersonal and irredeemable as the lightning that struck Caech, and perverted as the axe that clove Cild.

The image of the blood eagle burned behind his eyes.

He saw Emma spread and bleeding.

How did she feel?

She was still alive, sacrificed but still living, crucified but still alive.

Was she violated or sanctified? Nature's survivor or god's holy victim? Was what had happened a tragedy to rattle heaven or one of nature's accidents?

Age had not made him any wiser than he was before.

Emma returned with food and water. All he could say was:

"It was done for a purpose."

He had meant to comfort her, but her silence was more telling than a scream.

"For a purpose, Emma. If you don't believe me, we must find Dunstan."

"Dunstan?"

"Someone must answer for god."

VIII

A morning mist rolled over the isle of apples, the holy island in a sea of brambles, woods and marshes, where no horse trod, no hawk flew, no shod foot profaned the soil since it was trodden by a holy man whose master had sat at the Last Supper. But Glastonbury was old in worship long before St. Philip's disciples came and built the first church in Britain, whose wattle walls still stood ten centuries later.

The island and the tor were at the heart of an ancient mystery that had nothing to do with god and everything to do with Britain. Nature has her favourites, and islands are blessed and continents are cursed. Britain was blessed with a natural profusion of flowers and fruits, worts and woods, fish and fowls, crops and pastures, watered and wooed by the sun, wintered kindly, with gentle rivers and moderate mountains. Nature made her abode here and her oracle was in the watery pearl of Glastonbury. It was the spiritual well of England.

The first church was dedicated to the Virgin Mary. This too was a mystery. The mother of god was honoured first in Britain.

A little to the east, a small stone oratory was built four centuries later by St. David.

A hundred years on and a third chapel was added and attributed to twelve good men from the north.

In seven hundred, King Ine of Wessex built a square basilica with a tiled floor with strange geometric patterns where spitting was forbidden.

Saints abounded. Patrick, David, Bridget, Gildas among the remembered, countless others in the monks' cemetery presided over by two ancient pyramids between which a king was buried.

Clustered round the churches were the huts and hovels of the monks who continued the community above ground.

The mist rolled up and a town appeared on the skirt of the rising ground.

The two travellers coming from the north, rising from the marsh around the thickly wooded tor, could not see the town.

The old man saw nothing, and the girl watched the track of ancient tree-trunks laid from hummock to hummock.

"Yellow worts grow in soft ground, Emma, red are safe to tread on. The last time I came here, it was spring."

He was a boy and had carried the book for Cild. It was heavier when they left. Cild had copied the medical texts of Galen, Isaac Judaeus, Constantine the African, and Avicena, which lay buried in the library.

"There was a piece of Aaron's rod in the old church, and a little vial of something they said was the Virgin Mary's milk."

"Did you believe them?"

"There are greater miracles in nature. Milk itself. A cow only eats grass and yet it makes milk."

"Women can do anything." She laughed.

It was the first time she had laughed. He lost his thoughts and bumped into her. She turned and held him firmly.

"Careful, old man." She looked up at his pearled eyes. "Do you think we'll find Dunstan?"

"The apple doesn't fall far from the tree. Joseph was here, they say, who buried Jesus. Can you see the churches?"

Emma looked. There were three dingy little buildings in the mist and the rising bulk of the burnt-out basilica. Bald remembered.

"You see the little wattle church that looks as if it's grown from a tree with interlacing branches?"

She saw the roof had fallen in, and crazy rafters propping up the walls.

"Yes, uncle."

"It's nearly a thousand years old."

It looks it, she thought.

"The two chapels aren't much, but the basilica has a marble floor and the altar's covered in gold. There must have been a hundred books in the library."

A cock crew. The flock came flying out of the gaping doorway of King Ine's church. A boy in a tattered robe, his head roughly tonsured, swept out a drift of droppings.

A woman with baby at breast came out of one of the cells, yawning. She went to a well below a rock where a spring trickled red water over the moss and spat in it for luck or out of habit.

Somewhere a bell began to toll and a monk rose from the same cell like Lazarus pulling on his cerements.

Other monks in ragged habits emerged, a dozen or more, and a small rabble of children dispersing to collect sticks or eggs or chips of coloured tiles swept indiscriminately from the basilica.

"Isn't it magnificent?"

He could not see her rueful smile but heard the disappointment in her voice.

"I think we've come a long way for nothing."

They asked for Dunstan. A monk showed them a stone cell where a man could neither stand nor lie straight but could not say when or even whether Dunstan had ever lived there. He was staying in the town. They walked down to the line of houses along the riverfront. Most of them were new having been built of stones taken from the ruined churches. There was a quiet air of prosperity. Some ships were anchored in the river.

They were directed to a solid villa set in a pleasant garden where easter worts were flowering in the morning sunshine.

Dunstan himself answered the door.

He seemed confused to be discovered in such comfortable surroundings by two such biblical characters; Bald spare, barefooted, blind, and Emma ragged and withdrawn, a contemporary Tamar. He was plumper and had less hair than before, and Emma thought he looked like an ember goose.

The villa belonged to the widow Aethelfleda, a relation of the king, who could remember seeing Alfred when she was a girl.

"We live here in retirement. It's not far from the royal villa at Cheddar. You know our cousin Athelstan?"

Dunstan answered, "The king was sister Aelfgifu's sponsor at her christening."

"Aelfgifu the Viking girl? My goodness, what are you doing in Glastonbury?"

Emma was silent. Like Bald, she was uncomfortable in comfortable surroundings.

"I suppose you've seen what the Vikings did to our poor abbey?"

"The library?" Bald turned to where he thought she was.

"Burnt to the ground. Didn't you see?"

"I'm blind."

Dunstan told her, "This is Bald the leech who cured king Alfred."

"Is it? Then why doesn't he cure himself?"

Dunstan was embarrassed. Aethelfleda had the offensive candour of the rich and simple.

"I'm afraid some conditions are incurable."

"Well then, do a miracle!"

She was a crass and kindly soul, and insisted they stayed with her. When else would she have two such notorious guests to boast of to her friend Aethelwynn?

Dunstan took them out to the garden and showed them his retreat complete with desk and forge where he wrote and drew and created intricate jewellery. He was apologetic.

"Aethelfleda takes what I say too literally. She's a good Christian."

He took Bald's arm confidentially.

"But I can't perform miracles."

"I know." said Bald.

"Have you tried your own leechdoms?"

"We're not here for that."

"It's well-known doctors seldom treat themselves. Priests pray for their own souls all the time."

Bald lowered his voice.

"Can Emma hear us?"

"No. Aethelfleda's coming out and she's gone to help her down the steps. You must stop calling her Emma now she's sister Aelfgifu."

He watched the girl with pride. The garden like a bright enamel brooch bespoke his pride, as did his spotless habit. Bald gripped his arm and stopped him.

"She's not a nun and never will be now. She lost what faith she had."

"That's nothing, Bald, we all do every now and then. It's something you pagans don't understand. You think we're blind because we believe in what we cannot see. We see all right, my friend: ruin, poverty, hunger, murder, and the death of children. We doubt God exists, or if he does, is good."

His voice was happy, and he talked of horrors second-hand like a politician. He is blind, not me, thought Bald. He has seen nothing and I have seen almost everything.

"But if it was all fine and wonderful, there would be no need for faith at all. There can't be faith without doubt, or good without evil. When we realise that, we come back to God."

"She can't be a nun because she's not a virgin any more."

Dunstan drew in his breath with a hiss as if a cat had come into his garden, or a serpent.

"That's serious but it's not insurmountable."

"She was seized by a gang of robbers – seized – torn – violated –"

"No, no."

"I can't cure her, Dunstan, can you?"

Dunstan was silent. Bald heard a thrush whistle in alarm. The others were approaching. Dunstan murmured,

"Ah God, why is it always the children?"

Aethelfleda's voice came floating like the note of a flute.

"What are you talking about?"

"Bald's eyes."

"Damn my eyes. Woden closed my eyes so I wouldn't see what I have seen."

"God will open them for you." She might have said, "for me" because God was her friend. Dunstan intervened.

"Sometimes, Aethelfleda, it's better not to see, or hear, or know what's going on in the world. You for instance have kept yourself uncontaminated for sixty years, haven't you?"

"Fifty-two. Apart from the time I spent with my husband."

"Now Bald here is – how old are you, Bald?"

"Ancient." Said Emma.

"And perhaps we ought to leave him in peace."

I'm dying, thought Bald, drowning in unction. Ivarr would have been more merciful. The old lady was merciless in her goodwill.

"Shall we walk to the abbey before dinner and Dunstan can tell you how he dreamed it was going to be?"

Dunstan's vision was of a resplendent abbey enclosing the four churches in one, proclaiming prosperity and pride. It was entirely compatible with Athelstan's empire, a corpulent heart in a corporate body.

Bald could feel the mass of stone bearing down on him, and Emma pitied the poor little wooden church where Mary was at home. Nothing more was said about her by Dunstan and Bald as the treatment began.

In the book:

"For pearl, an eye salve; take ashes of broom and a bowl full of hot wine, pour this by a little at a time thrice on the hot ashes, and put that then into a brass or copper vessel, add somewhat of honey and mix together, apply to the infirm mans eyes, and again wash the eyes in a clean well spring.

For pearl on the eye apply the gall of a hare warm for about two days, it flieth from the eyes.

Against white spot, take an unripe sloe and wring the juice of it through a cloth on the eye, soon in three days the spot will disappear if the sloe be green.

Against white spot, mingle together vinegar and burnt salt and barley meal, apply it to the eye, hold thine hand a long while on it.

For pearl an eye salve; take seed of celandine or the root of it, rub into an old wine and into honey, add pepper, let it stand for a night by the fire, use it when thou wilt sleep."

Bald did not sleep much.

"This is the best eyesalve for eye pain, and for mist, and for pin, and for worms, and for itchings, and for eyes running with teardrops, and for every known swelling: take feverfue blossoms, and dills blossoms, and thunder clovers blossoms, and hammer worts blossoms, and wormwood of two kinds, and pulegium, and the netherward part of a lily, and coloured dill, and lovage, and pellitory, and pound the worts together and boil them together in harts marrow or in his grease, and mingle oil besides; put them a good mickle into the eyes, and smear them outwardly, and warm at the fire; and this salve helpeth for any swelling, to swallow it and to smear with it, on whatever limb it may be."

And when that failed to stop the burning:

"Rex glorie Christie raphaelem angelum exclude fandorohel auribus famulo dei + illi + mox recede ab aurium torquenti sed in raphaelo angelo sanitatem auditur componas + per."

Which did not do Bald any good at all.

He washed his eyes at the white spring near the red spring and it was this that, after several weeks, began the cure.

There was a bird, a sparrow, trapped in Dunstan's strawberry net. Emma saw it flutter from her window and ran down to release it. As she flew into the garden she saw Bald walk along the row of strawberries, stoop and untangle the sparrow and cup it in his hands. Her spirits leapt. She called out: "Dunstan! Dunstan!"

Bald turned. The sparrow flew from his hands and scudded just above the ground towards the steps just as Dunstan came running from the villa. It flew under his foot as it came down and crushed it, popping out its heart.

Bald came up to the steps and saw the sparrow and the tiny red heart still pulsating in the dust. His eyes filled with tears which lay translucent on the melting marble like water on ice. He looked up at Dunstan, whose own eyes widened at the sight.

"Bald, Bald, it's a miracle."

"Yes, master, you're the only man who ever trod on a sparrow."

Emma buried the sparrow and said a prayer for the first time since she left York.

Aethelfleda had a good influence on all of them. She refused to recognise anything that might disturb the peace of her well-ordered existence. Bald's grittiness was smoothed over by the pearl of her complacency. Dunstan found in her sublime confidence that comfort his nervous ambitious and creative soul required. Emma was mothered. The old lady's instinct divined her deep distress and provided an ample bosom, both physical and spiritual, for her to lie on.

Aethelfleda, however, had her own problems and one fine day when Dunstan and Emma had gone to climb the tor, she confided them to Bald.

In the book:

"For kernels or swelled glands which wax on the groin take this wort lapatium and pound it with old grease without salt, so that of the grease there be by two parts more than of the wort; make it very well mixed into a ball, and fold it in the leaf of a cabbage, and make it smoke on hot ashes, and when it be hot lay it over the kernels and wreathe it thereto. This is best for kernels."

"An infusion of the root is good for constipation." added Bald.

"I've lived a chaste and virtuous life, as my friend Aethelwynn or anyone will tell you." Athelfleda was not quite sure what constipation was.

Emma broke through the tangled thicket that covered all but the top of the tor. Looking round she saw the marshes and rivers shining like glass. There was no life on this bald tonsure of land but silence, stillness and purity. On the ascent, Dunstan had told her stories of an ancient people who lived on Ynis Witrin, the isle of glass, and sacrificed a virgin to the goddess Bel on the first day of spring. She stood on the highest point, a pile of stones from some early settlement, and raised her arms to the sun.

Dunstan toiling up the top slopes stopped and stared at the cross she made against the sky. He had been moved by Emma's violation and now was seized by the shuddering certainty this was a vision sent to him by God. Her suffering would save her.

There would be another miracle. He had forgotten the sparrow.

He had been reading on the subject, and quoted St. Augustine aloud.

"Thus the sanctity of the body is not lost provided the sanctity of the soul remains, even if the body is overcome, just as the sanctity of the body is lost if the purity of the soul is violated, even if the body is intact. St. Augustine said that, Emma."

She lowered her arms and turned with her head bowed. He thought how young she looked. Her voice was soft and clear.

"Was he ever raped?"

His world of worthy platitudes was shaken by the question of a child. All the wordy books of the fathers of the Church were outweighed by a sparrow's tiny heart.

Bald resented the return of the light and the sight of a world he thought he would never see again. Illness is a retreat from reality, like madness. Seeing is also exposure.

Each day after he endured the leechdoms and washed his eyes in the white spring, he saw a little clearer, and what he saw opened a pit of despair.

He knew Emma had suffered but never imagined the grey and haggard creature he now saw, like a ghost. Her childhood had fled. Her youth had been wrenched from her. She had changed suddenly like an animal of the forest from fawn to hunted deer.

Her eyes had lost their trust. He was more shocked by the sight of her because Aethelfleda had dressed her as a woman in her own royal purple-edged robes. It made her look to him like a mourner at a funeral, one of those elongated saintly women in the corner of a crucifixion. She was sixteen.

Sight and the soft life stirred his desires.

Aethelfleda gave him a tunic of Welsh wool and leather sandals for his horned feet. He bathed, and a slave shaved the stubble on his head. He began to dream again.

He dreamed he was following a woman dressed in black through an underworld of tunnels and caves. He never saw her face, but knew quite well who she was. Eneda had returned to him, and was leading him somewhere he did not wish to go.

It disturbed him all the more because the blackness had grown round him like the night, and he was too old for another dawn. His imagination had painted a kinder picture than he saw in the ruin of the little wooden church or Aethelfleda's blotchy complexion.

He would have left Glastonbury, had it not been for Emma.

She spent more and more of her time on the tor.

He asked her what she did up there alone.

"I'm not alone, uncle."

"Who's with you?"

"No-one."

He knew better than to ask further. There were more souls in Glastonbury than bodies.

He spoke to Dunstan, who was concerned.

"There's only one person who's never alone, and that's the devil."

"Do you think Emma's possessed by the devil?"

"She was possessed by devils, Bald."

"What can we do?"

"I don't know. It will shock her but I think we have to talk to Aethelfleda. She's a woman."

The old lady was unshockable.

"I knew something had happened to the girl. She'll recover."

"I regret to say it, but she'll never recover her virginity."

"Virginity is a nuisance!"

Dunstan was shocked.

"How can you say that, Aethelfleda? Christ was a virgin. His mother was a virgin. All the first rank of saints were virgins, men like John the Baptist, John the Evangelist, Paul, Clement, Gregory."

"All women have a problem with the virgin Mary, Dunstan, and the rest are men."

"You believe in the immaculate conception?"

"Conception yes, parturition no."

"The church has not pronounced on parturition."

Blind, thought Bald, blind.

"As for female virgins, there's a calendar of them. Agatha, Eugenia ..."

"She pretended to be a man and entered a monastery."

"Constantia, Anatolia, Victoria ..."

"Yes! And all the other silly girls who preferred death to marriage. Foolish virgins, Dunstan. The wise ones married and begot children. Where would the world be else?"

She was a stout old body and defended herself well.

"No! If to be a virgin was the height of virtue, I'd have been one, I assure you!"

Dunstan realised he was on soft ground and neatly turned the argument.

"But you are chaste, Aethelfleda, and chastity is only secondary to angelic beatitude. I'm celibate myself."

Ay, thought Bald, and so am I, worse luck. Aloud he said, "So you think she'll get over it?"

"Women are stronger than men, suffer more, endure more, and come to an everlasting glory in the halls of heaven. If you had to put up with it, you'd know!"

It was all, then, rape of a kind, blessed by the church or not. He knew it was in nature, the female seized, torn, violated. Creation was violent, an act of violence.

The violence of spring was all around him in the garden. Flowers and worts forcing a way upward and bursting open. A mushroom lifting a stone the size of a cathedral to it in its growth. A sparrow trampling its mate and flying off, whistling. Nature revelled in violence like a Viking.

He thought of Eneda. She had got over it several times, he thought. He felt better.

Then Emma disappeared.

It was evening. She had gone to the tor and not returned. Dunstan hurried to the abbey and asked if anyone had seen her. Some children had in the morning, but no-one since. He wanted to send the monks to search for her, but all refused. It was late, they said, and growing dark, and the ground was dangerous, but he knew they feared meeting devils. Aethelfleda's slaves returned to the villa swearing they had been to the top of the tor and there was no sign of Emma. Now Bald suspected they had gone no further than the lower slopes because the Britons still believed in Bel.

Bald would have searched himself, but his sight was bad enough by day and the tor was dangerous, loose rocks and deep fissures defending her fastness.

So it was Dunstan who took a lantern and a staff and went off into the dark bravely and fearfully.

He passed the four churches and the valley where the red and white springs splashed from overhanging ledges of rock. It was a summer night and a light mist hung like a curtain, veiling the mystery of the tor.

He gripped his staff and plunged into the thicket at its foot.

The lantern was of little use, frightening him with shapes and shadows, and he soon abandoned it, leaving it hanging on a branch as a guide for the descent.

He climbed steadily, following a track that wound around the tor, rising from one level to the next like a labyrinth.

He remembered the ancient myths of maiden sacrifice: in that respect, he was not safe himself, and of the Celtic mother goddess Matrona whose crystal cave was said to be somewhere beneath his feet. He murmured prayers to Mary and St. Michael and, as he breasted the last level and came out into the sky, he half-expected to see a dozen druids waiting for him. There was nothing.

He was breathing heavily and sat down on a rock to recover. There was nothing, and yet he was conscious of a presence, and rose again.

The mist lay beneath him on the surface of the marsh like breath on a mirror. He looked around in wonder and then drawn by a dream, down to where the four churches lay like tumbled stones.

He did not see stones.

He saw a white abbey with a central tower and a great nave rising in a sheer clerestory of crystal glass buttressed by flying arches of pure marble.

He saw his abbey, his vision, his ice-white edifice of purity, floating on the black mirror of the marsh.

"It is." He spoke aloud. "It is."

It was a moment before he remembered his mission and turned away to look for Emma who might have fallen among the rocks and cracks. When he looked back, there was only darkness, and the fires of the monks shining like fireflies.

He set out on the descent.

He found the lantern hanging on the branch and went down into the valley of the springs. He came to the cascading water of the white spring and stopped to drink.

He noticed an effect never seen by daylight because it was so faint, a little gleam of moonlight in the water. Yet there was no moon. What light was that?

He put down the lantern and peered into the water as if into a mirror, which it was by day, and saw through the water that the rocks behind it were not solid but formed a cave. The glistening walls of the cave emitted a faint white light.

There was the white figure of a woman.

At first it was a pale pencilled outline with a few delineated features. He used to draw like that in the margins of his books: Christ, Mary, himself.

As she approached she became more like an effigy in church enrobed in purple, her pale face serene and just about to smile.

He felt a reawakening of faith.

It was Emma, she was here, she was alive, she was at peace with herself. He stepped back and Emma came through the curtain of water into the night.

She was cold and wet and wanted to go home. She held a piece of crystal in her hand.

Bald and Aethelfleda were waiting anxiously when they returned to the villa, and harsh questions softened into wonder at her story.

"I was coming down another way between two stones like gateposts, and the ground suddenly slipped from my feet and I fell into a hole. There was a tunnel going into the tor and the rock glowed in the dark. It led me into the middle, where there's a big hall as high as York Minster, uncle, with long white columns hanging from the roof and rising from the floor, and water running everywhere."

"A calciferous cavern." Bald had the answer.

"That's where the stories of Bel and Matrona come from." So did Dunstan.

"I always knew the tor was hollow." said Aethelfleda. "How did you get out?"

"The lady showed me the way."

The ground slipped from under their beliefs. Now they were lost in a dark cave of unknowing and needed her help.

"What lady, Emma?"

"My mother, uncle."

"Dressed in black?"

Emma nodded.

"What way, my dear, did the lady show you?"

"To follow the stream, which I did, and there was Dunstan waiting for me."

"She has seen St. Mary." Said Dunstan. "Aelfgifu has come back to us."

She saw Eneda, thought Bald. And aloud,

"Emma has come back."

"Who did you see, my dear? Who was the lady?"

"Dear Aethelfleda, she was my mother, and she gave me this."

Emma held out the crystal which she had kept clutched in her hand. It was a small vial in a net of gold wire, and held a drop of white liquid.

Dunstan knelt.

Aethelfleda smiled beatifically.

Bald stared as if he did not believe his newly discovered sight.

He had seen the vial before.

It was the vial of the Virgin's milk.

IX

Dunstan wrote a letter to Athelstan telling him about the miracle of St. Mary's manifestation and asking for an endowment to build a new abbey. He mentioned two more miracles: Bald's sight had been restored and Aethelgifu had returned to the faith.

Athelstan granted the abbey twenty hides of land and sent officers to Glastonbury with some precious relics and orders to arrest Bald and Aelfgifu and bring them to him at Tamworth.

He was faced with a great threat to his kingdom.

The Scots, the Northumbrians, the natives of Strathclyde and the Welsh had united with Olaf Guthfrithsson and the Vikings from Dublin to assemble the greatest army ever seen in Britain.

Olaf had brought his ships through the Clyde and the Forth and down the Humber to York, where he was received with acclaim by Danes and Saxons alike. Athelstan's ambitions and exactions united the north in the final struggle for independence against the south. The great battle between the rival dynasties of Alfred and Ivarr, between unity and chaos, was about to be fought.

Athelstan needed the marriage of Ivarr's granddaughter to his brother Edmund to sway the Danish settlers in Mercia and East Anglia to his side.

So he sent his officers to arrest her.

Bald and Emma were unaware of the mighty armies converging in the centre of Britain.

Bald was conscious of fate in the form of a feminine demiurge determined to convert him to her worship. He was half committed but he wanted something in return. He wanted to keep Emma.

He knew if the Virgin claimed her she would be lost in a monastery and a sterile life of servitude. Her spirit would be subsumed by grace. The grace of God was the beginning of death.

He began to look in his heart for Eneda, for Matrona, the

Mothers, for the woman in nature, to save Emma from the suicide of chastity and the renunciation of the world.

He knew the destructive power of impotence.

His search for Fornjot's palm had been his own lost journey. Now he set out on a spiritual crusade, naked except for the book, an eagle in the army of old gods against the new, the dagger against the cross, the raven versus the dove. Emma prayed.

The precious vial had been replaced in the old church and there she prayed night and day, long fasting vigils that delighted Dunstan though he did not join in them.

"What are you praying for?" asked Bald.

"I shall know when it comes."

It came one dawn.

She hurried up the hill because it pleased her to be in her pew before the monks rose.

It was full summer, and the earth stirred with life and sighed contentedly in the soft breeze that comes before sunrise.

She walked lightly past the cemetery not to disturb the sleep of kings. She crossed the shadow of the basilica and the two stone chapels and approached the wooden church that lay like an ark where it had landed ten centuries ago.

She entered, and was a trifle annoyed to see someone there already hunched in a corner.

She dipped her fingers in the wooden font and went to her place on the left of the altar where the relic had been buried for safety.

She waited for the channel of prayer to be opened to her.

She heard a movement and saw sideways the other person rise and sidle along the row towards her. The person was no taller than the backs of the benches. A child, she thought with annoyance and closed her eyes tight against the distraction.

The person sat next to her.

She became aware of a smell that took her back to her own childhood in York, to Lyb and the pigs, to her little family, to her brothers Liofa and Ulf.

She unstuck her eyes and glanced – looked – stared!

It could not be! Liofa was dead, hanged by Edmund.

The boy's hunted desperate face stared back at her out of his rags like a fox out of a sack.

It could not be, and yet it was Liofa!

"Liofa! Ave Maria! You need a bath!"

Martha probably said the same to Lazarus.

"Thank God, thank God you're alive! Kneel with me and pray. Here, Liofa, where a great treasure is buried, Mary Mother of God I didn't know how great!"

They knelt together and now he was as tall as she was. He looked where she had pointed and seemed to get some comfort from her words.

Emma was too excited to pray.

"Tell me what happened!"

"Edmund changed his mind."

"God bless Edmund!"

"Woden take him. He gave me six years in exile."

"But you're alive!"

The dwarf glanced at her. He had the old Briton's ignorance clad in the tattered arrogance of youth.

"I'd rather be dead than live anywhere else but here."

"How did you escape?"

"They put me on a ship in chains but I could slip my hands out of the manacles. The crew got drunk the night before they sailed."

"Didn't they chase you?"

"They don't have to. I'm an outlaw. If I'm found, I'm dead, anyone can kill me. So I chase myself."

"How did you find me, Liofa?"

"I have to eat, so I go into the villages at night for food."

"How can you afford it?"

"I steal it."

She was hurt and looked down, but he was full of his own predicament and went on hurriedly.

"It's easy. Nearly all the men have gone to war. The women go to church and leave their houses open."

"Stealing is wrong."

"There are armed men moving everywhere. At first I thought they were after me, but like the fools they are, they're going to kill each other. I was going to follow them. I heard da' say once the best time for ravens and robbers was after a battle."

"Oh Liofa, you're so young!"

"I had to grow up quickly in my head."

Indeed, his head was bigger and older in comparison to the rest of his body.

"Then I heard people talking about a miracle, and they spoke your name, Aelfgifu. A girl had seen the Virgin in Glastonbury. I suppose it's a miracle to see a virgin anywhere."

She turned away with distaste.

"Ay, look away! I'm four feet of pigshit!"

"You're a Christian, Liofa. God gave his life for you as much as anyone."

"Then why am I in trouble?"

She could not answer without confirming his opinion of himself.

"Aelfgifu, that's Emma, I thought. And I'm right!"

"But what can I do? How can I help you?"

She turned to him with wide eyes. He stood up and seemed to be smaller standing than he had been kneeling.

"I need money."

Emma shook her head helplessly. He seemed annoyed to have to explain it to her.

"Do a miracle."

"You don't understand, Liofa. I don't do them: she does."

"Tell her I need a hundred silver pennies to pay wergild and take the curse of exile off me, for Emma, I'll die out of this country."

Big tears came into his eyes and Emma cried to see them. He and his kind were bred out of the earth and loved it better than other men.

The bell for matins tolled.

She hurried him out and hid him in Dunstan's deserted cell where he fitted comfortably, and then ran down to the town to tell Bald.

These days, Bald's brain woke a full hour after he did.

The body went about its daily functions, but the brain slept like an ancient monster on the verge of extinction.

When Emma ran in and whispered urgently that Liofa was alive and here and hiding in the abbey, he thought she had seen another vision, another sign from god.

In the book:

"This wort, which is named betony, is found in meadows and on clean downlands, and in shadowy places; it is good whether

for the man's soul or his body: it shields him against monstrous nocturnal visitors and against frightful visions and dreams: and the wort is very wholesome and thus thou shalt gather it in the month of August without using iron: and when thou have gathered it, shake the mold till nought of it cleave thereon, and then dry it in the shade very thoroughly, and with its roots together reduce it to dust; then use it and taste of it when thou needest."

She looked at him with gentle pity.

"Liofa doesn't need betony, uncle, he needs money."

The old man sighed.

"Ah, mistress, even the dreams of the young are becoming mercenary."

"Who are you talking to?"

"I wish I knew."

He was picking his sarsen teeth with a sliver of ash. She touched his shoulder and shook him.

"Come and see." He rose politely and she felt a flicker of anger. "And bring your wits with you!"

The warmth of the morning uncongealed his blood and by the time they reached the abbey a little plan was germinating in his head. He crawled into the cell and saw the boy crouching there.

"It's Liofa!"

Emma keeping watch outside looked up to heaven.

"Help me, uncle."

"Yes I'll help you, I'll help you."

He squatted inches away from the boy's bulging head.

"Listen my son. I know where there's money, don't you fear. Go towards the west to the forest of Andred. Look for the Roman road and the river. Where the edge of the forest overhangs a scarp you'll find the hamlet your father came from. Ask for the thane's house. Go there secretly, and in the pond there's a bar of silver and a forger's dies."

His eyes were bright with memories and then came the flowering of his plan.

"On second thoughts, Emma and I will come with you, and see you safe!"

He smiled as if he heard a happy reprise and saw the prospect of reliving the days he had spent with Lyb and Eneda. Besides, he would take Emma away from the baneful influence of Dunstan and the Madonna and back to the fields of nature and the book.

"I'll go alone."

Liofa's discord jarred.

"What?"

"I'm an outlaw, and if you're found with me, we'll all hang."

He had a plan of his own. "I'll stay here until it's dark and then I'll go. Thanks, uncle, and God bless you."

Bald growled.

"I give you to Woden."

He crawled backwards out of the cell with bad grace. Emma was waiting.

"Well?"

"I've given him the proper leechdom for a thief: a mouthful of silver. He'll leave tonight. But Emma, we mustn't let him go on his own or he'll be caught and hanged. We'll follow in the morning."

"Where, uncle? Where are we going?"

"To your mother's house."

He knew it would catch her imagination, and she talked about it all the way to the villa.

They opened a door and a white dove flew out. Dunstan was singing in the garden, and a lyre hanging on the wall responded to the antiphon as his pure voice touched the strings.

They made no active preparations for the journey though when they passed each other the excitement thrilled between them and Bald felt he was alive again.

Aethelfleda died.

She had not been ill or shown any sign of the approaching end, but that night she would not go to bed and sat in a chair and kept the lamps burning.

Towards dawn she suddenly cried out and clasped her head.

Her slave called Dunstan, who immediately sent for Bald and Emma. When Bald entered the room, Dunstan was bent over Aethelfleda listening intently and nodding. She stopped talking and he moved away and Bald saw the old lady's face was as purple as her robe and her eyes bulged like oysters. He answered Dunstan's look with a shake of his head.

Dunstan called Emma.

"She wants to see the sacred relic, and only you and I know where it's buried. I have to give her the Eucharist. Run to the old church and fetch the vial."

Emma ran off.

Bald examined Aethelfleda more closely. Her life was visibly draining away. He brushed the straggly hair away from her face, and she smiled.

"Don't worry; I'm only dying."

Emma ran up to the abbey. The night was not dark and the tor was black against the sky.

She stopped at Dunstan's cell and softly called Liofa's name. The cell was empty. She sent a prayer into the sky after him.

She ran to the wooden church and along the aisle to the little altar and to the left of the altar. She stopped.

In the faint light through the open roof, she saw a black hole where the relic had been buried.

She gasped.

She knelt.

She felt inside the hole and felt a black hole of sickness and wretchedness open inside herself.

She looked up wildly and around wildly but there was no hope, no vision, no answer other than the one she knew already.

Liofa had stolen the vial and gone.

She had to return to the villa. What could she tell Aethelfleda, her friend, her benefactress?

Only the truth.

But Aethelfleda already knew the truth.

She lay in bed inert and snoring quietly. A cross of oil glistened on her forehead. Dunstan knelt holding her hand. Bald stood waiting for the coda of her life to end.

Emma went up to him and whispered.

"It's gone. Liofa took it. Shall I tell her?"

"It's too late to tell her anything."

So they stayed until the dawn came and Aethelfleda stopped breathing and turned her head towards the light. A white shadow crossed her face and she died.

Out in the marsh, Liofa stopped to see what he had stolen. He was disgusted. He ripped the thin gold wire from the vial and pushed it into his pocket. For a moment he wondered what the white substance was the crystal held. Then he cursed it and tossed it away.

Aethelfleda was buried in the old church in the place where the relic had been hidden. Her friend Aethelwynn, prioress of the abbey at Shaftesbury, came to the funeral.

Afterwards, in the villa, Dunstan read her will. She left her money to the abbey, her property to Dunstan, and Emma to the care of Aethelwynn with the request she would be accepted into the community of nuns at Shaftesbury.

Bald watched as Emma went and knelt by Aethelwynn and knew that he had lost her.

No sooner had the Virgin claimed Emma for her own than the Mothers snatched her back for the world.

Aethelstan's officers arrived in Glastonbury and arrested her. Aethelwynn returned to Shaftesbury. Before she left, Emma asked for her blessing.

"My dear Aelfgifu, you should rather bless me. You have seen St. Mary. You can be sure she has a special care for you and you are destined to serve her, if not in this life, in the next."

Dunstan grieved to lose both Bald and Emma. His own journey was long and difficult. Saints do not know they are going to be saints or they would not be saints.

As the small party of guards and prisoners left Glastonbury and the tor dwindled behind them to a finger in the sky, Bald smiled secretly to himself.

That was dangerous.

Know more than the gods, someone had said, but do not let them know it.

They travelled north to Watling Street and then east to where it met Ermine Street in a great cross at the centre of England. All along the way they were passed by men in twos and threes armed with scythe blades and pitchforks. All around the standing crops ripened under the sun. A mounted thane came by with his retainers armed with swords and spears, and once they saw the battalion of an ealderman or bishop in the distance.

As they neared the great crossroads, they mingled in a crowd of west Saxons, south Saxons, men of Kent, Mercians, Angles and Danes. England was rising, and in the rising, becoming England.

X

“Here King Athelstan
the giver of rings
Edmund the atheling
with swinging swords
at Brunanburh;
hewed the wooden line
these sons of Edward
by noble birth
against their enemies
for treasure and for home.
the Scottish lewds
fell to fate:
with warriors' blood:
at morningtide
slid over the deep
everlasting god
sank to rest.
slaughtered by spears
struck over their shields
weary of the ways of war.
all the long day
in hot pursuit
cut down the fugitives
with well-whetted blades.
in hard hand-fighting
The warriors of Olaf
In their ships' bellies
Fought against fate.
On the battlefield
In the sleep of swords:
Jarls of Olaf
Of sea-pirates and Scots.

the lord of warriors
and his brother together
won lifetime glory
in fatal combat
broke the shieldwall
with hammered blades
as it became them
as often in the camp
they fought for land
The hated cringed
and sea-pirates
the field bedewed
since sun-dawn
the shining star
god's bright candle
until the royal creation
Here lay soldiers
warriors of the north
ay and Scotsmen too
Wessexmen fought
with horse-warriors
of the loathed enemy
who fled the battle
The Mercians
spared no-one.
over the waters
longed for our land
Five of them lie
young kings
aye and another seven
and unnumbered hosts
There fled the field

The chief of the Norsemen forced by his fate
To take to his ship with a few followers.
The ship fled to sea the king flew off
On the falling tide to save his life.
There too the old man in fearful flight
to his northern clan fled Constantine
The hoary warrior: he had no cause
to boast of this battle bereft of kin
his friends fallen on the battlefield
slain in strife his son abandoned
in the slaughter-place ground with wounds
a child of wardeath: he cannot boast
the grizzly devil of the sword-clash
the old malignant: neither can Olaf
or the ruin of his army dare to laugh
at the business of battle or boast themselves better
in the field of war or in the strife of banners
or the meeting of spears or encounter of men
or clash of swords in the slaughter-lea
playing the game with Edward's sons.
The Northmen went off in their nailed ships
The sad survivors to Dingmere
And over deep water to look for Dublin
And back to Ireland in deep shame.
Then the two brothers both together
the king and the atheling sought their home
the land of Wessex with great war-glory.
They left behind them to share the corpses
The black-sheathed swart raven
Horn-beaked the grey-coated
White-tailed eagle to join the feast
The greedy war-hawk and greywild animal
Wolf of the forest. Never was such slaughter
In this island never folk felled like this
By the sword's edge as books tell us
And old sages since from the east
The Angles and the Saxons came up
Over the wide sea seeking Britain.
Proud warsmiths overcame the Welsh
Earls eager for glory created a country."

The minstrel rested his harp.

Sitting by the fire in Winchester, Emma thought it was not like that at all.

They had been riding north towards Tamworth. For days the sky was streaked and the air acrid with the smoke of burning crops. The road was jammed with men and cattle, and they took to the fields. Soon they were riding over blackened stubble, crackling and smoking, the horses stirring up sparks of smouldering straw.

The smoke thickened over Tamworth and the rider sent ahead returned to say the town was in ruins. The army of the north had sacked Tamworth and gone eastward in pursuit of Athelstan who had marched away down Watling Street.

The two captains Alfgeir and Grodrek decided to cut across country to catch up with him in the vicinity of Northampton. Two days' riding brought them in sight of the fort without any sign of the army. The nervous garrison sent them further to the east from where they hoped to receive reinforcements. Their alarm was reflected in the faces of the officers and the urgency with which they shook their horses onwards.

Emma watched Bald riding with his head nodding and his arms hanging by his sides. Aethelfleda's death made her watch him more carefully. It had come so quietly while no-one was looking.

She had no fear for herself. What could happen worse than had already happened? The rape had exposed her to the blunt dagger, the death that was not fatal, and she had triumphed. The wound had healed and she was stronger than before. She began to understand the purpose of suffering, which was just as well.

They forded the river Nene and climbed the rising ground that edged the great plain stretching far to the north and east until it merged with the waters of the Wash where sometimes it was land and sometimes sea.

Away to the south lay the forest of Brunenswald like a great green sea itself.

Alfgeir and Godrek reined in their horses and one by one the others breasted the hill and stopped in sudden awe at the scene below them. Emma remembered the sound.

It was the humming of a field of insects on a summer day, a breeze among the leaves and flowers of summer, a thousand whirrings and stirrings.

What she saw were thousands on thousands of men encamped on the plain and the sound was their moving, talking and laughing, the whetting of scythes and swords, hammering of shields, sharpening of axes, cutting of spears, saying of prayers.

The plain shimmered and vibrated as if it was water and the weapons were reeds waving in the wind, and the men were midges and mayflies with one day to live.

There were birds she saw circling above the host, hawks and ravens, and high above them, eagles.

Bald rubbed his eyes.

"Athelstan?"

"No, leech. Olaf."

Olaf her cousin! Emma felt excitement as the old Sigtryggr in her stirred her blood. These were hers, these swords, spears and axes, to go Viking in a great adventure and go laughing to Valhalla! Bald watching her, and he watched little else, saw her lift her head as if to drink the red blood from the cup of the plain. She had lost her taste for Virgin's milk. He would have grinned, but his mouth was stretched to the limit by age and scepticism.

"Olaf, Emma. Olaf your cousin."

She knew him, and knew what he was thinking. Go down, no one would stop her, go down and ride among your kinfolk and be free! Live for the now and not the future because there is no future. Go by the book and not the bible because the book tells no lies and promises no promises. Be yourself and not the imitation of a tortured divinity denying your humanity. Be Emma not St. Aelfgifu!

She would!

Her body tensed. Her horse sensed her intention and stepped forward. Alfgeir leant down and took her reins.

"It's too late, lady."

He looked to where he had looked before and the rest were looking, towards the Brunenswald.

The sun flashed her eyes shut.

For a moment the retinas retained the light and she saw red sky, black forest, and bleaching from the black trees like sap a white line spreading on to the plain.

She opened them.

Athelstan's standards were all white and the shieldwall of white linden stretched all along the Brunenswald as far as she could see. The line came on to the plain slowly like the tide, rank on rank of levies interlinked with Saxon soldiers to strengthen their resolve. A block of horsemen moved in the centre around the high banner and cross of the king.

Step by step the line advanced towards the great mass of northmen on the plain.

Looking down, Emma thought she saw two monsters about to fight for the fate of the world.

The vast amorphous body of mad gods, red with rage, rushing against the all-encompassing white serpent, in the last great cataclysmic battle.

She turned to Bald like a child.

"Stop them."

He shrugged. It had been fated from the beginning. Brunanburh was always going to be fought and the outcome was already known. Down there, chance would decide which man was struck and which survived. Up there – he did not need to look because it was all in his head – the gods would play with the world until they broke it. Through the blazing morning, Emma remembered, the red mass was encircled by the white serpent, at times constricted, and times spilling out and streaming away like blood from a wound.

For hours of unreal time they watched the struggle.

The intense heat and light penetrated her senses and Emma felt herself detached from the battle on the plain. She watched the warbirds drifting in the sky in widening circles ascending to heaven.

Bright blazing heaven was where the true encounter between god and god was taking place, while men below in sweat and blood and mangled limbs were ground beneath the wheels. Woden, Thor and Freyja she could almost see, they were so familiar to her youth. Her Christ was a warrior too, slain in the war with evil and gloriously resurrected. Above all shone the high god in the sun.

She closed her eyes and looked for St. Mary. Burnt in the centre of the sunlight was a black-cloaked figure moving towards her, growing larger and larger, opening the folds of its wings to cover her in its shadow like an eagle with its prey.

She came awake.

The others had risen in their saddles and were leaning forward.

She looked. The black block of horsemen had forced itself into the centre of the heaving mass of struggling men. The pressure broke the ring. Red hordes poured out and fled away northwards across the plain. The horsemen rode straight through the broil and turmoil cutting a road through the fleeing masses. The white ring closed on those who stayed. It was the end, the kill.

Bald shifted the book on his back and fetched round his pouch.

"Emma, now we go down and do what we can."

He meant, to repair what chance had done. What god had done was irreparable.

They wound their way down the hill into the carnage.

Nobody gloried. Nobody triumphed. All had lost.

They began, she remembered, where the minstrel's song had ended, with the dying.

Bald knew there was no leechdom for wounds already putrefying in the heat and dirt. There was no water to cleanse them, no worts to cure them. He looked for broken limbs, blunt blows of axe and sword. He walked among the wounded so gaunt and grim men hoped he would not notice them.

Emma wanted to tend each dying man.

She forgot about herself. Her fate was settled. She was Athelstan's. She turned to prayer because she had nowhere else to turn.

A man said his name was Aelfwine and he was Alfred's grandson, and she kissed his forehead and signed him with the cross and closed his eyes. He was an old man.

Another, Sigfrid, she told he would drink tonight with the gods. A bearded Scot said the body he cradled was the boy Cellach son of Constantine. Later a Saxon robber cut his throat.

Every yard of ground had its portion of the dead and dying. Owain of Strathclyde and Gibleachen king of the isles lay head by foot with Harek and those whose names she could not put in her prayers. Theodred she found, the bishop, still alive under his horse, and called to men standing to come and free him. He swore it was a miracle and perhaps it was, for among the men was Edmund.

He did not seem surprised to see her. So much slaughter made everything banal, not least slaughter itself.

Bald came up to them.

"Come, there's flying venom in the air."

"The horse."

The horse had been hamstrung and was waiting with resignation for the axeman.

Bald looked round, took up an axe and struck its neck once. Emma remembered the sound it made.

It was a hollow toll that tolled the death of Viking, of Woden, of lawlessness, of freedom, and of the dream.

The old gods died at Brunenburh. In a sense, a part of nature died, that part of man that was an animal, the earth, the worts and flowers and the trees, that died.

Christ won, and men were uniformly nailed to the tree of hope.

This life, that they had so lived and loved, was lost. Bald knew it.

She remembered how grim and ghastly he had looked.

Now, in the firelight at Winchester, he just looked old.

After the battle, there had been a stiff reconciliation with Athelstan and then the journey south.

The king was smiling amiably at the company. His fine golden hair framed his rubicund face, fatter than Emma remembered it. He had achieved Alfred's ambition of a united Christian kingdom, at least in name. That was enough for one who believed in symbols rather than substance, in miracles, in relics, in the minstrel's song. He saw his glory reflected in every face except one: Bald had fallen asleep. Athelstan sent an attendant to wake him and call him to a council after dinner.

They met in Alfred's bedchamber. Athelstan slept in the new extension he had added to the palace.

Bald knew old Wulfhelm, archbishop of Canterbury, but not Odo his designated successor, a Dane by birth. He had met Theodred bishop of London at Brunanburh.

Athelstan was walking up and down to settle his stomach.

In the book:

"Of late digestion; nine little grains of the seed of rue rubbed small with three bowls full of water, add these to a cup full of vinegar, boil them, then administer to be drunk for nine days in succession. Of late digestion; take of the red nettle so much as with two hands thou mayest grasp, seethe in a cup full of water, drink

after a night's fasting. It is advisable if he taketh mallow with its sprouts; let him seethe them in water, give this to be drunk. They who care not for these leechdoms in this disease, on them then cometh dropsy, liver pain, and sore or swelling of spleen, retention of urine, inflation of the wamb, loin pain, stones wax in the bladder, and sand."

"You drink your old wives' water, Bald! I have a stone from the Saviour's tomb to put on my stomach. What? Don't you believe in miracles? Those oils that cured Alfred came from Jerusalem. Dunstan wrote to say to me your sight was restored by a miracle."

Bald was silent. It was unwise to question an act of God with one who had some difficulty distinguishing between God and himself.

"And Aelfgifu saw St. Mary who returned the sacred relic to her. How do you explain that?"

"It was a miracle she found me on the battlefield. I'd have been dead by now." Theodred spoke.

"There you are. Theodred believes in them."

"So I do, my lord – but then I'm a bishop."

Athelstan took another turn round the room. What was it about, thought Bald, if not indigestion? Suddenly Athelstan swung his head and shouted.

"Is Aelfgifu still a virgin?"

So that was it! His thoughts were started like a flock of birds – not pigeons, that all fly off one way, but crafty old rooks that scatter in all directions. Say yes, what then? All options stay open. But Dunstan could have written another letter, or even be behind the door. Say no, then what? Who knows? Say nothing.

Wulfhelm was talking.

"You must answer, leech, and truthfully. It's a matter of great importance to the kingdom. If she is, she may marry Prince Edmund. If she is not, she must go to a monastery for the rest of her life."

"Why can't she go free?"

"Don't question me!" Athelstan was angry. "Do you think I'd let her go – or you, if you lie to me?"

The rooks flew in a circle. If only they were eagles, one eagle!

Cild's words came suddenly.

In the book:

"Apply the leechdom according as thou seest the state of the body. For a mickle difference is there in the bodies of a man, a woman, and a child; and in the main or constitution of a daily wight or labourer and of the idle, of the old and of the young, of him who is accustomed to endurance and him who is unaccustomed to such things."

What was the leechdom for Athelstan? Bald answered loudly. "Yes! She is!"

Athelstan took a letter from his pocket and opened it and read a sentence that might have been a death sentence.

" 'Bald told me they were attacked by Welshmen and the poor girl was raped.' From Dunstan."

Wulfhelm, Odo and Theodred were shaking their heads sadly.

"That is true, my lord, but when Aelfgifu saw St. Mary her virginity was restored to her ... by a miracle."

Athelstan glowered at him suspiciously but behind the mask Bald saw his pale eyes wondering.

The bishops had their heads together and were murmuring in Latin lists of saints and martyrs. Wulfhelm was again the spokesman.

"My lord, we can find no precedent for such a thing among the saints and if it was true of Aelfgifu she would be a saint indeed."

"Masters, you're like the new leeches who forget their debt to nature. Remember St. Mary herself, the patroness of Glastonbury, a virgin, and no virgin, and an eternal virgin."

They nodded, and Bald thanked Aethelfleda in his thoughts.

"And I can prove it."

He felt the wings of the eagle bearing him upwards.

"How, leech?"

"The king himself will be the judge."

"No he won't!" Athelstan was adamant. "Let some good woman do it."

"Aelfgifu will submit to an ordeal."

As he said it, Bald had a sickening moment of doubt. What if Isaac Judaeus had been wrong?

But the bishops were taken, talking enthusiastically, and the king saw in this end-game a degree of glory.

Emma laughed.

"It's ridiculous; besides I don't want to marry Edmund, he's too young. You know I'll fail the ordeal, whatever it is."

A few days later, she was surprised to see Dunstan and Aethelwynn at court. There was also a scandal. A known prostitute called Elvira had been visiting Bald's room in the palace accompanied by two porters carrying a cask of wine. Emma became concerned for her uncle's health, and looked in the book.

In the book:

"Of venery; to all dry constitutions venery is not beneficial; but most to dry and cold ones; it harmeth not hot and wet ones; it is worst for the cold moist ones and them which have disorder of the gastric juices. To such men it is of benefit that they should seek to themselves exercise, and should dose themselves without bath, and with smearings smear themselves."

"Uncle, do you think you take enough exercise?"

"Quite enough."

"But you don't take any."

"Exactly."

"Why is Aethelwynn here and why hasn't she come to see me?"

She had her answer the following day.

She was summoned to the council room which was filled with grey eminent churchmen and ealdermen. Athelstan was sitting magisterially in the centre. Edmund was there, little more than a boy, she thought, and felt a small burst of resentment against him.

Aethelwynn and Dunstan had privileged places near the king, and Emma was surprised to see Elvira in this company.

Bald entered in his Glastonbury gown, looking, she thought, as shifty as Liofa when he lied to her. She wondered what unpleasantness and public humiliation she had to undergo.

Bald was speaking.

"My lords, it was long believed there was no way of proving virginity in a maid except by destroying it. It was, in short, blood on a sheet."

They are absorbed, she thought, these old men with grey faces and gaping mouths like the men who raped her. Was she going to be raped to prove she was a virgin? That was the principle of the ordeal: suffering brought out the truth.

"This was the case until the learned doctor Isaac Judaeus discovered an infallible way without touching the maid at all."

He clapped his hands like a magician and two porters carried in a cask of wine and set it upright before the king. They placed a spike and mallet on the cask, and went out.

"Air, my masters, is the least substantial of the four elements. If air passes through a body, it means the body has been broken open. But if air cannot pass, then the body is intact and perfect."

He took up the spike and mallet and broached the cask.

He nodded to Aethelwyyn who approached, lifted the skirts of her habit and stood astride the cask. She looked around complacently and squatted on the open top.

"Be good enough, your grace, to smell her breath."

Athelstan rose with some apprehension, went to the abbess and lowered his face to hers. She opened her mouth and breathed out. He smiled.

"Nothing, cousin, but sanctity."

Wulfhelm followed, and Odo, but when ealderman Turfrid came forward, Athelstan snapped.

"That's enough!"

She returned to stand by Dunstan, a model of virtue, looking around her like a lighthouse on a turbulent sea of sin.

Bald beckoned Elvira to come and sit on the cask. She was a handsome woman, knew many at court intimately, and had no hesitation in raising her dress to show she was naked underneath it.

Athelstan bent down to smell her breath and recoiled immediately.

"Wine! I smell the wine!"

Wulfhelm took his place.

"French wine."

Turfrid pushed Odo aside and sampled Elvira's mouth with relish.

"The thirty-five."

Bald turned to Emma.

"Come along, child."

"I'm a woman, uncle."

She spoke low, but those nearest her heard her confession. Bald shook his head slightly. She shrugged and strode out determined to face whatever indignity awaited her. She was smaller than the others and had to hold down her robe as she hopped up on the barrel.

Bald turned to the council.

"Let everyone smell her breath and if there's a trace of wine upon it, hang me and send her to a monastery."

And hang Isaac Judaeus, he added to himself.

Athelstan sniffed her several times, and was convinced.

"Pure, pure."

So were Wulfhem, Odo, Theodred, Turfrid and the rest. Dunstan at the last came up to her. She opened her mouth.

"No, Aelfgifu, not to me." He lifted her from the barrel and kissed the top of her head. "You are a saint already."

Her thoughts about Bald were not at all saintly.

When she could free herself from the crowd of congratulations, she went to find him in the New Minster.

He was measuring his shadow in the garden.

In the book:

"On the twentieth of September, that is the equinox, the shadow at nine and three is twelve foot long and at midday nine."

"How did you do it, uncle?"

In the book:

"If the sun shines on the twelfth day, men shall be weak, and there shall be much quiet on earth."

"How did you do it? I'm not a fool and I'm not a virgin."

"When Elvira came to see me the other night to learn what she had to do with the cask of wine – she drank most of it."

"Poor woman."

"It's her fate."

"And you changed my fate."

"I can't do that, Emma."

"I'm frightened of what you can do!"

"My love, it's not the leech who cures the man but the worts and his own body. It's the same with fate. Even Athelstan can't make you do what you don't want to do."

"You're cleverer than Athelstan. You use him like you use everybody. You want me to marry Edmund so you put me to the test to prove I'm something that I'm not!"

"How do you know you're not? The test was a proper test. How do you know there wasn't a miracle when you saw your mother?"

He stared at the sundial and the shadow slowly covering its face as the sun dipped below the tops of the trees.

"I won't always be here. I believe it's your fate to be a queen and the mother of kings and queens. More than that, Emma. When I die, I'll leave the book to you. It mustn't end, you understand."

She looked too young, too slight, for such a burden.

"I don't want it."

Suddenly the sky darkened so it seemed to him. He shouted, "What do you want?"

Her voice came small and from a distance.

"I want to be with God."

"There is no god!"

He thought, so that is where I am going: nowhere. I have climbed the mountain and now I can only look down. He cast around for her but could not see her. The garden was dark: night was coming quickly.

He heard a voice.

"The only one who can say that is God himself."

XI

Edmund was seventeen. He had grown up in a corner of Athelstan's glory where his red hair hardly glowed. In the autumn of this splendid year, as the leaves fell in a golden shower, people noticed the red boy had become a man. The younger courtiers began to drift, as new-antlered deer from the herd, towards the promise of a young pretender.

Bald had never paid him much attention, no more than to his position and Emma's prospects. He saw the boy doted on her, and that was enough. The lack of any close relationship in his own life left a gap in his experience which was impossible to fill with conjecture. He was conscious of the loss, but did not feel it. He was crippled young. His emotions had hardly grown before they were amputated at Thetford by Cild's sacrifice. The phantom pains were in his head and not his heart. His love for Eneda, and now for Emma, was intellectually contrived and could never be anything else. His body was dead, dry and cold, the book said, and no amount of exercise, doses and smearings could bring it to life. So his attempts to guide Emma into Edmund's arms were inspired by stupidity, aggravated by ignorance, and persisted in with an old man's obduracy.

There was nothing in the book about love, or living together, and while there was a great deal about the spleen, nothing about splenetics. Edmund was splenetic. He suffered from too much Athelstan.

In the book:

"For split wark, or acute pain in the spleen, and that the milt is on the left side, and tokens of the disease, how colourless the patients are, and there are wounds not easy of cure. The men are meagre and uncomfortable, pale of aspect, though ere this they were fat, and still are constitutionally disposed that way; and the wamb is not under control, and scarcely can it be that

the mie is healthy, but rather it will be swartish and greenish and blacker than its right is to be, and the breathing is very hard drawn."

Bald saw a colourless, meagre and uncomfortable young man and put it down to milt wark and not the more dangerous cause of the defect in his character.

Emma knew less but saw more and divined the restless energy and anger in Edmund that made her not so much dislike as distrust him.

This was apparent to her in his treatment of Dunstan. When Dunstan was out of favour with Athelstan, Edmund was his best friend. When Dunstan returned to court and Athelstan was pleased with everyone, Edmund rebuffed him.

"Why are you rude to Dunstan? Edmund?"

"We were out hunting yesterday and Dunstan suddenly told Athelstan he was riding with the devil and the courtiers running behind us had turned into goats."

Emma laughed.

"Of course Athelstan thought he meant me and called off the chase."

"Dunstan's your friend."

"I don't have friends, I have followers."

She was silent. It was true.

Emma was intrigued by Dunstan's vision and asked him what it meant.

"It's not good, I'm afraid."

"For Athelstan or Edmund?"

"Athelstan. He's not well. He relies too much on relics. He should see Bald."

"Don't you believe in miracles?"

"I believe in them but I don't rely on them."

That winter at Winchester, as it became apparent to everyone except Athelstan that he was overweight and apathetic, the urgency for Edmund to marry increased. Eadred his brother and the last of Edward's sons was a sickly boy, and nobody expected him to live long. Wulfhelm summoned Bald to the New Minster, where they mused about the succession over Alfred's tomb.

"My dear leech, there are men who are envious of us. I don't mean Danes but Saxons like Wulfstan of York who won't accept my authority. If Alfred's line dies out, heaven knows what strife and trouble we're in for! There's no longer any problem about the wedding, so what are they waiting for?"

"She doesn't like him."

"She doesn't have to live with him for long. Once she's had two sons, she can retire from the marriage like most decent women."

"She has too much spirit for that."

"Then tell her to do it for her country."

"Good master, Emma's country is York. Will she marry Edmund for York? No, Edmund will marry her for York. You tell him to get on and woo the girl if he wants her."

"Woo? You're not married or you'd know wooing has very little to do with it. What an old-fashioned word! Woo-woo! It sounds like an owl."

He tottered off, and Bald wondered what an archbishop knew about wooing. Then he remembered many of the old clergy were married and Dunstan's reforming zeal was meeting opposition in high places. He spoke to Emma in his room that evening. He was preparing a leechdom.

In the book:

"For milt pain; pound green sallow rind, seethe in honey alone, give the man three pieces to eat at night fasting."

"For Edmund?"

"Yes."

"Why?"

"He has milt wark."

"I didn't know that."

Emma wandered round the room which Bald had turned into a laboratory. Honey was seething in a crucible on a fire. Bunches of worts hung from the beams. A giant pestle and mortar stood near the open book on the table. Bald watched her, loving her.

"Uncle."

He was sitting upright. The fire cast his deep-lined features in bronze.

"I dreamt I was asleep under an apple tree and a hound came and lay down at my feet. It was a bitch and she was pregnant and the whelps were barking inside her. Two apples fell from the tree and a voice said, “Well is thee.” And though the tree was tall, the apples were small, and they fell into a river.”

She was silent and Bald waited. He was excited because he knew what the dream meant, but he did not want to press her too urgently. The coals glowed, the honey bubbled, Emma went and curled up by his chair with her head resting against his knee. He touched her hair. It shone like gold and he saw Eneda. His heart lurched and he almost wept. She was his child. He spoke softly, he thought, but it was loud.

“Can’t you see, my dear? The whelps barking inside the mother are your unborn children calling for you. And the apples are when they are born and fall from the tree. And it will be ‘Well with thee’.”

“What’s the river?”

“Life.”

She thought for a moment.

“I might marry Turfrid or someone else. It doesn’t have to be Edmund.”

“No, then the circle wouldn’t be complete. Emma ...”

He hesitated so long she thought he had fallen asleep.

“Your grandfather was King Ivarr, who led the Vikings, and on the other side, Cild, my father, was your great-grandfather.

We’re Saxons. At Thetford many years ago, Ivarr murdered Cild. For all my life since, there’s been war between us. Between your father, Sigtryggr, and Alfred. He’s in you, in those whelps you dreamed about, and Alfred is in the tree. We worship the tree in the centre of the world that holds up the sky. We meet again in you, in your children, but you must marry Edmund.”

She did not know whether she was dreaming again or whether it was real. The old man’s rambling, part story, part myth, part truth, only confused her. She reached for a certainty.

“I’m going to Shaftesbury Abbey with Aethelwynn.”

“Your mother gave you her milk, Emma. It means you’ll have children.”

“You make things mean what you want them to mean.”

“Me?” He seemed surprised there was such a person. “I’m nothing. I’m going nowhere. You’re the only part of me that’s left.”

She turned to look up at him.

The fire had burned down, and now he looked like iron, or stone, or the wood lying in the marsh at Glastonbury for centuries, black and acidic, which when dried turned to dust.

Edmund started wooing her. Perhaps Wulfhelm had a word with him or there was a crack in his angry nature. He gave her a dress embroidered with jewels which had belonged to one of his stepmothers. Emma was embarrassed.

"It's too big for me."

"Then you should eat more and get bigger."

"Did you give the dress to me or me to the dress?"

He was incapable of generosity. He resented his love for her and hated her for it. His lack of charm extended even to himself.

"Do what you like with it!"

She gave it away to a beggarwoman in Winchester who flaunted it and turned whore.

Emma was not unattracted by Edmund and her sense of destiny was strong. Aethelwynn left for Shaftesbury alone.

"Dear Aelfgifu, God will wait for you."

The approach of Christmas found her looking for a present for him.

"Uncle?"

"Marry him, then you won't have to give him a present."

"I'll have to give him two! One from me and one from his wife."

"Tell me one good reason."

"I shan't say I don't love him because you won't think that's good enough."

At least, he thought, she's forgotten God for the moment.

"I don't know."

"You don't know a reason."

"No. I just don't know."

That is how we live our lives, he thought, not knowing. He had once believed in knowledge, and Woden, and Fornjot's palm, and now he believed in nothing. He was going to live forever. The irony of it amused him.

Edmund gave her a ring from Alfred's workshop. She treasured it, not so much for the value of the jewel as for its associations. In return she gave him a sash she had embroidered herself with tiny flowers. He threw it into the bottom of his wardrobe and forgot it.

So the strange pair of reluctant lovers drifted round each other like bubbles on a mere, in an eddy of emotions, now attracted, now repelled, until everybody wished they would burst.

It was a mild grey winter and an early spring, and Bald ventured out, glad to be free from his cell, to gather worts.

In the book:

"Mugwort, waybroad which spreadeth open towards the east, lambscress, atterlothe, maythen, nettle, crab apple, chervil, fennel, and old soap; work the worts to a dust, mingle with the soap and with the verjuice of the apple; form a slop of water and of ashes, take fennel, boil it in the slop, and foment with egg mixture, when the man puts on the salve, either before or after. Sing the charm upon each of the worts; thrice before he works them up, and over the apple in like manner; and sing into the mans mouth and into both his ears the same magic song, and into the wound before he applies the salve.

Standeth she against venom
Stoundeth she head wark
Wreaketh on the wrath one
Whirleth out poison
This is the wort which
Fought against worm
This avails for venom
For flying vile things
Tis good against the loathly ones
That through the land rove.
These nine can march on
Gainst nine ugly poisons
A worm sneaking came
To slay and to slaughter
Then took up Woden
Nine wondrous twigs
He smote then the nadder
Till it flew in nine bits."

He grinned to himself in his skeletal skull. Believing in nothing, he could believe in anything.

He was accused of sorcery and arrested.

The man he cured of bloodrunning in the nether parts was Cynwulf, one of Athelstan's reeves. The days had gone when he could call on Woden with impunity and Cynwulf charged him with sorcery.

He was carried before the cathedral court and excommunicated under a recent statute "that those who commit perjury and practise sorcery shall be cast forever from the fellowship of God."

In one day he lost what rights he had and lay in Winchester prison at the mercy of the king.

At first nobody knew where he was, and when word got out, nobody dared come and see him.

Athelstan lay in his new bed, reinforced with great oak beams to bear his weight, clutching a crucifix in one hand and the coccyx of a saint in the other, waiting for time to ripen.

Emma heard from some informed attendant and knew what she had to do.

Athelstan made her wait a day before admitting her to an audience.

The smell struck her first, and she saw an array of stinking pots around the heavy bed with its abnormal burden.

A boy slave carried out a half-eaten meal of eggs and oyster patties, sweets and green apples.

Athelstan lay, pale and glistening, swollen and overblown with wind, like a beached whale on the bed.

Emma remembered the book.

In the book:

"Of their hue, or complexion, and of the navel, and of the dorsal muscles, and of the back gut or rectum, and of the lower belly and the milt and the share; they are horribly pale, and all the body is glazed, and an evil stench hath not control over itself, and the sore is on the right side, on the share and on the wamb, much troubled by it, and again from the navel to the spleen, and on the left dorsal muscle, and it reacheth to the anus, and to the lower belly, and the loins are girt about with much soreness."

Athelstan had wamb disease, between a swollen liver and a fatal dropsy. She ignored who he was and went to the window to open the shutters and let in the sweet spring air.

She drew back the heavy covers of the bed and looked aghast at the ossuary of relics surrounding the mountainous body like the remnants of some obscene feast.

There was a bundle of wrappings between the king's spindly legs and she had a sudden fantasy that he had given birth to a monstrosity.

It moved!

She screamed!

The boy ran in with a monk she knew was the king's confessor and bed-companion: Marcus, a sickly stick-like youth who looked like one of Athelstan's legs.

Marcus snatched up the bundle and unwrapped it.

It was a fat baby.

"We're trying to keep him warm!"

"You're wrong! He must be cool, and have wort drinks, and fast! He must be bled and cleansed inside with a wash! Go – get my uncle, quickly!"

"What – Bald the devil?"

"Bald the leech!"

"Do you want to kill the king?"

He stood there trembling. The baby began to bawl. Athelstan groaned.

"I need the pot."

Emma went out and waited. She had acted instinctively. If Marcus accused her, she would be guilty of violating the king's mund, his hand, and be condemned to death.

She shrugged. Death has no power over the very young and the very old. Marcus came out, still carrying the baby.

"I'm trying to do my best. He won't see a doctor. He's frightened."

He stood aside to let her into the room again.

The slave had closed the shutters and pulled back the bedclothes. He took out a foaming pot.

Athelstan was sitting up. He was gracious.

"I'm not as other men, Aelfgifu. I don't expect you to understand it."

He beckoned her closer.

"I've been promised."

"What, my lord?"

"I can't tell you. By God himself, immortal God."

He lay back. She thought of two passages from the book.

In the book:
"When the insensible hardening of the liver is of too long duration, then it forms a dropsy which cannot be cured.
If moreover the liver hardening, and the disease, and the upblowing, is kindled on the hulks and hollows of the liver, then it soon seems to the doctor that the humour descends downwards rather than ascends, and the man suffers swoonings and failings of the mind."

"Will you marry Edmund?"
"Yes my lord. Will you let my uncle examine you?"
"It's a waste of time. I have to go through a transformation to rid myself of all earthly corruption so that I can be given what I've been promised."
"Will you let him free?"
"Yes, yes, on your marriage day."
She thought better of him. He had achieved much. He would probably go to heaven. But he would not like it there because he would not be king. For herself, she thought – goodbye Emma.
Edmund and Aelfgifu were married in a Winchester ringing with bells and scattered with flowers. Athelstan was present having had a remarkable remission to everyone's surprise except his own.
Bald growled.
Dunstan had come to him in prison.
"There's a condition. You've got to be baptised and renounce Woden and all the devils. Otherwise, how on earth can you be related to the royal family?"
"I renounce Woden gladly, but why should I clutter myself up with Christ?"
"It's lucky I'm here and not one of the others because I know you like shock treatment. Jesus went before you. Is there one step he took that you would not take yourself?"
Bald thought.
"I wouldn't have had the courage."
"You're half-Christian already. That's more than most. Is it because you don't know or you don't believe?"
"The trouble is I don't believe what I know and I don't know what I believe."

"You're almost a saint."

"You have to be dead to be a saint."

Nevertheless he agreed. As Dunstan left, he called out:

"I won't take on sin! I was born – not guilty! I've lived – not guilty! I'm going to die - not guilty!"

Dunstan came back and spoke quietly in his ear.

"Sin isn't for us. We're healers. Sin is a disease of the mind and merely needs a leechdom. We have a greater problem than sin: doubt. It's easy not to sin. It's impossible not to doubt."

Edmund was carousing with his companions in the great hall.

The ladies of the court carried Emma up to the bedroom with shrieks of laughter and jokes that clashed with the chanting of a chorus of monks praying for increase. They undressed her and put her to bed. Bald strode into the room. The ladies giggled. He stared at them. They fled.

"Hello uncle."

"I haven't had the chance to thank you for saving my life."

"I think you did it on purpose."

"No, it was fate. Now you are a queen."

"And you're a Christian."

"I'll survive."

He grimaced. He went to the bed. He bent down and kissed her forehead.

"Goodbye Emma."

"Why?"

"I'm going away."

"Uncle!"

"I must."

He meant he could not bear to see her with a man though he knew he must.

"I must follow the book. The book's not wanted here."

"Where are you going?"

"To York. I'll go and stay with Lyb. I want to be where she was."

"My mother?"

He nodded.

"And then you'll come back?"

He shook his head.

"Come back!"

"My dear, my love, Emma ..."

What could he tell her? Only the truth this time.

"I don't want you to see me die."

He left.

She cried.

Edmund came up drunk and raped her.

He came to York in late summer. There were more marks of government here. The walls had been pulled down and many shops were closed. Few ships lay in the river. The city was silent. The king had shut the mint and much trade had moved to London.

Saxon soldiers sat in the sun outside the palace. Bald did not try to enter. He did not know ealderman Orm who governed York for Athelstan.

Workmen were carting timber to the blackened shell of the minster. The stone walls stood but the roof had fallen in. He climbed into the great crater over heaps of rubble and ash, and made his way up the nave past Guthrith's tomb. Here the floor was clear of debris and swept clean. Four tall candles burned in memorial. Why this and nothing else? Guthrith, Sigtryggr's brother murdered by Caech, was not a Christian but had a Christian burial and was now venerated.

Why?

Bald went to the part of the wall painted with the scene of the crucifixion.

Most of it had been obliterated by the fire. The Christ had gone, and the four evangelists. The Virgin's house remained but the woman inside had no face and her dress was black. She was the image of his dreams when Eneda was dead.

Ruin and death were all around him. He hurried away along Petergate and out of York.

It was evening when he saw Lyb's holding. The sky was an upturned bowl of deep blue above the saucer of land still filled with sunlight. Beyond the dark forest, the moors were purple and brown. Bald stood and thought: this is where I will die.

Ulf came out of the house in the hollow to fetch in the pig. He saw a gaunt black figure against the sky and cried out.

Lyb rushed out waving an axe.

"You know me, Lyb! Bald the leech!"

The dwarf dropped the axe and ran to him. Ulf cried out:

"Uncle! We thought you must be dead!"

Ginna and Toki shrieked with delight and two little girls, both taller than their brother, stood shyly in the doorway.

They wondered that he could see again.

"Where's Emma, uncle?"

"Emma is a queen in England."

He looked at the shining faces in the firelight. It was possible to be happy, to live with the earth and not against it, not to care who ruled the country, to be cautious, small and uninquisitive, to live and die unnoticed. Yet few had the talent to ignore their self-esteem and do so.

He envied the dwarf.

He had a dish of eggs and leeks for dinner and lay on the ground with the book under his head. Before he slept, he thought: this is where I will die.

He dreamed the old dream that used to torment his impotence. He thought as he was dreaming, if that part of the mind persists so long after that part of the body is dead, perhaps we never die completely?

He woke and went outside silently.

The night was warm and the earth was darker than the sky because there was no moon.

The earth was like a woman sleeping, a presence he could feel. From the side of his eye he saw a movement at the edge of the forest. On a summer night the deer would come across the fields to nibble the awns of barley.

A figure, too tall and slender for a deer, glided from the shadows into the lighter darkness of the field.

It was a woman in a black dress.

The second he moved his eyes she disappeared.

He felt the fear of the unknown winding like a cold sheet round his body.

No animal stirred, no bird of the night, no dog, no sheep had sensed a human: what was she?

Sanity said it was a shadow in his eye, the presage of returning blindness. It was not Eneda.

The days passed. Memory faded. In the old, memory wears thin in places, reflecting an incomplete picture of the past. Memory is a mirror, and the silver back is etched away with age. We always see ourselves, and less and less of that until all that remains is black and unreflecting and perhaps the truth. We were never there at all.

He was in the forest one afternoon in early autumn. He saw a wolf, and immediately remembered Dr. Oxa and the Quadrupedibus of Sextus Placitus.

"For devil sickness and for an ill sight, give to eat a wolf's flesh, well-dressed and sodden, to him who is in need of it; the apparitions which ere appeared to him shall not disquiet him."

First catch your wolf. He looked again and the wolf was gone. You seldom see a wolf twice, he thought.

He walked on over the drifted leaves. After a while, he saw a deer.

In the book:

"Against ill humours and swelling, take shavings off the horn of a hart, or meal of the horn, mingle with water, smudge it on, it doth away and driveth off all that ratten and the evil wet."

Everything in nature had a purpose and a use. Prayers and incantations, relics and signs only prolong the agony. Faith, he thought, only prolongs the agony.

He walked a little further and saw a dog. A wolf will kill a deer if he is hungry. A dog will hunt every deer he sees. Men are killing wolves and breeding dogs. They are turning from nature to politics and religion. The dogs of Brunanburh killed more young men in one day than all the wolves of nature in a year.

He was so engrossed in his thoughts he did not see the young man watching him until his horse chinked its bridle.

He turned quickly and for a second thought his memory, his wits and his eyes had all gone mad and he was looking at Caech! The impression was so strong, his fear so great that he flinched.

The young man laughed.

Caech would have laughed, he thought, and probably killed him, but this boy was young and had not grown to the full dog.

The young man raised his hand to his mouth and called: "Erche! Erche!"

In a moment there were huntsmen running and riders crashing through the forest, stirring up waves of fallen leaves. Two mounted men rode up. One he recognised at once as archbishop Wulfstan;

the other was a stout ealderman from his appearance and the rich caparison of his horse. A third rider halted a distance away.

Wulfstan was astonished.

"It can't be Bald the leech, can it?"

"Who?"

"Bald the leech."

The young man went a vivid red.

"The man who killed my father?"

"No, Cuaran, he was Caech's leech."

Bald thought, these Vikings always get the wrong man. I killed his grandfather. But what was Caech's son doing in Athelstan's York, with York's archbishop, and, if the ealderman was Orm, York's governor?

Wulfstan enlightened him.

"Did you ever meet Caech's son Cuaran? He's staying with Orm. What are you doing here?"

Bald shrugged. He had to be careful.

"Since Athelstan dismissed me, master, I had to come to the old Danelaw."

"The old Danelaw?"

The boy looked just like Caech.

"Ay, master, if you're safe here, so am I."

"I'm safe enough aren't I, Wulfstan?"

"As my guest."

Orm leant across to Wulfstan and spoke quietly. Wulfstan turned to Bald.

"Why did Athelstan dismiss you?"

Why? He wondered how much they knew about Emma.

"I couldn't cure him."

"That's true. Athelstan's dead. He died quietly at Gloucester two weeks ago. Edmund is King of Wessex."

How much did they know?

"And the girl they claim is Sigtryggr's daughter is queen."

Everything!

Cuaran was suspicious.

"What does he know about her?"

"He's her kinsman – aren't you, Bald?"

Wulfstan spoke politely but Bald felt the ambitious churchman was more dangerous than the hot-headed young Dane.

Cuaran rose in the saddle and shouted to a man in the distance.

"Olaf! We were hunting a deer and we've caught a fox!"

Olaf? Bald saw Wulfstan glare with anger and Orm put out a restraining hand to silence Cuaran.

There was only one Olaf – Olaf Guthfrithsson, King of York, defeated at Brunanburh! Olaf Guthfrithsson, Guthrith's grandson, and Guthrith was the son of Ivarr! That was why candles burned on Guthrith's tomb in the minster. Olaf Guthfrithsson in York with Wulfstan and Orm.

The Vikings were back!

They were looking at him with dispassionate concern as if he was indeed the deer they had caught and one of them was going to dismount and cut his throat.

Death, desirable at a distance, was less welcome the closer it got.

"Masters, I saved Sigtryggr's life! I'm a leech! I have no business with well men."

Orm spoke.

"We need a leech in York."

Cuaran's hand was on his dagger.

"I'd rather give him to Woden."

"Let Olaf decide."

Wulfstan turned his horse and trotted towards the man in the distance. Bald had no doubt what the decision would be. The Vikings' solution to every problem was death.

Cuaran was staring at him like a dog about to fight. Orm was impassive. Bald wondered what promise was great enough to make him betray his king. Wulfstan returned.

"He keeps his life, but we can't leave him free to go to Edmund. Orm, you take him and look after him."

Two huntsmen put a rope around Bald's neck and tied the end to Orm's saddle. The horses moved off at walking pace. As they cleared the forest, Olaf Guthfrithsson rode up and joined them.

He was young, no more than twenty-two or three, Bald thought. So he had raised the raven standard at Brunenburh, this tall young fair-haired Viking of the line of Ivarr. Guthrith had been a brave man before he became bloated with beer and ambition.

Bald glanced up and saw Olaf watching him. He felt he was being weighed in those grey eyes. He felt himself between the axe and the ring, that Olaf would give him either indifferently, but with justice. He felt this man was a king.

Orm lived in the gatehouse of the Roman fort which served the kings of York as a palace. Bald knew it well, and found himself in his old room. Orm's wife Eda was ill and Orm needed him nearby. He was guarded night and day, and Wulfstan sent a priest, Mael, to work with him. Mael was born in Dublin of the Danes the Irish still called foreigners even after a hundred years.

In the book:

"The maw is near the heart and the spine, and in communication with the brain, from which the disease come most violently from the circumstances of the maw, and from evil juices, humours venombearing. Then the evil humours get gathered into the maw and there they rule with excoriations within; especially in the men who have a very sensitive and soon sore maw, so that some of them suddenly die; they are not able to bear the strong excoriating effects of the venomous humours."

Cild's diagnoses sometimes stretched so thin you could see through them to the despair he must have felt for hopeless cases.

"There is good support in good wort drinks, as leeches work them, of vinegar, and of fennel roots, and of its rind, and of aloes, and of dumbledores honey; mix that up and administer a spoonful of it or two, then that maketh the wamb nesh and firm; and it is efficacious against breast wark, and heart disease, and epilepsy, and in case that a man be filled with inflammatory humour in the maw, and that is valid against many disorders which come of surfeit, and of various evil humours."

Bald dutifully supplied Eda with wort drinks he knew would not cure her.

"A leechdom for swelling of the maw; one shall in the morning hours squeeze hard the mans feet and hands, and one shall bid him cry or sing very loud, and one shall exhort him after his night's fast, and provoke him to spew; and in the morning smear him with oil on which has been sodden rue and wormwood, and let him diet on the afore named meats."

He knew he must never give up. He knew there were cures Dunstan would call miraculous because they came from the patient and not from the doctor. He knew he did not know enough to cure Eda.

There was a girl he used to see in Eda's room, her daughter Aldgyth. He asked her once if she knew what Olaf Guthfrithsson was doing in York. She blushed and fled. Mael told him.

"She's going to marry him."

So that was the reward for Orm's treason. Aldgyth would be queen of York and Dublin, and what else? Mael went on.

"Of course he's got a wife already but that doesn't matter."

Bald thought, Wulfstan will marry them as he married Caech and Eadgyth. But why?

Eda's condition suddenly deteriorated. She choked, and lost all powers of speech and movement. He shouted to the guard to fetch Orm and when the man ignored him, he went himself, hurrying along the corridors to the council chamber. He pushed open the door and saw the whole conspiracy uncovered as if he had lifted up a stone and seen the worms writhing underneath.

With Orm and Wulfstan, Olaf and Cuaran, were nearly all Athelstan's old ministers, the Saxon magnates of York, the Danish jarls of East Anglia, and the ealdermen of Mercia. Many of them Bald had last seen in Winchester. He stared as the extent of the conspiracy struck him. A half of England had deserted Edmund!

He called out:

"Orm, your wife is dying."

Orm hurried from the room. Bald followed, but before he left, looked back. Many of these men had fought against Olaf at Brunenburh. Some stared him out: some looked ashamed. Now they were Olaf's friends and Edmund's enemies – and Emma's enemies.

As he returned to Eda's room he tried to think how he could send word of the impending disaster south.

Before he reached the room, he was seized by soldiers, dragged down and flung into a dungeon.

He was not there long before he was released and taken to the council chamber. Orm was there alone. Bald knew Eda was dead. He said nothing. At last Orm spoke.

"I can just remember Alfred. I knew Edward and fought for him. I used to think he was right and the old kingdoms had gone forever, and we should be one England. But you must have seen it! What's good for the south isn't good for the north. You can only govern men with their consent, and Yorkmen don't consent to be ruled by Wessex! Mercians don't! Anglians don't! The unity of diverse peoples like ours can only be imposed by force. It isn't natural and it doesn't work. It's all right for taxmen and administrators because it gives them power, but it's no good for the people."

He looked at Bald for the first time since he came into the room.

"You can't grow one crop over the whole country, the conditions are wrong. The old kingdoms came about by common consent – Anglia, Mercia, Northumbria. We're going to restore them by common consent."

He waited for Bald to speak.

Bald had no intention of saying anything.

"My wife's dead. I don't blame you: you came too late. I can't let you go, you understand? You can either give me your word to stay here, or go back to prison."

Bald thought quickly. They did not know about Lyb. He would not be able to get word to Lyb from prison.

"Master, your wife's time had come. Mine will come soon. I don't want to spend my time in prison. I'll stay here."

"Swear it."

"In god's name."

Which god? Did it matter? Both were preparing for war.

When he left the council chamber, Mael stuck to him and the guard followed them back to his room.

Bald waited. It was only a matter of time before Lyb or one of the family found a way to reach him.

It was Ginna who came to clean his room.

Mael was watching Bald preparing a leechdom. The book was open on the table.

In the book:

"If thou seest a wolfs spoor ere than thou seest him, he will not scathe thee, if thou hast with thee a wolf's ridge hair and tail hair, the extremest part thereof on thy journey; without fright thou shalt perform the journey and the wolf shall sorrow about his journey."

Bald's hand shook and he spilt the solution he was holding on the open page. He cursed himself for an old fool and tore off the part with the leechdom on it and threw it on the floor.

Ginna swept up the scrap of paper with the old rushes, strewed fresh rushes and went out without raising her head.

Bald trusted Lyb to realise any message he sent was meant for Emma. Wolf and Olaf were the same word in Saxon.

Olaf came to see him.

Bald was surprised when he suddenly entered and dismissed Mael with a nod.

The bright young Viking's presence seemed to light the room. He smiled.

"I'm sorry you have to be shut up in here."

"It makes no difference to me."

"You're a man of the wilds. We're both out of our elements."

"What's yours, master?"

"War, I suppose. Or the sea. Did you ever meet Ivarr?" Ivarr! The image of the blood-eagle burnt in his brain.

"Not exactly."

"But you knew Sigtryggr?"

Bald nodded.

"And Guthrith?"

He nodded again.

"What were they like?"

"Sigtryggr was a pirate."

Olaf laughed. Bald had to be careful with Guthrith.

"Guthrith was a learned man."

He looked at Olaf under half-closed eyelids, like a cat.

"He practised reading and was interested in Christianity."

Olaf was listening intently. Tell him he was a saint.

"He was martyred. In fact he sacrificed himself by drinking a poison meant for his brother."

Olaf nodded wisely.

"I knew we weren't savages. We rob abbeys but it's only because they're wealthy."

Engaging, thought Bald, but simple. Kings should be simple.

"Sigtryggr's daughter."

Kings should be like the best of their subjects: brave, loyal and not too clever. Like Alfred. They should reward cleverness in others, but cleverness is never popular, and they should avoid it.

"Tell me about Sigtryggr's daughter."

"She was born after he died. I tried to keep her birth a secret."

"Why?"

"Happiness is the prerogative of the unrecognised, my lord."

"Isn't she happy?"

"Her life is not her own."

"What do you mean?"

"She's a child of fate. Like you, Olaf Guthfrithsson."

Olaf's brightness clouded.

"You must have been at Brunanburh." He was silent for a moment.

"I shan't make the same mistake twice."

But you are going to try, thought Bald.

"Did you know she had a son?"

Bald knew she would have two.

"Fate will have to decide between Edmund and me."

Olaf hesitated.

"I don't suppose you have any idea which one of us will win?"

Bald thought, god make me cryptic. God did.

"Your son will be king of England."

That was safe because Olaf would never know if it was true or not.

Olaf left.

When the period of mourning for Eda was over, Olaf and Aldgyth were married by Wulfstan.

The army of the combined kingdoms marched south.

Lyb was already on the road to King's Stone where Edmund had been crowned and his son Edwy was born. He bought a donkey, knowing Emma would repay him, and a week later was ushered into her presence by a disgusted courtier. To the courtier's horror the queen ran to embrace the dwarf and kiss his horrid face and call him "da'"

Emma read the leechdom and hurried to Edmund to warn him the wolf was in the north.

The army of Wessex and the south marched north.

They met at Leicester.

XII

The northern army made rapid progress through the unresisting boroughs until the Saxon garrison in Northampton refused to surrender. Olaf turned west along Watling Street to Tamworth which had been an easy source of supplies and money in the last campaign. He captured Tamworth after a bloody battle but his army was so heavily depleted he retired to Leicester. He showed no sign of returning the land he occupied to the original kingdoms, and the jarls and ealdermen who had planned to set up their own petty kingships began to drop away from him.

Edmund moved more slowly. His army pushed up to Leicester and encamped around the town, cutting off supplies, and prepared to resist any attempt of escape.

Bald was in Leicester. He had been brought south by Olaf and found himself sharing cramped quarters with Wulfstan, Orm and Aldgyth, who had accompanied her new husband without much opportunity of sleeping with him. From Olaf's point of view, Bald thought, she had served her purpose.

Outside the town, Edmund had Odo with him. Wulfhelm had finally been translated to heaven, and the forceful Dane was archbishop of Canterbury. Emma and her baby son Edwy had gone for safety to Polesworth Abbey where Caech's relict Eadgyth still ruled. Lyb went with them. Fate, having so organised affairs, sat back and waited for them to develop.

Edmund was eighteen and unpredictable. He wanted to assault the town, but Odo persuaded him to wait.

Olaf's great desire was to avenge Brunanburh in a glorious battle: victory or Valhalla, but Wulfstan gave him graver counsel of how to keep what he had won and make himself king of half England.

"We need someone Edmund trusts, a man without prejudice. Bald the leech."

"What for?"

"Bald will obtain a free passage for a sick man and his attendant. You and I will leave Leicester and go to some neutral place where we can negotiate with Edmund and Odo."

Olaf shook his head.

"There must be a battle."

"Why, my lord?"

"There always is."

Wulfstan was exasperated.

"Like Brunanburh?"

"If it has to be."

"The advantage of Christianity is that nothing has to be. We don't accept fate."

Olaf looked around with concern. Wulfstan was condescending.

"The idea of fate is merely childish, a lack of understanding. In this modern age, matters are determined by men, in this case the archbishop of Canterbury and myself."

He could not prevent a trace of complacency in his voice.

"I know where we'll go. There's an abbey near here where your cousin Eadgyth is abbess. She's Edmund's sister, so he can have no objection. We'll go to Polesworth Abbey."

Fate smiled.

Bald suspected Wulfstan was using him but took the opportunity to escape from Leicester himself. He left the town next morning, walking ahead of a horse-litter bearing a sick man and led by an attendant in a hood. He entered the king's camp and was taken to archbishop Odo, who gave him free passage for himself and his patient without hesitation. Bald was convinced Odo and Wulfstan planned to prevent a battle between the two youthful and hot-headed kings, and divide the country north and south.

He did not see Edmund and left the camp quickly with the horse-litter. When they were well on the way to Polesworth, Wulfstan pushed back his hood and Olaf climbed out of the litter to ride the horse.

Bald pretended to be surprised.

The late sun shone on the pointed rooves of Polesworth Abbey. Bald was sent ahead to inform the abbess of the arrival of an important visitor who required her hospitality.

He had not seen Eadgyth since Caech's death. She was matronly and secure in her position.

"I don't want to see another Viking as long as I live!"

"Wulfstan's with him, lady, and I expect Olaf Guthfrithsson will be King of England before long."

"Not while my brother Edmund is alive, I hope!"

She plumped the skirts of her habit complacently.

"Queen Aelfgifu is here, you know."

He felt the blood pulse as his heart leapt, part in the anticipation of seeing Emma again, part in the sudden intimation of danger. What danger he did not know, but it was so strong he rose in agitation.

"All in good time, leech. Go and fetch Olaf and the dear archbishop. I know how to treat royalty. I'm one myself."

Eadgyth welcomed Wulfstan and was struck by Olaf's appearance. He stood straight and called her aunt and, forgetting Aldgyth, Queen of York. Bald, watching, saw Alfred's granddaughter and Ivarr's great-grandson chatting amiably by the fire while Wulfstan penned letters of state in the corner.

As soon as he could, he went up to see Emma.

He came to her room and opened the door quietly.

Emma was holding her baby son, Edwy, by candlelight.

He saw the mother of his dreams, serene, ageless, all-knowing.

He saw what he had sought for all his life, fulfilment and peace. Lyb, sitting in the shadows, growled softly. Emma turned her head.

"Uncle, oh uncle! I thought I'd never see you again."

"It's fate, my love."

He went to her and she lifted the child for him.

"He's a little costive and I give him cheadle."

"Betony is better for a child."

"Cheadle grows in the garden."

"Betony grows in the woods."

He kissed her.

"How are you?"

"I'm better now."

She had a bad childbirth, he thought.

"And Edmund?"

She turned away but not before he noticed her distaste.

"I don't know."

Oh God, had he been wrong to make her marry Edmund? No, it was fate. A great void opened under his thoughts – what if there was no fate, and only god who lets us make our own mistakes? His mouth stretched in a humourless grin like a skull. Am I guilty after all?

"Olaf is here."

"Who, uncle?"

"Olaf Guthfrithsson, your cousin. His grandfather Guthrith was your father's brother."

"Oh, the wolf." She showed no further interest.

He stared into the light without seeing it – if there was no fate? His skull seemed to shine through his skin. Emma was concerned.

"What are you thinking?" She already had an inkling. "It wasn't your fault, uncle."

"Emma ..."

"Don't say anything. I'm quite content."

He returned to his cell and lay on the bed vacated by a nun.

How could she be content with half a life? In a bad relationship? In an intolerable situation? Only if she was a saint.

He awoke at dawn and went out into the woods to look for betony.

When he returned, Emma was kneeling in the garden.

In the curve of her back, he saw Eneda.

"What are you doing?"

"Picking cheadle."

"Fool!"

He stumbled in his annoyance and she laughed a stream of tumbling laughter and her face lit up like the morning sun, and that was how Olaf saw her for the first time.

He had been for a swim in the river and drops of water sparkled in his hair and on his face and his body glowed and that was how she saw him.

Bald immediately recognised the danger. They were so alike. They were so alive to each other. Face to face. Hand to hand. Blood to blood.

"Cousin Emma."

"My name is Aelfgifu."

"I give you your Viking name. Mine is Olaf."

He appealed directly to all that was Eneda in her and all that was Sigtryggr too. Maria Virgo was lost, Bald thought.

Messengers passed between Wulfstan and Odo.

Eadgyth was pleased with her company and remarked how well they got on with each other.

Bald watched as the affair unfolded. He soon exonerated himself from blame. Fate or no fate, the two archbishops had brought Olaf and Emma together. Let them answer to their god.

He felt the excitement and danger of the relationship. He was part of it: he had lived the past, and he was a party in their rides and rambles. They both trusted him, though had he been Loki or Judas they could not have done differently. Their love was immediate and overpowering. Bald felt alone when he was with them, they were so locked in each other.

The abbey was full of eyes, so they went out into the warm golden autumn days, into the wooded valley of the river Anker. Bald wandered away to pick worts, but was always within the leash of earshot. Emma's voice would tug him back if he went too far. He wondered at her restraint, knowing the whirlpool of a woman's desires, and blamed it on fear and Christianity. He wanted them to be lovers. He wanted her to know what he had never known. He knew the consequences would be disastrous. A violent love would have a violent end. But to have had it himself, he would have died a blood-eagle.

Their looks seldom left each other.

In the abbey, the baby slipped to the periphery of her life. Olaf was her prayer.

How long could it last? Contentment is never enough, Bald thought. Fear is strong, faith is stronger, but both would fry in the furnace of ecstasy. Olaf was waiting for her, a spirit of adventure and danger leading her to a laughing death and Valhalla. He was the skald singing in her blood. He filled the aspiration of her mind; how long before he fulfilled the passion of her body?

And for Olaf, who knows? She was a sister spirit and a challenge to a victory over Edmund, what else? A passionate woman, a Christian and a saint. Love is the ultimate sacrilege. The weather broke.

They were in the Anker valley and Bald, obsessed with betony, had waded across the river when the storm arose and he was trapped by a wall of tawny water, tumbling rocks and fallen branches twisting in the torrent as it rushed downstream. The wind whirled the last leaves from the trees and the rain stamped them like coins on the ground.

He clutched his few sprigs of bishopwort and began to trudge back to the ford below the abbey. The sky had darkened, but he thought he saw Emma in a shaft of yellow light falling on the edge of the forest. She looked lost, small and forlorn, and fallen.

Lightning cracked and burnt in his eyes. He thought he heard a cry before the thunder fell on him and he fled along the slippery bank towards the abbey.

Upstream, the river spread into the meadows up to the grey walls and slate rooves silver in the yellow sky.

He splashed across to look for shelter.

Wulfstan was waiting, and Bald caught the glint of suspicion like a drawn sword in an alley.

"Where do you go on these long walks of yours? He's got two wives already; how many more does he want?"

"It's only a drop of rain, master?"

The storm passed leaving darkness and dripping eaves. Olaf and Emma had not returned and Eadgyth sent out slaves with bunches of burning straw to search for them. Bald went too. He had the senses of a fox and knew where the chickens ran.

Branches glistened in the starlight and the woods smelt sharp and tarry. Bald moved silently, barely stirring the wet leaves underfoot. He went away from the river, knowing the Viking would have looked for higher ground and shelter.

He remembered seeing a heap of rocks in the distance on the edge of the heath north of the forest. He looked up to the stars to point the way.

In the book:

"Arctos hight a constellation in the north part, which hath in it seven stars, and it is by another name hight septentrio, which laymen call the churls wain."

As he came out from under the trees and the sky opened above him, he caught the acrid smell of smoke. The heath rose before him and on the rise among a group of rocks there was the glimmer of a fire. He walked up carefully not to surprise them.

The rocks had been built up into a rough sheepfold and the fire burnt low in a corner where clothes were spread on the wall to dry. He heard a fieldmouse scuttle and a silent shadow passed over his head.

Death, he thought, love and death.

He left the fold to look across the heath. A few yards away a great stone lay like a giant's gravestone, a fallen megalith, looming out of the earth.

There would have been an arch, and its fellow had been broken for the fold.

Men and women would have gone through the arch to another world.

They were lying in the heather on the far side of the arch naked in each other's arms.

The world begins here, he thought, on a breast of earth under a pall of sky – ay, and ends here, too, condemned by God to die.

He drew back and went as silently as he had come.

Olaf and Emma returned to the abbey next morning laughing at themselves for their stupidity in getting lost.

The sun came out again.

Bald noticed now Emma's happiness and found a little of his own in it. He was a complaisant uncle and kept his head down when they touched behind his back, and walked hand in hand, and kissed in the doorway. On their outings, he swore he had not picked enough betony and left them early and came back late, cracking twigs to warn them.

For a few days, Olaf and Emma lived in the other world of love.

The only thing the gods learned from man was how to love and even then they were not very good at it. Jesus never did, thought Bald, and forbade it in heaven. He would not go through that arch.

So far, Emma had not said a word about it.

The morning Wulfstan announced the negotiations were over and Edmund and Odo were coming to the abbey to seal the treaty, she came to Bald's cell.

"What shall I do?"

"What's Olaf going to do?"

"I'm my own master."

He heard Eneda speaking.

"I don't know, Emma."

She was seventeen, and a mother, and older in terms of love than he was.

"The only way I can leave Edmund is to go to Shaftesbury, and then I can't go to Olaf."

"You'll have to forget Olaf."

She laughed at this impossibility. She stopped suddenly.

"I could kill Edmund."

The words rang in his skull and amazed him.

She meant it. The enormity of the remark coming from such a child shocked him.

"Then Olaf would be king of England and marry me."

Bald was shaking his head. By God she was Sigtryggr's daughter! She was worthy of a saga. He heard himself saying:

"Emma, you're a Christian."

"When has that meant anything to you?"

"Now."

"Look at my life! No mother, no father, robbed of my maidenhood, married to a man I hate! Shall I kill myself?"

"No!"

"What, then? What shall I do?"

What could he answer? Leave it to fate? Leave it to god? Suffer and endure? Or kill! We all live with our own deaths, can we live with another's? How could he answer for her?

"Emma, you must be yourself."

That was it! That was the end! Go back to nature!

"Do what your nature tells you to do."

"Is that all?"

"I can't cure the world."

He meant to say, I am not god, but she knew that.

Edmund bad-temperedly tampered with the treaty and gave the lovers one last afternoon.

It was gloomy out.

Bald was boiling betony when they came to his cell.

In the book:

"If a man be inwardly broken, or to him his body be sore, let him take then of betony the wort by weight four drachms; boil it in wine much; let him the drink at night fasting; then the body grows light for him."

He got up to leave them together. Olaf held him back.

"No, friend leech, we only want to talk."

Bald was reluctant to stay because he was afraid Emma was going to ask him for poison.

"Emma and I have decided to wait. All will be well, you'll see."

Looking at them, bright creatures of the summer, he wondered at their dreams.

"There's a secret clause in the treaty between Edmund and me. Whichever of us outlives the other takes all England. Well, that's my chance!"

Olaf was cheerful.

"None of Edward's sons lived long. My father had a long life, and Guthrith was cut short, as you know."

That was true, thought Bald, but Olaf was like a dragonfly looking to live until December. And what about Emma?

"Are you both prepared to wait for Edmund to die?"

"I'm prepared to pray, uncle."

It was a different sort of Christianity to use faith like an axe. Olaf was agreeable.

"We'll wait a year or two anyway."

"One year."

Emma was firm. "One year, and I'll pray every day."

They stayed a little while just to be together.

The fumes of the wine filled the cell.

Bald tried to think of something to say. When he did, some trite optimism, he turned and could not say a word.

They were holding hands and gazing at each other as if to burn the beloved image into their minds and hearts for ever.

In the haze, they were the golden gods of the sagas, all made from the same strong mind, all valiant, all loving, all laughing, and all lost.

Edmund and Odo arrived that evening with a clutch of courtiers who crowded out the abbey.

The treaty divided the country along the lines of the old Danelaw of Alfred's time. Olaf gained everything north of Watling Street. Edmund lost everything Edward and Athelstan had won. Wulfstan and Odo created two archbishoprics for the whole island: York and Canterbury. There was one condition, and it applied to the secret clause: Olaf had to become a Christian.

He underwent the ritual with a smile.

Bald could not help comparing the two kings as they exchanged gifts. Red Edmund scowling as he gave Olaf a ring with bad grace, and Olaf giving him a sword, the point significantly upwards, in return.

Bald murmured to himself.

"I give you to Woden."

Which one of them would survive?

Emma stayed in her room and sent a message that Edwy was costive.

It took almost a month to disband the armies. The weather was warm, the abbey crammed with courtiers, the drains overloaded.

A nun succumbed to fever and died.

Five more died three days later.

In the book:

"For a tertian fever, let the sick drink in warm water ten sups of betony, when the fever is approaching."

Bald soon ran out of betony.

Ten more died, and the court prepared to leave the abbey. Bald hurried to Odo's room.

"Nobody must leave here, master, or you'll spread the fever through the whole land."

"Do you expect us to stay here and die?"

"You'll die anyway and take a few thousand with you."

"If it's a tertian fever, those still well after three days can leave."

"It's not a tertian, or a quartan, or a quotidian. I've seen the dead. It's lent addle come early."

"I can't risk the king's life, leech."

"Will you risk it on the road?"

Odo took his arm and led him away from the door confidentially.

"You don't know this, but if Edmund dies, Olaf will be king of all England."

"Olaf is in the same condition. He can't leave. Wulfstan must know it just as you do. We all have to take our chance."

He did not have to argue any more because Olaf collapsed that night with sweats and shaking limbs and a screaming pain in his head.

He had been swimming in the river.

Edmund stayed to watch him die.

In the book:

"For lent addle, or typhus fever, work to a drink wormwood, everthroat, lupin, waybroad, ribwort, chervil, atterlothe, feverfue, alexanders, bishopwort, lovage, sage, cassock, in foreign ale; add holy water and springwort."

The holy water was ominous, thought Bald, betraying Cild's lack of confidence in the leechdom. Nevertheless he mixed it with Wulfstan's blessing and carried it to Olaf's room.

"Take care of Emma."

"Her room is sealed and only Lyb goes in and out. He's a Briton; even the addle won't go near him."

"She's my sister and my love. Do you think the gods are punishing me for becoming a Christian?"

"Haesten was baptised three or four times and died of old age in Francia."

"I'd like to have lived in those days. I'd have given Edmund to Woden and had England and Emma. I'd have burnt this abbey to the ground instead of lying here dying in it."

Bald felt his skin was hot and dry and he cried out when he tried to move his joints. It was less like typhus than a synovia which was not at all fatal and could be cured with maythe and honey and, more obscurely, the bowels of an earwig and the smede of wheaten meal.

"Olaf, I might have been wrong."

"I never thought I'd hear a leech say that."

Bald left him and hurried back to his cell. The corridors were filled with makeshift beds, and Eadgyth moved among the sick, monumentally immune.

A group of monks was chanting a psalm outside Edmund's bedroom. Odo's priest rushed by carrying a silver paten, and went into the room. Bald followed him.

Through the smoke of incense he saw Edmund's closest councillors gathered round the bed. The priest had taken the paten to Odo who was writing at a table on which there was a stoup of holy water and a cup. Bald remembered something Cild had copied in the scriptorium at Canterbury.

In the book:

"A man shall write this upon the sacramental paten, and wash it off with holy water, and sing over it "In the beginning + +" (John I 1). Then wash the writing with holy water off the dish into the cup, then sing the Credo, and the Paternoster, and the lay Beati Immaculati, the psalm with the twelve prayer psalms 'I adjure you + +'. And let each of the two men, the priest and the sick, then sip thrice of the water so prepared.

Inde salutiferis incendens gressibus urbes
Oppida, rura, casas, vicos, castella peregrans,
Omnia depulsis sanabat corpora morbis.
Sedulius."

It was the exorcism for fever.

He pushed his way between the councillors to the bed.

Edmund was lying in a sweat, with chattering teeth and fixed eyes.

Bald stared. It seemed the secret clause, the deal with death between the two kings, would be over before it began, and one of them would certainly die at Polesworth.

Odo was praying over the cup.

He made way for him and quietly left the room.

Perhaps God would cure Edmund? Perhaps God would cure Olaf?

For three days Wulfstan and Odo prayed for their respective kings and Bald marvelled at the elasticity of faith compared to the obduracy of fate.

Olaf's synovia yielded slowly to his ministrations.

For a time it seemed that Emma's prayers would be answered, but Edmund stubbornly resisted the exorcism and recovered.

That was the end of the lent addle, which burnt itself out by Christmas.

Olaf left Polesworth without seeing Emma again; it was thought too dangerous for them to meet. He went back to York with Wulfstan and Lyb, who was going home.

Edmund was put on a litter for the journey south. Emma followed with Bald.

She had asked him to go with her because she was pregnant.

XIII

The royal villa at Cheddar had been Alfred's favourite residence from where he went hunting across the Mendip hills.

There Edmund found release for his pent-up rage after the humiliation of Leicester. Every morning he prayed aloud for Olaf's death, unaware that Emma, kneeling by his side, was praying for his.

Winter drifted into spring and the late snows ebbed from the hills. The deer came down from the forests and the hungry hounds bayed in the kennels.

Bald had seen more seasons than most men but spring continued to amaze him. There were one hundred and eighty five worts in his herbarium and they all seemed to appear overnight in a glorious jumble of colours and sizes. Nature never failed, whatever men did to restrict or pervert her course, and when they tormented her beyond endurance she turned and destroyed them. God was a comparative newcomer in these affairs, first as a personification of nature, then as one of man. The phenomena of sickness and death became God's will and not nature's course. So in sickness and death, men appealed to God and forgot nature. The knowledge of the book and the great pharmacy replenished every spring were replaced by prayers, relics and incantations. The natural lore collected by Cild and practised by Bald declined from use and lay dormant between the ox-hide covers. Doctors with theories of medicine flourished while simple leeches travelling the land vanished into folklore in the guise of witches and wise women. Bald's leechbook was the only one.

Dunstan came up from Glastonbury to try to persuade Edmund to pay for his new abbey. Edmund had lost half his revenues at Leicester and was not amused. Dunstan lingered at Cheddar hoping the king would change his mind.

Emma swelled with pregnancy, resentment, and fear that her child would betray her. Edwy was small like Edmund. The dread of a long-limbed baby drove her to a desperate remedy she remembered from her childhood. She had seen how Lyb had dwarfed Ulf and Liofa, and she went out at dawn, leaving black footprints in the dewy grass, to dig up the roots of daisies, which she chewed in secret.

The first morning of the hunting season broke sharp and bright. Edmund's daily anathema against Olaf over, he was striding towards the kennels with his young companions when Dunstan rushed up and shouted a warning not to hunt that day because he had dreamed there was going to be a terrible disaster.

Edmund laughed and told his bullies to throw the monk into the kennel-pond. Dunstan was hurled into the stinking pit and told, "There's your disaster!"

The hounds were loosed, the king and his huntsmen mounted horses, and the rest ran after them.

Dunstan scrambled out of the mire and followed until they vanished into the hills, then he turned to the theatre of his dream, the wooded cliff above the Cheddar gorge. There he saw a solitary figure stooping over some rare wort, and called Bald to go with him.

In the book:

"If a man dreams he is a-hunting, let him be well on his guard against his enemies. If he thinks he sees hounds and they bay him, let him be on his guard against his enemies. If he thinks he sees hounds run, that stands for much coming good."

"I dreamt I was hunting with the king and the hounds bayed me."

Bald moved upwind of him.

"Then the hounds were running through the woods and they disappeared!"

"They won't come this way, master."

As he spoke, Bald felt Dunstan touch his arm and he turned. A great red stag stood panting under an oak tree. If it saw them, it scorned them, and nibbled a few green shoots of grass. It trotted a dozen paces as if to display its indifference, or audacity as it turned out, and suddenly the wood was full of hounds crashing through the undergrowth.

Dunstan moved and Bald seized him and made him stand. The hounds might slobber them to death but nothing else.

The stag lifted its great head and sprang forward straight through the thicket protecting the clifftop and over – and the hounds, deranged by its powerful scent went pouring over after it!

Silence.

They stared.

They turned!

A rider at full gallop came hurtling by and took the same disastrous course!

They started up to stop any others, but none came.

It was a moment before either of them could speak.

Horror spoke first.

The scream of a horse.

"God Jesus," Dunstan spoke, "He had red hair."

Bald ran to the edge of the gorge and cautiously peered over. There was nothing to see but the pointed tops of the trees.

"We must get help!"

I must tell Emma, thought Bald.

They ran back to the villa.

It had happened so suddenly Bald wondered if it had happened at all. Dunstan had sped ahead, and he slowed to a walk to give himself a chance to think of the consequences.

Edmund would be succeeded by his brother Eadred, but Olaf would undoubtedly invoke the secret clause of the treaty of Leicester, and claim the whole island for himself.

The renewal of the war between north and south was inevitable.

Emma and her unborn child would be in danger. They would have to leave for the north before the news of Edmund's death reached Eadred. He was approaching the villa when Emma came running towards him, a figure of such frantic joy it frightened him.

She fell on him, crying hysterically.

"I can't believe it, oh God, I thank God!"

"Take care, Emma! Olaf's hundreds of miles away and the court's full of his enemies. Come inside and show grief."

"Uncle, I'll never cry again!"

She was so fiercely exultant she frightened him again. Know more than the gods, but do not let them know it.

He felt her trembling against him like a bird longing to be released.

They walked towards the villa.

Dunstan suddenly appeared in the doorway, waving his arms and shouting,

"God is merciful!"

Bald knew immediately that God could not be merciful to both Dunstan and Emma. He gripped her firmly to withstand the shock.

"Edmund's alive! He wasn't with the hounds! It was a groom, a man of no consequence!"

He came running down to them.

"God is merciful to his saints."

Emma had gone dead white. He did not dare look at her. Dunstan came up on the other side and they helped her back to the villa.

When he returned, Edmund was told she was too shocked and grieved by the false news of his death to see anyone. He was moved himself, and called Dunstan and embraced him. He was following his hounds when his horse faltered and he sent the groom ahead. The boy had loved the king and dyed his hair in his honour.

"God spared me, Dunstan. I'll build your abbey and you'll be the first abbot. We'll go to Glastonbury to give thanks tomorrow."

Bald was concerned for Emma and feared the double shock might derange her. Her condition restricted her to her room where she stayed, pale and silent, sitting out the final months of pregnancy. There were no leechdoms for despair and the charms were of little effect on someone who already knew them. She had bewitched herself, as he had brought the knot on himself, and these self-inflicted wounds were incurable. He turned to Dunstan, who came back from Glastonbury fresh in his abbacy.

In the book:

"Write this writing, "Scriptum est, rex regum, et dominus dominantium Veronica, Veronica ..."

"Why Veronica?"

"Not Veronica, leech, the face of God on her handkerchief."

"sanctus sanctus sanctus dominus deus sabaoth amen alleluiah."

"Then what?"

"Work up a drink thus; font water, rue, sage, cassuck, dragons, the netherward part of the smooth waybroad, feverfue, a head of dill, three cloves of garlic, fennel, wormwood, lovage, lupin, of all equal quantities."

"Is that all?"

"Write across three times with the oil of unction, and say "Pax tibi." Then take the writing, describe a cross with it over the drink, and sing this over it.

"*Dominus omnipotens, pater domini nostri Iesu Christi, per impositionem huius scriptorae et per gustum huius expelle diabolum a famula tua Aeflgifu."*

"Wet the writing in the drink and write a cross with it on every limb, and say, *'Signum cruces Christi conservet te in vitam aeternam. Amen.'* This craft is powerful against every temptation of the fiend."

"It might cure the devil, Dunstan, but what good can it do Emma?"

In summer the court moved to Winchester.

The birth of a son in July did something to restore her spirits. The boy was small and fair and the living pledge of her love for Olaf. He was christened Edgar.

Dunstan claimed an angel told him, "Peace to England so long as this child shall reign and our Dunstan survives."

Emma laughed.

Bald woke from his afternoon sleep.

She was sitting in the window embrasure illuminated like a gospel.

In his mind he saw the Maria Virgo in York minster. The circle was almost complete: Eneda and Emma were one.

"Why are you laughing, my love?"

"I feared god would take my baby for that boy's life."

"Which boy?"

"The one who died at Cheddar."

"That was fate."

"I wanted it to be Edmund."

"The baby's well: small but well. The strange thing is, I once told Olaf his son would be king of England."

"I'll never see him again."

He looked at her sharply. She seemed composed, almost serene, and absolutely certain. Once again he saw the woman in the crucifixion scene, smiling though her son was dying, knowing he would live again. That was the secret of the Mothers and what he sought in all women, rebirth, the secret of nature.

Time missed a heartbeat. That was the moment Olaf died.

He was bold and young, the best of Ivarr's line.

He could not stay in York, and when the wind and sea called him, he went a-Viking round the coast of Lothian.

The serpent-ships put in to Tyne mouth to attack the church of St. Bealdhere. They sailed on to Tyninghame and there he was killed in a raid.

The king of Dublin and York and ruler of half England died in a fool's raid on a tiny settlement on a wild and barren coast.

His companions sent his corpse, with the scrap of gold from Ivarr's helmet on the breast, out into the Firth of Forth, and his soul to Valhalla, laughing.

His and Emma's son was Edgar, the darling of the English and father of a long line of kings.

It took a month for news of Olaf's death to reach Winchester.

Edmund was elated. He immediately sent orders for the army to assemble, and prepared to travel north.

Emma asked permission to retire to Shaftesbury Abbey.

She came to him already dressed as a nun.

Edmund was nineteen and eager to regain his kingdom. She was two years older and thinking of the next. They parted amiably enough.

"Dunstan always said you were a saint, Aelfgifu."

"Call me St. Emma."

She concealed her grief from everyone except Bald, and even to him bore it with composure.

He was worried about her health and went to Shaftesbury with her. The abbess Aethelwynn welcomed them both.

"I knew you'd come."

Ay, thought Bald, but not why.

Emma had left her two sons in the care of a Saxon lady, Aethelflaed of Damerham. She entered fully into the life of a nun. Bald thought there was more self-mortification than commitment to God in it. She wore a black habit and her pale youthful face gave her the appearance of a saint in a missal.

Bald saw her as he had seen her before in dreams and visions.

Aethelwynn asked him: "Why is Aelfgifu always so sad?"

"Great loves have great griefs, lady."

The abbess wisely asked no more.

News came to Shaftesbury of Edmund's swift success. Cuaran had succeeded Olaf as king of York, but he was unpopular and had no support outside the city. Edmund occupied all the country south of the Humber before winter.

The year closed round the abbey and the farms and hamlets within its purlieus. People came to the hospital for treatment and there Emma found her true vocation.

She is a good leech, thought Bald, watching her.

Her face, her voice, her touch, calmed the most fractious child, eased the suffering of the sick, reconciled the dying. Women especially asked for the young nun. In the abbey, they forgot she was the queen. She seldom spoke except to counsel, comfort and console.

She prayed seven times a day with the others. Bald wondered whether she was herself reconciled to God?

She asked him one night,

"Can a woman go to Valhalla?"

She had come to his room late, and woken him up. He saw a woman in black in the doorway and for a moment thought he was dying.

"Freya's there: why not?"

"Do you have to die in battle?"

He came to his senses and grinned at her.

"Do you want to spend eternity in a beer-hall with a bunch of drunkards?"

"I don't want to spend it here in heaven."

She smiled a smile he recognised as Eneda's.

"No my sweet, the battles are over and the old gods have lost."

"What then, uncle? When we're dead?"

"I believe we're reborn as earth, or grass, or worts, or bees, or chickens, or oxen, or even men."

"Or gods?"

"Thought perhaps."

"Or gods?"

"Some of us."

He had to say it. She was young.

She kissed him and left.

Next morning Aethelwynn called him in alarm. He rose and hurried after her to the queen's room. A frightened nun stood by the door.

He pushed past her and entered the room with Aethelwynn.

Emma lay on the bed, her arms by her sides, as if laid out ceremonially on a catafalque.

He knew before he went to her she was dead. He knew there was no reason why, no taint of poison, no mark of rope or dagger, no sign of death's struggle. The blow that killed her was the same one that killed Olaf in battle. She was in Valhalla.

There was something glinting in the winter light lying on her breast. He thought it was a cross until he looked closer and saw the small engraved panel of gold from Ivarr's helmet. Olaf must have given it to her, he thought.

Aethelwynn asked him,

"What is it, leech?"

"A token of love."

Of love and death.

She was buried in the abbey to the left of the altar. Bald laid the book at her feet before the tomb was closed.

It was all he had to give her.

He stayed in Shaftesbury.

Edmund's campaigns in the north followed the pattern of previous campaigns. Successes were followed by truces in which the principal mover was seen to be not Cuaran the king, or Olaf's brother Ragnall, but archbishop Wulfstan. He fought doughtily for York.

Edmund finally took York and burned it. Cuaran fled to Dublin.

He was the last Viking king and ended a long life as a monk on Iona.

A year after Emma's death, Edmund married Aethelflaed of Damerham, his children's nurse. He oversaw the building of Dunstan's abbey at Glastonbury, gave it a charter, and endowed it with land, and relics looted from Northumbria. He was on the way to becoming a king in the Alfredian mould when he met fate.

It was in the spring and he was twenty-four. He had begun a journey north and stopped at the village of Pucklechurch on the road to Gloucester for St. Augustin's day.

There was a feast in the moot hall and among the company was a dwarf who was lavishly spending silver pennies stamped with King Alfred's head.

The ale flowed, and Edmund kept seeing this dwarf and wondering where he had seen him before. The longer it took to remember the more angry he became, and when it finally struck him, he was in a rage.

This was the villain he had exiled, and here he was, flaunting himself at the king's table!

He did not reason that the exile was for six years and eight had passed. Edmund and reason seldom sat down and never got up together. He leapt from his chair, hurled himself at the dwarf and grappled with him, rolling onto the floor.

The dwarf drew a dagger and stabbed him to the heart.

So Liofa killed King Edmund and was cut to pieces by his guards.

In the fastness of Shaftesbury, Bald heard of Edmund's death but not the manner of it, and so he was deprived of the pleasure of talking about fate.

He was now very old, and Aethelwynn was concerned about the propriety of a layman living in the abbey, particularly as she suspected him of practising wortcunning and starcraft.

She called Dunstan, who came from Glastonbury where he had just buried Edmund in the new north tower.

He showed his usual good sense.

"I'll make him a monk. I should have done it years ago. He's the most religious man I know."

"I don't think he's a Christian."

"On the contrary: I baptised him myself."

"I mean he doesn't believe in God."

"He does better than that. He believes in God's creation. We pray for help. Bald helps."

Aethelwynn sighed.

"I wish he'd wash a little more often."

"He'll make an excellent monk, and he'll call you mother!"

When the abbess told him his duty would be to attend Aelfgifu's tomb, Bald agreed. He made a habit out of plaid and carried a wooden cross without a crosspiece.

Dunstan saw him before he left. They stood before the tomb.

"She was a saint, brother Bald."

"Ay, master. You know she saved a criminal from hanging?"

He meant Liofa.

"She gave away her dress to the poor in Winchester."

To the poor whore.

Dunstan was interested. A royal saint would be a great acquisition.

"There would have to be miracles performed at her tomb."

"How many?"

Dunstan looked at him closely. Bald was not smiling but you never knew.

From then on, the sick coming to Shaftesbury found an ancient monk leading them in single file up the nave to kneel at a tomb on the left of the altar. He gave them each a flower or herb to lay on the tomb. Then he let them go home with their leechdoms.

After a while it became customary to visit the tomb before going to the hospital.

Then some of those who were ill were cured at the tomb and did not have to go to the hospital at all. Even those who did gave credit for their cure to the saintly queen who lay in the abbey. Those who were not cured had no opinion.

Pilgrims began to come to Shaftesbury from all over England.

Some came from as far as York.

One spring, two tall girls arrived leading a donkey ridden by an old dwarf. He was gross and had a hoofmark on his head. They helped him down and those around saw his short legs were crooked and crippled, his feet were swollen, and he could hardly walk.

He joined the line of pilgrims and hobbled into the abbey.

So great and noisy was his pain that everyone stood aside to let him waddle slowly along the whole length of the nave, groaning and muttering and cursing – "Faul! Faul!"

A monk was squatting by Queen Aelfgifu's tomb like a gargoyle. He was so grey and angular many thought him made of stone. His black rat's eyes opened and stared out of cobweb skin at the dwarf, who took the last few painful steps and touched the tomb with gnarled fingers.

"Lyb."

The dwarf started at the whisper as if the dead had spoken.

"Lyb!"

The dwarf jumped round to see if the devil was behind him.

"LYB!"

The dwarf fled – back along the great nave past the gaping pilgrims, out of the doors, startling the girls and alarming the donkey, and almost half a mile on the road to York before they could catch up with him.

"A miracle!"

The cry went up and was repeated.

"A miracle! God bless St. Aelfgifu, it's a miracle."

In May, Aethelwynn came to tell Bald that Queen Aelfgifu had been canonised, and her feast was to be celebrated on the eighteenth. She was old now, and it took her quite a time to walk up the nave. She was annoyed to see the tomb swept clean but no sign of Bald. She went outside and asked the boy who kept the sheep if he had seen him.

The boy pointed to the woods.

"He went to get some worts, mum."

He never returned.